THE MAN WHO WAS NEVER THERE

William Arthur Wheatley

W&B Publishers
USA

W & B Publishers

For information:
W & B Publishers
9001 Ridge Hill Street
Kernersville, NC 27284

www.a-argusbooks.com

ISBN: 9781635541342

This is a work of *fiction*. All of the characters, organizations and events portrayed in this novel are either products of the author's imagination or used fictitiously.

Book Cover designed by Dubya

Printed in the United States of America

There are two essential rules one must follow to be a good clandestine agent. The first is being there, fully aware. The second is being invisible; not *being there.*
NEVER BLOW YOUR COVER!

The Intelligence Manual
(Author Classified)

TABLE OF CONTENTS

AUTHOR'S PREFACE

How does a young man become an intelligence officer? There are several paths he might follow. You may be curious about the path I followed, but I don't want to have to kill you, so I can't tell you my own story. However, I can tell the story of Arthur Cornwallis Harris, whose fictional story is based on my own experience.

The story of this book begins in the childhood of Arthur Cornwallis Harris, and chronicles his entry into the world of intelligence operations. After yearning to become a spy and a Navy officer when a child, he becomes an officer with the Naval Office of Special Intelligence (NOSI), a super-secret sub-unit of the Office of Naval Intelligence (ONI). The story includes events of his childhood, but it is not a book for children.

The story of this book is drawn from events in my life, experiences I have had, and experiences of others I have known, including other clandestine intelligence operatives. Having said that, this work is fiction, based very loosely (but very directly) on the real world and times in which I have lived. However, some of the events are described exactly as they happened, using fictional characters. If you were to guess which are accurate stories and which are pure fiction, you would probably be wrong, because in many cases, the truth really is stranger than fiction.

For the most part, the real world of intelligence work is rather un-interesting to one not involved directly in it. It consists of endless hours of analysis of documents, photographs, reports, statistical data, and other materials, in order to try to find the hidden truth behind it all. It amounts to "reading between the lines." The vast majority of such data comes from public sources available to anyone who wants to dig for them.

Even clandestine operatives usually lead relatively boring lives. They live under cover, employed in a bland cover occupation, but their role is quietly to collect information without "making waves," without anyone knowing they are there. Although an occasional intelligence officer has adventurous, exciting experiences at occasional times, James Bond is fiction. Indeed, some operatives, at some times, lead exciting lives, especially when involved in covert operations, or when caught up in historic events. Some give their lives in service; but most lead fairly humdrum lives. My own work in intelligence was no exception – at both ends of that spectrum.

When I had excitement in my life, it was because I was in a certain location when life in that region was disrupted by significant events, not because I was involved in the gathering of intelligence. It had to do with where I was and when I was there more than with what I was doing – although it is unlikely I would have been there at all but for intelligence purposes. In most cases, officially I was never there, hence the title of this book.

The personalities of the characters in the book are based on people I have known, but the roles they play in this story may be quite different from the roles they played in real life. I have used the real people in my life and then subtly altered them to develop characters that fit the story and that I hope will appear realistic; but they are now fictional characters.

When senior-level public officials appear in the story, I have used their actual names in order to provide historical context and authenticity. For example, when the Director of the ONI appears in the book, he is given the name of the real Director, ONI, at the time in which the book is cast, and the story is cast in the midst of the real events of history. When I name a U.S. President, or a Soviet President or Premier, or any senior government official, I am naming them only for "historical" purposes, to place the story in a real historical context. When a senior official plays an actual part in the story line, I have provided a fictional identity.

The genuine historical people I name never met Arthur Harris, because Arthur Harris is not a real person, and so they did not say to him what they do in the book nor did they do precisely what the book has them doing. I did meet Nguyen Cao Ky and certain other historical personalities, but not necessarily under the same circumstances as Arthur Harris. Events in the book that involve my characters do not necessarily depict any real events, and when they do, the real events may not be in the same time-frame or location as in the story in this book. In telling the story, I have been careful not to reveal actual means, methods and events of the intelligence community, unless they are already well-known, although the events I describe bear some sort of relation to events in real life, to people I know, and to events of history.

There are many people I should thank for the assistance they rendered in certain aspects of this book, but who must remain nameless here, because they are still "in the business." Thank you, my nameless friends. You know who you are, and you know I couldn't have completed this work without you.

Some of you who know me may think that you see yourselves in the story and may be surprised at the things I have you saying and doing. If this applies to you, you should just pretend that you have entered a parallel universe in which you are not quite yourself, and in which everything around you is subtly (or dramatically, as the case may be) different.

The characters, events, and circumstances have been scrambled to protect the innocent (or guilty) people whose personalities I have borrowed and transformed, and to protect my friends and me from the guilty. Nothing I have said in this book is dependable historically, except for the actual historical events that are generally well known. That having been said, the events in this story *MIGHT* have happened, at some place, in some time, to some real people – but all is illusion. It's just a story.

So, once upon a time, in an alternate universe, was born Arthur Cornwallis Harris III. Now, please continue reading.

I hope you enjoy this story. If you do, I have more stories to tell you.

--William Arthur Wheatley
(From an Undisclosed Location)
10 August 2019

FOREWORD

Throughout history, stories of intelligence and espionage have always aroused the imagination of the public. The simple truth of how most individuals of outstanding character and ability are brought into the realm of secrets is, however, decidedly less intriguing. Today, most who will enter the world's second oldest profession apply online for consideration to be hired into one of the 17 government entities that comprise the Intelligence Community (IC). In 2010, the Washington Post reported that there were 1,271 government organizations and 1,931 private companies in 10,000 locations throughout the United States engaged in some type of counterterrorism, homeland security or intelligence-related tasks. As a whole, in 2010 the IC included more than 854,000 individuals with top-secret security clearances. By virtue of the magnitude of the numbers and the impersonal, technical means of entry, the IC is hardly the stuff of Bond or Bourne-like daring and intrigue. Yet for those mature enough to understand how states compete with one another, the exceptions to the norm are both possible and exhilarating.

Among the most intriguing characters in the long history of intelligence and espionage are those who enter the craft via a non-traditional route. These pages provide a fictional account of one such character named Arthur Harris, recruited while in his first year of college, the beneficiary of some significant on-the-job field training, and only then sent through the traditional training of a CIA officer. As is the case with all good works of fiction, this one entertains the reader with highly unusual, if not unbelievable, exploits made all the more intriguing because they are based upon the real-life experiences of the author, my friend, William A. Wheatley.

As someone with intimate familiarity with the world of clandestine operations and daring intelligence operatives, Wheatley's Arthur Harris is a character known to me in many guises and names throughout the years. Harris begins his career with the Office of Naval Intelligence (ONI) where he is recruited to be one of the first intelligence officers in a new, super-secret (and fictional) sub-unit. There he does things that ordinary Navy Intelligence Officers don't do. Could it be that Harris, while just a Midshipman on summer training with the Navy, would be assigned to participate in aerial surveillance during the Viet Nam War over a neutral country, which then would lead to his having been shot down, and then fighting his way through the jungle to survive? Only those who have not had the benefit (and honor) of meeting Cold Warriors of the Vietnam era could doubt such a story. For the rest of us, the Viet Nam War, like so many throughout the ages, routinely made the unbelievable all too real.

Harris doesn't realize it in real-time, but ONI's orders cause him to intrude on territory claimed exclusively by the CIA. Like so many patriots before (and since) Harris finds himself as both beneficiary and victim of the rivalries that too often lead colleague entities to compete against one another for bureaucratic sovereignty over "territory" as vigorously as they do against foreign adversaries (the 9-11 Commission's overview of the FBI-CIA rivalry before the attacks of that day are instructive as an example). All of this makes for a fascinating story which, while portrayed by the author as fiction, has too often broken through the barrier of the make believe into reality.

I enjoyed this book, because it struck the chords of memory and experience for me, and I believe that you will as well.

--Edward A. Turzanski

Edward A. Turzanski is an historian of intelligence and espionage and a national security analyst with nearly four decades of direct field experience and academic research and teaching activity. He is a Life Member of the Association of Former Intelligence Officers (AFIO), having served with the U.S. Intelligence Community in postings throughout the Middle East, Central Asia and Eastern Europe during the Reagan Administration, and he also served as a member of the U.S. Department of Justice's Anti-Terror Advisory Committee throughout the George W. Bush Administration. Since 9-11, Turzanski has regularly offered commentary on national security, political, intelligence and terror-related issues on more than four-dozen media outlets throughout North America, and has been a frequent contributor to Fox News Channel, Canada's CTV News in Toronto, the Canadian Broadcast Corporation, LBC radio in London, CNN and CNN Headline News, the British Broadcasting Corporation, Turkish National Television, and other international outlets. In 2011, he was named the first-ever Templeton Fellow of the Foreign Policy Research Institute (FPRI) where he specializes in threats to national security, and is also co-chairman for its Institute for the Study of Terrorism. He is also the first-ever Scholar-in-Residence for the World Affairs Council of Philadelphia. Turzanski is a Life Member of the National Association of Scholars; and in addition to his academic, media and occasional government-related national security work, serves as a Vice President and Member of the Board of Directors of the Union League of Philadelphia, and a Trustee of Thomas Jefferson University Health System.

PRELUDE

23 September 1944
Knoxville, Tennessee

Arthur Cornwallis Harris, known as "Art," folded the newspaper and placed it in his briefcase. On second thought he removed the paper from his briefcase and carried it to the trash bin. It was old news, anyway. He returned to his table in the all-night Knox Diner and finished his coffee. He looked at his watch. It was 2:00 in the morning. He put some change on the table to cover the cost of the coffee and walked tiredly back to the trash bin to retrieve the newspaper and verify that the date of the paper, yesterday, was September 22, 1944. Dates and days had been blurring together lately for him. An engineer in charge of around-the-clock work on the construction of Norris Dam, he was worn down by long hours and overtime. Dropping the newspaper back into the trash bin, he picked up his weathered brief case and walked out the door.

The Knoxville street was empty, except for a few cars parked at the curb, including his wife's 1939 gun-metal-grey Oldsmobile sedan. He had driven her to the hospital in it because it was more comfortable for her than his 1936 Chevrolet pickup truck. He looked up at the sky. The air was still and cool, with the temperature in the upper-sixties, a relief from the heat and humidity of yesterday. The sky was very clear, despite the proximity of the

Great Smoky Mountains. A front had passed through early the previous day, moving from northwest to southeast, so the air was becoming slightly chilly. Fall was on the way. Arthur looked up and admired the brilliance of the Milky Way. He picked out several constellations but couldn't remember them all. He began walking back up the low hill to St. Mary's Hospital.

The doorman nodded at Arthur and opened the door for him. Arthur took the stairs to ascend to the maternity floor because the elevator was too slow. He walked to the nurse's station, and asked the head nurse, Sister Mildred, if there were any news.

"Mr. Harris," she said, smiling, "you are the father of a boy, born just fifteen minutes ago. You will be able to view him soon in the nursery, but he is not there yet. He has been taken to his mother to nurse. They are in Room 312."

"Thank you, Sister," said Art. He walked up the hall to Room 312 and knocked lightly on the door. There was no response, so he opened the door and looked in. He saw his wife, Linda Marie Deville Harris, asleep in the bed, with a small bundle attached to her breast, her curly, dark-brown hair mussed by her ordeal. A nurse was sitting by the bed. He motioned to the nurse and stepped back into the hallway. She followed him.

"Sister, is everything all right?" he asked.

"Everything is wonderful, Mr. Harris. You have a healthy son! Your wife is, to say the least, fatigued, after the lengthy labor, but she is well and strong. She is sleeping while your son nurses. Would you like me to awaken her?"

"No, no – let her rest. She has had a bit of an ordeal. I am just sorry that I was not here when she gave birth. Because my wife had been in labor for over twelve hours and had not dilated much, the doctor suggested that I go get something to eat. I should have eaten faster and returned quickly." He felt guilty that he was not there at the birth.

"He had no idea that the labor would produce its results so quickly after that."

"Thank you, Sister," said Art. "What should I call you?"

"I am Sister Marie," she responded, her plump cheeks dimpling with a smile. "Would you like to sit with your wife?"

"Yes, Sister Marie, thank you very much." Art entered the room quietly, taking the chair that Sister Marie had vacated. He gazed fondly at his wife and the fuzzy head of his son and felt himself being shaken awake.

"Mr. Harris, are you all right?" he heard. Sister Marie who was shaking his shoulder. He blinked and rubbed his eyes to clear the sleep from them.

"Your wife called us because she thought you had collapsed."

"I'm well. I must have fallen asleep."

"She awoke, and saw you, but could not awaken you, so she pulled the nurse call cord." Art looked toward the bed, and saw Linda, wearing a worried look on her face.

"I spoke louder and louder, but you didn't answer," she said. "I was afraid you'd had a heart attack, like Father."

"Darling Heart," said Art, "you know I am a sound sleeper."

"Yes," she replied, "but usually, you snore loudly. I couldn't even hear you breathing and so I grew afraid." Art stood, approached the bed, leaned over and kissed Linda, savoring her red lips.

"Darling heart," he said, "I am so happy that you are all right and that our son is all right. May I hold him?" Sister Marie lifted the bundle and handed it to Arthur.

"Be sure to support his head," she said. Arthur accepted the bundle, placing his large left hand under the baby's head. He gazed lovingly at his son.

"I'm sorry I wasn't here when he was born," he said. "Doc sent me to eat, thinking you would be in labor a bit longer than you were. I was tired, or I would have eaten faster and been back sooner."

"Darling," said Linda, "I couldn't have stood it if labor took longer than it did. It took all the strength I had to see it through." She looked fondly into her husband's eyes, seeing the worry in his.

"Have you decided on a name?" asked Sister Marie. "We need a name for the birth certificate."

"Darling," said Linda, "I think we should name him after you."

"He would be Arthur Cornwallis Harris III," said Arthur. "I hesitate to do that. I was always nicknamed 'Corny,' and I wouldn't wish that on my son."

"It is a proud name," said Linda. "The honor associated with it would undo all the teasing that might result." Art was silent, for a while, looking at the bundle cradled in his arms. Finally, he bowed his head and kissed his son on the forehead. Immediately, the infant awoke and began crying. Art noticed the deep indigo of his eyes. Both he and Linda were brown-eyed, although his own eyes tended toward hazel.

"Arthur Cornwallis Harris III, welcome to the world," said Art. He handed the infant back to his wife, who placed him on her other breast, and the crying immediately stopped.

"He's a hungry babe," said Linda, worrying again. "I just hope my milk production is up to his appetite."

Art napped in the chair while his wife and son slept. Early in the morning, barely an hour after he had met his son, Art got to watch his son be "processed" —

footprinted, weighed, etc. Art waited for the somewhat rotund and balding attending physician to enter the room. Dr. O'Malley shook Art's hand warmly and congratulated him.

"You have a fine bouncing boy," he said, with a trace of Irish brogue.

"One thing bothers me," said Art, worrying. "His arms seem a bit short. He can't reach the top of his head!" Both husband and wife were worriers. Art ran nervous fingers through his hair. He, too, was balding on top, although his dark brown hair showed little grey.

"Perfectly normal, Mr. Harris, perfectly normal. His arms and legs are short in relation to the length of his torso. That conserved space in the womb. They will grow faster than the torso and soon he will be in proper proportion. You sound English."

"I was born English, but I am an American now. Don't you think he should be given growth hormones?"

"I don't think growth hormones are necessary. He'll be fine without them."

"I hope you're right, Doctor." Arthur looked at his son. After all, he did look like a normal baby.

"I just hope," said Art, "that he has a better world to live in than we did."

"I hope so, too," said a new voice. Arthur turned and recognized his parish priest, Father McGrory. "I wouldn't count on it, however, because the world has not been a better place for millennia. Read the Bible, and you'll see what I mean."

"I know, Father," said Art. "However, we must hope, and that is my hope."

"God bless you, my son," said Father McGrory. There was irony in the wording – Art was old enough to be the young priest's father. Not a tall man himself, but built like a football player, Art towered over the short, slender priest. Art had started his family late in life. He had served briefly in the US Cavalry at Fort Bliss, El Paso, right at the end of World War I. He had tried to enlist for World War II, but he was rejected because of his age. Linda was proud of him for trying to enlist, but greatly relieved that he remained a civilian.

"Please pray for us," asked Art. "Pray for the health of my wife; pray that I will be able to continue supporting my family; and pray, especially, that the world will turn a corner and be a better place for my son. May there never be another Hitler."

"Amen," said the priest. "I will include that in my prayers every day this week and the next." His bushy eyebrows bobbed up and down when he spoke. Art turned and looked fondly on his wife and son. Linda was already asleep again, Arthur III snuggled contentedly to her breast, making happy slurping sounds.

"Sister Marie," said Art, "I have to go to work. Will you tell my wife I'll be back after the end of the shift?"

"I will," said Sister Marie.

"I'll see you later, Son," he whispered. "I wonder: what will you be when you grow up?"

CHAPTER 1

ARRIVAL

July 1955
Location: Northwest Florida and Southeast Alabama

"You're on my side of the seat," complained Matthew, Arthur III's younger brother.

"No, I'm not," snapped Arthur. "My feet are still on my side of the seat."

"But you're using more seat than I am!" Matthew exclaimed.

"I'm bigger than you are," explained Arthur, "but I'm still all on my side of the seat. You can use more of your side if you want to. Besides, Butch is between us." Butch was their little dog, a mix that looked like a Fox Terrier but that was too small to be purebred. Their father called Butch a "Toy Fox Terrier."

The boys' grandmother, Marie Deville, sitting on the passenger side of the front seat, turned back toward them. "Stop quarreling," she said. "When we stop for a rest you won't have any treats if you continue this childish bickering." The boys curbed their desire to taunt each other and remained silent. Tempers easily grow hot in the oppressive, humid air of a Northwest Florida summer.

"*In principio*," said Arthur, "*creavit Deus caelum et terram.* And eventually He created Matthew to irritate me."

"What did you say?" demanded Matthew.

"In the beginning, God created heaven and earth," said Arthur.

"What you said," said Grandmother, "was designed to put down your brother because he doesn't know any Latin yet. Apologize. Now."

"Sorry, Matthew," said Arthur. "I didn't mean to insult you. I just wanted to let you know how much you are irritating me right now."

"Huh!" exclaimed Matthew, turning away to look out the window.

The trunk was filled with luggage, carefully placed like pieces of a Chinese puzzle to completely fill the space. If they had a flat tire, all of it would have to be taken out to reach the spare tire. So far on this trip, this had happened only once, between Houston and Beaumont.

Cardboard boxes filled with household goods filled the space between the front and back seats on the floor, so the boys had to ride with their feet up on the boxes. Matthew was small enough that he could ride with his feet straight out, but Arthur was tall enough to have to bend his knees. It was an uncomfortable position, so he changed it at times, drawing his feet up onto the seat beside him. He had been in that position when Matthew complained.

The heavy, steamy, hot summer air of the Mississippi coastal plain in July blew on them through the open windows, bringing them the salty, fishy smell of the Gulf of Mexico. Arthur's Davy Crockett T-shirt clung wetly to his skin and increased his discomfort. The blazing sun baked the dusty skin of the '39 Olds so it was burning hot to the touch. The heat rose in energetic, shimmering waves from the asphalt pavement ahead. Melted tar pooled in spots along the white sandy-clay shoulders where it had trickled out of the pavement.

Arthur's father had bought the car originally in Tennessee and drove it to Mexico when he moved the family there after World War II. They lived in Puebla, but that city did not have commercial airline service. When it came time to move to Dothan, Alabama, Art drove them to the airport in Mexico City, saw them onto their plane, and continued the drive to Brownsville, Texas. Their household goods had gone ahead of them by train. He had driven with Butch as his passenger and companion, while the rest of the family had flown to Brownsville First Class on Pan American Airways.

In Brownsville they traded places. Art flew ahead to Dothan, and Arthur's mother now was driving the car to their new home. While they were on the road, Art had picked out a house for them and started his new job as a construction engineer at U.S. Army Camp Rucker.

The Olds made steady progress toward Dothan with all the windows open. Arthur's mother kept it to a steady speed of between 55 and 60 miles per hour, despite the impatience of the other drivers. She was a stickler for obeying the law, and the maximum legal speed was 60 miles per hour. The hot, sticky air poured in on them through the open windows, but it would have been worse had the windows not been open. Nevertheless, they were damp for nearly the entire journey.

Neither Arthur nor Matthew stuck an arm out the window because the hot metal of the car would burn them – but also because the boys were mindful of a story their grandmother had told them of a boy who had rested his arm out the window of a car and had his elbow torn off by a passing truck. Arthur had guessed that the story was invented as an object lesson; but he had decided to play it safe by keeping his arms inside the car.

The land on both sides of them changed from coastal plain to woodland, forested with tall pine trees of uniform height as they left Mississippi and entered Alabama. A large billboard greeted them: "Welcome to Alabama" and on the second line, "Y'all Come!" Grandmother explained that the woodland was probably a tree farm, and that the trees were destined to become lumber or paper. She explained that if it were not a tree farm, they would see greater variety in the tree heights and in the species of trees.

The shade provided by the trees was a relief, when it existed. They were travelling from west to east, so most of the time they were in full sunlight, except on the rare occasions when the road curved. The land was very flat, with low hills rising no more than about fifteen feet above the valleys. They were still tracking along the coastal plain of the Gulf of Mexico, and on occasion they were still close enough to the Gulf to smell a trace of the salt air.

They arrived at Aunt Mary's house in the Mobile suburbs in the late morning, staying until early afternoon, enjoying a light lunch and the "coolth" on her breezy, screened-in, two-story, back porch with its tall, Greek-Revival Ionic columns. They washed down their sandwiches with Aunt Mary's "sweet tea" – iced tea Southern style, overly sweet to the tastes of non-Southerners. They rested briefly, napping on the porch, while the sky drizzled, providing a little more "coolth." When the drizzle turned to mist, Mother and Grandmother continued their nap and the boys explored the large back yard, with a crystal-clear brook running through it in a rocky bed, under massive magnolia trees festooned with dripping Spanish moss. The boys pretended they were Tom Sawyer and Huck Finn, that the other side of the creek was the island, and the creek was the mighty Mississippi.

Their interlude of coolness soon ended, though, and the clouds parted to let the heat of the sun make the air steamy and oppressive once again. They resumed their grueling journey towards Dothan, hoping to reach the city by nightfall.

When they stopped at a gas station after leaving Mobile, the attendant had told them that a new "Interstate Highway 10," a super-highway, was planned. It would parallel US 90, but that construction had not yet started. A long line of cars trailed behind them, and at each chance to pass, one would zoom past their car, honking in frustration at Mother's practice of never exceeding the speed limit. It was not long after leaving Mobile that they found themselves in the Florida Panhandle.

"Oh, look," said Grandmother, "there's a farmer's produce stand ahead. Let's stop and see if he has any watermelons. A watermelon would be very refreshing now and would reward the boys for their good behavior." Mother slowed the car. Drivers behind them started honking. She extended her left arm out the window with the elbow bent and her forearm vertical, in the classic right-turn signal. The honking stopped for the moment as she slowed more and pulled off onto the white clay shoulder at the farmer's stand. The family waited in the car until the line of cars had accelerated past them.

"Both of you get out on the right side of the car," said Grandmother. "You don't want to be run over." As she opened her door and got out, Matthew opened his door and slid to the ground. Arthur clipped the leash onto Butch's collar, slid across the seat and followed him, closing the car door after he and Butch had jumped out. Mother opened the driver's door and got out, closing it quickly and walking around in front of the car. The four of them walked to the farmer's stand, which was manned by a tow-haired boy of about 14, tall, gangly and freckle-faced.

"Do you have," asked Grandmother, "— oh, I see you *do* have – watermelons. How much are they?"

"They's 15 cents for one, two for a quarter, or three for forty cents," he said in a deep Southern drawl. "Y'all ain't from 'roun' here, is y'all?" Grandmother laughed.

"How can you tell – from our accents?" she asked.

"Yes, Ma'am," he said politely.

"No," she said, "we're not from around here. We're moving from Mexico to Dothan, Alabama."

"Y'all don't look Mexican," he observed.

"We're not," said Grandmother. "We're American, but we've been living in Mexico."

"Is y'all Army?" he asked.

"No," said Mother, "but my husband works for the Army."

"Figured it was somethin' like that," he said. "Nobody moves to Dothan 'ceptin' they be Army or workin' for the Army. Well, almost nobody. They's got a new factory in Dothan, and for a while folks was movin' to Dothan to work there, but that all stopped a few months ago."

"How long will it take us to get to Dothan?" asked Mother.

"About six hours, as slow as y'all was drivin'," he said. "Y'all can get there in 'bout four hours if you drive like everybody else 'round here. Y'all gonna buy a watermelon?"

"We'll take three," said Grandmother, handing him four dimes. "Have you any chilled?"

"Yes, Ma'am," he said. "I've got a bunch on ice in the cooler." He motioned toward a large chest cooler emblazoned on the front with the Coca-Cola logo. "Got ice cold Cokes, too."

"We'll take one chilled watermelon and two unchilled watermelons," said Grandmother.

"There's a rest stop with a picnic table 'bout a mile down the road," he said. "It's got good shade and y'all can stop there and eat your chilled watermelon."

"Thanks," said Grandmother. "Can you help us put the watermelons in the car?" Matthew tugged on Grandmother's sleeve.

"Where are we going to put the melons?" he asked. "Car's already full."

"We'll put one in the front on the floor," said Grandmother, "one on the seat between the two of you and one on the luggage, between your legs. Butch can sit on your laps for a while." Arthur thought how uncomfortable he would be for the next six hours and how cramped his legs would become, but he didn't say anything. The boy carried the watermelons one by one to the car and put them where Grandmother directed him. She handed him a dime tip. "Thanks for your help," she said.

"Thank you, Ma'am!" he said. "Y'all come back now, y'hear?" Arthur remembered the "Welcome to Alabama" Billboard. They all piled into the car and Mother drove it back onto the highway. The watermelon boy stood looking after them.

About a mile down the road, Mother pulled off at a small clearing with a picnic table in it. She and grandmother carried the chilled watermelon to the table, and the boys followed closely.

"How are we going to open it?" asked Arthur. "We don't have a knife."

"We don't need one," said Grandmother. "This melon is ripe enough to split open on its own." She brought the edge of her hand down sharply on the top of the watermelon and it split in half, lengthwise, with a cracking sound. She leaned her weight on the two sides of one of the halves, and repeated this with the other half. The watermelon lay there divided roughly into four quarters. She handed a quarter of a watermelon to each of them.

"How do we eat it?" asked Arthur. "We don't have any spoons."

"Just hold it like this," she said, "and bite into it." She demonstrated. "Lean over so it doesn't drip onto your shirts. On second thought, take off your shirts first."

Soon all four were devouring the melon. Arthur had never tasted anything so sweet, juicy and refreshing, nor had he experienced anything messier to eat. He wondered if the manna God served up for the Israelites in the wilderness was as good as that watermelon. He and Matthew held a contest to see who could spit seeds the greater distance.

After each of them had gone behind the bushes in turn ("Watch out for snakes, and don't pee on your shoes!"), they all piled back into the hot car and resumed their journey, much refreshed. Mother kept the speed of the car under the speed limit until someone passed her, and then sped up to match speed with the other car. Arthur noted that they were driving faster than 65 miles per hour. Soon, they turned north on US Highway 231, and the terrain changed. The hills became just a little higher, and the clay shoulders of the road changed from a sandy white to an orange color. The orange clay was cracked and fissured by the heat. Soon they arrived at another "Welcome to Alabama" sign and knew they were almost home.

When they arrived in Dothan, it was still light. Arthur's father had described Dothan to them as a hot little sleepy Southern town. As they drove up St. Andrews Street and Foster Street toward the downtown area, Arthur thought how apt the description was. No people were visible. All were in their homes. It was hot – very hot – and muggy, besides. The town was small, although it was the County Seat of Houston County. In no time they were crossing Main Street, and a moment later they were parking at the Houston Hotel. At eight stories, it was the tallest building by far in Dothan. Mother locked the car and they all walked into the lobby, which was cooler than the outside, and had a high ceiling with ceiling fans guaranteeing air movement. Mother walked toward the desk. Standing by the desk, chatting with the desk clerk, was Arthur's father.

Arthur always thought of his father as a big man. He was about five feet eight inches tall, slightly taller than average for men his age, and he was solidly built, but not fat. He had been a football player in college. Aging now, he was 54 years old, developing a bald spot, and starting to turn grey at the temples. His warm brown eyes and warm smile greeted his family as they rushed to his greeting embrace. He helped them unload the luggage they would need for the next few days and carried it to their rooms. He and Mother had one room, Grandmother had another, and Arthur and Matthew shared a room, as they had in Puebla.

The next day was Saturday. Dad drove them all in his "new" car, a used, but immaculate, 1953 Chevrolet Bel Air sedan, to see the house he had picked out. It was a cozy-looking brick house with large pecan trees in the yard and a chimney extending above the middle of the roof. The lot on one side was vacant, and another brick house about the same size was on the other side. In fact, the whole area around for several blocks was filled with comfortable brick houses on large lots with abundant trees.

Mrs. Seay, the owner of the house, gave them a tour. The house had three bedrooms and two baths across the back. A hallway, called a "breezeway," that ran the length of the house, separated the bedrooms and bathrooms in the back from the kitchen, dining room and living room in the front. The kitchen was large, with a kitchen table in the middle of the room big enough to seat the family. It was just big enough. It would do. They were home.

Before they could occupy their new home, however, the Seays had to move out. For a month and a half, the family lived four blocks away on Highland Street in a smaller, frame home clad with asbestos siding. It backed up to open cotton fields, and about a half-mile through the cotton fields behind the house was a freight rail line. They soon learned to sleep through the considerable amount of noise it made.

CHAPTER 2

STRIKING OUT

July and August 1955
Dothan, Alabama

During the summer, Arthur and Matthew made friends in the neighborhood, but Arthur was a curiosity – an outsider who "talked funny" and didn't know how to play baseball. Young Matthew had quickly picked up an Alabama accent and fit right in. To Arthur's amazement, his father also quickly adapted his "King's English" accent to an Alabama drawl. Arthur, however, had difficulty shedding his British accent.

Boys from the neighborhood came around one morning a few days after the family had arrived at their temporary new home to recruit "the new kid" to play sandlot baseball on the vacant lot at the corner. The "new kid" was Arthur. Matthew was considered too young for the game.

They divided into teams and Arthur's team batted first. The first batter got a base hit on the first pitch. The game continued for two full innings before Arthur got his first turn at bat. So far, all outs had been batted balls that had been caught; no one had struck out. Arthur was the second batter up that inning. The bat was slippery in his sweaty hands. He swung three times and missed the ball each time. The boy doing umpire duty called each strike.

"Strike one."

"Strike two."

"Strike three – you're out!" Confused, Arthur turned to the "Ump".

"What does that mean?" asked Arthur.

"It means you had three chances to hit the ball and missed, so you're out. Get out of the way and let the next batter try."

Disconsolate, Arthur left the field and plopped down cross-legged on the ground at his team's sideline area along the first base line. He watched the next batter get a base hit, advancing the first batter to second base. He walked the long half-block home, assuming that "out" meant he was out of the game. It was all he could do to keep from crying. He slapped his thighs and the seat of his pants to shed the dust from the playing field before entering the house. No one was home.

Apparently, his Mom had taken Matthew and their grandmother shopping. It was too hot inside, so Arthur went back outside and sat on the ground under the small shade tree in the front yard. After dozing there for a while, he woke up, dusted himself off, and went inside to get a drink of water. In Mexico the tap water was not potable. It had to be boiled before one could drink it. To Arthur, it was a novelty to be able to drink water straight from the tap.

After a while, a couple of his new friends, John and Ralph, came by the house. They knocked on the kitchen door and Arthur opened it to let them come in.

"Why'd you leave the game?" asked Ralph in the region's heavy drawl. "Are you sick?"

"No," said Arthur. "The umpire said I was out."

"He didn't mean y'all was out of the game," said John. "He meant that your chance at bat that innin' was over. Ain't you never played baseball before?"

"No," said Arthur, "I don't know anything about the game."

"Y'all got lemonade?" asked Ralph. "I'm terrible thirsty."

"I think so," said Arthur, going to the refrigerator and opening it. He took out the pitcher of cold lemonade, put it on the oilcloth-covered kitchen table, and retrieved three glasses from the cupboard. He lifted the pitcher from the ring of water that had already condensed and collected on the oilcloth. He poured lemonade into the three glasses, handing one to John and one to Ralph and took one himself. All three boys sat down, drank thirstily and set their glasses on the table. Arthur's family ate breakfast and dinner at that table, but supper was always "formal," in the small dining room.

"See here," said Ralph, sketching a diamond on the oilcloth with the condensed water. "This here's the baseball diamond. This here's the home plate. There are three bases, first here, second here, and third here. The team in the field has a catcher here, behind home plate; a first baseman, who stands 'bout here; a second baseman 'bout here; a shortstop, who stands 'bout here; a third baseman, 'bout here; and three outfielders, who stand here, here, and here. The pitcher's mound is here. The pitcher stands on it to pitch. The ump stands here, behind the catcher. One guy from the other team comes up to bat. He stands here, if he's right-handed, or here, if he's a leftie. You got that so far?"

"Yes," said Arthur.

"Good. Now the first batter comes up to bat…" He proceeded to give Arthur a short course in the rules of baseball, and a little bit of strategy.

He concluded the "class" by saying, "If a batter gets all the way 'round the bases without gettin' out, an' runs to home plate and touches it before the ball gets there, he scores a run, and that counts one point for his team. He can also get a point if he hits the ball so hard it goes outa the ball park. In real ball parks, they got a fence out back of the outfield, and if the ball goes over the fence without hitting the ground first, it's called a home run. At our corner lot, if it goes into either of the neighbor's yards, on either side, without hittin' the ground first, it's a home run…and iffen it breaks a neighbor's window, we *all* run home." The boys all laughed.

After an hour of baseball talk, Arthur understood the basic rules of the game, and had been given an introduction to base-running strategy and base stealing, which confused him a bit. Now, however, he felt confident that he could play the game without making too many embarrassing mistakes. He could gradually stop being the "outsider."

The next day he took some of his stash of silver dollars and walked downtown to the sporting goods store and bought a glove, ball, and bat. On second thought, he bought a second glove, for Matthew. After that, at any spare moment, he and Matthew would retire to the back yard and practice their baseball skills.

Arthur played often after that, even joining Little League, but he was good only at two things: hitting the ball and running. He couldn't hit very hard but he was good for a base hit often enough that he always made the starting lineup. He ran fast enough to steal bases – but he couldn't catch very well unless the ball started its trajectory close to him. He couldn't throw the ball very far, and his throws were somewhat inaccurate. He was determined to improve, with practice.

Logically, he was assigned to left field, where he would be less likely to be called on to catch, but if he did catch or field a ball, he only had to throw to second base, third base, or shortstop, so if he threw inaccurately, there were three chances someone would be able to catch it. Still, he loved the game – but when he came up to bat, the field chatter was all about "the stinkin' Yankee tryna hit a ball but got none," and other disparaging remarks. It didn't bother him once he understood that every batter was bad-mouthed, and he did his share of chatter when the other team was at bat.

He was accepted by the kids in the neighborhood and had friends but remained an outsider. His parents hadn't grown up with the local parents, and so his family remained outsiders – well-liked, respected, and even admired – but outsiders, nonetheless. Arthur worked hard to try to erase his somewhat British accent, but never completely succeeded.

Arthur and Matthew had been tutored when the family lived in Mexico. Suddenly, in September 1955, on the day after Labor Day, at the age of ten, he was in Alabama, sitting in a classroom in public school for the first time. When school started, it became evident quickly that he was several grade levels ahead of his class in academic knowledge. He was able to coast through his classes, and his original friends started drifting away from him, except for those who were really struggling with their studies, and his fellow "geniuses." Arthur was happy to spend time with those who needed help, tutoring them, and they rewarded him with firm friendship. He became the champion of the poorer children who did not have the advantage of educated parents. Nevertheless, he continued to feel like an outsider who didn't belong, and was classed, even by his friends, with the geniuses. There was one other student in Arthur's class who was something of an outsider and also a genius: Freddy.

CHAPTER 3

A QUESTION OF CAREERS

October and November 1956
Dothan, Alabama

S. Frederick Jefferson, Jr., was the eldest son of
County Judge S. Frederick Jefferson, and quickly became
Arthur's best friend. The "S" stood for Samuel. He didn't
want to be called Sammy, so everyone called him Freddy.
He and his family lived just down the street two blocks, at
the very edge of town, on an estate that included a
comfortable large house, small cattle farm, and a small,
swampy forest they called a tree farm. They also kept a
couple of horses.

Freddy and Arthur were in the same classroom at
Cloverdale Elementary School in the sixth grade. Freddy
and Arthur competed for top-of-the-class ranking. Freddy
might not have been as intelligent as Arthur, but he
worked hard, and made straight As. Arthur made good
grades, but not straight As. Freddy was something of an
outsider because his family was wealthy, and because he
made straight As, so he was considered the "teacher's
pet" and somewhat resented. The two outsiders naturally
gravitated toward each other.

By tradition, when a new family moved in, everyone
in the neighborhood paid a visit, usually bringing a

prepared dish of food for the family. Freddy's mother had come to visit shortly after the Harrises moved into their house and discovered that Arthur's mother liked opera. His mother listened every Saturday to the weekly radio broadcast of the New York Metropolitan Opera, and so did Mrs. Jefferson. On Saturday afternoons, the two women would get together either at the Jefferson home or the Harris home to listen to the opera together. Because the Jefferson home had an air conditioner in the living room and the Harris home did not, in hot weather they listened to the opera at the elegant Jefferson home. The two boys would usually play in the barn or the pasture at such times. Arthur loved music, but he didn't understand the words of the operas, so he preferred to play rather than to listen to songs he didn't understand.

On a warm Saturday in October, they were in the barn, becoming acquainted with a young colt that had been born the week before. A flaky mix of dust and hay fibers floated in the air, making scintillating sunbeams where the sun came into the barn through cracks in the siding. The colt soon grew hungry and was feeding noisily at his mother's teats. The boys sat on a bale of straw and watched. It was a hot day (Dothan had a lot of those, even in late autumn) and the barn, with its high roof, offered a measure of protection from the heat. Its hay-hoisting door at the loft level allowed the rising hot air to exit, creating a gentle breeze in the hayloft. After a few minutes, the boys climbed the ladder to the loft and lay back on the hay that had broken free from the bales.

"Why did your family live in Mexico?" asked Freddy, lying back on a bale of hay and picking his teeth with a straw.

"My Dad was born in Mexico," said Arthur, sitting cross-legged on the next bale, "and after the War, Dad moved us back there where he got a job building power plants."

"Do you want to build power plants when you grow up?" asked Freddy. "Are you going to be an engineer?"

"Maybe," said Arthur. "I'd rather be a Navy officer. We saw a movie a few weeks ago about submarines during the War, and that looked exciting. I want to do something exciting in my life."

"I'm probably going into the army," said Freddy, "and I'll go to law school after and become a lawyer, and maybe a judge, like my Dad. All the men in my family have been army. My great-great-granddaddy fought under General Lee, and we're related to Thomas Jefferson." He said the last sentence with obvious pride.

"My great-grandfather fought in the Texas Army during the Mexican-American War," said Arthur, "and fought in the Confederate Army. He was a colonel and won the last battle of the Civil War. We're related to General Lord Cornwallis." Freddy looked confused.

"The Yankees won the last battle of the Civil war," said Freddy. "They defeated General Lee and that's why we're now in the United States of America instead of the Confederate States of America."

The mare whinnied and stepped away from the colt, who followed, clamping firmly on the teat. The mare reached behind with her head and gently shoved the colt away. He looked confused. She turned to face him, and after a while he turned away and plopped down on the bed of straw in the stall.

"That wasn't the actual last battle," said Arthur. "The actual last battle was fought after the war was over, at Brownsville, Texas, and the Confederacy won it. They didn't know the war was over yet. It was called the Battle of Palmetto Flats."

"I didn't know that," said Freddy. "Was your Dad in the Navy?"

"No," said Arthur, "he was in the Army – the horse cavalry right at the end of World War One."

"Sounds like the Harris men were all Army," said Freddy. "Will your Daddy let you join the Navy?"

"We had one relative in the Navy," said Arthur, "Commodore Truxton. He commanded the USS Constellation."

"Oh," said Freddy, "then there is precedent." Arthur had heard the word used before by Perry Mason on TV, so he understood what it meant, but he would not have used it -- but Freddy was the son of a lawyer who was a judge, so he tended to pepper his conversation with important-sounding legal terms.

"If I don't go into the Army," said Freddy, "I'll go into the FBI and help track down and capture Communist spies."

"Maybe I'll be an American spy," said Arthur, "and go spy on the Communists." He had never thought of being a spy before, but the words came out naturally in the flow of conversation.

"You might get killed," said Freddy.

"Not if I'm careful," said Arthur. "They'll never know I'm a spy."

"You'll have to be devious and misleading," said Freddy, "and you'll be able to get by without people knowing you're a spy. Are you good at lying?"

"No," said Arthur, "lying is a sin."

"You'll have to learn to lie if you're going to be a spy – or a lawyer. My Dad says lawyers lie a lot."

"I'll have to think about it," said Arthur. "I guess lying to the bad guys might be considered a good thing."

Thanksgiving that year was also warm weather, which is not unusual in southern Alabama. Arthur had adjusted to school, after his first difficult weeks, and was doing well. Matthew had started in the first grade but didn't do well at all. One of the teachers had suggested testing him. When he tested at third grade level, the school bumped him up to second grade, and he started doing well, too. It seems he had been bored in first grade. By Thanksgiving of their second year, both boys had settled into the public-school routine.

The Thanksgiving table was set with their mother's fine china, crystal and silverware, with two silver candlesticks holding tall wax tapers. Because it was a special day, the boys and their father were wearing suits and ties. It was reasonably cool in the dining room. Arthur's father had installed window air-conditioning units in the living room and kitchen, and the air circulated easily into the dining room, which was between them. Grandmother sent the boys to wash their hands. When the boys returned, they all gathered around the table. Matthew reached for a fresh, hot, dinner roll and put it on his plate.

"You lack patience, child," said Grandmother to Matthew.

"But I'm hungry. Why can't I start?" asked Matthew. Matthew was only seven years old. Arthur was eleven – a virtual adult, by his own reckoning. His age had two digits, and in two years he would be a teenager. Arthur lacked patience, too, but knew better than to try to start eating before everyone was ready and Dad had said the blessing.

"Because we haven't said Grace yet," said Grandmother. Arthur believed that God would understand. Once, he had earned his Grandmother's ire by saying just, "Grace," when she asked him to say Grace, but he said nothing and waited. He didn't like to wait. His grandmother had told him many times that he lacked patience. She also liked to remind him that patience is a virtue. Putting the two statements together, he assumed that he lacked virtue, because he lacked patience. Nevertheless, he exercised patience, and so he believed that he was acquiring, even if he did not yet have, virtue.

But if he became a spy, he'd have to lie, so he'd have to be careful not to get too much virtue.

Father Jones had taught him in Catechism Class that the conscious, deliberate exercise of a virtue does not make one virtuous unless it becomes habitual. He was determined to become virtuous, by the conscious exercise of virtue until it became habitual. He wasn't quite sure what virtue itself was, but he knew it was good to have. He knew a virtuous act when he saw – or did – one, so he was determined to do virtuous acts, and to avoid un-virtuous acts, even if he didn't understand what it was to *have* virtue.

Father mumbled the usual blessing: "We thank thee, O Lord, for these thy gifts, which we are about to receive from Thy bounty. Bless them to our good and ourselves to Thy service – in the Name of the Father, and of the Son, and of the Holy Ghost, Amen." He crossed himself, and all did the same. After that, they all sat and began eating. Arthur dug in hungrily, largely ignoring the flow of adult conversation around the table.

After dinner, Arthur and Matthew went to their bedroom. The room was furnished with two twin beds that their father had made, plus two bedside tables and two dressers. It contained narrow floor-to-ceiling bookshelves built on either side of the large double window. The bookshelves were varnished pine, the same color as the knotty pine that paneled all the walls of the bedroom. The lower portion of each bookshelf was constructed as a small desk, and there was a chair for each desk. It was there that the boys did their homework and worked on their craft hobbies.

On the first shelf above Arthur's desk was a plastic model of the USS Missouri, halfway constructed. Matthew had a simple model airplane under construction on his desk. On the wall above the headboards of the beds hung two small pictures, one by Arthur and one by

Matthew, both framed in somewhat rustic frames made by the boys themselves. Arthur's was a picture of a ship he had painted with watercolors on a square of white cotton cut from an old sheet. Needless to say, the colors had bled a little bit. Matthew's was a picture of an airplane drawn on blue craft paper in red Crayola. Arthur found it hard to focus his eyes on the red lines on the blue paper – they seemed to vibrate. Matthew had defended his choice of colors. "If you can't focus your eyes on the lines, you won't see what a bad picture it is," he said.

Given a choice, Arthur would not have his picture hanging for all to see. He had been much younger when he had painted it. In the picture, the smoke from the smokestack billowed backward and the flag on the flagpole at the stern of the ship blew in the opposite direction. His father had pointed that out to him after he had framed the painting and hung it on the wall of his bedroom in Puebla. He wondered how he could have made such a mistake. He worried that it made him look stupid.

Arthur started into his homework, but his mind kept thinking of his conversation with Freddie. He put his thoughts aside and charged through his homework in record time so that he could enjoy the rest of the Thanksgiving weekend. After completing his homework, he opened the book on geology he had borrowed from the Dothan Public Library. He found the spot where he had stopped reading a couple of days ago, backed up one page, and began reading. Geology didn't have problems of virtue. Maybe instead of becoming a spy, he would become a geologist.

CHAPTER 4

CAREER PLAN

March 1957
Dothan, Alabama

Arthur was an avid reader. He read every magazine that came to the house and every book in his parents' library. His parents had a decent library and had always bought books for their sons to read. They had all the classics for children – *Treasure Island*, *Black Beauty*, *Le Morte d'Arthur*, and dozens of others, as well as all the classics for adults. Arthur read them all.

He had learned to read at age three and soon was reading everything available. Uncle Henry and Aunt Mary were impressed with his reading skills when they visited the Harrises in Puebla in the spring of 1953, when Arthur was eight, and read them several pages from Shakespeare's *Macbeth*.

They found him one morning reading the Spanish-language newspaper, *El Sol de Puebla*. They asked him about the news and he gave them a synopsis. At age nine, he read the Bible, cover-to-cover. Soon after that, his father unpacked some boxes that had arrived and arranged *The Encyclopædia Britannica* on the new bookshelves he had built for the purpose. He read the 24 volumes of the Encyclopædia Britannica, starting with the first volume, "A to Aardvark." He read *Merriam Webster's*

International Dictionary, a large, two-volume set, after getting half way through the first volume of the encyclopedia, because there were too many words he had to look up while reading the encyclopedia. He was in Volume 12 of the Encyclopædia when they moved from Puebla to Dothan, and he continued after the books were back on the shelves in Dothan. He skipped over the parts for which he lacked the math, but he got most of the concepts. By the age of ten he had a very large working vocabulary.

His parents subscribed to several magazines: *Time, US News and World Report, National Geographic, Look, Life, Popular Mechanics, Parents' Magazine, Construction Methods and Equipment, The Smithsonian, Sports Illustrated, Atlantic Monthly, The Saturday Evening Post, Vogue, House and Garden, Readers' Digest,* and *Coronet.* He and his brother subscribed to *Children's Digest* and *Boys' Life.* He read all these magazines cover-to-cover.

In one issue of *Parents' Magazine* he paid particular attention to an article on how to explain the "facts of life" to a young teenager. As a result, he didn't have to ask his parents to explain any of it.

He started noticing the ads in *Parents' Magazine* for boarding prep schools. The only two that interested him were Valley Forge Military Academy and Farragut Naval Academy. Because he wanted to be a naval officer and a spy, he longed to go to Farragut Academy, although he had not broached the subject to his parents. He began to form a plan.

It was a rare Alabama day, a cold day in March, and Matthew had moved from the boys' bedroom into the dining room to do his homework, because he was cold in the bedroom. The heating system of the house consisted of a floor furnace in the hallway that separated the living spaces from the bedrooms, supplemented by a fireplace in the living room. To save on fuel, the bedroom doors were left closed, and, therefore, the bedrooms were unheated, except at times of intense cold. Arthur's father had arranged for regular deliveries of coal to a bin he built in the carport, and in cold weather a coal fire was always burning in the living-room fireplace.

Arthur, despite the cold, was still in the bedroom. He treasured these moments of privacy. He pulled on a sweater and took a book from the shelf above the desk, opening it to the bookmarked section. He continued reading where he had left off the day before, instead of working on his ship model. It was his first spy novel; he had graduated from *Hardy Boys Mysteries* to James Bond. He was reading Fleming's *Casino Royale*, which he had checked out from the Dothan Public Library.

As he read, he thought about how exciting it would be to have a career as a spy. James Bond was a spy with the British intelligence agency, MI6, but also a Commander in the Royal Navy. Arthur had read the *Hornblower* novels in serialized form in *The Saturday Evening Post* and would have loved to travel back in time and be an officer on a sailing warship. Arthur's love of ships convinced him that he, too, should enter the Navy and pursue a career as a spy.

After reading a couple of chapters, he placed the bookmark and closed the book, and took out from the drawer under the desk a three-month-old *Parents' Magazine*. He had dog-eared the page toward the back that had ads for boarding schools, and studied again the ad he had memorized long before – the ad for Farragut Naval Academy, a maritime academy for boys that took boys his age and educated them all the way through high school, preparing them for entry into Annapolis, from which they emerged as officers in the U.S. Navy.

From the drawer under his desk he took out a large manila envelope. He had written to Farragut Naval

Academy, carefully typing the letter on his grandfather's old Remington typewriter, which he had "inherited." He had asked for information on sending a young boy to the school, and the Academy had responded with this envelope. He had memorized the contents and had even begun filling in the application form that was included with the school information. He decided the time had come to raise the subject with his father. Because he was still an outsider in Dothan, he didn't fit in easily with the other kids. He wanted to attend Farragut, and he was now old enough to do so.

The next morning, Arthur awoke early. It was still dark night outside. His father worked at Fort Rucker, which was on Daylight Savings Time, although Alabama was not. His father had to be at work at 6:00 in the morning Alabama time, which was 7:00 in the morning Daylight Savings Time, and so he would arise at 4:30, eat a quick breakfast, shower and shave, and leave for work while the rest of the family still slept. That morning, Arthur arose early and joined his father for breakfast.

"To what do I owe this honor?" asked his father, smiling.

"I wanted to discuss something with you," said Arthur.

"Having trouble in school?" asked his father.

"No, I'm doing fine there, but I do want to talk about school, because I want to talk to you about my career." His father regarded him for a moment, a small smile on his face.

"Don't you think you're a bit young to be worrying about that now?" asked Father.

"No, Father," said Arthur, "because the choice I am making requires early preparation."

"So, what do you want to be when you grow up?" asked Father.

"I want to be an intelligence officer in the U.S. Navy."
His father's smile faded and he regarded his son seriously.

"It sounds like you have given this some thought," he
said.

"Yes, Dad, I have," said Arthur. "To achieve that
goal, I will need to be able to win an appointment to
Annapolis. To do that, I must be well prepared so I will be
considered for the appointment. I do not believe I can get
the necessary preparation in public high school. I think I
need to go to Farragut Naval Academy, which takes boys
my age and prepares them for maritime careers. A high
proportion of boys graduating from Farragut go on to
Annapolis and to careers in the Navy."

His father regarded him seriously. Arthur laid the
manila envelope on the table next to his father's cup of
coffee. "This is the information on Farragut Naval
Academy. It includes an application form. I have started
filling it out, but the rest you will have to do."

"There are other paths," said his father, "to a
commission as a naval officer. You can go to any of a
number of colleges and join the Navy Reserve Officers'
Training Corps, the NROTC. I earned my commission as
a U.S. Cavalry Officer by joining the ROTC when I was
in school. I chose not to follow a military career, but I
served for a term in the cavalry."

"I'll think about that, Father, but I think Farragut
would provide me the best preparation available."

"I'm sure you're right," said Father. He was silent for
about twenty seconds, his head bowed. He raised his head
and looked seriously at Arthur. "I agree that Farragut
would provide excellent preparation. However, I don't
have the money to send you to Farragut, and I cannot get
the money. I'm very sorry about that, but that's just the
way it is. Do you remember anything of the circumstances
surrounding our move from Puebla to Dothan?"

"Some," Arthur shrugged. "I know you were worried that you would lose your job because the Mexican government was going to nationalize your company."

"That's right, Son. They did nationalize the company, and they made it illegal for non-Mexicans to hold management positions in the company. Do you understand what nationalization of an industry is?"

"Yes, Dad," said Arthur. "Socialist governments move to take over and control the major means of production and distribution. When a government takes over a business, it is called 'nationalizing the business.'"

"Yes," said his father, "the Mexican government took over the company for which I worked. They seized it, without paying the owners of the company the value of their ownership. The company was a corporation. Do you know what that means?"

"A corporation is a form of company in which the ownership is vested in shares that can be bought and sold. Investors buy the shares, and the company can use that money to build its business. The profits of the company, or at least some of the profits, are distributed to the shareholders as income. The investors can keep their shares or sell them to others."

"Yes," said his father. "I invested a lot of the money I had saved in shares in *Luz y Fuerza de Puebla*, hoping that the shares would provide income for my retirement. I lost my investment when the government nationalized the company, and so I do not have that money any more. We are living now at a much-reduced status compared to the way we lived in Mexico, as I am sure you are aware. My salary at Fort Rucker is much lower than my salary was in Mexico, and the cost of living here is much higher than it was in Mexico. I'm sorry, but you'll have to make do with public school. If you work hard, make excellent grades, and keep out of trouble, you'll be able to get into the college of your choice with a scholarship, and even

into Annapolis. If I had the money, I would pay for you to go to Farragut, if your heart were really set on it; but that is something I just can't do. I don't have the money, and I can't get the money. I just can't pay for private schooling for you. I won't even be able to pay for college for you. I had to earn my own way through college, as my father, your grandfather, was dead and the Mexican government had nationalized our family's silver mines in their revolution. I paid my own way through college with a scholarship and with full-time work, and I also supported my mother and my sister while doing that. You won't have it *that* hard, but you'll have to work your own way through college. I'll help all that I can, but my funds are limited, and I'll have to save some to help Matthew. I'm very sorry, son, but I don't have the money to pay tuition at Farragut."

Arthur felt like crying but bit the inside of his lower lip to prevent that from happening. He felt as though his dreams had just been crushed. He felt really sorry that he had asked his father for the private schooling. He loved, respected and admired his father very much and didn't like having put his father in the position of having to tell him that he could not send him to the school of his choice. He sighed and straightened his shoulders.

"Dad," he said, "I understand what you have told me, and I understand the sacrifices you and Mother have made for Matthew and me. I hope that I never let you down. I'll do the best I can in school, so that I can go to a good college, one with a good Navy ROTC program." He and his father solemnly shook hands.

"Son," said his father, "If you do your part, I'll do everything I can for you."

"I know you will. Thank you, Father." Arthur left the kitchen and returned to his room, forcing himself to a firm determination to achieve excellence in school, so he could follow the career of his choice.

His father gazed after him solemnly, tears forming in his eyes. *What have I done,* he thought, *to deserve such an intelligent, thoughtful, mature son?* When he got to his room, Arthur cried, feeling very immature.

And yet, although he was determined on a career in intelligence, Arthur wondered: *Is a career as a spy a virtuous career?* A visit to Father Jones in the confessional before Mass the next Sunday helped him to resolve his doubts. He made his usual confession, admitting to lying to his mother about something, lusting after a girl in class and masturbating that night, omitting his daily prayers on a couple of occasion. After this regular confession, he confided that he was considering a career in espionage but was uncertain whether he could remain virtuous and still be a spy, because of the level of deception required. Father Jones was silent for a minute.

"My son," he said, "In ancient times, while the Apostles still headed the churches and St. Peter was still Pope, there were many converts among the Roman soldiers, including both officers and men. They were allowed to continue in their careers as soldiers, even though their careers involved killing. Killing in the name of the State in wartime, when one is ordered to kill, is a just act under the laws of civil society, and this was recognized as an exception, if you will, to the Fifth Commandment, 'Thou shalt not kill.' A better translation would be, 'Thou shalt not murder.' Murder is killing that is not justified under the law. Exceptions to the Fifth Commandment were always recognized, in that some sins were punishable by death from the earliest days of the acceptance of the Ten Commandments, and so killing under those circumstances was justifiable. The Ten Commandments are not absolute rules; they are guiding principles that must be applied to actual events and situations of life, but exceptions are allowed based on circumstances. As a spy for your government, you would be in the shoes, as it were, of an early Christian who was a Roman Centurion. That places you in between; you are subject to the commands of your government, but you must determine for yourself that the commands are just. If you are ordered to kill, you must conclude that the killing is independently justifiable. You may kill enemies of your country who would otherwise kill your countrymen. In that killing, you are preventing killing. If the country engages in a war that is just, as I believe the wars in which the United States have engaged have been just, the Christian soldier may fight in that war. Similar rules apply in peacetime. We know that our country has enemies who would destroy us, given the opportunity. The use of deceit to learn about them so we can prevent our own destruction is justified. Moses himself sent spies ahead into the Promised Land before the Children of Israel came out of the desert to conquer it. Does all of that make sense?"

"Yes, Father, it does," said Arthur. "Thank you. I will think on this and guide my choices accordingly."

"I'll pray for you, my son. I had hoped that you would feel a calling to the priesthood – but a military calling, and I include the espionage services of our country in that category, is honorable and acceptable unto God. Remember that Jesus told his disciples, 'Behold I send you as sheep in the midst of wolves. Be ye therefore wise as serpents and simple as doves.' You will, in a way, have to do things that in other contexts would be considered unvirtuous and even sins, to follow that career choice, but you can serve your country without really losing your virtue. You need only lose your naiveté and exercise your judgement. You must be able to distinguish between immoral deceit and justified deceit. And now, my son, is there more you need to confess?"

"No, Father, I think that is all."

"Now make your Act of Contrition."

"O my God," said Arthur, "I am heartily sorry for having offended Thee and I detest all my sins because of Thy just punishments, but most of all because they offend Thee, my God, Who art all good and deserving of all my love. I firmly resolve, with the help of Thy grace, to sin no more and avoid the near occasion of sin. Amen."

"*Dominus noster Jesus Christus te absolvat;*" said Father Jones, "*et ego auctoritate ipsius te absolvo ab omni vinculo excommunicationis et interdicti in quantum possum et tu indiges. Deinde, ego te absolvo a peccatis tuis in nomine Patris, et Filii, et Spiritus Sancti. Amen.*" Arthur made the sign of the Cross. Father Jones continued with another prayer.

"*Passio Domini nostri Jesu Christi, merita Beatae Mariae Virginis et omnium sanctorum, quidquid boni feceris vel mali sustinueris sint tibi in remissionem peccatorum, augmentum gratiae et praemium vitae aeternae. Amen.*" Arthur made the sign of the cross again. "For your penance, pray five Our Fathers and five Hail Marys. I hope you will learn the Act of Contrition in Latin. You do plan to take Latin in High School?"

"Yes, Father, I do. I already know a little Latin, the Latin of the Mass. I'll start learning the Act of Contrition now."

"God bless you, my son."

Arthur left the confessional feeling like a new person, fresh and acceptable to God, and determined more than ever to pursue a career in naval intelligence. Now, when someone asked him what he wanted to be when he grew up, he would say, "I want to be an intelligence officer with the Navy." He began collecting information on NROTC programs, and on the universities that hosted them. One school rose immediately to the top of his list: Rice Institute. Rice did not charge tuition. Anyone who could qualify for acceptance could attend tuition-free; and it had a good NROTC department. It also had an excellent reputation as a science and engineering school. First, he would join the Boy Scouts, to learn military drills and wilderness survival skills.

CHAPTER 5

BOY DETECTIVE

September 1958
Dothan, Alabama

The bicycle rode bumpily over the rutted, dusty path. Arthur had taken this path every day since starting at Young Junior High School in September of 1956. He started on St. Andrews Street, continued to Foster Street, and cut left up the driveway of the nursing home. He continued into the former field behind, now growing just grass and weeds. The trail wound up the hillside to Franklin Street, on which he would take a left, crossing Oates Street to Dusy Street. He would then pedal up Dusy Street to the school. The path through the field was a short cut with no traffic. Once he had passed the nursing home, it angled left, a copse of woods filling the space to his right. As usual, a small plume of smoke was rising from the heart of the woods, and a branch of the trail angled into the woods.

Arthur was early, so he applied the brakes, coming to a quiet stop. He was alone this morning. Usually, he rode the trail in company with his best friend, Freddy, but Freddy had a strep throat and would be out of school until it was cured. Arthur decided to investigate the smoke, as a way of practicing to become a spy. He walked his bike quietly into the woods and off the path into the dense trees, where he found enough space to lay it down on the ground. He placed his backpack beside it, and, opening it, removed his Kodak Brownie Camera. Grass wouldn't grow in such dense shade, but there was an abundance of pine needles covering the ground, with tall ferns straining to reach the sunlight. No one would spot his bike and backpack lying there.

Walking carefully and quietly through the trees as he had learned to do in Boy Scouts for stalking prey, and paralleling the pathway rather than on it, Arthur remained hidden as best he was able, flitting from tree to tree. Soon, he approached a clearing and lowered to a crawling position, still shielding himself using trees. Lying face-down on the ground behind the trunk of a large pine tree, he peered around to see what was in the clearing.

He saw a large, green-stained, copper tank, standing above the ground on angle-iron legs about four feet high. The tank had a conical top whose narrow end terminated into a copper tube that spiraled down like a cork-screw to a smaller tank sitting on a wood pallet on the ground. There was a fire burning brightly under the larger tank, and a man knelt beside the tank, feeding split logs into the fire. A double-barreled shotgun, presumably his, leaned against a crate beside him, which held burlap sacks. Several more crates were stacked behind it, a tarpaulin covering their tops.

A small copper pipe rose from the ground beside the tank on the left side of the tank, rising to the top of the tank and turning 90 degrees, joining a copper flange welded to the side of the tank. Between the 90-degree joint and the flange was the bulge of a gate valve, with a valve handle protruding above. A ladder leaned against the tank beside the pipe. Above the pipe connection, about a foot up the inverted cone that formed the top, was a round hatch, with clamps placed around its perimeter to hold it tight to the top of the tank. To the right of the tank, several dozen gleaming, glass milk jugs with cork stoppers sat empty. Arthur took in the scene, listening idly to the mocking bird singing and warbling in the tree above his head.

This must be a moonshiner's whisky still, he thought. The man tending the fire placed the last piece of firewood into the fire and stood up, backing away. He sat down on the crate against which his shotgun leaned and removed a pipe from his right pocket and a leather pouch from his left. He carefully filled and tamped the pipe and placed it in his mouth. He took a match, struck it on the rough wood of the crate, and lit his pipe, blowing clouds of blue smoke that rose to join the larger stream of smoke rising above the clearing from the fire under the still. The pungent aroma of pipe smoke mixed with the smell of the wood smoke from the fire under the still.

Very carefully, Arthur leaned to the left and raised his camera to sight through the little aperture at the top. *Good. I'm just far enough away to get the entire scene in one shot*, he thought. He clicked the shutter lever, its sound lost in the crackling of the fire and the whispering of the breeze in the pines overhead. Arthur pulled himself behind the tree just as the man turned to look in his direction. Arthur held his breath, but nothing more happened. After what seemed like five minutes, he looked warily around the tree. The man was still sitting on the crate, smoking his pipe and watching the fire. Arthur turned and made his way carefully from tree to tree, taking care not to step on any twigs on the ground. He circled the still, taking pictures from several different angles. Finally, he reached his backpack, stowed his camera, put his arms through the backpack and settled it onto his back. He lifted his bicycle and rolled it carefully out of the woods and back onto the pathway.

At school during the morning recess, he went to the Principal's office and found Mr. Turk sitting behind his desk, shuffling paperwork. He knocked on the open door.

"Mr. Harris," said Mr. Turk, "Come in and tell me what you have done to get into trouble."

"Mr. Turk," said Arthur, "I'm not in trouble – at least not yet. I witnessed something that I think the FBI needs to know about."

"Well, well, that sounds serious. Close the door behind you and have a seat."

Arthur closed the door and sat on the straight-backed wooden chair that sat facing the desk.

"Now," said Mr. Turk, "start from the beginning and tell me about it, and together we'll figure out what to do about it." Arthur took a deep breath and began.

"Do you know the little patch of woods behind the old nursing home on St. Andrews' Street across from Southside Elementary?"

"Yes," said Mr. Turk.

"Do you know the pathway that cuts through the field behind it?"

"Yes," said Mr. Turk. "Judge Jefferson and I used to ride our bikes up that path to come to Young Junior High School when we were students here."

"Did you ever notice smoke coming up from the middle of the little woods?"

"Yes," said Mr. Turk, nodding.

"Did you ever wonder what caused it, and investigate it?"

"Yes," said Mr. Turk. "I wondered, and asked my Dad, and he said it was probably a still. After that I made sure I rode past the woods without looking into them or stopping. I didn't want anyone to shoot at me." Arthur grinned.

"This morning," said Arthur, "I was early, so I decided to take a look. I hid in the trees and watched a man tending the fire under the still."

"Mr. Harris," said Mr. Turk, "that still has been there a long time. It's illegal, of course, but it provides cheap whisky to all the bars in the area and to a lot of the citizens as well. That's why nobody has reported it to the federal authorities. It's a federal matter. There's no local office for the Alcohol and Tobacco Tax Division of the Internal Revenue Service, but they have an office in Montgomery. If you report it, and they come take out the still, and anyone finds out that it was you who reported it, you'll make a lot of enemies in this town and trouble for your family."

"What if I report it anonymously?" asked Arthur.

"They might not pay attention," said Mr. Turk. "In order to make the trip down from Montgomery to investigate, they would want some evidence."

"I see," said Arthur. "Well, it was a thought, anyway. I'd better go – the bell already rang and I'll be late for math."

"I'll give you a note to give to Miss McClendon," said Mr. Turk. He scribbled a note on his note pad, tore off the sheet and handed it to Arthur.

"Thank you, Sir," said Arthur, taking the note and standing. Mr. Turk's office was in the northeast corner of the building, which was rectangular, with a single row of classrooms all around a central courtyard, and a covered but open cloister connecting all the classrooms. Arthur hurried down the cloister to Miss McClendon's classroom, handed her the note, and took his seat. Miss McClendon resumed her talk at the blackboard.

The next morning, Arthur rose early, fed himself some cereal for breakfast, left a note on the kitchen table for his mother, and rode his bike rapidly to the start of the pathway. He had learned to read and make maps while working on the Pioneering Merit Badge in Boy Scouts. Note pad and Boy Scout compass in hand, he paced off the length of the driveway at the nursing home and sketched it on his pad. He paced off the distance to each turn in the pathway, using his Boy Scout compass to gauge the direction of the path at each turn. He marked the location of the fork in the path, sketched in the woods, with a clearing in the middle, and a bold X in the middle of the clearing. Just above the X, he wrote, "Here lies the still."

By the time he got to school, he had a rather accurate map showing the location of the still in the woods behind the old McPherson house. On his way home that afternoon, he used the rest of his film to take pictures of the trail, the fork, the spot at which it entered the woods, with the smoke rising above them, and the front of the nursing home from the street.

At home that evening, he re-drew the map carefully, rendering the features carefully with ruler, compass, French curve, and triangle. He clearly labeled each feature, including the address for the nursing home. He drew an old-fashioned north arrow in the lower left corner.

He climbed under the covers of his bed with his camera, and opened it in the dark, removing the film and sealing the paper tab on the end of the film roll to keep it protected from the light. Arthur had been developing and printing his own pictures for three years, since his father gave him the developing kit. He pulled his darkroom kit from under the bed, cleared his little desk, and laid out the developing pan, the fixing pan, and the rinsing tank. He measured the chemicals carefully into the developing and fixing pans, capped the bottles and put them away in the box. He went to the kitchen and filled the teakettle with water. Returning to the bedroom, he taped a sign to the door saying, "Do Not Enter – Darkroom in Use."

He plugged in his red light, hanging it from an eyehook screwed into the side of the bookshelf, pulled down the shades to minimize light infiltration from the moon and stars, closed the door, and poured water measured with his mother's measuring cup into the pans. While the chemicals dissolved, he returned the teakettle to the kitchen. Returning to his room, he closed the door, used a plastic spoon to stir the water in the pans until the chemicals were thoroughly dissolved and mixed, and turned off the room lights. The vinegary aroma of the chemicals filled the room and tickled his nose.

He broke the seal on the film and unrolled it from the spool. He began dipping it through the fluid in the developing tank until the images stood out in stark negative. He repeated the dipping, this time in the rinsing and fixing tanks. Using a thumbtack, he tacked the strip of film to the edge of a bookshelf over the rinsing tank to let it dry.

He turned on the room lights and carried each pan in turn carefully to the bathroom, where he emptied the fluids into the toilet and thoroughly rinsed each pan. He flushed the toilet and returned to his room. He dried the pans with an old, stained dishtowel that he kept in his darkroom kit and put the pans back on the desk.

Mixing fresh chemicals, he prepared to make prints. He turned off the room lights, leaving only the red light burning. He placed the printing lamp on the desk to the left of the pans and took from his kit a package of photographic paper. He could only make contact prints; he did not have an enlarger. He removed a sheet of photographic paper from the package and inserted it into the printing frame. Taking down his film, he cut it into strips a little shorter than the width of the photographic paper, five pictures per strip. He laid them carefully on the paper and pressed a piece of window-glass down on top of them, clamping it into the frame. Next, he turned on the lamp in the printing rig, timing the exposure carefully with his glow-in-the-dark wristwatch.

Removing the glass, the film strips and paper from the frame, he dipped the paper through the developing solution repeatedly, watching the pictures appear as the developer washed out the unexposed silver. He examined the pictures, deciding that he had timed everything correctly and that they would do the job. He dipped them through the rinse and fixer several times. He used clothespins to hang them to dry from a string he had strung across the space between the bookshelves above the two desks. He returned to the bathroom with the pans, emptied and washed them, flushed the toilet, and returned to his room to dry them and put away the darkroom kit. He took down the sign he had put on the door and sat at his desk to do his homework.

The next day, Wednesday, he rode downtown to the bookshop after school, where he bought a package of 9" X 12" manila envelopes. Back at home, he used his grandfather's typewriter to type a letter to the Alcohol and Tobacco Tax Division of the Internal Revenue Service at their Montgomery address, making a carbon copy for his records. He signed the original, "Anonymous." He used a pen to label each picture with a number, and he marked the map with the location from which each was taken with an arrow showing the direction of view.

He placed the map, the pictures and the letter into a manila envelope, sealed it, and carefully hand-lettered the delivery address. For the return address, he labeled "Anonymous, c/o Mr. Turk / Young Junior High School," and the school's address. He weighed the letter using the scale from his chemistry set, applied the appropriate number of postage stamps, and put it with his homework and books into his backpack. He made an early start the next day, pedaling first downtown on North Oates Street to the US Post Office, where he mailed his envelope, and returned south to school.

He waited impatiently, day by day, waiting for something to happen. He wished he could be patient, but that was not one of his virtues. Finally, exactly one week later, Miss Jernigan, his home room teacher, handed him a note when he arrived in the morning. Opening it, he found a message from Mr. Turk, asking if he would kindly stop by his office at the lunch break. When he did, Mr. Turk handed him an envelope.

"This could only be for you," said Mr. Turk, smiling. The cover of the envelope bore the engraved return address of the Alcohol and Tobacco Tax Division of the Internal Revenue Service in Montgomery. It was addressed to "Mr. Anonymous, c/o Mr. Turk, Young Junior High School," with the school's address.

"Thank you, Mr. Turk," said Arthur.

"Be careful, Mr. Harris," said Mr. Turk.

"I will, sir," said Arthur.

After lunch, Arthur went out onto the playing field with the rest of the kids from his lunch period. The post-lunch break would last about fifteen minutes before the bell rang for the next period. Arthur wandered away from his friends to the bushes along the fence on the north side, and there, alone, he opened the letter.

Dear Mr. Anonymous:

Thank you for bringing to our attention the location of the still in Dothan that has been in operation for generations. Please stay clear of that area next week, as we would not want you to get into trouble if you were found near when we do our raid. If what you have told us is true, you will have earned a $100.00 reward, which you may claim anonymously by calling our office, using the code words 'Anonymous Bravo Charlie,' and giving us an address to mail the reward money, or arranging to meet and receive it, at your option.

Sincerely,

[signed] *Agent Jeffers*

Every morning and evening the following week, Arthur made it a point to listen to the news broadcast on the radio and to read the newspaper every day.

He had just gotten home from school on Wednesday when the phone rang. He answered. It was Freddie.

"My Dad just told me that the Revenuers made a raid in the woods today behind the old McPherson home and destroyed a moonshine still," said Freddy. "Isn't that exciting? We should have used the trail coming home from school, and we might have seen the action, but you wanted to come home straight down Oates Street. Why did you do that?"

"We can get home faster using Oates Street," said Arthur carefully. "Even though there's more traffic, we can pedal faster."

"Oh," said Freddy. "But we missed all the excitement!"

"Sorry about that," said Arthur. "You didn't want to get shot at, did you?"

"No, but they wouldn't have shot at kids," said Freddy.

"If they thought the kids might have turned them in, they might."

"What are you not telling me?"

"I'm just speculating," said Arthur.

"Did you find the still and turn them in?"

"Now, you're just speculating," said Arthur. "Don't say that to anyone else, or they might think I did it."

"Did you?" asked Freddy.

"That would have been crazy," said Arthur. "I would have made enemies in Dothan and caused my parents a lot of trouble. Why would I do something like that?"

"Yeah," said Freddy. "I guess you're too smart to do that. I would have done it and they might come shoot my Dad. They arrested two men – the man running the still and the owner of the still."

"Who were they, do you know?" asked Arthur.

"I never heard of the guy running the still, but the owner of the still is Deputy Sheriff McPherson. He owns the property."

"Ah, yes, the old McPherson home."

"The McPhersons are going to try very hard to find out who turned them in. McPherson's dad started the still a long time ago."

"Well," said Arthur, "I hope they don't come after you. Your Dad and the Sheriff have been enemies ever since your Dad became County Judge and put one of the Sheriff's deputies in prison for lynching a Negro. My Dad says Deputy McPherson is the head of the Ku Klux Clan in this area."

"That's right," said Freddy. "They say he's the Grand Wizard."

"They might figure out that it was you who turned them in because you and I usually use the trail to go to school," said Arthur.

"Me?" said Freddy, "but I didn't turn them in!"

"Maybe you should talk to your father and let him know that we usually take the trail to school."

"I will. You should tell your father, too."

"I will," said Arthur.

The *Dothan Eagle* arrived at the Harris home before Arthur's father got home. Arthur read it immediately. The story, complete with photos, was all over the front page. Agent Jeffers was quoted as saying that they made the raid based on an anonymous but credible tip. The Deputy Sheriff would be in prison for more than a few years. They had arrested not only him, but his brother and two nephews as well. The man who operated the still, a Mr. Lang from Enterprise, had cooperated in return for the promise of a lighter sentence, and had named everyone who was involved in the still business. The Sheriff was not directly implicated but had resigned, and the county would have to elect a new Sheriff. In the meantime, a Federal Marshall was being sent to oversee the Sheriff's Office. Judge Jefferson's brother, George Jefferson, had announced that he would run for Sheriff in November's election. He was quoted as saying that he would work to eliminate the criminal element among the deputies and to clean up the Sheriff's office.

"The Klan in southeastern Alabama will be a thing of the past," said the story. "The list of the Klan members was confiscated from the Sheriff's desk drawer, and they are all being rounded up as I write this."

The phone rang again, and Arthur answered it. He was the only one at home – his father had not yet come home from work, his mother was out doing the grocery shopping, and his brother was playing touch football with Freddy's younger brother and their friends.

"Mr. Harris?" said a gruff-sounding male voice.

"This is Arthur Harris, Junior," said Arthur. If you are looking for my Dad, he hasn't gotten home from work."

"No, it's you I want to talk to," said the voice. "I am Agent Jeffers. I suppose you heard the news of the raid today." Arthur's heart skipped a beat.

"Yes, Sir," said Arthur.

"I would like to meet with you privately and confidentially tomorrow," said Agent Jeffers. "After school, can you come to the Houston Hotel? I can meet with you there privately."

"Yes, Sir. I can be there at 3:30."

"Good. I'll see you then."

The next day after school, Arthur pedaled his bike downtown and parked it behind the Texaco station next door to the Houston Hotel. He stepped into the lobby and looked around. A tall, craggy-faced man wearing a suit and hat approached him.

'Mr. Harris, I am Agent Jeffers." He held out his hand, and Arthur took and shook it. "Please come with me." He led the way to the elevator. They rode it to the sixth floor and walked down the corridor to Room 611. Agent Jeffers unlocked the door and they entered. Agent Jeffers locked the door from inside. "Please take a seat and make yourself comfortable," he said, indicating a chair at a small desk in the outside corner of the room. It was by the open window. A pleasant breeze was blowing, alleviating the heat of the day. An open transom over the door to the room allowed the air to circulate into the hallway. Arthur walked across and sat in the chair, taking off his backpack and placing it on the floor. Agent Jeffers sat on the bed. He looked at Arthur for a moment without expression and reached for a brief case that sat on the floor beside the bed. He opened it and took out a Manila envelope. Arthur recognized it as the one he had sent.

"Mr. Harris," said Agent Jeffers, "you did some impressive detective work. I knew it was you because I had a conversation with Mr. Turk and required him to identify you. What you mailed us enabled us to plan and execute our raid flawlessly. We sent an agent to Dothan to search property records for the owner of the property and staked out Deputy Sheriff McPherson's house. He left the house in the morning, but instead of going to the office, he visited the still. We moved in, made the arrests, and destroyed the still. Your map was perfect, and the photographs showed us that your tip was worth following up." Agent Jeffers took another envelope out of his brief case. "This is for you," he said, handing it to Arthur. It was a plain white business envelope, with no return address and no address. Arthur used his penknife to slit it open. Inside was a crisp one-hundred-dollar bill.

"Thank you, Sir," said Arthur. "This is a lot of money for me." Agent Jeffers smiled.

"I suggest you hide it in a safe place for a while. We wouldn't want anyone to connect you with the raid. There are still some members of McPherson's family whom we could not connect with the still and who might seek revenge. Just keep it safe for a couple of months and you may take it to your bank. Do you have an account?"

"Not yet, Sir. I have a piggy bank, and it's now full. I'll take this and the piggy bank to my parents' bank and open a savings account."

"That's being smart," said Agent Jeffers, "but I knew you were smart from the excellent detective work you did, and the material you sent us that clinched the case. We were able to move in with arrest warrants and search warrants in hand because of the work you did. We were able to search the old McPherson home, the Sheriff's house and his office, where we were able to get enough evidence not only to shut down the alcohol ring but also the Ku Klux Klan in this area. Have you started thinking of a career? Would you consider a career with the FBI or with our office?"

"I have considered that," said Arthur. "I want to be an intelligence officer with the Office of Naval Intelligence. If I can't do that, I'll become an FBI agent."

"I see," said the agent, "you have thought it through already. Will you try to go to Annapolis?"

"If I can get an appointment, I'll go to Annapolis. If I cannot, I'll go to a university with a good Navy ROTC program. There are a number of them around the country." Agent Jeffers stood.

"We'd better get you out of here and on your way home before people start wondering where you are," he said. "Again, thank you for what you did, and be assured your secret is safe with me. Mr. Turk and I are the only ones who know who you are. As I said, I made him tell me. He had to, so don't be angry at him. I threatened him with arrest as a material witness unless he identified you." Arthur laughed.

"Mr. Turk would have been very upset with me if that happened," said Arthur. "I'll make sure that he knows I don't mind that he told you."

"I don't want to encourage you to put yourself in danger with any more investigations," said Agent Jeffers. "However, if you come across any information that would be helpful to me or to the FBI, don't hesitate to call me. I'll always take you seriously and follow up. I'll also keep your identity secret."

"Thank you, Sir," said Arthur, standing up. He placed the envelope in his backpack and closed the flap, slipped his arms through the straps and shrugged the backpack into place in the middle of his back. He held out his hand, and Agent Jeffers shook it.

"Good luck, son," said Agent Jeffers, "but I get the impression you won't need a lot of that. You're the type who makes his own luck."

"I hope so, sir," said Arthur, grinning. He whistled the "*Toreador*" theme from *Carmen* as he rode his bicycle home.

CHAPTER 6

SURVIVAL

July 1959
*Chattahoochie and Appalachicola Rivers – Alabama
and Florida*

The hot wind blew into the '53 Chevrolet. Arthur's
dad was driving with Arthur in the front passenger's seat.
It was a muggy Saturday morning, and Arthur and his dad
were returning from Sears with a load of things they
would need for the Boy Scout Troop 130 camping trip.
Arthur had earned his Eagle Scout medal that spring, and
his father had taken over as Scoutmaster when Grady
Jones, the previous Scoutmaster, had been transferred out
of town by his employer. Arthur had persuaded his father
to take the troop on a "survival camping trip," living off
the land in survival mode, carrying with them a minimum
of "stuff." His father had agreed, and with the members of
Troop 130 helping, had built a flat-bottomed boat in the
back yard.

They planned to put into the Chattahoochie River just
above the Walter F. George dam in Lake Eufaula, go
through the lock at the dam, and travel down the river
through the "jungle" of southeastern Alabama and north-
western Florida for two weeks, living off the river, and

ending in the beginnings of Lake Seminole. The previous summer they had put in just below the Jim Woodruff Dam that forms Lake Seminole and floated down the Appalachicola River to the bay, using canoes borrowed from the Boy Scout Camp, but that was not a "survival" trip. They had carried food with them.

Once home, they unloaded their "loot": four oars, twelve pith helmets, water sterilization pills, a bottle of Clorox (in case the sterilization pills ran out), a cast iron Dutch oven, a large cast iron skillet, lanterns, pup tents, and the prize of all, US Army Surplus jungle hammocks. These hammocks had a canvas bed, a canvas roof, and screened sides. Once the hammock was strung up and the Scout was zipped in, mosquitos would not bother him. Of course, they also had a case of mosquito repellent, suntan lotion, and other essentials like toilet paper, soap, and toothpaste.

Just after they arrived, the members of the troop who were going on the adventure arrived with their back packs, and the supplies just purchased were divided up. The plan was to take only what would fit in backpacks, except for the hammocks, tents and large pots and pans, which would be packed in duffel bags.

Harvey Boggs, the Assistant Scoutmaster, arrived in his pickup truck with the canoes borrowed from the Scout camp. The Scouts unloaded the canoes, and together lifted the new boat onto the bed of the pickup. Into the boat went the duffel bags and their "emergency" food supply – dried beans, garlic, cheese, dry sausage, pancake mix, and syrup. A bottle of Clorox, as well as the cooking pots and pans, axes, and fishing gear joined the food in the boat. The oars went into the boat as well. The canoes were loaded next, each with two backpacks and two paddles. After they finished packing the boats, they broke for lunch: hot dogs roasted over a fire in the back yard, washed down with soft drinks – the last soft drinks they likely would have before the end of their trip.

While they ate, Arthur's dad explained that this was not really a survival camping trip. If it were, they would bring no tents or bedding, no fishing gear, and no food. They would depend on their skills at scavenging, trapping, making primitive tools, and making shelter from vegetation for their survival. On this trip, they had emergency supplies and were bringing shelter with them. They would learn survival skills but would not depend on them entirely for their survival.

After lunch, the boys together reviewed the river maps that Arthur's father had bought from the Army engineers and planned each stop. The river snaked its way in lazy curves through the wilderness, and on the inside shore of each curve was a sand beach. These would be perfect for beaching the boats and camping. They would go downriver for about a week before reaching the first bridge, and another week to the next bridge. Along the way were woods and jungle, with an occasional farmer's field on the Alabama side in the first week's stretch. Just north of the second bridge was an island. They planned to spend their last night on the island, and exit at the bridge the next day, where Harvey with his truck and several parents with cars would meet them to ferry the adventurers home.

After finalizing their plans, they all went home to their parents. The next morning, they attended Mass in their Scout uniforms, received a blessing from Father Jones, had a group picture taken by a photographer from the *Dothan Eagle*, loaded up and headed for the river.

They had originally thought to find a place to enter the river just below the dam, but the river below the dam had steep banks. A reconnaissance trip during the planning phase persuaded them to put in at a boat ramp above the dam, on the Alabama side of the lake. The lock was on the Georgia side of the dam. They parked and unloaded at the boat ramp. The canoes were light enough to be lifted out with the backpacks on board, but the boat was too heavy and had to be unloaded, taken off the truck, and reloaded.

Arthur and James Bryson were assigned to the boat, as they were the largest and oldest of the Scouts and both had taken and passed the rowing and canoeing merit badges. All on the trip had taken the canoeing merit badge, but only a few had taken rowing. While Arthur and James slid the boat down the boat ramp and into the water, Arthur's father and the canoes began departing for the short paddle to the boat lock. Arthur and James hurriedly packed the boat and shoved off, rowing to catch up with the canoes. The lock, built to accommodate river barges, was large enough to take all the canoes and the boat at once. They back-paddled while the great lock doors opened toward them. They paddled and rowed into the lock. Gradually they sank down in the lock as the water was pumped out. The second set of doors opened, letting them paddle and row into the channel leading to the river. They paddled out onto the river and began their journey.

Their first stop was just an hour downstream, where they beached the boat and the canoes at a sand bar and ate the sandwiches they had prepared at home and brought with them. It would be their last such meal until the end of the trip.

So far, so good, thought Arthur. This had been easy. They didn't have to do much rowing and paddling. They just drifted with the river and guided their craft around obstacles in the water – fallen trees, rocks, shallows and other obstructions. Sitting cross-legged and munching on his sandwich, Arthur looked up and saw his father standing with hands on hips looking into the boat. He turned and motioned Arthur over. When Arthur was standing by his side, he pointed into the boat.

"I see the hammocks and all the camping gear except for the tents," said his father. "Where are the tents?" Arthur stared, open-mouthed, a sinking feeling in his stomach.

"I – I guess we left them on the boat dock," he said. "I'm sorry, Dad. I guess James and I will have to go back upstream and get them."

"I guess you will," said his father. "Take my canoe and I'll take the boat. I don't think you'd make it in the boat, against this current. You'll find that the current is slower on the inside of a curve close to the bank. You can catch up with us at the camping site downstream."

Arthur found James and delivered the bad news. Together they emptied the canoe that his father had paddled, placing their backpacks into the boat. His father and Freddy, who was the other paddler in that canoe, would take a turn in the boat. Pushing the canoe into the water, Arthur and James got in and began the tiresome paddle upstream. It took them three hours to cover the distance it had taken them one hour to cover on the way downstream. The lock operator laughed when they told him the story, but he opened the locks for them and soon they were on the lake, at the boat ramp. Their tent package was still there, on the side of the ramp, partly hidden by a patch of weeds the same color as the duffel bag containing the tents. Wearily, they threw themselves onto the grass beside the ramp, breathing heavily.

"Man!" said James, "we're going to remember to check everything twice from now on. It's almost dinner time, I'm hungry, and we still have a half-day's journey ahead of us."

"I know," said Arthur. "I'm thirsty and we didn't bring our canteens with us back upstream. Downstream will be easier. We can even paddle to make up time instead of drifting with the current. Come on, let's load up and get going. We can rest a little in the canoe. The sooner we start, the sooner we'll get there." James groaned, but he hoisted himself to his feet and together they loaded the tent duffel bag into the center of the canoe. Pushing the canoe back into the water, they hopped aboard and paddled to the locks.

For the first ten minutes or so, they rested, letting the river carry them. They began paddling steadily, breaking every twenty minutes for a brief rest. Three and a half hours after they set out, they spotted the rest of the troop just starting toward the sand bar at the curve ahead, the sand bar where they planned to camp for the night. The others already had started setting up camp when Arthur and James arrived.

"You made good time," said Arthur's father as he helped them unload the canoe. "I'll give you guys the easy job, because I am sure you are exhausted. Rustle us up some grub. Start a fire, put a package of beans in the big pot, fill it half full of water, and put in a little salt, some salt pork, and a clove of garlic for each camper. Hang it over the fire just above the flames, on a tripod, and watch it cook. When it starts to boil, raise the pot. If it tries to boil over, raise it higher. If the beans absorb all the water, add a little more water. Use the river water, and filter and treat it before putting it in the pot."

"Aye, aye Sir," said Arthur, saluting.

"First," said his father, "change out of your uniforms to keep them somewhat fresh and wear jeans and tee shirts." The boys changed, folded, rolled and packed away their uniforms, and began the cooking process. They gathered dry sticks from the woods beyond the sand bar, and some Spanish moss for kindling. They stacked the smaller sticks in a teepee formation over the handful of Spanish moss. Arthur tried starting a fire using the bow-and-stick friction method, but the wood was damp and wouldn't generate enough heat to start the little bundle of Spanish moss he was using as tinder.

Using his iron and flint fire-starting kit, Arthur struck sparks that finally started a few tendrils glowing in the ball of Spanish moss. Blowing carefully on it, Arthur enlarged the flames until the sticks caught. When the sticks were burning steadily, he placed larger sticks on the fire until he had a healthy campfire. Using a stick, he collapsed the teepee into a bed of burning sticks. The fire kept burning, but less rapidly. He used three long sticks to rig a tripod over the fire and tied a piece of sash cord to the handle of the pot. He ran the cord over the top of the tripod, pulled the cord while James held the pot steady until it rested an inch off the burning sticks. He tied the end of the cord to a stake to the side of the fire. He filled a bucket with water and dropped in the specified number of water treatment pills, poured some of it through a piece of bedsheet used as a filter and into the pot, and turned his attention to the beans and garlic.

"Is this a clove of garlic?" Arthur asked James, holding up a head of garlic. Their supplies included a web bag filled with little garlic heads, smaller and, therefore, cheaper than the larger garlic in the store.

"I guess," said James. "My mom doesn't use any garlic, so I don't know about garlic." Arthur counted out twelve little garlic heads and sat, looking at the little pile of garlic.

"Sure seems like a lot," he said. James shrugged. Arthur gathered up the garlic and dumped it into the pot, followed by the beans, a small pile of salt poured into the palm of his hand, and some more of the freshly-treated river water, strained through their filter cloth, and half a dozen slices of salt pork. They lowered the pot to almost touch the glowing coals and chatted about fishing while the beans cooked. When the pot came to a boil, they raised it about a foot and fed more sticks into the fire.

By this time, the other boys had finished setting up the camp – pitching the tents, setting up the hammocks, digging a latrine ditch – and Arthur's Dad took them all out into the river to fish while Arthur and James cooked the beans, which took about two hours. When the fishing party returned to camp, Arthur's dad walked up and looked into the pot.

"Are you boys sure you used enough garlic?" he asked, grinning.

"I think so," said Arthur, "I did what you said – one per person."

"It looks like you put in heads of garlic instead of cloves," said his dad, stirring the pot with the large, wooden spoon. "It will be quite flavorful. In a way, that's good; it should help keep the mosquitos away. They can probably smell this a mile away." The boys gathered around the fire, cleaned their fish, placing the waste into the fire to burn, spitted their fish fillets on forked sticks, and held them over the coals to roast.

The beans were, indeed, flavorful – too flavorful – but the hungry boys wolfed them down anyway, along with the fish they had caught. They gathered around the campfire after eating and washing the pots and mess kits in the river and sang a couple of camp songs. They were all exhausted, so they smothered the fire with sand and went to bed early. Several of the kids volunteered for the hammocks, and the rest took to the tents. The hammocks were strung using bipods of sticks tied with cord, with the leaders stretched over the tops of the bipods and tied down to stakes in the sand. They all slept soundly.

With the dawn, the heat started to build, and the brightness of the sunshine woke the kids. Two were deputized to prepare pancakes while the rest packed up the camp and loaded the canoes and the boats. All sat around the campfire and ate large stacks of pancakes with sorghum molasses. Drowning and burying the fire, they washed up the pots and mess kits, packed up the last of the camp items, filled in the latrine, and set out for their second day's journey, leaving a clean beach behind them.

The going was easy. All they had to do was guide the boat and canoes, which left plenty of time for fishing. They caught bream, catfish, bass, crappie, sunfish and some fish they failed to identify. After an hour, Arthur realized that he was getting sunburned, so he donned a long-sleeved shirt over his tee shirt and applied sunscreen to his face, ears, and the back of his neck. He made sure to wear the pith helmet to shield his head, neck and face.

They stopped at a sandbar for lunch. They cleaned the fish and spitted them on sharpened sticks which they strung over the fire, turning them slowly. The fish cooked fast. They ate them off the sticks, like strange giant lollipops, accompanied by beans from what Arthur dubbed the "perpetual bean pot," so they had little cleanup to do before they took to the water again.

The afternoon went like the morning, except for a pop-up thundershower that caught them in midafternoon. The day was so hot that they welcomed the rain and its cooling effect. After it passed, their clothes dried quickly in the summer sun. They stopped at the next beach to overturn the boat and canoes to get the rainwater out. They drank copious amounts of water – treated, of course – to avoid dehydration.

The second night started like the first, except that before supper the boys swam in the warm river water, taking turns standing life guard and making sure they were always paired up in the buddy system. Arthur discovered that despite the long-sleeved shirt, his arms and back were sun-burned. The strong summer sun had burned him through the light-weight fabric of the shirt.

Two boys were tasked with "enhancing the beans." They took the pot with the leftover beans in it, added more beans and water, and placed it over the fire, stirring it until the old and new beans were well mixed. This diluted the garlic somewhat, but they still tasted more garlic than beans. Some went fishing as before, and others tried snaring rabbits. They caught two, skinned them, and stretched the skins on a stick frame to dry. They cleaned them and burned the offal in the fire. They spitted the rabbits and roasted them. After dinner, they went to bed as before and slept soundly.

Sometime in the middle of the night, Arthur awoke needing to pee. He heard rustling under the hammock, so he looked down before getting out of the hammock. There was an alligator directly under the hammock. One of the younger boys awoke, looked out of his tent and saw alligators all over the sand bar and started crying. Arthur's dad called out softly, "Boys, hold very, very still, and make as little noise as possible and they won't bother you." The crying boy stifled his sobs and in a moment the camp was quiet except for the rustling noise the alligators made crawling on the sand.

Finally, Arthur could hold it no longer, unzipped his screen siding, and pissed over the side onto the sand. The splashing noise seemed loud, and Arthur saw an alligator ambling over toward him. He finished, zipped up his screen siding and lay very, very still, watching the alligator. It ambled up to the wet spot in the sand, nuzzled it with his nose and ambled off toward the river. Immediately, the other boys in hammocks followed Arthur's lead, watering the sandbar.

The boy sharing a tent with Arthur's dad whispered, "I have to pee, too. Can I pee in the tent?"

"Yes," said Mr. Harris, "the tent has no floor, so it will soak into the sand – but don't pee on the sleeping bag. Pee on the sand." In a moment, there were pissing noises all over the camp, but the alligators paid no notice. The sound blended with the rustling noises made by the alligators. No one got any more sleep that night, but soon the sky started getting lighter, and the alligators meandered one by one into the river, leaving the sandbar clear. At breakfast (fried fish), Arthur's dad commented that they should probably look for signs of alligators on the next sandbar they considered using for a camp ground. "We could camp in the woods beyond the sand bars instead, but we'd have to worry about snakes," he said. "Alligators leave signs. Look for their footprints in the sand next time, with sinuous lines made by their tails dragging in the sand. I should have been more careful last night."

They only found signs of alligators one more time and went on to the next sand bar to camp. When swimming, besides the life guard on the shore, they posted an alligator lookout in a canoe out in the water. However, they did not see another alligator at their campsites, although they occasionally spotted one while drifting down the river.

On the fourth night, Arthur's dad gave a demonstration of safe use of the axe. He had the scouts gather at the edge of the forest, where there was a fallen log on the ground. He showed how to hold the axe, how to swing it back, slipping the forward hand down toward the handle and swinging it over and down onto the log. On his second stroke, however, the axe hit a slender, springy tree branch on the backswing, and rebounded to strike Mr. Harris on the top of the head. Arthur rushed to his dad and saw a gash in the scalp clear to the skull bone. He washed the cut with sterilized water from his canteen and doused it with antiseptic. He began pressing the skin to try to close the gash. He took hairs from each side and tied them together, pulling the gash closed. Soon, the gash was neatly closed, and the bleeding had stopped. Mr. Harris deputized Arthur to be the one to go find a doctor when they reached the bridge, which they were due to do in two days. They were a day ahead of schedule. As the senior Scout present, Arthur took the axe and proceeded to give the safe axemanship lesson, pointing out that it was necessary to make sure that the backswing area was clear before taking the backswing.

When they reached the first bridge two days later, Arthur climbed up the embankment to the road and found a country store about 100 yards from the bridge. He ran to it, explained to the old man who ran the store that his father was injured, and they needed a doctor. He asked the man to call a doctor.

"You're lucky, Son," said the old man, "The Doc hereabouts still makes house calls. Got a nickel?" Seeing Arthur's blank expression, he said, "All's we got here's a pay phone. Calls cost a nickel. Got a nickel?"

"No, Sir," said Arthur, "but my Dad does. If you'll make the call, I'll go get the nickel."

"Good," said the old man, "Y'all go get the nickel and *then* I'll make the call." Arthur ran down the embankment and reported to his dad, who shook his head, laughing, pulled a nickel from his pocket and gave it to Arthur. Back up in the store, Arthur handed it to the old man, who walked to the front of the store and onto the porch, where he put the nickel in the pay phone, told the operator to connect him to Doc Givens, and handed the handset to Arthur.

"This is Doc," said a husky voice on the phone, "Who're you and who's sick?"

"I'm Arthur Harris," said Arthur. "My Scout troop is taking a trip down the river and my dad, who's the Scoutmaster, got hurt with an axe. Can you come treat him?"

"Where?" asked the Doc.

"Hopkins General Store," said Arthur.

"I mean, where did your father get hurt?"

"About two days up river."

"Uh ... what part of his body got hurt?"

"He hit himself on the top of the head with the axe and got a big cut."

"I'm coming," said the Doc, hanging up.

The store had a chest cooler bearing the "Coke" logo. It was filled with ice with Cokes embedded in the ice. By the time he arrived, the whole troop and its Scoutmaster were enjoying ice-cold Cokes on the porch of the store. The doctor looked at the top of Mr. Harris' head, snipped away some hair to get a better view, and applied some tincture of iodine to the healing wound.

"I got two questions," said the Doc. "First, how the hell did the accident happen, and second, what genius tied the hair together?" Arthur explained, and the doctor started laughing.

"Sir," he said to Arthur's Dad, "remind me never to ask you for a lesson in axe safety." Turning to Arthur, he said, "If I ever do something stupid like that, I hope you're around to treat me. You did a beautiful job of cleaning and closing the wound. It's halfway healed already, and will barely leave a scar at all. I couldn't have done a better job myself. Have you considered being a doctor when you grow up?"

"Thank you," said Arthur, "but I want to be a Navy officer and a spy."

"Well, Son," said Doc, "I have the feeling that whatever you set your mind to do you will accomplish." Mr. Harris paid the doctor his $3.00 charge for a "house" call and thanked him. "I should be thanking you," said the doctor. "You've given me a good story to tell." Laughing, he drove away in his puttering 1935 Cadillac sedan.

The rest of the trip was uneventful. At each night's stop, the boys practiced new survival skills: making snares for small animals like rabbits, squirrels, opossum and muskrats (they tasted good roasted over the fire on a spit, and several of the boys had animal skin trophies to take home); how to make shelters from sticks and leafy branches; how to recognize and avoid alligator nesting areas; how to avoid snakes; how to tell the difference be-

tween a water moccasin and a blacksnake; how to catch
snakes, kill, clean, roast and eat them (they tasted like
chicken white meat); how to recognize animal tracks; how
to track animals and stalk them; how to tell direction
without a compass using a watch and the position of the
sun; how to boil water in a paper bag; how to recognize
poison ivy, poison oak and poison sumac; how to recognize edible plants and roots in the wilderness; and many
other lessons. One evening they captured a large snapping
turtle and had delicious snapper stew with their dinner.

On the twelfth night, they camped on the little island
they had spotted on the map. They dined early. Arthur,
James and Freddy decided to explore the island to make
sure there weren't any dangers like snakes or alligators.
When they reached the middle of the island, they found a
clearing, and in the middle of the clearing were about a
hundred five-gallon glass jugs with corks in the top and a
clear liquid in them. Arthur pulled out one of the corks
and took a sniff.

"That's alcohol," he said. "We'd better report it. This
is a moonshiner's stash." They walked back to camp and
told Mr. Harris, who decided they should move their
camp. They packed up the boats and paddled across from
the island to the riverbank, where there was a small pier.
Tied up to the pier was a boat with a large outboard motor. They landed at the pier, beached the canoes, tied their
boat to the opposite side of the pier from the motorboat
and followed a trail up the bank to a "fish camp" – a large
shed with tables and chairs, and another shed with wood-
en slop sinks for cleaning fish. In between the fish-
cleaning shed and the eating shed was a large cast iron pot
hanging from a wrought iron tripod over a charred area of
soil. It was a "fish camp" – a place that sold catfish din-
ners.

A man in coveralls without a shirt was hosing down
the concrete slab under the tables. They approached him,

and Arthur asked him please to call the sheriff, because they had found something suspicious. The man turned off his hose and looked at them.

"Well, boys," he said, "I happen to be the Sheriff around here. Why don't y'all just tell me what you found?" Arthur proceeded to tell the story, and Mr. Harris asked if they could camp there for the night to avoid trouble with the moonshiner.

"I reckon y'all can do that. Sounds like a good idea."

They camped there that night. In the middle of the night, Arthur heard the motor boat start up and sat up to watch it go out to the island. After a short while it went up river and out of sight and after twenty minutes, returned. It made several such trips up the river before returning to the pier. The next morning, Arthur told his father what he had seen.

"I think our friend, the Sheriff, is a moonshiner himself or is friends with the moonshiner. I think they moved their product to another location."

"Can we go see?" said Arthur.

"I think we've had enough excitement already involving moonshiners. We don't know anyone around here, so I think we should leave well enough alone."

"OK," said Arthur. "You're probably right." The Troop loaded up and continued their journey, after finding the sheriff and thanking him for his hospitality.

At the end of two weeks, they arrived at the second bridge early in the day, and Arthur climbed the bank to the ubiquitous country store and called for their transportation home. As the time arrived for their ride home, the boys all changed back into their uniforms, posed for the news photographer from *The Dothan Eagle*, showed off their animal-skin trophies and the large turtle shell, and bombarded their parents with their stories all the way home.

Arthur rode home quietly, reflecting on his experiences on the trip, and concluded that he was now ready to survive alone in the wilderness, should he ever have to do so.

CHAPTER 7

PRISCILLA

November 1960
Dothan, Alabama

Toward the end of the football season, for Homecoming, Dothan High School scheduled the Homecoming Parade on Saturday morning before the Homecoming Game in the afternoon. Saturday night would be the Homecoming Ball, ruled over by the Homecoming King and Queen. The students would gather at various places after for unofficial dancing and partying late into the night and until the morning. The Martin Theater scheduled an all-night movie marathon with free admission for Dothan High School students. Arthur looked forward to the weekend, washing and waxing his mother's old car, which she seldom used, and for which he was the principal driver. It was his pride and joy. He loved that car.

Arthur, who was in his third year of Latin, was a member of the Latin Club, *Latini Socii,* and had been for three years. Dothan High School offered French and Latin as foreign language subjects. Arthur had opted for Latin, based on his parents' advice that Latin, being a foundation language for all Western languages, should be his first choice.

Priscilla Holmes was President of *Latinii Socii* and a Senior, a year ahead of Arthur, who was one of the youngest members of his class. Most of the members of his class were a year older than he, so she was almost two years "ahead," being a year and a half older than he. Arthur was Vice President of *Latinii Socii*. He and Priscilla had run together for the leadership positions. They were unopposed, so they were elected.

It was general knowledge that Arthur was a talented artist. He was good at drawing, had taken both drawing and painting classes at Wallace Junior College. He drew and painted posters for the various high school clubs. His artistic talents had been recognized when he was in Junior High School, where he had painted the "NO SMOKING" signs for the new gymnasium the last year he was there. Calligraphy, drawing, and painting were hobbies of his.

At the end of the third year Latin Class in early November, Priscilla pulled Arthur aside. "You must design our float for this year's Homecoming Parade," she told him. "You are the best artist in our class. You have always illustrated your term papers, in every subject, with wonderful drawings. *Please* design our float this year! We have always been the laughingstock of the school on parade day! I want us to produce a winner this year!"

"OK," said Arthur, "but I will need your help, and help from a lot of students, to do it. I'll design it, but it has to get built."

"Don't worry," said Priscilla, "I'm in this with you. We'll sink or swim together. Design it, and I'll get the people necessary to help you build it."

Priscilla's father owned Holmes Hardware Store. Their advertising slogan was "Holmes for Your Homes"vvvvvvvv – and they sold everything any hardware store sold. Holmes Hardware had been a fixture in Dothan for over 100 years. Mr. Holmes' business sold the usual range of hardware store items, but he was also the dealer for several lines of farm equipment made by International Harvester. He had as many customers in the farms around Dothan as he did in the town.

Priscilla coerced her father into contributing to the effort. International Harvester made a utility truck that was sort of like an open-top jeep that was inexpensive. Farmers could use it to haul stuff around their farms when they didn't want to use their tractors, and it could also go on the open road and pull a trailer of produce, grain, or cotton to market. He loaned one to *Latinii Socii* for the parade. Arthur designed a float around it. He produced a design that would have two full-size cutouts of horses attached to the sides of the vehicle, almost completely masking the vehicle, which was not very long. The horses would pull a chariot, on which a Roman Centurion would ride, *pilum* (spear) in hand, *gladius* (sword) at his side.

Charlie Cherry, whose family owned a farm just outside of town, found the front axle, wheels, and tongue of an old farm wagon in his barn. Priscilla and Arthur drove out to the farm with the Harvester truck and attached the wagon tongue to the trailer hitch and hauled it to Holmes Hardware's warehouse. They shortened the tongue by sawing it off and re-attaching the business end of a trailer hookup to the stub.

Working with Priscilla in the warehouse portion of Holmes Hardware, Arthur produced full-size horse cutouts from hardboard. Priscilla was as good an artist as Arthur was. He and Priscilla carefully painted them and mounted them to a frame of 2X2s. They mounted them to the Harvester truck. Together, they built from plywood and 2X2s a platform with a curved front rail that they mounted on the wagon axle to make a chariot. They wrapped a piece of hardboard around the curved front rail, fastened it in place, and trimmed it with a sabre saw. After they painted it, the assembly looked just like a Roman chariot. When they mounted it to the trailer hitch with the horses in place on the International Harvester vehicle, they had a very convincing Roman chariot with its horses.

Tony Howard, who was both a good friend of Arthur's and student body Vice President, took his football 'armor' and mounted a breastplate and backplate made from cardboard and *papier-mâché* to his shoulder guards. He made cardboard greaves for his legs, and his Mom made him a Roman tunic with strips of cardboard attached to the skirt. His mother made him a red cape, and he added a crest to his football helmet, using ostrich feathers from an old boa his grandmother had. Arthur made a Roman *gladius* sword for him from wood, a Roman shield from hardboard and a Roman *pilus* (lance) from a broomstick with a hardboard spear point. Together they carefully laminated tin foil to cover the armor, the helmet, the *gladius*, and the point of the *pilus*.

The afternoon before the parade, Priscilla, Tony and Arthur rigged up the float in the warehouse behind Holmes Hardware, and Tony donned his armor and weapons and stood in the chariot holding the "reins" made from long strips of brown leather Priscilla had found in the warehouse.

Their creation was perfect. Arthur, Tony and Priscilla, its creators, were themselves impressed with how real it looked. After they took some pictures, Tony excused himself, put his clothes back on, and Priscilla drove them home, first dropping Tony off at his house, then Arthur at his house.

"Do you have a date for the homecoming dance," she asked, parked in his driveway.

"No, I don't," said Arthur. "I haven't done much dating since I arrived at Dothan High School." Actually, he had done none.

"Let's change that," she said. "I don't have a date for the dance. I have turned down several invitations. I have been waiting and hoping for you to ask me."

"I'm sorry," said Arthur, "I would have asked you if I thought there was a chance you would say 'Yes'. She laughed, gave him a quick kiss on the cheek.

"Would you go with me? I'd really like that," said Arthur. She put her arms around him.

"Yes!" she said. "I thought you'd never ask."

"I almost never did," said Arthur.

"But you did," she said.

Saturday morning, the parade went off without a hitch. Tony looked splendid in his chariot. Arthur drove the "horses" with Priscilla beside him. The homecoming game that followed was also spectacular. The Dothan Tigers won the game, placing them third in the conference.

Saturday night, dressed in his finest (and only) "evening wear," a white linen jacket similar to a summer dinner jacket, with black slacks, black shoes, and a black bow tie his mother resurrected from a trunk in the attic that also contained his Dad's old tuxedo, Arthur drove the Olds to Priscilla's house. He had hand-washed and hand-waxed the Olds so that it looked to be in mint condition.

He rang the bell. Her Dad let him in and told him she would be ready in a minute. He told him how impressed he was with the chariot. He had gone into the warehouse before closing the store to look at it.

Priscilla walked in, wearing a traditional "Southern Belle" evening gown, pink chiffon with hooped skirts and bare shoulders and back. With her pale skin, blonde hair and blue eyes, she looked as if she had just stepped off the porch of an ante-bellum plantation house. Arthur blushed because she was so beautiful and because he had never seen her before in a strapless gown with a low-cut back. He couldn't help wondering what held it up.

The high school band played waltzes for the dance. None of the kids knew how to waltz except the few who had taken dancing lessons, but they all got out on the dance floor and moved around. Arthur had never really held a girl in his arms before, and he was quite tongue-tied. However, he got through the night, and after the first fifteen minutes on the dance floor, his tongue loosened up a little and he could engage in small talk.

As was customary, after the first few dances, they were given dance cards and were required to dance with each of the people listed on the cards. Arthur's card had six names on it. He danced with all six girls, even though he had never danced before. Then, the band director announced, "Ladies' Choice," and the girls had the opportunity to pick the boys of their choice to dance, so he danced with six more girls. By that time, he was at ease holding a girl in his arms, swirling on the dance floor.

After the dance he drove Priscilla home. She sat close against him on the front bench seat. He pulled up in front of her house and parked. She reached her arm around his shoulder and pulled his head down and she kissed him.

"Thank you, Arthur, for a special evening," she said.

"It has been special for me, too," he said. "Wasn't our float wonderful?"

"It was *your* float," she replied. "It was your design, and mostly your work. But I wasn't talking about our float. *You* made it special for me by being my date for the evening." She kissed him again in the car before she got out. When Arthur started toward the front door, she led him around the side of the house to a side entrance.

"This is the side door to my bedroom," she said, unlocking it. "It used to be the garage before my Dad converted it into a bedroom and bathroom."

"Is it all right for me to be here with you?" he asked. "Shouldn't we tell your parents you're home?"

"They're at the country club this evening," she answered. "They're at the Fall Ball. They won't be home until late. I know they're not home because their car is not in the driveway." It was then that he remembered that her father had been wearing a tuxedo when he picked her up earlier. He followed her into her room, his heart racing and a trickle of fear running down his spine. The room's décor was very feminine, with flowery curtains and bedspread, lots of pink, with stuffed animals on the bed and pictures on the wall. Priscilla sat on the bed and patted the bedspread beside her.

"Come sit down," she said. Timidly, Arthur obeyed. He had never been in a girl's bedroom before, let alone sat on her bed – and this was only his first real date. As he sat, she turned toward him and put her arms around his neck. he put his arms around her and kissed her, and kissed her again, a long, lingering kiss. It was the first time he had kissed a girl in that manner. Soon, they were French kissing, and he discovered when she lay back on the bed that there really wasn't very much holding up the top of her gown. He thought he had died and gone to heaven, but he heard a car in the driveway and she quickly disengaged.

"Come on, quickly," she said, pulling up her top and taking him by the hand and leading him down the short hallway to the living room. When her parents entered through the kitchen, Arthur and Priscilla were sitting together on the couch looking at an album of family pictures.

"Arthur, I want to join the other kids at the theater," she said. "May I, Mom?"

"Yes, but don't go alone," said her father.

"I'll take you," said Arthur.

"I want to change first. Hooped skirts don't work well in a theater. Arthur, why don't you go home, put on something comfortable, and come back and pick me up?"

"OK," he replied. "Mr. and Mrs. Spann, good night."

Arthur hurried home, changed into slacks and sport shirt, and returned to Priscilla's house. She was waiting for him on the swing on the Holmes' front porch, wearing a dress that stopped above the knees, with a low top and spaghetti straps over the shoulders. They drove downtown and parked and walked a block to the theater. The all-night marathon consisted of old, black-and-white romantic movies from the 1930s. After two movies, kids started leaving.

"There are several parties going on," said Priscilla. "Let's go find them." She and Arthur returned to his car and he drove to Doctor Wallace's house. His son, Charley, was in Arthur's class. The house was large, and Arthur and Priscilla found the party going on in the family room and kitchen. There were trays of nachos, popcorn, bottles of soda pop in coolers, chips and dips. They stayed there for about an hour, and then Charlie suggested that they adjourn to the pasture behind Dobbs' Barbecue. Arthur and Priscilla joined a caravan of cars and soon they were in the field. The cars formed a circle with all cars facing the middle of the circle, their headlights illuminating the space between. All cars tuned their radios to WBAM, and the sounds of Rock-N-Roll filled the air. Kids were dancing in the illuminated circle. Arthur and Priscilla joined them, and Priscilla taught Arthur how to do the twist, the latest dance rage.

Finally, as the sun rose, they trooped into Dobbs' Barbecue for a good breakfast of eggs, grits, barbecued ribs and biscuits. After breakfast, Arthur drove Priscilla home. Her parents were up.

"Priscilla," said her Mom, "hurry and get dressed or we'll be late for church."

Priscilla gave Arthur a quick kiss and ran to her room to dress. Arthur drove home, did a quick change to his suit, and went with his parents to Mass. He didn't take communion because he had eaten breakfast, and fasting was required before communion. He had trouble staying awake during Mass.

The next week Priscilla started going steady with a halfback on the football team. Arthur's best friend, Freddy, told him that she had been dating Mike for over a month, but that they weren't going steady. When he asked her to the Homecoming Dance, she told him that Arthur had already asked her. Freddy told Arthur he thought that she had dated Arthur to make Mike jealous enough to ask her to go steady. She remained a good friend, though, and during his senior year while she was at Auburn they wrote each other from time to time.

Toward the end of the school year she didn't answer — and he didn't write during the summer, because she was home. He didn't see her during the summer, except casually. She worked at her Dad's store during the summer. He went in to see her a couple of times and took her to lunch at the lunch counter at Woolworth's, a block up the street. He took her to a movie — she was no longer going steady with anyone. She told him that going steady was a sophomoric thing to do, and that she would not go steady with anyone until she was ready to get married. Besides, he had started dating another girl, JoAnne McKinley, toward the end of his Junior year.

CHAPTER 8

JOANNE

April 1961
Dothan, Alabama

On a Friday in early April of 1961, Arthur was in the classroom used by the staff and faculty advisor of the high school newspaper, *Dothanhi Sootzus*. The masthead name was corny, but appropriate; most of the students felt that Dothan High suited them. Arthur wrote occasional editorials and a column on the arts, and he was assistant makeup editor. It was his job to paste up the mockup of the paper that went to the printer for composition before it was printed. Today, however, he and JoAnne McKinley were going over the list of merchants they would approach for ads. JoAnne, a cheerleader, wrote stories about the girls' sports teams. She and Arthur both sold ads for the paper.

"These five are all in the same area," she said, indicating five names on the list that she had circled with her pencil. "We could call on all of them in one afternoon." She and Arthur were sitting close together at a wooden table that was used for the newspaper work – very close together. Their shoulders and knees were touching, and both heads were bent over the list, close together. Arthur could smell the scent of her perfume. It was a warm day, and JoAnne unbuttoned the top three buttons of her blouse. Arthur glanced down and then concentrated on his work. He could see her bra.

Arthur had a crush on JoAnne ever since he had met
her in the summer between sixth grade and junior high
school. He was entranced by her warm brown eyes, her
cute figure, and her outgoing, bubbly personality. She was
one year behind him. He had met her at a city-wide, inter-
faith social sponsored by the Methodist Youth Fellowship. He had never dated her because she seemed always
to be going steady with one or another of his friends. In
fact, he did very little dating at all because she was the
only person he really wanted to date. Actually, he also
had a crush on Elizabeth Steinberg, who was probably the
most beautiful girl in the high school. She was in his
class. He had met her in the 7th Grade in English class.
However, she was Jewish, and while she was friendly to
him and he and she were "buddies," they didn't date because Jews didn't date non-Jews, and Catholics generally
dated Catholics, sometimes other Christians, but not Jews.
He would hear that JoAnne had broken up with a boyfriend, and by the time he screwed up his courage to ask
her out, she was already going steady with someone else.
Now, he was at the end of his junior year and she was a
sophomore.

"OK," said Arthur, "Let's do them together. We could
split them up and do them separately, but I think we
would be more effective working them together. If I run
out of things to say, or forget to say something, you could
chime in, and vice versa."

"Yes," said JoAnne, "let's do them together. Do you
have your car?"

"It's not my car, it's my mother's, but, yes, I have it."

The bell rang and they walked out together. They separated to visit their lockers and met at the front door of the
school. The student parking was to the right. They walked
to the Olds, and soon they were downtown in Holmes
Hardware, talking to Mr. Holmes.

"We're here to talk to you about advertising in the *Dothanhi Sootzus*," said JoAnne.

"Everyone in Dothan who has kids at Dothan High School reads the paper," said Arthur. "It has nearly as many readers as *The Dothan Eagle*."

"Our prices for ads are less than a tenth of the cost of ads in the *Eagle*," said JoAnne, "and the *Sootzus* doesn't become fishwrap because people tend to keep the issues, especially when their kids are in the stories. They don't put it on the floors of birdcages either. So, your advertising dollars go a lot further with *Sootzus*."

"We can print ad copy that you provide us," said Arthur, "or we can create an ad for you using data that you provide. Here are some samples of ads for which we have done the artwork." He opened the copy of the *Sootzus* that he had brought with him and pointed out three ads that he had created and two for which JoAnne had done the artwork.

"Besides," said JoAnne, "your daughter, Priscilla, is a Senior at the school and you would be supporting her student newspaper."

"You kids are good at selling," said Mr. Holmes. "If either of you would like to sell hardware, I could use another salesperson to call on farmers in the area."

"Does that mean you'll buy an ad?" asked JoAnne.

"Yes," said Mr. Spann, looking over the press kit they had given him that showed the different sizes and configuration of ads and listed the prices. "I'll take a half-page ad. What would you charge me to create it? I want you, Arthur, to do the artwork. I was impressed with your work on the chariot and horses."

"The artwork we'll create is included in the price of the ad," said Arthur.

Within minutes they had closed the sale, obtained the information to use in creating the ad, and moved on to their next merchant. Within an hour, they had sold all six of their targets, and were sitting on stools at the soda bar at Nip & Ernie's, the student hangout just over a block from the high school. Arthur and JoAnne both were eating chili dogs with the famous Nip & Ernie's secret recipe chili sauce. Soon, they said good-bye; they both had to go home and do their home-work.

The Dothan Public Library was not yet open, but Arthur was waiting on the front steps on a Saturday morning shortly after their ad-selling trip. His Junior year of high school was about to end, and he was confident he would do well in all his courses. As a result, he would be able to spend the weekend reading instead of studying.

Although he thought of himself as a thin, scrawny weakling, Arthur had even done reasonably well in Phys. Ed. He was a fast sprinter, so when they played baseball, he could usually make it to first base after hitting the ball. Ever since his childhood, he had been a weak hitter. He was not a strong thrower, so he played left field, as he had when he was in Little League. When a ball came his way, he would throw the ball toward the shortstop, which gave him three possible players to catch his throws – second baseman, shortstop, and third baseman. He was not good enough, however, to try out for the varsity baseball team; his throwing was accurate, but not strong enough to cover the necessary distance. The core of the varsity baseball team had played on the Dothan Little League All-City team that had won the regional championship, so there was very tough competition to make the team.

He was no better at football, but good enough to play it in Phys. Ed. He could run the ball, weaving expertly between attacking players, but he could neither throw the ball accurately nor catch the ball dependably. They played only touch games in Phys. Ed, but even so, when a lineman hit him he would go down and on one occasion he was knocked unconscious. He was lucky not to have gotten a concussion. He would never have been able to make the school's football team. He was no good at basketball, either, never being able to coordinate walking and dribbling at the same time.

He was a good marksman, however. There was a shooting range in the basement of the gymnasium, and students brought their rifles and pistols to school and keep them in lockers in the basement. The sport of target shooting was very popular, although the school did not field an official team. Arthur was the school champion both in pistol and rifle shooting, having learned to shoot at Boy Scout Camp.

At track and field he also excelled. He was not good at javelin or shot put, but he was a good sprinter. He didn't have the endurance for the mile run, but the quarter mile was his event. He was good at high jumping, his light weight and wiry frame being springy enough and limber enough to dive over the bar. He could never master the art of diving over the bar backwards, but he could beat everyone in his class simply by diving forward over the bar. He was also good at swimming, being fast at any stroke he attempted. He practiced yoga exercises in the morning before school, and the breath-holding exercises enabled him to swim the length of the Olympic-sized pool underwater without surfacing for air. He could do three laps that way, taking a large gulp of air after each lap.

While waiting for the library to open, he planned a strategy for trying out for the track and field team the following week. He could practice over the summer and be ready for competition in the following season.

Soon, Miss Alexander arrived and unlocked the doors to the Dothan Public Library.

"You're here early for a Saturday, Arthur," she said.

"I have already done all my term papers and I'm ready for the exams. I'll ace them. I'm going to spend the weekend reading."

"Anything in particular?"

"I don't know," said Arthur. "I have already read all the science fiction and junior literature in the library. I have now started on the science section. I have studied astronomy, and I am already pretty good at Egyptology. I can read hieroglyphics, although I don't yet know Coptic, the ancient Egyptian language. Still, I know the sounds, syllables, and words represented by many of the glyphs. I think I'll get a book on geology this time. I read a book on geology when I was in sixth grade but didn't get a lot of it."

Miss Alexander smiled. She liked Arthur – everyone seemed to like him – and he had read more books in her library than any young person she had ever met. He would check out between three and five books each Saturday and bring them back the following Saturday. By their conversations, she knew he had read and absorbed everything in them.

"George Wallace College," she said, "will be offering a course in geology during the summer. You might want to take the course. If you like geology, you'll find it interesting."

"Thanks," said Arthur, "that's great! I think I'll do that. I took painting there last summer, and don't want to take it again, so the geology course sounds like just the thing I'd like."

Arthur made his way to the science section and quickly found three books on geology. He leafed through them at the library table in that section. He browsed for other books and took one on astrophysics, thinking that the study of the earth in the context of the universe was a good idea. Finally, in the late morning, he carried them to the check-out desk and handed them to Miss Alexander, along with his library card.

"Hello, Arthur," said a feminine voice behind him. "I kind of thought I'd find you here this morning." Arthur turned, and immediately found himself tongue-tied. The speaker was JoAnne McKinley. Recently, she had been going steady with Don Cohen, the football quarterback, which had placed her off limits. Therefore, although she had been very friendly working with him on the *Sootzus* staff, Arthur had made no moves.

"It – it's good to see you, Jo Anne," stammered Arthur. He could feel his face starting to blush. "I only get to talk to you in *Sootzus.*"

"As soon as I heard you were on *Sootzus,* I signed up," said Jo Anne, smiling up at him. Arthur couldn't think of a response for a long moment.

"I'm glad you did," he finally said. "I really enjoy working with you."

"Did you know that Don and I broke up?" she asked.

"No, I didn't," he replied. "I thought you two were pretty close. What happened?"

"He started dating Elizabeth Steinberg," she said. "His Mom told him he should only date Jews."

"That's silly," said Arthur. "Are you upset?"

"No," she said. "In a way, I'm relieved. We weren't in love; I think I was just attracted to him because he was the football star. He's not very bright, you know."

"I didn't know," said Arthur. He did know, but didn't want to speak ill of Don.

"Since I'm not going steady, would you like to go with me tonight to the Spring Hop?" she asked. Arthur was struck dumb, unable to say a word.

"It's tonight, you know. Can you come?" she asked.

"I – I guess so," he said haltingly. Actually, he was overjoyed.

"I have been looking for a way to get to know you better," she said. "Mrs. Kinsey says you're the smartest boy she's ever taught." Mrs. Kinsey taught World History at Dothan High School. They both were taking the course, although they were in different class periods. "She said you can even read Egyptian hieroglyphics."

"Well, yes, I know the glyphs – and the words and sounds they stand for, and I know the hieratic equivalents for the glyphs, but I don't know the ancient Egyptian language so I can't translate very well. I know the English words for the glyphs that stand for words, but the writing is a mixture of words in which the glyphs are used alphabetically and words that have single glyphs. Only some of it makes sense to me that way."

He was still holding the pen he would use to sign out the books. Miss Alexander had made herself busy with something, appearing to ignore the two teenagers. Arthur opened his notebook.

"Here, I'll show you," he said, drawing a cartouche and some glyphs in the cartouche. "This is your name in Hieroglyphics." He placed some glyphs outside the cartouche. "And these glyphs stand for words. The glyphs inside the cartouche spell your name alphabetically."

"What do the glyphs outside the cartouche mean?" she asked. He blushed.

"That's for you to find out," he said. He had drawn the glyphs for the first person singular, "I," a man seated on the ground with one knee raised and pointing to his chest, and the verb, "love," a group of three glyphs – a stylized plough, a mouth, and a seated man pointing at his mouth. She smiled at him.

"Did you know that you're cute when you blush?" she asked.

"Does that mean I'm not cute when I'm not blushing?" he asked. "I blush because I'm really shy around pretty girls."

"You don't blush when you're working with me in *Sootzus*," she said, a coy smile dimpling her cheeks.

"That's because our attention is directed at the work, rather than at each other -- but I have more trouble concentrating on the work when you're around," he replied. "I like you too much." She smiled.

"I guess we have a date for tonight. Can you get your parents' car?"

"I can get my mother's car, the old Oldsmobile," he replied.

"I like that car. I think it looks romantic, like a car Greta Garbo might have driven. Pick me up about 6:30."

"I'll do that," said Arthur.

"Bye," she said.

"Bye," he said. He felt like he was in heaven as he drove home.

He was in the clouds all evening. He was a very poor dancer, never having been with a girl at a dance except for the Homecoming Ball last year with Priscilla, but he was a quick learner. Other boys were constantly cutting in, however, so he spent about half his time watching her dance with others. He danced with a few other girls – self-consciously. He was not experienced at dancing and didn't know anything other than a simple two-step – and the twist. JoAnne was very popular – bright, pretty, cute, a cheerleader, and friendly.

Joanne taught him several steps that night. After the dance he drove her home. The Oldsmobile had a bench seat in front, so she sat in the middle of the seat, close to him. As he drove, she laid her lovely head against his shoulder, her curly brown hair brushing his cheek.

"I heard you are going to Rice University," she said.

"That's right," he said. "At least, I would like to. I have applied, but I won't hear until sometime during the Summer. My PSAT scores were pretty good, so if my SAT scores come back reasonably high, I think I have a good chance of being accepted. You know, Rice used to be 'Rice Institute' and recently became 'Rice University'."

"Have you decided on a major?"

"I'm going into the architecture school, but I'll also be in Navy ROTC. I want to be a Naval Officer."

"I think you would look stunning in a Navy uniform," she said. He blushed, but she couldn't see that in the dark.

"I would love to be a Navy pilot," he said, "but you have to have 20-20 vision without glasses for that, and I have to wear glasses, so I can't be a pilot. I really want to work for the Office of Naval Intelligence, so I'll start out as a regular line officer until I can get into the ONI." She lifted her head from his shoulder and looked up at him.

"You mean you want to be a spy?" she asked.

"I think that would be an interesting career," he said, "but there's a lot to intelligence besides spying. Naval Intelligence mostly tries to keep up to date on the status of the navies of other powers. There's a lot of observation from ships and planes, and a lot of detailed analysis and code-breaking. For the most part, real spying is done by the Central Intelligence Agency."

"Do you want to be a spy or an analyst?"

"I want to be a spy."

"I think you're so smart that you can be anything you want to be. Do spies have families?"

"From what I understand, most of them do. They must look and act like something other than spies – so they are Embassy attachés or appear to be civilians working in a foreign country. Having a family helps with the cover story."

"I'm glad that you would be able to have a family, but I hope you would have one because you want one and not just for a cover story."

"I would only marry if I were in love. I'll have a family because I want a family, not because I need one for my cover. I just meant that families are allowed because they help with the cover, not that they are required."

"Oh. Do you think you would marry right out of college?"

"That depends on whether I find a girl I love who wants to marry me." She was silent for a while and laid her head back against his shoulder.

Soon they arrived at her parents' house. As he turned the key to shut off the engine and set the hand brake, she turned toward him, pressing against his arm. She tilted her head up towards his face. He turned towards her and she snaked her right hand over his shoulder and behind his neck in the beginning of an embrace. He reciprocated, happy confusion filling his mind. Their lips met in a long, tender kiss.

"Arthur, I like you very much," she said, finally breaking the kiss. "Do you think we should go steady?"

"I would love that because I like you very much, too. But in just over a year I'll be going off to Texas to Rice University, and you're going to Auburn the year after. It would not be fair to compel you not to date while we are separated." *Why did I say that? Why couldn't I just say, "Yes?"* he thought.

"Well," she said, "let's go steady unofficially until you leave for college. We'll see what happens during college. We can write, and we can see each other on breaks and vacations, if we still want to. I am pretty sure I would want to." Their lips met again, and the kiss this time was more passionate and less tender. Arthur felt like he was melting – that he was made of soft wax that she could shape any way she wanted to. The top of her strapless gown had slid down and she put his hand on her breast. If she were to ask him to change his mind and go to Auburn instead of Rice, he would do that. But she didn't ask. After a while she broke the kiss with a little moan.

"You're the best kisser I ever kissed," she said, pulling the top of her gown back up to a position of modesty. In the dim light he could see that her face was flushed. He could feel that his own face was flushed. He stroked her cheek gently and lovingly with the palm of his hand, and kissed her again, but just a short, tender kiss.

"I'd better return you to your father," he said, "before he comes to investigate why we are in the car so long. If we keep doing this, we might do something that we would come to regret. We don't want to lose our virtue."

"That's a funny, old-fashioned way of saying it," said Jo Anne.

"Those are the words my Grandmother used when I was in sixth grade and a neighbor girl got pregnant. Grandmother said she had lost her virtue."

"I feel so safe with you," said Jo Anne. "You are so mature and so strong in character. You seem much older than your age. If we had kept kissing, I would have done anything you wanted me to do. It's good that you stopped. I don't want to … lose my virtue. At least not yet." She giggled and he laughed gently. *Not yet?* He thought.

He walked her to the door and they kissed again before she knocked on the door. Her father opened the door immediately.

"Good evening, Mr. McKinley," said Arthur. "I had a wonderful time with JoAnne tonight."

"Was the dance good?" asked Mr. McKinley.

"With Jo Anne as my dance partner, I was dancing in the clouds," said Arthur. "Good night, sir. Good night, JoAnne. I'll call you tomorrow, if that's OK."

"Please do," she said. "I'll be home from church by half-past noon and through with lunch by 2:00. Call me any time after that." She squeezed his hand, turned and disappeared into the house. Mr. McKinley stood in the doorway, regarding Arthur solemnly.

"Good night, Arthur," he said, backing up and closing the door. Arthur turned and walked back to the Oldsmobile, his heart on fire and his mind in a fog. He knew that he was in love, and he thought she was as well. He had been in love with her for a long time, but she had only recently noticed him.

CHAPTER 9

FRESHMAN ORIENTATION

August 1962
Houston, Texas

Sunday, August 19, Arthur boarded Southern Airways' DC3 in Dothan well before dawn to fly to Houston. The rumbling old plane landed at Eglin Field (an Air Force Base between Dothan and Panama City, Florida) and at Panama City, and then took the "long" hop to New Orleans, where Arthur changed to a more modern Eastern Airlines flight, a DC6, to Houston. He was excited to be making a major transition between adolescence and adulthood. For him, it was a great adventure to be leaving the security of home to live separately in a far city.

He was headed to "Freshman Orientation." Two weeks before the official resumption of classes for the fall semester, Rice required its freshmen (and "freshwomen") to arrive for a week of orientation. Some upperclassmen and many faculty also attended, acting as mentors and guides. Each freshman or freshwoman was assigned to an upperclass "big brother" or "big sister" who guided him or her through the week, answered questions, provided advice, and for off-campus events, provided transportation.

When Arthur arrived at Houston International Airport, his mother's second cousin, Brad Austin, met him at the gate and gave him a warm welcome. He accompanied Arthur to baggage claim where they waited for Arthur's luggage to arrive. Brad was dressed in a business suit, and sweating; the day was hot, even by Houston standards, for a mid-August day, and the humidity made the air feel thick and wet. Arthur was also wearing a suit and tie, which was standard dress in those days for air travel. Daytime temperatures in Houston were hovering near 100° F, with relative humidity also near 100%. Because the air was saturated, as soon as temperatures cooled a little in the late afternoon, Houston would experience thundershowers, a typical daily late Summer event.

"After we get your luggage," said Brad, "I'm taking you home for a late lunch. My daughter, Hilda, will be joining us. I've asked her to help you ease into Houston's social life. She's less than a year older than you are and working for a year before starting college. She plans to go to the University of Texas to study accounting or business. Your mother tells me that you will be studying architecture?"

"That's right," said Arthur. "Dad wanted me to be an engineer. I love music and won a scholarship in music, but my parents pressed me to pick a field of study that was more readily employable, so I picked architecture as a compromise between engineering and art. I'll also be in Navy ROTC and am considering a career in the Navy, but you can't major in Naval Science."

"Linda, your mother, was always very talented in music," said Brad, "but she took a double major in Spanish and English Literature so she would be able to be a teacher."

"I considered that, but teachers make so much less than architects that I decided on architecture. My Dad wants me to consider a double major, both in architecture and in engineering, because an architect always must hire engineers to do the structural, mechanical and electrical design for the buildings he designs. If I were both an architect and an engineer, he says, I could do it all myself and not have to hire anyone."

"Maybe he's right," said Brad.

"I don't think so," said Arthur. "I visited an architect's office when I was in Boy Scouts, working on the Architecture Merit Badge. He had five people working for him, doing the details of the design. He would sketch out the design concepts for buildings himself, and have draftsmen and engineers work out the details while he sketched the design concept for the next building. He told me that he made more by employing architects and engineers because the firm could do so much more work than he could do alone. Oh, there's my suitcase."

He retrieved the suitcase and they walked to the air cargo counter where they retrieved several cardboard boxes, carefully taped and labeled. Using a luggage cart, they took them to Brad's car. As they drove to Brad's house in the southern Houston suburbs, Brad talked about his daughter, Hilda. She was working in a bank as a bank teller, in training for loan officer. Arthur was thankful that the car was air conditioned. By the time they reached the Austin home, he was no longer sweating.

He sat across the table from Hilda at lunch, admiring her long blond hair, sky-blue eyes and provocative smile. Hilda's father ate quickly and excused himself to go to his golf club. Her mother, Helen, got busy in the kitchen with the dishes. Arthur's mind retrieved memories of Jo Anne, but he was very aware that they had agreed to resume dating others while separated for college. Hilda was quite attractive, as tall as Arthur, with a perfectly feminine figure, and she engaged him in very pleasant conversation. He was entranced, transfixed.

"What sorts of things do you like?" she asked. "Do you have any hobbies?"

"Well, I like reading, drawing – especially buildings – studying science, military and naval history, and things like that. I also read a lot of fiction – science fiction, historical fiction, spy stories. I like reading about mathematical theory, although I don't really turn on to arithmetic." She laughed.

"Numbers," she said, "are my thing, although I don't really enjoy algebra, calculus, trigonometry and the like. But I like the orderliness of numbers and accounting. I guess that's why I'm working at a bank and will likely become an accountant." Her voice had grown animated, and she punctuated her words with hand motions – sort of drawing a spread sheet with her fingers when talking of the "orderliness of numbers."

"I also like to study theology," said Arthur. "I like the philosophical depth of Catholic theology. I thought of becoming a priest, but I'd like to get married some day and have kids."

"Besides," she said, "I never heard of a priest who was a battle fleet commander." It was his turn to laugh.

"You're right," he said. "If I were a priest in the Navy, I'd be a chaplain. But I really love science fiction and so I dream of flying a space ship to exotic planets. I can't become a pilot, however, so I'd never be accepted into the astronaut program." Hilda's mother, Helen, a quiet, mousy, unassuming but pleasant woman, brought in a coffee pot and cups, and served them coffee, taking a cup herself and sitting beside Hilda.

"How much do you know about Houston?" asked Helen.

"Very little," answered Arthur. "I know that it is a growing, medium sized city of a few hundred thousand, with a thriving seaport that has made it the hub of the American oil industry." He took a sip of his coffee, trying not to burn the roof of his mouth.

"It was founded as a real-estate venture by the Allen brothers from Pennsylvania. It was a swamp," said Helen. "They began draining it by digging deep ditches that drained to the bayous, and then produced brochures with renderings of a beautiful town. They used these to sell lots in their swamp to Easterners with a sense of adventure. They had trouble with malaria for a while. It was just a small town until the Galveston hurricane of 1901, which destroyed the Port of Galveston. Dredging the ship channel turned Houston into a busy inland port, and Houston was off and running." Arthur was smiling.

"You sound like a salesperson for Houston," said Arthur. Hilda laughed.

"Mother's family was one of the first families to move to Houston," she said. "Dad's family moved here from Austin, Texas, and the rest is history."

"So, what will you study at Rice?" asked her mother. She sipped her coffee, the steam clouding her glasses. She wiped them on her apron.

"I'll be an architecture major, but I'll also be in the Navy ROTC and go into the navy after graduation. I'll have architecture to fall back on after the Navy."

"Will you go for a career in the Navy or just for the one enlistment?" asked Hilda.

"I'm not sure yet," Arthur replied. Hilda drank some of her coffee. "I'll probably try for a career, but if that doesn't work, I'll go civilian and practice architecture." Hilda's mother was smiling. Arthur tried his coffee again, and it was now cool enough to take a drink rather than a sip.

"That sounds like a plan," said Helen. "Your mother was a very talented amateur musician. Did she teach you to play the piano?"

"She started, and then decided someone else should teach me. I took piano lessons in Puebla from a family friend, and then in Dothan I continued them with a man who taught piano and conducted the Glee Club at the high school. He took me last year to the Alabama Music Festival at Auburn, where I won the offer of a scholarship in music composition, but my parents persuaded me to pursue something more marketable. Besides, I really wanted to do the Navy thing. Still, I can continue writing music and might someday be able to get it performed and published. At least, I hope so."

"I'm impressed," said Hilda. "We'll have to get you to play for us here. But I know you must get to the campus and get settled. We'll have you over soon, and you can play the piano then."

He was surprised at how easily conversation came with Hilda. Even though he was being interrogated, in a way, it didn't feel like an interrogation. Hilda was open and friendly, but not intense, as was her family. He got the impression not that they were probing for information but that they were genuinely interested in him. Arthur usually didn't talk much, especially around girls. It was as if he were talking to an old friend whom he hadn't seen in a decade and who wanted to learn all about what he had been doing while they were apart. He felt drawn to her.

She drove him to the campus, straight up Main Street from the outer suburbs, pointing out landmarks along the way. There were several that he burned into his memory for future reference. First, on the left, at the corner of Main Street and Holcombe Boulevard, was the Shamrock Hilton Hotel, a grand looking, tall hotel in tan brick with a green-glazed, Spanish tile roof. Hilda told him that the restaurant in the hotel was good and not too expensive, and that the hotel had a swim club used by hotel guests but open to neighbors who bought annual memberships for a nominal amount. Included in the Shamrock Swim Club membership was access to the bar. Harris County, in which most of Houston was located, was a dry county, and one could only enjoy hard liquor at a "private club" or at home. There were many such clubs, and membership fees were nominal, with some clubs charging as little as $5.00 per year in dues. Her father was a member of the

Shamrock Club. Hilda said they would give him their membership number and list him as a family member so he could use the club on occasion.

"But I'm just seventeen," Arthur said. "I can't legally drink until I'm 21."

"Don't worry," she said. "The club doesn't sell memberships to minors, so minors who get in are members of a family that has a membership. You could drink legally in Louisiana. It's silly that someone who's old enough to go to war for his country isn't old enough to have a beer legally. Do you have moral qualms about drinking?"

"Oh, no," he said. "I just have qualms about getting into trouble for breaking the law."

"That's the beauty of private clubs. If no one complains and if no one gets drunk or disorderly, the club discreetly serves people who are 'adult minors' like you and me." She went on to explain that a member had to maintain his own stock of liquor at the club, and he was served from his own liquor for a small "serving fee." There was a liquor store at the club that was open only to members, who could buy bottles of their choice, and the club would keep them labeled with their member numbers for them and serve them from their own bottles.

There were several "lounges" along the drive as well. Hilda explained that a lounge could serve beer and wine, but no hard liquor, and did not have to be a private club. Appropriately licensed restaurants could also serve beer and wine.

Just a short distance from the hotel, but on the other side of Main Street, was Bill Williams' Famous Restaurant, which served superb fried chicken, steaks and seafood at reasonable prices, and close to it was The Red Lion Inn, a Tudor-English-themed pub that was actually a very fine restaurant and lounge that maintained an antique London black taxi and a double-decker London bus to transport customers. Guests at a hotel could call, and the restaurant would pick them up in the taxi. Groups, like weddings, would be picked up in the double-decker bus. The food was very good, but much more expensive than most restaurants in the area. The restaurant was the only Zagat-rated five-star restaurant in Houston, and it had a private club bar within it.

A short distance north along Main Street was Delmonico's Italian Restaurant, and immediately across from the Main Street entry driveway to Rice University was the Herman Professional Building, housing the offices of doctors associated with the Houston Medical center, which occupied a large tract of land just beyond, with world-class hospitals. The sprawling Herman Park surrounded the Medical Center and contained the Houston Zoo as well as a good public golf course.

On the first floor of the Herman Professional Building was a little fast-food restaurant called "The Dutch Kettle" that was open 24 hours a day. It was famous for its Belgian waffles and bottomless cups of coffee. It also served eggs, bacon, sausage, French fries and hamburgers, with a "soup of the day" on the menu as well. It was a favorite hangout for Rice students and medical students doing late-night or all-night studying. They could pay ten cents for one cup of coffee, and drink coffee all night while they studied for exams.

Rice University did not have dormitories; it had residential colleges, mimicking the Oxford model, and did not allow fraternities or sororities. The residential colleges served as a (mostly) sedate substitute for fraternities. All incoming freshmen were assigned to a residential college and remained members of that college for the rest of their lives. Arthur had been assigned to Wiess College.

Hilda turned her car into the service driveway to Wiess College, and found a place to park it out of the driving lanes. There was no parking lot, but a loading dock for deliveries. She parked just past the end of the dock. She went with him to the Commons, a large room outfitted with a variety of living-room-like clusters of furniture, a magazine rack, a TV, and a piano. The Commons was air conditioned – a pleasant respite from the heat outside. Arthur took a deep breath of the cool air. Here a desk had been set up for registering the arriving freshmen. It was manned by the upperclassmen who had "freshman orientation duty." A tall, lanky, muscular senior with a blond crew cut and blue eyes introduced himself.

"Hello, Arthur," he said. "I'm Bill Daugherty. You're one of my freshmen for Orientation." He shook Arthur's hand. "I'll be sort of a mentor for you, showing you the ropes here at Rice." As he spoke, he was looking at Hilda.

"This is my cousin, Hilda Austin," said Arthur. She extended her hand for a handshake and Bill took it. "Her dad picked me up at the airport, and I had lunch with the family. Hilda volunteered to deliver me here and make sure I got settled in properly."

"Real cousin or kissing cousin?" asked Bill.

"Her father is my mother's second cousin," answered Arthur.

"Kissing cousin, then," said Bill, smiling, and still holding her hand in his. "I wish I had a kissing cousin as pretty as Hilda. Arthur, you must be a real 'ladies' man.' You arrive on campus for your first day of college already with a beautiful woman on your arm." Hilda blushed slightly, but turned to Arthur, smiling and withdrawing her hand from Bill's. She put her hand in Arthur's hand.

"I guess I'll have to kiss you when we say goodbye today," she said to Arthur. Now it was his turn to blush.

"I guess I'll have to take you up on that," he said.

"Come, I'll take you to your room," said Bill.

"Are girls allowed to come along?" asked Hilda.

"Yes – check-in day is an open house," said Bill. "Most of the women accompanying the men today are mothers, however. Arthur, you'll be the envy of the College with such a pretty girl helping you move in."

He led the way out to the court, up an open flight of stairs, to an open balcony that connected to all the rooms on the second floor of that wing. There was a similar balcony for the third floor, above. As Arthur would learn, Wiess College was the only college on campus with that sort of open, "garden apartment" design. All the other residential colleges had internal corridors with rooms on both sides. Wiess was a better design for the Houston climate, because the rooms had windows at both ends to allow cross-ventilation. Air conditioning had not yet arrived at Rice's residential colleges, except for the Commons and Dining Halls.

"There's one room that is an exception to that layout. Here's your room," said Bill as they turned onto the balcony from the stairs. It was the first room on the right at the top of the stairs. "Unfortunately for you, your room is called 'the handball court' because it has no windows at the other end. It is the only room like that in Wiess College. I had it my freshman year. You can survive it, but I advise that you buy a window fan and persuade your suitemates to let you leave the bathroom doors open so you can get some airflow from their room." Wiess College was arranged in suites of two rooms, each with two beds, with a bathroom between the two rooms that was shared between them.

"When we're through here and you're all unpacked," said Hilda, "I'll take you to Fed-Mart to buy a fan and anything else you might need."

Arthur inserted the key that Bill gave him into the lock. *This is the first time I'm unlocking a bedroom door in the company of a girl*, he thought. The image of the key entering the keyhole took on erotic connotations, and Arthur knew he was starting to blush. Arthur opened the door, and saw another young man already in the room, sitting in his underwear at one of the two small study desks, reading a book and taking notes. When he saw Hilda, he jumped up, grabbed his pants, and hurriedly put them on.

"Henry?" asked Arthur.

"Yes, that's me," replied Henry, abashed but grinning. "I wasn't expecting a beautiful woman to walk in or I would have kept my pants on. I'm Henry Cartwright."

"That's OK," said Hilda, laughing and extending her hand. "You don't have anything I haven't seen before. I'm Hilda Austin, Arthur's kissing cousin." As they shook hands, Arthur knew he was blushing; he could feel the heat in the skin of his face.

"I'm your roommate, Arthur Harris," said Arthur, as they shook hands. He and Henry had become acquainted by correspondence during the summer, having been given each other's name and address by the Admissions Office.

"Welcome to the Handball Court," said Henry.

"I'm pleased finally to meet you," said Arthur. "I'll be right back with my things."

"You look sunburned," said Henry, who was deeply tanned. You might want to put something on that face before it blisters."

"He's just blushing," laughed Hilda. "He blushes easily." Arthur joined in the general laughter.

"I can understand that," said Bill to Hilda. "You're beautiful enough to make any man blush." She smiled prettily and took Arthur's hand.

"Let's go get your luggage, Kissing Cousin," she said. Arthur removed his suit jacket and tie, placing them on his bed, and rolled up his shirt sleeves.

Arthur and Hilda returned to the car, holding hands. They made three trips to the room to deliver Arthur's luggage and the four boxes of "furnishings" Arthur's Mom had packed for him. The suitcases contained his clothing, and the boxes contained sheets, a blanket, a bedspread, a hooked rug made for him by his grandmother, books and other necessities for a college student. The suitcase had come with Arthur on the airplane, but the boxes had been shipped as cargo on the same plane, for which Arthur's Dad had paid a fee.

Finally, everything was deposited into the room. Hilda helped him unpack everything and put it away. He carefully folded his underwear and socks before putting them in the drawer. She helped him make the bed. As she leaned over to tuck in the sheets, he couldn't help but look down the top of her low-cut dress at her beautifully formed breasts. It was a light, summer dress with a floral pattern, a low-cut back and front, and spaghetti straps over the shoulders, and she was wearing it without a bra. It was also short, revealing her slim, shapely legs.

Above his built-in desk were three stacked shelves mounted to the wall. He started placing books from the pile on his desk onto the shelves, and Hilda came up behind him to help. As she took a book and reached over his shoulder to put it next to the book he had just placed there, he could feel the warmth of her breasts pressing against his back. With a sigh, he knew that he would start blushing again any moment. He did, as she continued helping him with the books, their physical contact very present in his awareness – and very pleasant. He thought guiltily of Jo Anne, but he was unable to keep his mind off Hilda.

Once everything was put away, Hilda drove him to Fed-Mart, a dusty, cavernous discount store that sold something of everything at reasonably low prices. They had a variety of fans, and Arthur picked out a square window fan.

"Are you sure there isn't anything else you need," said Hilda.

"I don't think so," said Arthur. "I have toothpaste, bath soap, towels, washcloths, shaving cream, shampoo – I don't think of anything I need that I don't have."

"You're a typical man," said Hilda, shaking her head.

"I would hope so," said Arthur smiling.

"Men don't think of housekeeping. You have a cleaning service as part of your dormitory fee, but you don't have laundry service. There's a laundry in the basement with washing machines, dryers and an ironing board. I know, because a cousin of mine – not a kissing cousin – was at Wiess College for a year before he decided to transfer to an easier school. You will need laundry detergent, fabric softener, Clorox, a laundry bag, a mesh sock bag to keep your socks from being eaten by the washing machine – do you have an iron?"

"You're right," Arthur said, laughing. "I didn't think of housekeeping items. I do have a small travel iron, however."

"It would be your Mom who got the iron for you. You will need distilled water for the iron, or you'll get mineral stains all over your clothes. You'll need some spray starch and sizing. Also, given the configuration of your room and the lack of air conditioning, I recommend a can of Glade air freshener. Your room already smells rather rank." As they talked, they walked up and down the aisles, selecting the items Arthur would need.

When they were through shopping, Hilda helped him carry his purchases to the car and drove him back to the campus. They continued their conversation in the car.

"Did you have a girlfriend in high school, anyone special?" Asked Hilda. This took Arthur by surprise, reminding him of JoAnne.

"I...I...I did almost no dating at all, until my junior year." He didn't like how this sounded. "First of all, I spent a lot of time studying, and my parents wouldn't let me date if I had any unfinished schoolwork," he said defensively. "Second, I'm very shy by nature and have trouble talking to girls about anything personal. I just freeze up and can't think of what to say. I can talk about schoolwork – I did a lot of tutoring of girls, and some boys, who needed help with their studies – but I would freeze if the subject changed to something more personal. By the time I got up the courage to ask any particular girl for a date, she would be going steady with someone. Then, when they broke up, by the time I got up the courage again, she would already be going steady with someone else." Hilda was smiling sympathetically.

"You said a lot without answering my question. It sounds like you never figured out that when a girl stops going steady with a guy, it's usually because someone she likes more has asked her for a date. Was there ever anyone special?"

"For a cousin, you sure ask a lot of questions," Arthur said, grinning. "That's OK; I like answering them. I like you, and I like talking to you. I feel comfortable with you."

"So, who was your special love?" she asked, frowning and grinning mischievously at the same time. "Stop being evasive! Spill it! Inquiring minds want to know!" Arthur laughed.

"OK, OK. I always wanted to date JoAnne McKinley. She was a year behind me, a brown-skinned, brown-haired, brown-eyed girl with a cute turned-up nose and dimples when she smiled. I met her at a multi-church social sponsored by the Methodist Youth Fellowship when I was in seventh grade. She was extremely cute, and I got to square dance with her at the social. When I was in the eighth grade, she was in the seventh grade at my school, Young Junior High School. I had a boyhood crush on her that never went away.

"She was the one I always wanted to ask for a date but didn't because she was always going steady with one or another of my good friends. She was very popular – a cheerleader, a National Honor Society member, on the staff of the high school newspaper with me, the *Dothanhi Sootzus*..." Hilda started laughing.

"Yes," Arthur said, "Ii *is* a corny name for a newspaper, but Dothan High 'suited us.' Dothan is a small, tightly knit, Southern town. Anyway, I never got a date with her until the end of my junior year. She asked me to the spring hop. We dated through my senior year and this summer and we were unofficially going steady. We didn't make it official because we knew we would be separating for college and decided it would be better if we were free to date others. I may be in love with her. Only time will tell."

"Was JoAnne the only girl you dated?" asked Hilda

"I did a few dates with a couple of other girls," he replied. "Melba Scarborough's father made her break up with her boyfriend and she was without a date for a Prom as a result. She asked me to take her, and I did. I had a couple of dates with Priscilla Holmes, as well, before I started dating JoAnne." By that time, Arthur and Hilda had reached Wiess College and were sitting in the car together at the loading dock with the motor and air conditioner running.

"Why so much interest in my adolescent love life?" asked Arthur, grinning at her.

"Just curious," she replied. "I like to know a little about the men I know, especially when I'm thinking of dating them." Arthur thought of JoAnne, but dismissed the thought, telling himself he had every right to consider dating Hilda. He felt his heart beating faster in Hilda's presence, and was aware that she was very sexy. Suppressing his guilty conscience, he returned to the scene at hand.

"I'm as curious of you as you are of me," he said. "I'm not going to use the corny approach of asking you what a pretty girl like you is doing without a boyfriend, but what are you doing without a boyfriend?" She laughed.

"I've had several," she said. "Each one turned out to be either a bore or a boor. I'm in between now, and attracted to you, so I'm exploring the possibilities. I'm not in a rush to get married, but I'm not discounting the possibility."

"Gee – we barely know each other," he said, "and the subject has already turned to marriage." He laughed. She looked down.

"That's not what I meant," she said. "I meant that I like you, want to get to know you, but I'm not going to rush serious involvement, which will come when and if it will, in its own time."

"OK," he said, "I can go with that. You're the only girl I know in Houston, and I'm sure you won't be the last, but I like you and want to get to know you better."

"We'd better get your room set up," said Hilda, changing the subject before it became more awkward than it already was. They carried Arthur's purchases to the room. Henry was in the room, dressed in grey slacks and shirt with a tie, his blazer hanging on the back of his chair.

"You didn't have to get dressed up just for my sake," said Hilda.

"I would if I had thought of it," said Henry, laughing, "considering how I was dressed when we met. I'm waiting for my father to arrive. He's taking me to dinner before flying back to Wilmington." He smoothed his curly brown hair with his hand and straightened his tie.

"Indeed I am," said a deep voice from the doorway. "You must be Arthur," he said. Arthur and Hilda turned to see a tall, round-faced, slightly rotund man with horn-rimmed glasses, wearing a brown suit, white shirt, and regimental-striped tie.

"Hilda, Arthur Harris, this is my father, Wilfred Cartwright," said Henry.

"Mr. Cartwright, Hilda Austin is my cousin and lives in Houston," said Arthur.

"It's a pleasure to meet you both," he replied.

"The pleasure is mine," said Hilda.

"And mine," Arthur echoed.

"You are both invited to have dinner with us," said Mr. Cartwright.

"Thank you so much," said Hilda.

"I made a reservation at the *Red Lion Inn* for three, intending to include Arthur, but I didn't know you'd be here, Hilda, or I would have made it for four. There's no telephone in the room here, so I'll go downstairs to call them and increase it to four while Arthur dresses. Hilda, you're well-dressed just as you are. That dress is beautiful on you." Arthur put his bags of purchases on the floor beside his bed.

"I'll go with you," said Hilda. "I need to call my parents and let them know I won't be home for dinner."

"Please give me a few minutes to clean up and change," said Arthur, taking blazer, slacks, dress shirt, a change of underwear and socks and retreating to the bathroom, where he quickly showered and dressed. When he returned to the room. Hilda was plugging in the window fan, which Mr. Cartwright had already installed in the window. It whirred to life.

"This is going to make a big difference," said Henry. I can already feel the air coming through. Thank you for getting it."

"Don't mention it," said Arthur, tying his tie. "I would have died without it."

Arthur thought the prime rib at the *Red Lion* was wonderful. Mr. Cartwright ordered a bottle of good French Malbec wine, and a second one half way through the meal. After dinner, they said goodbye to Mr. Cartwright in the Commons, and Arthur walked Hilda back to her car. After she opened the driver's door, she turned to him, put her arms around his neck, and they kissed – a long, lingering kiss, their bodies pressed together in an intimate embrace. Finally, they broke the kiss.

"Hilda," said Arthur, "I very much like the fact that we are kissing cousins."

"So do I," said Hilda. "Should we plan something for next Saturday? I promised Dad I'd show you around Houston."

"The college has a very full schedule for us until Labor Day weekend," said Arthur. "This Saturday we are going to a musical, *Bells are Ringing*. They have paired us with girls from Jones College – sort of a managed, mandatory date." Hilda laughed. "Why don't we get together sometime during Labor Day Weekend?" asked Arthur.

"Perfect," said Hilda. "I'll pick you up that Friday evening at 5:00. You're going to spend the weekend with me. Pack your swim suit, casual clothes for Saturday, a jacket and tie for Saturday evening, and casual clothes for Sunday and Monday. I'll have you back to Wiess College by midnight Monday, Labor Day."

"It's a date," said Arthur. He decided he was going to enjoy college.

"Arthur, remember to call me if you need anything," said Hilda. "I don't live far away and work closer. I can run errands for you when you need me to."

"Thank you. I will," said Arthur, meaning it.

"Good luck, Arthur. Give me a call every few days to touch base."

"Thanks, Hilda, I will. I can't wait to see you again."

"Your Mom made Dad promise to keep an eye on you and make sure you didn't fall into dangerous company. She's convinced that colleges are filled with Communists." Arthur laughed.

"I'm sure there are some here," said Arthur, "But I have no interest, other than academic, in Communism."

"Dad told me he was delegating his 'oversight' role to me. I'm going to enjoy keeping an eye on you and keeping you…out of trouble." She winked.

"So instead of waiting for me to fall into dangerous company, he is providing it. I'm really glad we're not more closely related," he replied, laughing.

They kissed again, long and lingering, then again and again. Finally, Hilda broke the kiss.

"I'm going to have to go home and take a cold shower," she said. Arthur laughed.

"That's supposed to be my line," he said. She sat, closed the car door and drove away into the night. He stood in the dark for a minute, enjoying the afterglow, before walking into the college.

The ensuing two-week orientation period was filled with seminars and activities for the incoming students. Professors with Orientation Duty were on campus, along with the upperclassmen mentors.

Every five freshmen had one upperclassman who would help them become "acclimatized" to Rice's culture. Arthur and Henry were both registered as architecture students. They were both assigned Bill Daugherty, along with three other freshmen. At the start of the freshman year, freshmen were grouped as Science, Liberal Arts, Engineering, and Architecture students, even though majors would not be declared until the end of the freshman year. Henry and Arthur were the only two architecture students assigned to Bill Daugherty.

Bill took his freshmen to Kay's Lounge the next night to get acquainted. Although the legal drinking age was 21, the drinking age was not rigidly enforced in the lounges around the University provided the college students behaved themselves and didn't cause trouble. Kay's was the favorite off-campus hangout for Rice students and was a short walk from the campus.

Bill also was in the Navy ROTC program, and would be commissioned as an officer upon his graduation at the end of that year. He was a mechanical engineering major. Arthur peppered him with questions about the NROTC program. Bill told him he was opting for nuclear school after his commissioning and would serve his time in the nuclear submarine fleet. Arthur quickly became more and more excited about the possibility of undertaking a career as a US Navy officer.

CHAPTER 10

NAVAL OPTIONS

August and September 1962
Houston and Galveston, Texas

The next morning, Arthur attended an orientation session at the School of Architecture. The new department chair, Bill Caudill, who was also head of the largest architecture firm in Houston, Caudill Rowlett Scott, welcomed the new students – all 35 of them – and discussed how he and his faculty were transforming the way architecture was taught at Rice. Students could complete a Bachelor of Arts in Architecture in four years, or the Bachelor of Architecture, the "professional degree", after five years. In the fifth year the students would complete their "thesis projects" under the guidance of the faculty, with very little class work otherwise, because all other requirements for a degree would have been completed in the first four years. The five-year option would cut two years off the period of apprenticeship they would have to serve after graduation before becoming licensed architects, allowing them to become licensed after two years of apprenticeship instead of four.

Immediately after that morning orientation session, Arthur visited the Navy Building and inquired about the NROTC program. He learned that he could join the NROTC Contract program, and if he completed his BA or BS degree within five years, he would be commissioned as a Reserve Officer. He would do a minimum of three years of active duty, and serve another three years in the reserves, for a total of six years.

There was also a Regular Navy program as part of the NROTC, which was the pathway to a Navy career, like that provided by the Naval Academy at Annapolis. If he qualified for it, he would receive a scholarship and would be commissioned in the Regular Navy, rather than the Reserves, on graduation. He would be required to serve a minimum of six years' active duty. After that, he could re-enlist to continue serving, or be transferred to the reserves. Once he had served at least twenty years of active duty, he would be eligible to retire, with a pension and lifetime medical and other privileges, and he could start a second career at the age of forty-two. Almost all career officers came from Annapolis or from the Regular NROTC program.

The idea of a Navy career grew on him. He filled out the official application for the Contract NROTC Program. Once he was in it, he could apply for the Regular NROTC Program. He kept the carbon copy of the application form and gave the signed original to Captain Butler, the CO of the NROTC unit. Captain Butler accepted him for the program and sent him down the hall to the NROTC Wardrobe Room to be measured for uniforms.

The sailor running the wardrobe, Seaman 1st Class Roberts, rummaged around and found a full complement of uniforms that would fit him. He outfitted Arthur both with officers' uniforms and enlisted work dungarees. Although as a Midshipman Arthur would be part of the officers' corps, during his first summer training cruise as a Midshipman Fourth Class he would be working with the enlisted sailors to learn shipboard operations from the bottom up. For his last cruise, as Midshipman 2nd Class or 1st Class, he would live and work as an officer.

For the remainder of the two-week orientation period, Arthur attended NROTC Orientation on Tuesday and

Thursday mornings at 7:00 AM for an hour and a half. His Naval Science classes would meet throughout his college career on the same schedule. Others would be assigned to the Monday-Wednesday-Friday schedule, also at 7:00 am, but for an hour each.

In NROTC Orientation, he learned basic Navy protocol and etiquette, the history of naval warfare, how to recognize a service person's rank from his or her insignia, the different classes of ships used by the contemporary navy and the various career paths available to US Navy officers.

On the first day of class, Marine Master Sergeant Cutler gave the 40 incoming Midshipmen an introduction to Navy etiquette. His shaved head sitting on his shoulders like a bullet, the neck as wide as the head, his uniform entirely wrinkle free, he appeared formidable. *He must sleep at attention*, thought Arthur. Muscles bulged under his uniform. He gave the class an overview of Navy etiquette – how to recognize ranks by insignia, whom to salute and how to return a salute given by an inferior, and how to address an officer. In the army, for example, all officers are addressed by their titles – Lieutenant Jones, Captain Stevens, Major Clark, General Grant. In the navy, officers below the rank of Commander are addressed as "Mister," while Commanders and above are addressed by rank. When asked a question by a superior officer, the answer always begins and ends with "Sir!" One says, "Sir! Yes Sir!", "Sir! No, Sir!", "Sir! It is my opinion that thus and so. Sir!" On the other hand, when given an order, one replies, "Aye, aye, Sir." The first "Aye" indicates that the order is understood and the second that one will comply with the order.

When Master Sergeant Cutler had finished his talk, Captain Butler gave an introductory address to the incoming class of 40 Midshipmen. He was a tall man with close-trimmed greying hair, distinguished-looking in his white dress uniform. The curve of his nose reminded Arthur of an eagle's beak.

"This morning," said Captain Butler, "I will give you a brief overview, a summary of the material included in your textbook, *Introduction to Naval Science*, in the first chapter. Your first assignment also includes the next two chapters, which give you an introduction to Naval etiquette, insignia, uniforms and procedures. You will also learn the equivalent uniforms and insignia of the other services.

"The 'classic' career path for naval officers is that of a Line Officer. Line officers work on board ships and rotate to shore duty, and back again, in the command structure of the branch of the navy that goes to sea and fights wars. They will progress up the ranks from the initial commissioned rank of Ensign, through the ranks eligible to command at sea, and ultimately to the sea-command ranks of admirals, and on up to the land-based admirals who command whole branches of the navy.

"Line officers are either Surface Warfare Officers or Submarine Officers, although some are qualified as both. Naval Aviation is a second career option, and, unless they were also qualified as Surface Warfare Officers, Aviation Officers cannot command ships. In today's navy only an officer can be the pilot of an airplane. Enlisted members of the Aviation Corps are mechanics, technicians, flight controllers, flightline personnel, or perform other roles within the Aviation Corps. The Admiral who commands an aircraft carrier is usually qualified as both, wearing both the wings of the Aviation Officer and the ship-and-crossed-sabers of the Surface Warfare Officer on his uniform.

"Alternatively, a Midshipman can opt for Supply Corps. Supply Officers are the 'businessmen' of the navy. They manage the purchase, stockpiling and supply of food, fuel, ammunition, and other supplies used by the navy. Every ship has at least one Supply Officer on board. A supply officer is not eligible to command at sea, but, nevertheless, could rise all the way to the rank of Admiral within the Supply Corps.

"There is a general grouping of engineering-related members of the navy as well. The Seabees – CB stands for Construction Bureau – are engineers and construction personnel who maintain and build navy installations. Some of you architects and engineers in the group might opt for Seabee commissioning. Seabees also are not qualified to command at sea.

"In addition, any of you thinking of medical school following graduation may want to opt for the Medical Corps and defer your active duty until after you earn your MD degrees. Most ships have doctors and medics on board to take care of shipboard illnesses, injuries, and battle wounds. In the old days, the ship's surgeon was also the ship's barber, but that is no longer the case." General laughter greeted this last remark.

"If you want to be a lawyer," he continued, "you can defer your service after graduation to go through law school and serve in the Navy as a lawyer in the Judge Advocate General's Corps, which contains both lawyers practicing in the Navy and judges for the justice system in the Navy.

"There is an elite group of navy officers and men called the UDT, for Underwater Demolition Team. Trained as frogmen and qualified by rigorous training for explosives demolition and close combat, UDT officers and sailors, also called Seals, are trained to swim underwater to clear mines anchored to the bottom, deactivate stalled torpedoes, blow up enemy docks, place magnetic mines on the hulls of enemy warships, and even to sneak ashore for combat raids and demolition of enemy installations. Their emblem is the trident. Many Seals are also qualified as Surface Warfare Officers and eligible to command at sea. They are the Navy operational equivalent of the Army Special Forces – the Green Berets. Seals also man speedy gunboats called PT Boats for special missions in the Brownwater Navy, the branch that patrols rivers in Vietnam, but most PT Boats are commanded and crewed by Surface Warfare Officers and sailors. President Kennedy was a PT boat commander when he was in the Navy. Opting for the Brownwater Navy is a short cut to command of a vessel. A PT Boat is usually commanded by a Lieutenant, and a squadron of PT Boats by a Lieutenant Commander. Larger ships are always captained by an officer of Commander rank or above.

"Finally, a Midshipman can opt for the US Marines. Your second cruise is not really a cruise. You will do your training at a Navy Aviation base, where your time will be divided between Aviation Familiarization and a short preview of Marine Boot Camp. You will learn the fundamentals of flying planes and you will drill like Marines. You can declare yourself for the Marine Option after your second summer training. The Marine Corps is part of the navy, but with its own independent command structure, using ranks that mirror army ranks. Marines originated as combat fighters assigned to navy ships. They can be slipped ashore for onshore surveillance, often under the command of a Navy Intelligence Officer, or they can be used to storm beaches. They are elite fighters, but without the UDT training of the Seals. It is not unusual for Marines and Seals to work together. When the USA invades another country, the Marines are usually the first to storm and take the beach, holding it while the army comes onshore.

"Finally, there is also the Chaplain Corps. Those of you with a religious calling can defer active duty after graduation for seminary study and ordination, after which you will serve your term in the Navy as Chaplains.

"That is a summary of the common career options you will have in the modern navy. You'll learn more detail in your Naval Science classes. Be sure to read through the material in the first three chapters. There will be a quiz on it next time you have a Naval Science class."

Arthur raised his hand.

"Mr. Harris, do you have a question?" asked Captain Butler. Arthur stood to attention.

"Sir! Yes, sir!" he said. "You have not yet told us anything about the Office of Naval Intelligence. Will you be doing so, Sir?"

"Mr. Harris, you are the first Midshipman to ask me about the Office of Naval intelligence," said Captain Butler. "The Office of Naval Intelligence is the oldest intelligence service in the United States. It was formed initially to gather intelligence about the naval technology of other countries, both friend and foe, so our Navy could begin upgrading its ships to be prepared to fight a naval war. Every ship has an officer who is trained in intelligence. Most are both Line Officers and Intelligence Officers. Most Intelligence Officers are Line Officers who have been assigned as Intelligence Officers and given some training in intelligence. Some, however, opt early for careers in intelligence. Without undergoing the training necessary to attain command at sea, they go through more intensive training in intelligence operations. These are considered Restricted Line Officers. They wear insignia indistinguishable from line officers but are not eligible to command at sea, and do not wear the ship-and-crossed-sabers badge of the Surface Warfare Officer, unless they have qualified for such. One of our faculty, Lieutenant Thayer, is both a Surface Warfare Officer and an Intelligence officer. I suggest that you arrange a time to see Commander Thayer privately. He can answer your questions in more detail, if you are interested in more information."

"Thank you, Captain," said Arthur.

"Class dismissed," said Captain Butler.

Here endeth the first lesson, thought Arthur. That afternoon, he sought out Lieutenant Thayer.

"Commander Thayer, Sir," said Arthur, "I want to speak with you about the possibility of becoming an Intelligence Officer."

"Captain Butler told me you might want to see me about that. Why are you interested in intelligence work?"

"Sir, to be perfectly honest, I got the idea after reading some James Bond novels. He was both a naval officer and an intelligence officer, and the idea of following that sort of career fascinates me."

"Are you aware that James Bond is fiction, and the life of an Intelligence Officer is really quite different?"

"Sir, yes, I understand that, sir. It appeals to me, nevertheless. While I would prefer clandestine operations to analysis, I will do whatever it takes to make a career in intelligence."

"Mr. Harris, I reviewed your file after Captain Butler talked to me. I know all your work in high school, including at George Wallace College. I happen to have a good friend in Montgomery who heads the Alcohol and Tobacco Tax Division office there, and he had given me a heads up about a certain Dothan kid who wanted a career in naval intelligence. He told me about your detective work, and I must say, I was impressed. Are you sure you understand what you are asking for?"

"Sir, I believe so, but I want to start learning what I can about that career option so that I can make an informed choice by commissioning time."

"Very well, Mr. Harris. I will give you some reading assignments. The material is available in the NROTC library. The books and papers I am assigning you will give you an overview of the history and current work of the

ONI. After you have read the material, contact me to schedule a private meeting."

"Aye, aye, Sir," said Arthur. He took the list Lieutenant Thayer handed him.

"Dismissed, Mr. Harris."

"Sir! thank you, Sir." Arthur left Thayer's office and walked next door to the NROTC library room where he collected and signed out the books, papers and reports Thayer had assigned.

In the pale, early morning light of Friday, 31 August 1962, Arthur packed his suitcase. Into it first went his slacks and blazer, followed by the shirts Hilda had folded so neatly. Two pairs of jeans went on top of the shirts, followed by two pairs of khaki shorts and three sets of underwear, socks and tee shirts. He packed his tennis shoes, his swim suit, and three polo shirts. Next, he packed up his shaving gear, toothbrush, toothpaste and deodorant and put them in the suitcase. Henry arrived while he was doing this.

"Giving up early and going home?" he teased.

"I'm spending the weekend with relatives," said Arthur, grinning.

"You lucky dog," said Henry. "I wish I had a kissing cousin as cute as Hilda." Arthur felt his face starting to flush.

"Careful, Arthur; you need to do something about that sunburn," said Henry, grinning.

"You're just jealous," said Arthur. Just then, the door opened and Bill stepped in.

"Going somewhere, Art?" he asked.

"I'm going to spend the weekend with relatives," said Art.

"Don't forget to wear your rubbers," Bill said and grinned. "It might rain." Arthur flushed again. "Wouldn't want your feet to get wet."

Arthur finished packing without saying anything and picked up his suitcase and headed for the door.

"Enjoy the weekend," said Henry and Bill in unison.

"You too," said Arthur, "or, I should say, you two, too." They laughed at the pun.

"Yeah, we'll try to enjoy the weekend," said Bill. "You won't even have to try, you lucky bastard."

Arthur carried his suitcase downstairs to the Commons. Hilda was already there, waiting for him. She greeted him with a hug and a kiss, while thirty or so other men in the commons stared and grinned.

"How did Arthur get so lucky?" asked one, in a voice loud enough for all to hear. Hilda broke the kiss.

"He was born into the right branch of the family so we could be kissing cousins," she said in a voice that carried throughout the room. Everyone laughed.

Arthur and Hilda departed, laughing, arms around each other's waists. Arthur was wearing khaki slacks, a blue short-sleeved shirt with button-down collar and brown Weejuns over white athletic socks. Hilda was similarly dressed, but with a short khaki skirt instead of slacks, and loafers with no socks.

"How did we coordinate our wardrobes so well?" she asked after they were both in the car and headed south on Main Street.

"I think our minds are synchronized," said Arthur.

"Well, if you are thinking what I am thinking, this is going to be a *fabulous* weekend." They grinned at each other.

"Yes," said Arthur, "bards will write *fables* about it." Hilda laughed. She turned on the radio and they listened to Houston's KLEF classical radio station while driving south.

"You missed your turn," said Arthur as they passed the turn-off from South Main Street into the subdivision where the Austins lived.

"No, I didn't," said Hilda. "I told my parents I was spending the weekend at our beach house in Freeport. They are going to Austin to spend it with Dad's brother. They're going fishing."

"Is there a relationship between the name of the town and your family?" asked Arthur.

"Yes. The town was named after our ancestors. We're related to Stephen F. Austin." He slid down a little in his seat and laid his head back, listening to the music, but his mind was racing. *What am I getting into? Most kids my age do have sex, but it is still against the teachings of the Church. What am I going to do?*

"Hey, don't go to sleep on me!" she said.

"If I were on you, there is no way I could sleep," he said. "But after, I'd be very happy to fall asleep on you." She laughed.

"You have a wit, Mr. Harris. What makes you think you're going to be on me?"

"Well," he said, "I'd just as soon be under you." She laughed again.

"Mr. Harris, I think we're going to have fun." They were both silent for a while. The radio was playing Mozart's *Requiem*.

"Arthur, this music is beautiful, but I don't want to listen to a requiem on the way to a romantic weekend. Do you mind if I change stations?"

"Go right ahead," said Arthur. She turned the dial until she found a rock station. They began listening to the music of the Beatles, a new, up-and-coming rock band recently imported from England. About thirty minutes passed.

"Arthur, I think you are a virgin," said Hilda.

"Yes, I am, but not by choice. I was born that way." She laughed. He knew it would be pointless to try to lie to Her.

"After this weekend, you will no longer be a virgin," she said.

Here we go. I'm about to lose my virtue.

"I hope you are right," he said.

She was right, he thought, as they lay together on the bed, facing each other and kissing. She had unbuttoned her blouse and had placed his hand on her breast, and he was fondling its silken smoothness and its pert nipple. His other hand found her leg and moved up her thigh under her skirt. Her hands moved to undo his belt and unzip his pants. *Adam tasted of the forbidden fruit,* he thought, *offered to him by the woman. Now I'm losing my virtue for real.* Her hot breath panted in his ear as they matched each other's thrusts.

It was a wonderful, romantic, sexy weekend.

When she dropped him off back at Wiess College just before midnight Monday, they embraced and kissed passionately.

"Well, I guess that this weekend I finally lost my virtue," said Arthur.

"Do you think what we did was wrong?"

"I don't know. It felt right, but it is against the moral rules taught by the Church. However, I believe that I love you. I think sex in that context isn't that great a sin. I really like you, I think I am in love with you, but I also think we need more time to get to know each other."

"Arthur, I could easily be in love with you, but I agree – we need to get to know each other well before getting too serious. One of the things I love about you is your seriousness and your strong sense of morality. I'm not Catholic, but Methodist, as you know, but I'm not as serious about religion as you are. Sometimes I feel guilty for being a Christian only on Sundays. I need to learn more about Catholicism. May I start going to Mass with you on Sundays?"

"Of course!" said Arthur. "There is a chapel just off campus called the Rice Newman Center, run by the Dominicans, that has daily Mass for Rice Students, and anyone in the area who wants to attend. Officially, it's an extension of Holy Rosary Parish, also run by the Dominicans. Sunday Mass is at 10:00 am."

"So, we have a date for Sunday," she said. "Do you want to set one for Saturday night?"

"Of course. Dinner at 7:00, followed by something else?"

"I accept," She said. They kissed again, and Art stood in the darkness after she drove away before going into the Commons.

Almost every weekend he saw Hilda. He met her friends, some of whom were insufferable bores, and she met his friends, some of whom were unmitigated social disasters. They would laugh together over the foibles of their friends. Whenever Arthur did not have an intense study weekend, they would sneak off together to the beach house. Arthur was having the best time of his life. Arthur found himself going to confession every week, and he was not confessing venial sins. Each time, he resolved to "sin no more," but the near occasion of sin kept getting him. Over and over again. He knew he was in love, and had found his Eve, his life mate.

Classes started immediately after Labor Day. He had a rigorous schedule that crammed the usual freshman program of Calculus, American History, English Literature, a foreign language, Physics, Naval Science and Phys Ed into the mornings. The language choices available to him had been Spanish, Latin, French, German, Japanese and Russian. He knew some Spanish from his childhood in Mexico and he had taken Latin in high school, so he wanted to try something different. He signed up for German 101. In his second year, Physics would be replaced by Chemistry.

His afternoons were occupied by Architecture Lab, except for Thursday afternoon, when he had Physics Lab. The academic portion of the Architecture curriculum was crammed into the mornings as well – a course called "Architectural Technology" that covered the basics of Engineering Statics, Engineering Mechanics, Mechanical Engineering, Electrical Engineering, and Structural Engineering. All of these, as well as the lab, were counted as a single course, Architecture 101, for nine credit hours.

Every day his academic day began at 7:00 AM. American History was Monday, Wednesday and Friday at 7:00 AM. Tuesdays and Thursdays at 7:00 AM he had Naval Science, followed immediately by one hour of Phys. Ed. Every Saturday morning, he had Navy Drill for two hours, in full uniform and shouldering a rifle, in which he learned all the intricacies of marching in formation, called "close order drill." This part came easy for him because his Boy Scout Troop had drilled on marching at the start of each of its monthly meetings, and his Patrol, the Wolf Patrol, had practiced close order drill at their weekly meetings.

Architecture Lab took place in the drafting room, which occupied the entire second floor of Anderson Hall. The freshman students did design exercises, drafting exercises, in effect learning the art of producing lines of different weights on a sheet of paper, producing sketches of massed geometric shapes, and other drawing and drafting exercises that Harry Ransom, the professor in charge of the Freshman architecture class, called "The Elements of Design." They were told that as soon as they were all adept at drawing they would start actual design exercises.

Two weeks after Labor Day, Arthur and the other Midshipmen reported to the Navy Building in dress khakis. Captain Butler gave them a short congratulatory speech, saying that because they had been selected for the officer program, they were now "officers and gentlemen by Act of Congress," and he expected them to behave accordingly. He administered the officer's oath, in which each pledged to support and defend the Constitution of the United States against all enemies, foreign and domestic, and to obey the lawful orders of their superior officers. He pointed out that to be an order demanding obedience, it had to order a lawful act. "For example," he said, "if I were to order you to murder the President of the University, that would not be a lawful order and you would be bound by your duty under your oath to refuse the order." He also told them that some of them might not make it through the program, but that they should give it their all, because if they didn't make it through, they would go into active duty as enlisted sailors.

"You're in the Navy now, for a minimum of six years," he said. "I assume you had rather spend your time as officers and gentlemen rather than as swabs. So, work hard, study hard, do the best you can, and good luck."

After his swearing-in as Midshipman 4th Class in the Contract program, he applied for the Regular Navy Program.

A bright student who was somewhat bored by the slow pace of education at the public high school in Dothan, Arthur had always looked for ways to learn more than the high school curriculum provided. While still in high school, Arthur had taken the geology course that was offered at the local George Wallace College, along with art classes. In the geology course, he had learned to read the rock layers and formations revealed in clear, three-dimensional detail in stereoscopic aerial photos. When he entered the NROTC program, Arthur had filled out a detailed summary of capabilities – a thirty-page questionnaire. He had duly answered all the questions. One of them was, "List all subjects studied and specialized skills acquired." He listed his high school classes, his science fair awards, the art and geology classes he took at George Wallace College, and his skill at reading aerial photos for geological mapping. He was told that all of this would be entered into a computer database at the Pentagon that contained the records of every Navy officer, and those records would be used to find assignments that best suited the needs of the Navy, and that used his talents and skills. The database would be updated quarterly as he progressed through his Navy career. He was also aware that Lieutenant Thayer knew all about his background, including even his "detective" work.

He settled into his class and study routine well. He was, he told himself, on his way to a career as a U.S. Navy Surface Warfare Officer and Intelligence Officer. He did find college much more demanding than high school and had no time for pursuing independent study on his own as he had in high school. He had particular trouble with calculus, because he had no introduction to it in high school, and his calculus professor took the position that all his students should have had introductory calculus in high school and it was not his fault that they had not.

CHAPTER 11

THE BRINK OF ARMAGEDDON

October 1962
Houston, Texas and Guantanamo Bay Naval Base,
Cuba

On Sunday, October 14, 1962, CIA U-2 spy planes, assigned to the Air Force for cover purposes and operating from Florida, photographed what were clearly large missiles being unloaded in Cuba. It was the middle of the first term of Arthur's freshman year at Rice University. On the evening of Monday, October 15, there was a knock on the door to Arthur's room, where he and his roommate, Henry, were studying. Arthur opened the door, and Lieutenant Thayer stood facing him.

"Mr. Harris, please come with me -- we must talk privately," he said quietly. Henry seemed oblivious, concentrating on his calculus studying.

"Sir!" said Arthur, also speaking quietly. "Now, sir? If I don't study like Hell tonight I'll flunk my calculus exam tomorrow."

"Mr. Harris, this is a direct military order. Come with me." Arthur followed him out the door, down the stairs, and across the grass to the middle of the Phys. Ed. playing fields that separated Wiess College from the Gymnasium. Luckily, it was not raining, although it had been raining and the sky was still heavily overcast. The wet ground filled the air with the fetid swamp smell typical of Houston when the humidity was high.

"I think we can talk here without anyone overhearing us," said Mr. Thayer. "I have been tasked to start putting together a special clandestine group within ONI and I want to recruit you for it. At present, it is very small, but it will grow as our involvement in Vietnam grows. You indicated in our last meeting that you have read the material I assigned you and still want a career in Naval Intelligence. Are you ready to commit now?"

"Sir! Yes, sir," replied Arthur.

"In that case, I have special orders for you. You will be detached temporarily from the NROTC unit and temporarily attached to the ONI. I can use you for some special work, based on the commitment you just expressed and your ability in reading aerial photos. Your studies will have to be interrupted, but you will be able to make them up after you return. At that time, I will personally recommend you for the Regular Navy Program, which I know you have applied for, and I am sure you will be accepted for it. What I am about to tell you is Top Secret. The ONI is clearing you temporarily for Top Secret." He briefed Arthur on the presence of Soviet missiles in Cuba, discovered on aerial photos, and told him that the US was on the verge of a nuclear confrontation with the Soviet Union.

"Tomorrow morning," he said, "you have Phys. Ed. before Calculus. In the Phys. Ed. class, you will undergo the Physical Education Capabilities Tests." (All freshmen took these halfway through the first semester to gauge their physical abilities.) "When you get to the standing broad jump station, you will jump and land awkwardly. You are to collapse on landing with one leg bent under you. You will do this carefully so that you are not actually injured. You will complain that your knee is injured and that you cannot walk on that leg. Your friends will help you to the infirmary, where an ambulance will take you from the campus. As far as anyone at the University is concerned, and as far as anyone outside the intelligence community will know, you will have injured your knee and will have been taken to the hospital for treatment or surgery. The story of your injured knee and hospitalization will explain your absence from classes. However, there will not be a record as to which ambulance service picked you up or which hospital they took you to. The university will allow you to make up the missed work on your return, so you won't need to worry about the calculus exam tomorrow..."

As Mr. Thayer spoke, Arthur's mind raced. He memorized instantly the instructions he was receiving. He believed that this was his chance to prove himself to the ONI. Now, his Navy career might have exactly the options he wanted!

The next morning, following Mr. Thayer's instructions, Arthur slipped out of his dorm room without waking Henry. He reported to the Navy ROTC building at 4:30 AM. He carried with him his US Navy issue duffel bag, packed with his Navy uniforms and five changes of underwear. He was dressed as usual for a day of classes at the University, his gym clothes in a satchel.

Mr. Thayer met him there and handed Arthur two manila envelopes: one containing travel orders to Guantanamo, and the other containing his mission orders, to be opened after he arrived in Guantanamo. He asked Arthur for a list of people who might ask questions about his absence, so they could notify them with a calming message. Arthur gave him telephone numbers for his parents and for Hilda. He asked if he could call Hilda himself, and was told that he should not. The Navy would take care of that for him.

Arthur discussed the mission in detail over breakfast at the Navy Building with Mr. Thayer and left for his Phys. Ed. class. Half way through class, it started to rain, so the class was moved into the gymnasium. Arthur did his standing broad jump on the wood gymnasium floor with wet sneakers. When he landed awkwardly with his right knee doubled under him, his feet had actually slipped on the polished wood floor and he actually did hurt his knee.

After his staged injury, two friends helped him hobble to the infirmary, where he departed by ambulance. Mr. Thayer was in the ambulance with Arthur's duffel bag. Arthur changed into his dress khaki Navy uniform. The ambulance took them to Ellington Air Force Base just outside of Houston, where he took a pair of crutches from the ambulance to prevent injuring his knee more. He and Mr. Thayer boarded a Navy C-3 that took them to Eglin Air Force Base in the Florida Panhandle and then, after refueling, to the US Navy Base at Guantanamo Bay in Cuba.

High-level aerial surveillance was being performed by U-2 planes flying from Florida, and low-level surveillance by Navy Crusader jets stationed at Guantanamo. For two weeks, Arthur, working with about a dozen other photo analysts under Lieutenant Thayer's command, reviewed photographs that came off the Navy Crusader jets as soon as they could be developed and printed. Arthur had two principal jobs: do whatever Thayer told him to do, and man the radio that connected to ONI headquarters by a scrambled, encrypted channel that connected Guantanamo Naval Base with the Pentagon through ONI. All Top-Secret communications between Guantanamo and the Pentagon went through that radio, because the ONI was considered a safer channel than the Navy in general. The analysts worked in the back of the same building that housed the Guantanamo Command.

Most of the photographs showed nothing of military interest. Any photo that showed anything that looked like military activity, especially if it showed anything looking like missiles, was duplicated and flown to Washington, where specialists with the ONI at the Pentagon and the CIA at Langley did the next round of analysis. Arthur's role, and the role of the other screeners at Guantanamo, was to select out the photos that would be sent to Washington.

Occasionally, U-2s would land at Guantanamo to have their photos processed when there was a backlog in Florida. Arthur met several of the U-2 pilots – in particular, Air Force Captain Robert Bull, who was actually a CIA officer, not an Air Force officer. After they met, Bull suggested they go to the Officers' Club for beer. They both ordered Budweiser, found a table in the corner and sat down.

Arthur didn't let on that he was not an experienced beer drinker. His family didn't drink, even though his maternal grandmother, who lived with them and was a tee-totaling Methodist, had a nightly shot of whiskey "for medicinal reasons." His father was Catholic and had nothing against drinking, but deferred to Arthur's mother, who was Methodist, like her mother. The widow of a doctor, Grandmother was convinced that the daily consumption of a small amount of alcohol was good for the heart and circulatory system and she used it only for that purpose. Arthur knew from watching his roommate that six beers at a sitting was probably too much and determined to limit himself to three.

"Robert, how did you become involved with the CIA?" asked Arthur.

"After high school," said Robert, "I wanted adventure. My Dad was a CPA and his whole life was involved with columns of numbers. He wanted me to go to college, study accounting, and take over his business. I wanted nothing to do with that. So I left home after high school and joined the crew of a freighter taking cargo from Elizabeth, New Jersey, to Spain. I signed on only for the one-way journey. That gave me enough money to live on for a while after we reached Spain."

"Why Spain?" asked Arthur

"I had decided to try to become a bull fighter. One of my heroes was Ernest Hemingway, and while not trying to follow in his footsteps, I loved reading his stories about Spain."

"How does an American kid with no background in bullfighting become a bullfighter?"

"Well, I spoke Spanish well. I took Spanish in high school and practiced speaking it with our Mexican gardener and our maid. I also picked up several other languages, studying them on my own and practicing them in immigrant neighborhoods in New York. In Spain, I rented a room in *Sevilla* and enrolled in the Royal Bullfighting School. I registered my name as '*Roberto Toro.*' It seemed I had a real talent for the sport, and I progressed rapidly. I took only enough chances to encourage applause from the crowd, and I was good and precise in my movements. Before my money ran out, I took my *Alternativa*, the ceremony at a bullfight in which I became a full-fledged *matador de torros*. In *La Suerte de Matar*, the veteran *matador* who gave me my final instruction approached me in the ring. I gave him my novice's cape and he gave me the professional cape and sword of the full-fledged *Matador de Torres*. He gave me his final instructions, and I fought my first fight as a professional, as a *Toreador*."

"How exciting," said Arthur. "I grew up in Mexico and my father took me to a bullfight once, but Mother wouldn't go. She thought bullfighting cruel."

"It is cruel, and it's not really an even match, but bullfighters often get injured in the sport. For a year, I fought bulls all over Spain, and earned a name in the sport. I earned good purses. After I had started earning real money, I gave up my small room for a full apartment. Soon I received an invitation to the Presidential Palace from *Generalissimo* Franco."

"I guess that was the signal that you had made it, like when President Kennedy invites the World Series winners to the White House."

"I suppose so, but not even an hour after the invitation arrived at the door to my apartment, I heard a knock on the door. When I opened it, a man introduced himself as an agent of the US Central Intelligence Agency and told me to call him Bob. They needed me to work for them...By the way, since you're an intelligence analyst here, I assume you have a security clearance."

"Yes," replied Arthur, "Top Secret."

"OK, so I can talk to you, but I won't tell you anything really secret. The idea of working for the CIA appealed to my sense of adventure and patriotism, and I agreed to help the CIA. 'Bob' rigged me with a hidden microphone and broadcasting unit, and I went to the audience at the Presidential Palace wired for sound. As an anti-Communist, Franco was an ally of the US, but as a Fascist dictator, he was also an enemy. Call it a love-hate relationship. I never did know what the CIA was looking for, but on a number of occasions I wore a wire to receptions at which government officials were expected. They paid me by the assignment, so I was really a 'Contractor' rather than a CIA employee."

"How long did that continue?" asked Arthur.

"Not long – about six months. There came a day that a bull got the better of me. He gored me in the face, breaking my cheekbone and jawbone and knocking me down, and turned back around and gored me in the leg before I was pulled away to safety. The injuries were not life-threatening, but they were serious. This scar on my face is a remnant of that. The scar on my leg stretches from my upper thigh to my kneecap. They stitched me up and I healed, but I decided to quit bullfighting. I asked 'Bob' to make me a regular CIA agent. The fact that I was fluent in Russian, Italian, Spanish, Catalan, Basque, German and Chinese, I think, helped. The CIA shipped me to Virginia, put me through a year of intensive training at The Farm, and then gave me a year of flight lessons. Soon I was flying U-2's."

"The Farm?" asked Arthur.

"Camp Peary in Virginia is the CIA training campus. Once upon a time it was a farm, and that's what we all call it – 'The Farm.' It's public knowledge that the CIA uses it for training, but it's not officially admitted. I flew two missions over the Soviet Union, and Gary Powers flew the next mission. His downing and capture ended U-2 flights over Russia, and we shifted to flights over other Communist countries. About a year ago, the Soviet Union provided Red China with the same type of missile that shot down Powers' U-2, and so we discontinued most flights over China. We began relying heavily on spy satellites over Red China and USSR. We shifted the U-2's to fly over 'Communist Expansion States' – Cuba, Ghana, Nicaragua, Viet Nam, and other hot spots. That's how I got here.

"I haven't told you anything you're not entitled to know as an ONI officer in Cuba – but I can't tell you anything else. If I can get assigned to CIA headquarters after this, I'll pick up a law degree at George Washington University in Georgetown, and then when I get too old or nervous for CIA assignments, I'll retire and practice law. My plan is to practice in the international arena. The contacts I will have picked up around the world through the intelligence community would be very valuable to such a practice."

They talked late into the night, and then, having drunk three beers, Robert excused himself to get some sleep before his morning flight.

"I'm not allowed to drink any alcohol for 24 hours before I fly," said Robert, "but I ignore that rule. The other U-2 pilots do, too. Nobody says anything so long as I don't drink too much and don't show up too drunk to fly. The CIA is known for its hard drinkers – often there is little to do and a lot of stress when on covert assignment, so drinking is popular. We also spend a lot of time in bars listening in on conversations."

Arthur, too, had drunk three beers, and felt a little light headed. He reminded himself to limit himself to no more than three beers at a sitting. That night, he dreamed about Hilda. He and she were together in the barracks, and he was trying to conceal her in his bed with extra pillows, because she was not supposed to be there. In his dream, he had no chance to do anything with her except to keep her hidden. When he awoke, he realized how much he missed her, despite a lack of time to spend missing her.

The next day, October 18, Arthur spotted pictures of a Soviet freighter off-loading very large missiles at Matanzas, Cuba's port with the deepest water, and five more freighters at sea heading toward Cuba with similar cargo, one of which appeared to be carrying large warheads. He tried to find Thayer but could not. He placed them in a special "High Alert – Rush – TOP SECRET" envelope and drove a jeep to the airfield where a C-3 was waiting to take off the next morning with that evening's batch of photos for analysis in Washington. He found Robert hanging out in the pilots' lounge.

"Robert," he said, "these photos that came from your U-2 this morning have to get to Washington immediately. The regular photo flight doesn't leave until the morning. How can I get them to ONI headquarters by the fastest route?"

"Give them to me. I'll take them. I'm not scheduled to fly for the next week except to take my plane to Florida for service tonight. I'll just fly to Bolling Air Force Base

in DC, deliver them, and fly back to Eglin in Florida."
Arthur handed him the envelope.

"When you get there, please stress the importance of
these photos," said Arthur.

"May I see them?" asked Robert.

"I don't have time to get authorization for you to see
them, so I didn't ask. At the same time, I don't have orders for you not to see them. The envelope isn't sealed."

"Walk me out to my plane," said Robert. Together
they walked out across the tarmac. "My flight plan is already filed, so I can fly when ready. I'll radio in the modi-
fications to it from the air when I'm in civilian air space."

Half way to the plane, Robert slipped the photos out
of the envelope and leafed through them. He whistled,
and started running toward the plane.

"I'll contact you from ONI in Washington," he called
back over his shoulder. Arthur waved, turned and walked
back to the jeep and drove it back to the Analysis Building, where Lieutenant Thayer asked him where he had
been.

"You weren't here, Mr. Thayer," he said, "and I
couldn't find you, so I had to make a command decision
and act on it without authorization. The latest batch of
photos showed ICBMs being unloaded at Matanzas, with
several more ships at sea, with similar cargo, following
them. The last ship of the train, instead of carrying missiles, was carrying cargo that I interpreted to be nuclear
warheads. I duplicated the photos and took the most critical ones to Captain Robert Bull. He was scheduled to fly
his plane this evening to Florida for service. I felt it was
extremely important to get the photos to Washington as
soon as possible, and having Captain Bull take them was
the fastest way. Without authorization, I permitted Captain Bull to view the photos so he would know their importance, and he is now on his way to Washington with
them."

Thayer regarded him silently for a minute.

"Mr. Harris," he said, "the action you have taken either will save the world from nuclear holocaust, will start a nuclear war, or will end your career in the Navy. I want you to be aware that it might both save the world and end your career. At the same time, I believe that you made the right decisions."

"I'll wait here tonight," said Arthur. "Capt. Bull will call me from Washington."

"I'll wait with you, "said Lt. Thayer, "but first I'm going to go get a beer. I'll bring one back to you, although I will be violating protocol. There isn't anything about this operation right now that is following protocol."

Arthur tuned the radio to pick up the secure channel from Langley for transmissions involving the U-2 program in Cuba and connected the radio to the descrambler device. Any traffic coming in from Langley would be scrambled. He would need to type a specific code for the descrambler to activate. He drank coffee while staring out the window at the stars. After about thirty minutes, Lt. Thayer was back, carrying two six-packs of Budweiser.

"Mr. Harris, this is going to be a long night. Pace yourself with the beer. We'll need to be ready to jump into action at a moment's notice. Put on a pot of coffee, too. We'll need that to offset the beer."

"Aye, aye sir," said Arthur. Thayer pulled out a deck of cards.

"How much money do you have on you?" he asked.

"About five dollars, sir," said Arthur. "I'm just an NROTC Midshipman Fourth Class. I don't get paid much for this – just $40 per month." Thayer smiled.

"I know you don't, Mr. Harris," he said. Reaching into his pocket, he pulled out a wad of currency. He counted it out. "Here's $50.00," he said. "I'll loan it to you, to be repaid from your first active duty pay if you lose it. Now, let's play poker. That's what Mr. Kennedy and Mr.

Khrushchev are going to be doing." They played poker as the night wore on, the money shifting back and forth across the table.

At about 0500 hrs. on the morning of 19 October, the radio crackled into life with the code numbers that indicated a message from Langley for Guantanamo Bay. Arthur turned up the volume so they could hear clearly despite the droning, grinding noise of the air conditioner and typed the activation code for the descrambler. It was the Director, ONI. He gave the appropriate code words to identify himself.

"This is Rear Admiral Vernon Lawrence, Director of Naval Intelligence. Identify yourself." Arthur gave the required code words.

"This is Midshipman Arthur Harris, manning the radio. Present with me is Lieutenant Nelson Thayer."

"Robert Bull is here with me. Mr. Harris, you know you took a risk in taking initiative in the absence of your superior officer. However, what is more important is that you took the right initiative. I hereby make your detachment from the NROTC at Rice University to the Office of Naval Intelligence permanent, if you are willing to accept such assignment. Should you choose to accept it, you will now have a career with the ONI, with the special unit header by Mr. Thayer. You will continue serving as a Midshipman member of the NROTC Unit, but Mr. Thayer and the Officer in Charge of the unit – and only they – will be aware of your status. Upon leaving the NROTC, you will be commissioned as a Lieutenant, Junior Grade, in the U.S. Navy. You will perform the role of Intelligence Officer on Navy ships until you have qualified as a Surface Warfare officer eligible for command at sea. Your sharp eye and quick thinking have rendered critical service to your Country. Now stand by to receive coded orders to the base, which you are to broadcast immediately..."

The orders that Arthur decoded from the code manual placed all units of the US Military on high alert. Several units were being mobilized. Arthur ran next door to the Command and obtained authorization, and then retransmitted the appropriate portions to the different units at Guantanamo and to the ships in port and offshore. He poured himself a cup of coffee.

"Deal, Mr. Harris," said. Thayer. "and welcome to my unit, the Naval Office of Special Intelligence, NOSI. No one knows of its existence except the Director, ONI, the Chief of Naval Operations, the President, and the handful of men serving under me. It's just Friday and we have to work. We can relax if and when the weekend hits, and I'll brief you more fully on NOSI."

On the Base Commander's order, Arthur activated the "battle stations" claxon and the PA system, and made the announcement that the entire base was on full alert and all hands were to man their battle stations. Only then did he deal the hand. When they were relieved by the next watch, they counted their money. Arthur had $55.00, so he handed $50.00 back to Lt. Thayer.

"Mr. Thayer," he said, "I won $5.00. Next time the beer's on me."

The tension at Guantanamo for the rest of the weekend was palpable. Orders flew over the airwaves as units were positioned for possible military action. It was clear that the US was preparing for two possibilities: invasion of Cuba, and/or full nuclear exchange with the USSR.

Few slept. All reviewed and re-reviewed procedures for various situations they might face at the base. The entire base stood battle watch, known as "watch on watch off," meaning that everyone on base stood four hours on watch at their duty stations, stood down for four hours and then returned to their duty stations for another four hours. This went on around the clock, with half the personnel at the base on watch and at their duty stations at any given time.

Marines were offloaded from ships in the bay and dug in along the perimeter of the base, ready either to repel a Cuban attack or to initiate an attack on Cuba. Artillery – guns, missile launchers and tanks – were moved to the perimeter of the base and targets in Cuba were selected. The primary targets were the known missile installations, with Cuban and Russian military units in position to attack Guantanamo as second targets. Anti-aircraft batteries, both guns and missiles, were armed and prepared for action. Two more ships steamed into port and offloaded yet more Marines. A large contingent of naval forces had taken up positions around the island after missiles were first detected. Ships in the port steamed to sea and joined the task forces already in position. They collected into battle groups rather than continuing what had been routine picket duty.

On Sunday evening, 21 October, orders came through mobilizing for a naval and air blockade of the island. No ships, other than US Navy ships, were to come to the island without stopping for inspection by the US Navy to ensure they were not carrying offensive weapons. Ships in port were to be allowed to depart without interference. Russian military aircraft would be intercepted and turned back or shot down if they refused. Arthur and the others in his unit worked fast and furiously decoding and encoding messages to and from the various units.

The next day, Monday, 22 October, President Kennedy addressed the nation and announced the "quarantine" of Cuba. If the Russians challenged the blockade militarily, there was the possibility that all-out nuclear war could result. Tensions continued to build as Russian ships and US ships maneuvered in the waters around Cuba. The Russians kept trying to find a way through the blockade without being intercepted, and the Americans kept making sure that a Russian ship couldn't slip through without being stopped and searched. It was a naval chess game in which both sides were trying to accomplish their purpose without provoking an attack.

On Thursday, 25 October, the level of alert nation-wide was raised to the highest level short of full-scale nu-clear attack on the Soviet Union. The next day, a Russian tanker successfully evaded the blockade, but the US Navy allowed it to continue without attacking it because they were certain it did not carry any offensive weapons. Later that day, a Lebanese freighter was intercepted, boarded, inspected, and allowed to continue.

On 26 October, Arthur processed and sent to Wash-ington a set of photographs proving that several missile sites in Cuba were fully operational and fully manned. With no sign that the Soviet Union was going to back down, later the same day the US began full-scale mobili-zation for an invasion of Cuba, with plans for nuclear launch against the USSR if the USSR responded militarily to the US attack on Cuba. SAC B-52 bombers, loaded with their full complement of nuclear bombs, began con-tinuous bombing runs toward the Soviet Union, turning back at the last minute if they did not have secure orders at that point to proceed. Intercontinental ballistic missiles equipped with nuclear warheads were prepared and armed for launch.

On 27 October, Arthur was listening to radio chatter between surveillance planes and the base when he heard a distress call from an American U-2 plane launched from Florida. The pilot reported that he had been hit by a sur-face-to air missile (SAM) and was going down. He later learned that the pilot had been killed in the crash, and he was relieved to learn as well that it was not his friend, Robert Bull. Later that day, several US Navy Crusader aircraft on low-level reconnaissance seeking SAM sites were fired upon and one was hit, but it was able to return to base safely. Intelligence contacts in Cuba got a message through to Arthur's unit that the order to shoot down the U-2 was made by a Soviet commander in Cuba without authorization from Moscow, and, in fact, against orders from Moscow, and that he had been relieved from command and imprisoned. The Crusaders were hit by nervous Cuban troops who thought they were under attack. Arthur encrypted and sent the message to Washington, and the Pentagon called off the retaliatory attack it was about to launch.

On 27 October, President Kennedy sent a message to Moscow accepting, with qualifications, an offer made earlier by the Russians to de-escalate if the US would remove certain missiles from Italy and Turkey. President Kennedy's response did not mention the specific missiles in Italy, but mentioned the type of missiles deployed in Turkey, which the US regarded as obsolete but the Soviets thought were state-of-the art. The US was prepared to remove them even without the Cuban Missile Crisis but had left them in place at the request of the host government. The condition attached to President Kennedy's message was that Russia, in turn, had to remove all of its missile capability from Cuba; that if Russia did not agree to do so, the US would employ military action to remove the missile threat from Cuba; and that if the USSR interfered with such military action, a full-scale nuclear attack would be launched against the USSR. Arthur received the transmission from Washington, with instructions to use his unit's contacts in Cuba to get the message to the Cubans and their Russian allies on the ground in Cuba. Arthur passed the message to Thayer, who got the message through to the Cuban contacts.

The next day, the US Navy dropped warning depth charges on a Soviet submarine that was attempting to run the blockade, unaware that it was carrying nuclear-armed missiles. They were warning charges, not intended to do damage, and did no damage. The submarine did not respond except to halt its progress toward Cuba and turn back. An aerial confrontation later in the day occurred between US planes and Soviet planes over the eastern tip of Siberia. Both the Americans and the Russians were nervous and President Kennedy and Khrushchev were both worried that inadvertent nuclear war could happen. Both were determined to find a way to de-escalate the crisis.

On 28 October, as was reported in the US newspapers, "Khrushchev Blinked." He accepted President Kennedy's proposal and issued orders to deconstruct and remove the missile stations from Cuba. Kennedy issued orders for the blockade to stand down, but to continue monitoring. Units that had been on high alert preparing for invasion demobilized. Arthur was sent home to Rice, enjoined to remember that he was never at Guantanamo. He was the man who was never there.

As soon as he was back at the dorm, wearing a knee brace and using crutches to continue the cover story of his injury, he called his parents. His father answered the phone.

"Hello, Harris here."

"Harris here, too," responded Arthur.

"Arthur! Are you all right?" asked his father.

"I'm fine, Dad," said Arthur. "How are all of you?"

"We're fine, but I have been worried about you. Your Lieutenant Thayer briefed me with an outline of what you were doing. I have a Top-Secret clearance for the work I do at Rucker, and I guess he decided I have the need to know. All I know is that you were on a special assignment at Guantanamo Bay. You'll have to tell me all about it when and if you are allowed to."

He spoke with his Mom. All she knew was that he had hurt his knee, and that his father had been in touch. He also spoke with his brother, who asked about his knee.

Arthur called Thayer, asked for, and received, authorization to tell Hilda that he had been on special duty with the Navy, without telling her any details. He called Hilda, who immediately left her job and rushed to see him at Wiess College. After Hilda arrived, he told her that he had been on special assignment with the Navy and couldn't talk about it. She had assumed as much because she had not been able to contact him while he was away, and the Navy had contacted her to tell her Arthur would be out of touch.

"Were you in the blockade of Cuba?" she asked him as they sat on a bench in the court under the leaves of a live-oak tree.

"No, I wasn't," he said.

"Were you at Guantanamo?" she asked.

"I can't tell you where I was."

"OK, so you can't tell me where you were," she said, "but you can tell me where you weren't, so that means you were at Guantanamo." He realized immediately that he should have told her nothing. He refused to say anything else to her about where he was or what he had been doing.

"I'm sorry Hilda," he said, "that I can't tell you anything else, but you are jumping to conclusions. I was officially *not* at Guantanamo. I missed you and thought and dreamed about you while I was on duty, even though I had very little time to think about anything other than what I was doing." She was a little distant with him for a couple of weeks after that, but then their relationship seemed to return to normal.

Arthur returned to classes and made up his missed work. Ostensibly, he was like any other Midshipman undergoing officer training. But in reality, he was operating from that time forward as part of NOSI. His career as a clandestine officer with the Office of Naval Intelligence had begun.

ONI was divided into two groups: Intelligence, and Thayer's new Special Intelligence group. Intelligence Officers operated relatively openly in the regular navy, assigned to various units to gather intelligence data about enemy naval capability, and served as Naval Attachés at foreign embassies. They also worked in Washington doing analysis work on intelligence information received, and communications intercepted. The handful of officers of the newly formed Naval Office of Special Intelligence, NOSI, were organized to operate in deep cover on clandestine operations when they weren't working as ordinary Intelligence Officers. Arthur could speak English (in various dialects), Spanish, and German. He also spoke Latin, but that would be of no use unless he were assigned to spy on the Vatican. His ability with languages, he hoped, would help to keep him in NOSI.

CHAPTER 12

ANTI-SUBMARINE WARFARE

June and July 1963
Pacific Fleet

Midshipmen undertake three summer trainings in the summers while they are in college – two cruises and one land-based exercise. At the end of his Freshman year, Arthur received travel orders to Long Beach Naval Base in California, and service orders to report for training duty to the destroyer USS Ingersoll in the Third Fleet, the US Navy Fleet covering the eastern Pacific. The Ingersoll was a WW II era destroyer, re-commissioned to enlarge the Navy as tensions between North Viet Nam and South Viet Nam escalated, along with Cold War tensions between the Soviet Union and the US.

Arthur had a two-week break before he had to report for duty, so he spent a long weekend with Hilda at the beach house. Her family was there, so it was a "subdued" weekend – but Arthur enjoyed being with Hilda. On Monday, he flew home to visit his family. His proud mother insisted he wear his dress white uniform to Mass and then to brunch after. Arthur felt like he was on display, but he enjoyed the attention he received. His proud parents and his brother all went to the airport to see him off, two days before he was required to report to the ship.

He flew the familiar Southern Air Lines route from Dothan on a DC-3 to Eglin AFB, to Panama City, Florida, Mobile, Alabama, and on to New Orleans, where he changed planes to a TWA DC-7 to St. Louis, and another change of planes for the long flight from St. Louis to Los Angeles on an elegant Lockheed Constellation, the sleek airliner with three tail rudders and four powerful propeller engines.

He discovered on the Constellation that there were three Navy officers sitting together, in a section in the middle of the plane that had pairs of seats facing each other over small tables attached to the hull, like in a dining car on a train. They invited Arthur to join them, so he did. They bought him a cocktail and offered him cigarettes. He accepted gratefully and spent the rest of the flight chatting, drinking and smoking with them. The flight took them right over the Grand Canyon, which was a spectacular sight from their altitude. The pilot circled the plane a few times so everyone who wished could get good pictures.

Upon leaving the Los Angeles International Airport, he took the bus to Long Beach. Dressed in his summer dress khakis, wrinkled from the long trip, with his duffel bag over his shoulder, he stopped at a dry-cleaning shop and sat in the back with a towel wrapped around his midsection while his uniform was pressed, and then walked the long walk from the base gate to the dock at which the Ingersoll was berthed. There was a cruiser docked against the pier, and outboard from the cruiser were four destroyers.

Arthur walked the gangway to the deck of the cruiser, lowered his duffel bag, stood at attention facing the aft end of the ship, saluted the flag, and turned and saluted the Officer of the Deck.

"Permission to come aboard, Sir," said Arthur, handing over his envelope of orders. The officer, a young, newly-commissioned Ensign, was backed up by a seasoned Master Chief, who saluted Arthur at the same time that Arthur saluted the officer. The officer returned his salute and looked briefly at the orders.

"Mr. Harris," he said, "the Ingersoll is the outermost ship berthed here. Please pass through and proceed to the next ship." He handed the envelope of orders back to Arthur, who saluted, receiving the officer's return salute, and marched through the midships passage to the next ship. This process was repeated until he reached the outer ship, where the officer of the day, an Ensign named Timothy Luke, welcomed him aboard and directed him to his berth. Because he was just a lowly Midshipman 4th Class, he would sleep in crew quarters, rather than officers' quarters, and would be under the supervision of the petty officers (enlisted, non-commissioned officers) while he learned shipboard routines. He was assigned first to the Deck Crew, known as Bosun's Mates, and berthed in the forward hold with the rest of the Bosun's Mates. "Bosun" was a contraction of "Boatswain," a job description originating in the British Navy. Mr. Luke was assigned to oversee the group of four Midshipmen who would be on board for this cruise, complementing the eight regular officers on the ship. The officer corps on board consisted of the Captain (a Commander), the Executive Officer (a Lieutenant Commander), the Engineering Officer (a Lieutenant), the Assistant Engineering Officer (a Lieutenant, Junior Grade), the Deck Officer and Intelligence Officer (Ensign Timothy Luke), the Supply Officer (a Lieutenant), the Chaplain (a Lieutenant Commander), and the Ship's Doctor (a Lieutenant).

The Deck Department is responsible for operations on the deck and maintenance of the hull of the ship. The head crewman of the Deck Department is called the Chief Bosun's Mate and reports to the Deck Officer. All who work under the Chief Bosun Mate's direction are called

Bosun's Mates. The Chief Bosun's Mate is generally assisted by at least one Bosun's Mate for each shift, and the remainder of the Chief Bosun Mate's crew consists of Seamen (their rank) also known as Bosuns Mates (their rating, or job description).

That night would be their last night in port for a while, so Timothy Luke rounded up the four Midshipmen on board and suggested they hit the town with the other officers for a round of bars, minus the Captain, who never fraternized with his officers except formally, at the Officers' Club.

"Mr. Luke, Sir, what should I wear?" asked Arthur.

"Did you bring any civvies with you, Mr. Harris?" asked Mr. Luke.

"Yes, Sir."

"Well, you probably won't need them on this cruise. Your dress for going ashore is to be the dress uniform of the day. You will wear civilian clothes only if you go onshore for an overnight stay, and you will change from your uniform after you are onshore. For this whole cruise, the uniform of the day will be either your Dress Whites or your Dress Khakis. Here in California the uniform is khakis. When we steam out of port, we will be in khakis for the duration, until we approach Pearl Harbor, where the uniform is whites. We will change to khakis after we leave Pearl and will be in khakis until we dock again in California. Oh, but you Middies will be wearing dungarees under way, just like the rest of the crew, because you will not be functioning as officers. To enter and leave port, you will wear your officers' uniforms, and you will wear officers' uniforms when on watch on the Bridge and for dress inspections. Otherwise, you will wear dungarees.

"While you are technically, and by law, officers and gentlemen, you will be doing the work of crewmen. On shore, however, you will be officers and gentlemen. You will not fraternize with the crew, but with the officers. On board, you will take your mess with the crew, except that you will dine in the Wardroom with the officers on a rotation basis. To command effectively as officers, you must know both the officers' world and the world of the crew. Now, let's all go get dressed to hit the beach. See you on deck at 1800 hours. We'll mess at a restaurant near here, and cruise the bars after."

At about midnight, the officer corps of the Ingersoll returned to the ship, not quite sober but not quite drunk, either. They slept well.

Most of the next day was spent in preparation for getting underway. Arthur's first assignment was with the deck crew. Working alongside the crew under the stern but jovial eye of the Chief Bosun's Mate, Arthur scrubbed the deck, inspected the safety rails and safety lines, touched up the battleship-grey paint, polished brass, and received instructions as to what to do, how to behave, where to stand, and what to wear as the ship steamed out of port. At 1400 hours, the crew broke work to shower and change into clean dress uniforms for the passage to sea. They were in port, so they would be able to shower with fresh water, but at sea they would shower in salt water.

Shortly, all were back on deck, standing at attention along the safety rail that bordered the main deck. Arthur and the other midshipmen, along with the officers not on watch for the start of the voyage, gathered on the first deck above the main deck and one level below the Bridge, wearing their dress khakis. The crewmen were on the main deck, lining the rails, wearing their enlisted dress whites. Crewmen did not have a dress khaki uniform, just a heavy blue wool uniform for winter and a white, cotton uniform for summer and, of course their work dungarees.

The shrieking pipe of the Bosun's Mate sounded over the loudspeaker, followed by the announcement, "Ingersoll arriving." The Captain was coming aboard. The pipe shrieked again, another pattern, and the deck crew began untying from the ship next to them. The funnels were belching black and smelly smoke from the boilers as the ship built a full head of steam. The twin screws began churning water. Side thrusters were in use, and the ship drifted out from the adjacent ship. When she was about twenty feet out, "Anchors Aweigh" began playing at full volume from the loudspeaker system and the ship began moving forward, with foaming white water, churned up by the screws, surging from the aft end of the ship. The ship accelerated rapidly to 12 knots, the legal speed limit for maneuvering in port and harbor channels, and began steaming away. All hands stood at attention along the rails, the officers included.

Glancing back, Arthur saw the next ship also beginning the process of getting underway. Soon, the group that had been berthed together – the cruiser and three destroyers – was steaming single-file from the harbor. As soon as they had cleared the port, the Bosun's whistle squealed the order to man their duty stations, and all except those on duty went below. Officers exchanged their formal covers for Navy-blue ballcaps with the ship's name emblazoned on the front, and changed into working khakis. Arthur changed to dungarees – a pair of bell-bottomed blue denim trousers, white web belt, blue chambray shirt, and white sailor's hat – and joined the deck crew for his first duty watch. At sea ahead of them appeared soon the remainder of the task force with which they would be operating – a carrier, loaded with helicopters, five more destroyers, and a conventional submarine.

Soon, they were steaming in formation westward. The carrier and the cruiser were in the middle, the cruiser leading the carrier, with a circular screen of destroyers around the formation about two miles from the center.

The submarine brought up the rear, outside the screen ships.

They were in formation as an anti-submarine-warfare (ASW) task force. When they reached the location for the start of their exercises, about 30 miles out, the submarine submerged and disappeared from radar, and then from sonar, and the task force began trying to find her and "force" her to the surface with a dummy attack. All the while, they stayed alert to detect any Soviet submarines that might try to collect data on the exercise.

Arthur wandered around on deck with others of the deck crew. There was nothing for them to be doing now. Most were at the aft end of the ship, called the fantail, where the ship's superstructure shielded them from the wind created by their forward speed, which was about 25 knots, but Arthur and three other Midshipmen were on the forward deck near the prow, a location called the Fo'c'sle, a contraction of "Forecastle."

The seas were choppy at first but soon gave way to steady linear waves of about four feet in height, called swells. Ingersoll rolled gently as she made her way through the swells. She was cruising roughly parallel to the swells with the cruiser to the starboard, and with the carrier behind the cruiser; but the swells were also in motion, crossing their path, and this resulted in the steady rolling motion of the ship as she rose and fell over the swells. Behind the Ingersoll, on the port side, was another destroyer, and ahead to the starboard side, another.

As the seas got heavier, the direction of the swells had changed so they were crossing the swells head-on, and salt spray started blowing over the prow with each swell. Arthur and his companions made their way aft to the fantail. By late afternoon, thunderheads appeared ahead of them, and the Chief told him they were going to have a little storm. When the rain began to fall, those of the deck crew who were on watch, including Arthur, made their way to the Fo'c'sle and to the Bosun's Locker below, the forwardmost compartment in the ship, at the prow. It contained coils of stored cable, rope, chains, tools, cleaning materials, cans of paint, paintbrushes, and the other things that the deck crew would use. It smelled of tar and turpentine. The watch crew lounged around on coils of rope or cable. Some played cards, some read pocket-sized paperback books, others chatted, bragging about their exploits with women in port. Some napped, snoring gently. Arthur merely observed, practicing patience.

When the Bosun's pipe sounded mess call, their watch shift was over. Other members of the deck crew arrived, relieving those who had been on duty. Arthur and his fellow watch-standers made their way to the crew mess for dinner. Each steel table rested on a central pedestal that was bolted to the floor. Chairs were mounted with a swivel mount to cantilevered arms fastened to the central pedestal. The dishes and silverware were tin-plated, magnetized iron, and the tabletop was steel. The dishes and silverware clung to the table and did not slide off when the ship rolled. Arthur learned quickly not to fill his metal "glass" too full or it would spill.

The crew went through a serving line as at a cafeteria, and the cooks – mostly Filipinos – slopped generous servings of mashed potatoes, stewed beef in gravy, and vegetables on their plates. Filipinos, having once been residents of an American Colony, had special privileges that allowed them to join the US Navy and become US citizens by that service. They served as clerks, stewards, and kitchen crews. Arthur found a place at one of the tables and began eating. The mood in the mess was jovial.

After dinner, Arthur went to the forward crew billet along with the rest of the deck hands who were not on watch. They were on what Arthur was told was an easy schedule – six hours on watch, twelve hours off watch, and another six hours on watch, followed by twelve hours off, etc. Arthur's watch had ended at 1600 hours, so his next watch would begin at 0400 hours the next morning.

Arthur lounged in his rack, the topmost of three narrow, cot-like beds stacked above each other, attached at the side to the hull, and suspended on chains from the overhead. He watched a poker game underway at a card table in the small clear space at the base of the ladder into their compartment from the mess deck above.

Some of the men were moaning as they lay in their racks and made occasional dashes to the head. They were seasick. Arthur had not felt any seasickness yet, and seeing the misery some were experiencing, he counted himself lucky.

Gradually, the ship rolled and pitched more and more violently. The seas were heavier with the thunderstorms full upon them. Arthur could hear the muffled crackling of the thunder through the hull of the ship and could hear the waves crashing against the hull next to his rack. He gathered that his rack was roughly at water level.

At 2200 hours, the bosun's whistle signaled "Lights out," and the lights were extinguished except for red lights that remained on. Sailors began sacking out in their racks to sleep. Despite his excitement at being at sea, Arthur fell asleep quickly, lulled by the rocking of the ship.

Arthur awoke suddenly, the shriek of the Bosun's pipe in his ears. "Now hear this – now hear this," blared the loudspeaker. "Battle stations, battle stations – all hands man your battle stations. This is not a drill. I repeat, this is not a drill."

Arthur tried to sit up too quickly, and his forehead hit the underside of the steel deck above him. As instructed, he had slept in his underwear so he could dress quickly. He swung his legs and upper body out so he was sitting in the middle of his rack. He dropped to his feet onto the deck and dressed hurriedly. Men hurried from their racks and into their duty uniforms and ran up the ladder, Arthur among them. His battle station was on the Bridge. Because this was Bridge duty, he was wearing his officer's work khakis – khaki cotton twill trousers, with a khaki web belt and tan open-necked cotton shirt, with insignia pinned at the appropriate places. Some wore watch sweaters over their khakis and knitted watch caps. He carried with him his watch sweater and watch cap, putting them on as he entered the bridge. Even in summer, the wind at sea could be cold. He performed look-out duty, standing on the Flying Bridge, a semi-circular extension of the deck outside the Bridge, scanning the horizon and the seas between the horizon and the ship with binoculars. He was glad for his sweater and knitted watch cap. The air was chilly and felt even colder in the 35-mph wind caused by the combination of a 10-mph wind and the speed of the ship.

They were still on station with the carrier as before, and the whole formation executed a 45 degree turn to port. Sonar had picked up a suspected Soviet submarine on the port side paralleling their course. The task force had turned to intercept her. Helicopters were in the air, low over the waves, dipping sonar microphones into the water. The task force's submarine was submerged, somewhere in the area.

The sonar room informed the Captain that the Ingersoll was about to intercept the suspect submarine and would pass directly over her. After conferring with the Admiral on the carrier, the Captain ordered that unarmed torpedoes and depth charges be prepared. He ordered torpedoes launched at the submarine, and as the Ingersoll passed overhead, he ordered depth charges dropped. Each depth charge exploded at a pre-set depth with a small charge insufficient to damage a submarine, but loud enough to declare its nature.

After they passed over the submarine, she surfaced and identified herself by radio. She was, indeed, a Soviet, nuclear-powered attack submarine, a November-Class attack submarine, K-42. The Ingersoll turned to starboard and slowed to parallel the submarine. The Captain ordered the crew to the rail. The crew of the submarine had come on deck and saluted the Ingersoll, whose crew returned the salute.

"Flank speed," ordered the Captain, "and play Anchors Aweigh." The orders were "telegraphed" to the engine room. On the Bridge was a dial mounted on a pedestal with a handle and pointer. The handle could be rotated around the dial, and the pointer attached to the lower end of the handle would point to the word indicating the engine speed the Captain was ordering. There was an identical device in the engine room, and it would repeat whatever was done to the device on the Bridge, thereby communicating the Captain's orders to the engine room. There was also a telephone connecting them, and a speaking tube, but by tradition (and practicality) the orders were transmitted instantly using the "telegraph."

The Ingersoll began to gain speed quickly, a rooster tail of water at her Fantail. She steamed away from the submarine with "Anchors Aweigh" playing over the loudspeakers. She was doing about 35 knots when she resumed her station point, at which time the Captain reduced the engine speed to "full" and returned Ingersoll to her screen station. He ordered the sonar room to track the submarine and report its position every five minutes. The submarine made way rapidly, remaining on the surface, and turning away from the task force, sailed away over the horizon and out of sonar range.

"Secure from battle stations," ordered the Captain. Arthur left his lookout station and walked into the Bridge, on his way back to his compartment.

"Mr. Harris," said the Captain, "Did you enjoy your first sub kill?"

"Sir! Yes, Sir, Captain," said Arthur.

"I hope we never have a situation where we need to make a real kill."

"Sir, would that mean war?" asked Arthur.

"Yes," said the Captain, "it would. What we just did carried some risk, but the Russian had to know we were engaged in antisubmarine warfare exercises and must have thought we had confused his craft with our own target submarine. But he wasn't sure, so he surfaced just to indicate his non-hostile intent in the event we were really trying for a kill. Enjoy what's left of your sleep." The time was 0200. Arthur had slept two hours and had been at battle station for two hours. In two more hours he would be back on duty for his next turn at watch.

Work for the deck crew underway was relatively easy. Their first task was to hose down the deck to remove the accumulated salt buildup from the sea spray. They would repair anything that needed repairing (little repair was needed) and would spend the rest of the time lounging on deck or in the Bosun's Locker, ready to jump into action when needed. Midshipmen assigned to the Bosun's crew were made to practice all the varieties of knot used by the Bosun's Mates. Once they had mastered their knots and bights, they were taught how to braid lanyards that they could wear around their necks to which their Bosun's pipes would be clipped.

As the days wore on, exercises against their target sub would take place sometimes in the daytime and sometimes at night. Arthur learned that finding the sub was difficult when she was submerged. She would find a boundary between warm and cold water and stay below that boundary, and the sonar would deflect at the boundary and not find the sub. Once, the sub sneaked up behind the formation, obscured by the wake of the carrier, and positioned herself directly beneath the carrier. There, she was virtually invisible to sonar, but one of the ships finally found her. The carrier, after she was informed, dropped depth charges and the submarine surfaced beside the carrier. She submerged and made way at right angles to the course of the task force. She would go out beyond sonar range and return submerged to give the task force an opportunity to catch her again.

Arthur wrote both to Hilda and to JoAnne, describing his days, but without giving details of the antisubmarine exercises that would reveal any classified information. They wrote back. Once every couple of days, by helicopter from the carrier, a mail package was picked up, and a mail package delivered to each ship in the task force. Hilda's first letter told of her promotion to loan officer at the bank, and Jo Anne's spoke of regularly dating the Auburn quarterback. Arthur responded to JoAnne, suggesting they get together for a date when he got home in August. He wrote back to Hilda congratulating her. Jo Anne didn't write again. Hilda did, suggesting they visit the beach house together when he returned.

Apparently, JoAnne was now a part of his past, while Hilda remained a part of his near future, at least. Arthur had mixed feelings about that. He had experienced strong feelings for JoAnne, but those had waned, to be replaced by stronger feelings for Hilda. He was in love with Hilda.

Duty rotation for the Midshipmen had them spend part of the cruise working in each of the different shipboard departments. After working with the deck crew, Arthur worked next in the sonar room, where he learned about the two types of sonar – active and passive. Active sonar sent out a high-pitched sound beep and picked up the echo returning from any objects in its path – other ships, whales, seamounts, and anything that would return a solid echo. The time it took for the echo to return allowed calculation of the distance to the object. A change in pitch of the echo relative to the original sound, taking into account the Doppler effect, told the listener whether the relative motion of the object was away from or toward the ship, and at what relative speed. The sounds were plotted on a cathode ray screen, showing the relative positions of all the objects that returned echoes, with the ship being in the center of the screen.

Passive sonar simply listened for sounds, picking up the sounds made by other ships and the songs of whales. He learned that the sounds made by different ships were different. After a week in sonar, he could identify some of the ships of his task force by the sounds they made. He started printing paper charts of the sound patterns, shown as a squiggly line on a graph. He labeled each with the identification of the ship producing the sound. He folded the charts and kept them in his "study file" in his ring-bound notebook in his locker.

For his next duty rotation, he worked a week in the Combat Information Center (CIC), which was located on top of the Bridge and just under the main radar and microwave antennae. The CIC monitored radar, ran the fire control computer, and coordinated with Sonar. The fire control computer was a rectangular metal prism about three feet square and four feet high. Several cranks protruded from its sides and there were various dials on its top surface. During gunnery exercises, two men would man the cranks, cranking in numbers representing the ship's heading, its speed, the sighted direction and distance to target, and the wind speed and wind heading. The central readouts gave them the exact bearing and elevation to point the guns to hit the target. It was a purely mechanical calculating computer, with no electrical or electronic parts. It worked by gears and cams.

For targets over the horizon, radar would give the bearing and distance, and the computer would give the aiming instructions after all the relevant information had been cranked into it. They did gunnery exercises using an inflated float towed on a long line behind a destroyer, and on a small unmanned glider towed behind a plane from the carrier. They also did anti-submarine warfare exercises every day in pursuit of, and in defense against, their target submarine.

Soon, the task force steamed into Pearl Harbor at Honolulu on Oahu Island for a three-day break. The four Midshipmen were given shore leave and together rented a suite at the Hilton on the beach. They spent their days exploring the island, watching (and making passes at) the girls on the beach, and climbing the Diamond Head volcanic cone to look down into the inactive crater. They spent their first night-on-the-town in Don Ho's famous restaurant, enjoying the food and drinks and watching the show. Their second night was spent visiting strip joints. They returned to the ship a bit jaded and ready for some clean sea air.

For the first week of the homeward-bound part of the cruise, Arthur worked in the forward gun turret for a live gunnery exercise. A ship that was being scrapped was towed out from Pearl Harbor to the target area on a long cable behind another ship. The ships of the task force lined up in single file and steamed past the hulk at a distance of five miles, emptying their guns at her.

Arthur worked in the forward-most turret. Elevators lifted metal powder cartridges and bullets to the turret, and Arthur and the seamen working in the turret worked hard lifting the heavy projectiles and powder cartridges and loading them into the breeches of the guns.

Arthur was surprised that it took three passes by the entire task force before the hulk sank. The Chief Gunner's Mate pointed out that she had no munitions or fuel on board, and so there was nothing except metal to hit. Over 200 shells had hit the target, but over 600 shells had been fired. That meant that only 1/3 of the shells hit their target, which wasn't a very good ratio. But that was what gunnery practice was for.

In an actual battle situation, she would have sunk faster, because either the engine room would have exploded, or her fuel stores would have exploded, or her magazine, the ammunition store room, would have blown up. Arthur was still amazed at the number of direct hits she took from the Ingersoll's four 5-inch guns without sinking. The cruiser, USS Galveston, had six five-inch guns in two triple mounts and six five-inch guns in three double mounts, along with the Talos missile launcher (the missiles weren't used in this exercise), and she didn't seem to do any more damage than the Ingersoll's guns.

Following his tour of duty in gunnery, Arthur worked in the forward engine room. By the end of the week he could draw from memory the steam cycle diagram for the engine room, indicating pipe routing, pipe sizing, and each valve and instrument. He knew how to change a burner for the boiler, and how to adjust fuel flow and build proper steam pressure for the engine speed called for by the captain.

For his final week of the cruise, he worked on the Bridge mainly as a navigator. He got to "take the con" (take command of the ship) for a whole watch under the Captain's watchful eye several times. He learned rapidly and performed well. Since he was doing "officer work" at that time, he dined in the officers' Wardroom. Every evening after coming off a day watch, he would remove his work khakis, shower, and change into his dress khakis, before wandering up to the Wardroom. It had newspapers, reading materials and board games. He would try to catch up on the news, although they received newspapers only when they pulled alongside the carrier once a week for package delivery, so the news was often several days old. At time to eat, he would take his place at table with the other officers.

At the appointed time, the officers behind their assigned chairs until the Captain entered. He would take his
place behind the chair at the head of the table. All would
bow their heads, and the Chaplain would say a prayer of
blessing from the Episcopal Book of Common Prayer and
sit, followed by the rest of the officers. The table was set
with white linen tablecloth and napkins, real china and
real silverware. The meal was served in courses by the
Filipino stewards. Conversation was begun by the Captain. He would begin by engaging each officer in turn in
conversation. Once he started chatting with the officer
immediately to his right or his left, others would begin
chatting with each other.

Mr. Luke sat directly across from Arthur and did everything he could to make Arthur feel at home. He explained the customs of the Navy and of the Ingersoll. The
ship provided the food for the crew, but the officers had to
pay an assessment which was used to purchase their food.
Often it was similar to the fare of the men, but had spe-
cialties that only the officers got, like filet mignon and
other delicacies that would be outside the budget for crew
meals. He told Arthur that when the weather was stormy,
a bit of dexterity was required to hold one's plate in position with the silverware not in use, and to avoid spilling
one's glass. China, crystal and silver couldn't be magnetized, and neither could the wooden table. Available drinks
consisted of iced tea or water. With the dessert course one
could have hot tea or coffee. Officers ate with the crewmen on rotation, and in stormy weather there were always
officers who chose to eat in the crew's mess because of
the magnetic tables and dishes.

The perimeter of the wardroom consisted of built-in,
leather-upholstered couches with built-in end tables in the
corners of the compartment. Once the meal had been
cleared away, officers either went to their berths or hung
out for a while in the wardroom. Four officers usually

played bridge at the table, and Arthur often played chess with the Ship's Doctor in a corner of the wardroom. Arthur had thought he was a pretty good chess player until he started playing the doctor. He learned otherwise and lost every game. The doctor would sit, reading a book and smoking his pipe. After Arthur made a move, the doctor would glance up quickly, make his move and return to reading. He never lost.

On their last day at sea, the Captain asked Arthur to visit him in his stateroom after dinner. Arthur knocked on the door upon arriving.

"Sir! Midshipman Arthur Harris reporting as ordered. Permission to enter, Captain."

"Come in, Mr. Harris," said the Captain. Arthur entered to find the captain seated at a desk against the forward bulkhead. "At ease," said the Captain. "You may be seated." Arthur sat on the chair indicated.

"As you know, I am aware that you are in training not only for surface warfare but also to be a Naval Intelligence Officer. Accordingly, I have made sure that you have undertaken every exercise that an officer must master to qualify for command at sea. I have made the appropriate entries in your record. Upon commissioning, I am sure you will be qualified to wear the Surface Warfare Badge.

"Your performance on this cruise has been exemplary, and I have given you the highest marks available. You will make a superb officer, and I wish you luck. I hope our paths will cross again, Mr. Harris. It would be a pleasure to have you under my command as a commissioned officer."

"Thank you, Captain," said Arthur.

"Get a good night's sleep and enjoy the rest of the summer. Dismissed."

"Aye, aye, Sir," said Arthur, rising to attention. He made an about face and left the stateroom, returning to his rack in the forward crew compartment.

He had to change planes in Houston, so he stopped overnight with the Austins, bringing Hilda up to date. She was warm and welcoming, kissing him soundly on the lips when she collected him at the airport. Early the next morning she drove him to the airport, and soon he was in New Orleans, changing planes to the Southern Airways DC-3 that would deliver him to Dothan and home.

That flight home was an adventure. As they were approaching Panama City, Florida, in the Southern Airways DC-3, one engine started belching fire, and the pilot shut it down. Smoke kept pouring from it. The pilot landed the plane using just the one engine and the passengers all disembarked, to wait in the airport lounge while the mechanics looked at and tinkered with the engine. Finally, the pilot came into the lounge to inform them that the plane would not be resuming flight that evening. It would require a new engine. The airline would provide rental cars for them to travel the 90 miles to Dothan, with four passengers per car, including the designated driver; and those who were headed for Atlanta would be met at the Dothan airport by another plane that would take them on to Atlanta. They all headed out, four to a car. Arthur's car was driven by a man in a hurry, and the night was foggy, so the ride was somewhat exciting. Despite the fog, they made Dothan in under an hour and a half.

At home, he spent hours telling his family of his adventures. His mother made him change into each of his uniforms in succession and stand at attention in the sunlight for photographs. His brother, Matthew, took the pictures.

Arthur loved his family deeply, but felt a separation developing between them. He was becoming a man, but to them he was still their boy. It was as if the family was frozen in time, but he was not. Their conversations were replays from a script, except when he talked about his cruise, when the family listened with rapt attention. While he loved his time on the Navy cruise, he regretted not being able to spend more time with his family. He felt like he was moving on without them, and in a way he was. He was beginning to leave the nest and test his wings.

Arthur called Jo Anne, and asked her out, but she declined, telling him that she was getting serious about her quarterback boyfriend. Although this brought sadness to Arthur's heart because he still had feelings for her, he also felt relieved, because he was in love with Hilda. He called Hilda and told her about his call to Jo Anne, and he confessed that he was in love with Hilda. She confessed strong feelings for him, but suggested they not go too fast with their feelings, because they were both still quite young. "Feelings will do what feelings will do," said Arthur. "I can't really control them."

"I know," said Hilda, "but you can remind yourself not to surrender to them until you are ready. You can't control your feelings, but you can control your actions."

"OK, I'll do that," said Arthur, "but when you do that, be careful you don't smother your feelings."

"I'll be careful not to do that," she said. "After all, I *like* these feelings."

"So do I," said Arthur. "Now, you sleep tight and have pleasant dreams."

"You, too," said Hilda.

"That's easy," said Arthur. "I'll be dreaming of being with you." The call was not a long call, because long distance telephone service was expensive.

It had been a good summer, but within two weeks he had to return to school. While he wished he could spend more time with his family, he was looking forward to getting back to his new life and to Hilda.

William A. Wheatley

CHAPTER 13

FLIGHT

June 1965
Corpus Christ Naval Air Station, Texas

The school year flew by rapidly. Arthur was just behind the top-ranked member of his architecture class, and he was in the top ten percent of his Navy class. He studied hard and dated Hilda on the weekends, spending the occasional weekend with her at the house on Bryan Beach.

When they weren't at the beach house for the weekend, Hilda accompanied him to Mass at the Newman Center. He went to confession before every Mass as he had been taught, and felt guilty confessing the same sin every time, while being thankful for the absolution. Hilda began taking instruction from the Dominican priest, Father Joubert, and Arthur accompanied her to the instruction sessions. She took the course seriously, apparently intending to convert. She asked questions, debated issues, and studied the required readings.

She balked a bit (as did Arthur) at the sexual teachings of the Church. Both she and Arthur were aware that most teenagers engaged in sex before marriage, and they were no exception. Father Joubert was aware of that, as well.

"Yes," said Father Joubert, "I understand that most kids don't follow the rule, but it remains the teaching of the Church, and always will, that sex outside of the marriage between one man and one woman is a sin. Intentionally engaging in such activity is objectively sinful."

"That means that most Catholic youth are sinners," said Hilda.

"We are all sinners," said Father Joubert. "St. Paul reminded us that 'all are sinners and have fallen short of the glory of God,' and that he, also, was 'the chiefest of sinners;' and yet through God's grace and the sinners' penitence, all sins can be forgiven and ways can be mended. Tell me – have you ever had a puppy, and gone through the housebreaking procedure?"

"Yes," she replied. "I have."

"You loved the puppy and were determined to housebreak him so he could share your house with you. He didn't understand any of that, and peed when and where he wanted to. You patiently corrected him when he did so, taking him outside at the first sign that he wanted to pee, and keeping him there until he did. You gave him a swat when you caught him in the act of peeing in the house. You took him outside after feeding him until he did his business. You kept him in a box in the bathroom. He didn't foul the box, because no animal will foul its own bed. Even though you punished him when he peed on the doorjamb, you did it because you loved him and wanted him to share your house with you. Correct?"

"Correct, so far, except that my puppy was a girl, and didn't pee on door jambs, she peed on the carpet." Father Joubert laughed.

"Gradually, the puppy came to understand that she was allowed to pee and do her business only outside. Yet there were occasions when she failed to live up to that – moments of extreme excitement, times when you were away too long and she couldn't wait for you to return. Right?"

"Yes, Father," Hilda replied.

"But you kept loving the puppy, and eventually she became housebroken and was allowed to share your house. Right?"

"Right."

"Your relationship with God is like that of the puppy to you. Life is a housebreaking exercise to prepare us to share Heaven with God. He loves you and corrects you. He asks of you what you think is impossible. Yet, if you keep trying to conform to God's will, and keep asking for his grace to do so, eventually you will be able to lead a moral life in accordance with God's law. When you fail, you will be sorrowful and will confess the sin, pledging to try to avoid the occasion of sin. Ultimately, you likely will marry, and then be able to have sex with your husband without guilt."

"It's not easy, Father."

"I know." The elderly priest smiled kindly at her. "All of us sin and fall short of the glory of God, yet he sticks with us, forgives us, and works with us toward our perfection."

"I always thought it was hypocritical," said Hilda, "for a person to keep doing the same sins and then going to confession for absolution."

"The puppy is sorry for having peed on the rug, and although you punished her, you forgave her and stuck with her, working to get her housebroken."

"The analogy makes sense," said Arthur. "I never thought of it in those terms."

"The two of you," said the priest, "need to try to save yourselves for each other in marriage, if marriage to each other is what you want, or to save yourselves for marriage in general, if you are not to remain a couple. It is not easy – I know, because I was once young myself. I truly understand your dilemma. Life presents us dilemmas, but we must still choose the right way."

Arthur walked back to Wiess College beside Hilda, holding hands. Neither spoke for a while.

"We need to try to do as Father said," said Arthur, when they had crossed half the campus on their way back to Wiess.

"I agree. It will not be easy. There will likely be times when we succumb to temptation, but God will still love us and help us."

"I hope we can get through all of this and find happiness together," said Arthur. He glanced sideways at Hilda. She turned to face him and took both his hands in hers.

"Arthur, I think I love you," she said, "but I don't think either of us is mature enough for such a commitment as marriage yet. We'll just have to follow the path and see where it leads." She kissed him, and then they turned and continued walking toward Wiess.

Arthur would have three summer cruises with the Navy during college, which left one summer for other things in the five-year architecture curriculum. Arthur planned to complete the four years of Naval Science courses by the end of his senior year, but to work in an architect's office during the summer after his sophomore year to meet the work experience requirement for the architecture degree. He would take his final training cruise after his senior year and before his fifth year.

Arthur's Sophomore year at Rice was almost routine. He studied, he worked his classes, and he enjoyed his time with Hilda. Knowing that he needed to learn to act, he joined the Rice Players, so he could study acting. He knew he would need to be able to act to be a good spy. The Rice Players were the campus "drama club." There was a faculty member assigned to develop it, but there were no classes as such in drama. If one were a student at Rice, and wanted to learn acting, one joined the Rice Players. He learned much by being in the Players. He played many minor roles, often three or four in any given play. He learned to switch quickly from one *persona* to another. He also designed and helped build sets, which put his architecture skills to use.

After his sophomore year, he took a summer off from the Navy and worked in the architecture office of his sophomore professor, Clovis Heimsath. As luck would have it, Heimsath was designing a beach development for Bryan Beach, near the Austins' beach house. Model beach houses were under construction already, and Arthur had to inspect the construction, usually on a Friday. As a result, he and Hilda saw each other almost every weekend, and Arthur enjoyed his work. It was a small office, so he got to do design, detailing, specifications writing, and field inspection of work under construction. He learned a great deal of what was required for an architectural practice. Although he enjoyed it thoroughly, by the end of the summer he was still committed to the idea of a Navy career. Architecture would be his fallback career, or his second career after he retired from the Navy.

He applied himself hard to his studies in his junior year, making sure he got top marks in Naval Science. He continued his relationship with Hilda, but it was growing somewhat strained, and Hilda often seemed distant. He could not understand why, and he couldn't get Hilda to open up to him about it. It seemed as if the relationship had become stale, routine.

"Hilda," he said one evening after they had seen a movie, "Do you still think you love me? You seem to be a bit distant these days."

"I still love you and I always will," she responded, "but I don't know if I want to marry you. As I said, we'll follow the path and see where it leads. Once you're commissioned and ready to take your place in the fleet, I'll have to make a decision. Will I want to be a Navy wife, seeing my husband only when he's in port, or do I want to marry someone who will come home from work every night to share my bed?"

"I understand," said Arthur. "That choice will not be easy. I will face the flip side of that coin. I don't like the idea of spending months at sea without you, but I won't have a choice in the matter, at least through the first six years. I am already in the Navy, and I can't turn back now." They had reached the parking lot across the road from Wiess College and were standing beside Hilda's car.

"Arthur," said Hilda, "I care very deeply about you, and I understand that the dilemma you face has already been decided by your oath as a Midshipman. I will face the dilemma when the time comes for us to say goodbye when you head off to sea duty after college. I don't know now how I will feel then or what I will decide then."

"Let's live life as we find it, one day at a time, trusting in God to show us the way."

"Yes. It's the only right way forward," replied Hilda. They kissed, long and passionately, and then Hilda drove away.

During the summer, the dorm at Wiess College was not available. Arthur took a small and inexpensive efficiency apartment near the campus, an apartment building occupied mostly by Rice students and medical students at the Medical center.

His apartment was on the second floor. It had a reasonably large, "L" shaped room that had the living-dining area in the long part and the bedroom in the short side of the L. A louvered folding partition separated the two legs of the "L." Enclosed by the "L" were a bathroom, opening to the bedroom, and a kitchenette with a small refrigerator, a counter with sink and a small amount of storage under it, and a small range. Cabinets overhead provided some additional storage. A louvered, folding door could be used to close the kitchenette off from the dining area. The side wall of the bedroom was wall-to-wall closets.

The apartment came furnished – with a square table and four chairs in the dining area; a couch, coffee table and two end tables, with a single easy chair, in the living area; and a king-sized bed in the bedroom area (but no bedside tables). A recessed alcove in the wall by the door to the bathroom provided a shelf on which he placed his alarm clock, prayer book and rosary.

He decided to remain an "off campus" student for his Junior year, staying in the apartment. He enjoyed the freedom that it gave him. His monthly stipend from the Navy, combined with his earnings from making posters for campus organizations, provided just enough money to pay the rent and meet his expenses.

The second training "cruise" for Midshipmen was "Flight Indoctrination" combined with a short version of Marine boot camp. At the end of the summer, those who wanted to be Marines would be asked to commit to the Marine Option. They would skip the third cruise and do Marine boot camp instead. Those choosing the aviation option had until the time of their commissioning to make that choice. Arthur took this training after his junior year.

Arthur wished he could become a pilot, but he knew that his glasses would prevent him. To be a Navy pilot, one had to have 20/20 vision, uncorrected. Arthur's was 20/40. Wearing glasses would interfere with wearing the flight mask pilots had to wear. Although contact lenses would have worked, Navy regulations had not yet caught up with the times. Arthur was determined to learn all he could and to progress as far as he could, and was wearing contact lenses, hoping they would not be noticed.

Hilda dropped him off at the Greyhound station in downtown Houston. Dressed in his dress khakis, required wear for naval officers traveling for Navy duty, Arthur tossed his duffel bag into the luggage compartment on the Greyhound bus that would take him from Houston to

Corpus Christi. He kissed Hilda goodbye and boarded, showing his ticket to the driver. He found a seat halfway back. He put his uniform cap onto the overhead luggage rack, along with his attaché case. For his birthday the previous year, Hilda had given him a sturdy, black leather attaché case with a combination lock. He used it to carry books and notebooks on campus, and for this trip, he had packed into it all the flight manuals he had been able to find in the NROTC library, along with his study notebook, orders and slide rule. The NROTC librarian had allowed him to check out the books with a late return time of twelve weeks, commenting that no one had checked out those particular books in more than a year.

The bus took him to downtown Corpus Christi, where he took a taxi for the six-mile ride to the Corpus Christi Naval Air Station, which was on the coast just south of Corpus Christi. There were six auxiliary air fields in the area around Corpus Christi that were also part of the station. The taxi dropped him at the main gate. Arthur exited the taxi, retrieved his duffel bag from the trunk, and presented himself to the gate guard, who checked his orders against a list, and motioned him through the pedestrian gate, directing him to the office of the Commanding Officer.

"You must rate," he said. "All the other Middies are sent to the Chief Drill Instructor. You're reporting to the CO. What are you, some kind of hot shot?"

"I don't know," said Arthur. "You know as much about it as I do. Maybe I'm in trouble and don't know it."

He walked the quarter mile in the broiling heat of the Texas summer sun, wearing his dress khakis, with the strap of his duffel bag over his shoulder. The air was very humid, and he could smell the salt water of the Gulf just a short distance to the east. His uniform was blotched with sweat by the time he arrived at the Admiral's office. He entered the building, presented himself to the duty clerk, and handed him his orders. The clerk glanced at them and told him to take a seat. The clerk wrote for a moment on a slip of paper, and gave it to another clerk, who carried it down the hallway and out of sight. After about fifteen minutes, the clerk returned, and said something quietly to the desk clerk.

"Mr. Harris," said the desk clerk, "please proceed to the Admiral's office. Fourth door on the right." Arthur stood, straightened and smoothed his tunic, picked up his duffel bag, and started to walk toward the corridor. "You may leave your sea bag here," said the clerk. Gratefully, Arthur dropped his duffel out of the way in the corner, and walked down the corridor to the fourth door, which was open. He brought himself to attention, executed a right face, and stepped to the doorway.

"Sir! Midshipman Second Class Arthur Harris, reporting as ordered, Sir. Permission to enter."

"Enter," said the Admiral, sitting at his desk. "At ease. Close the door behind you." Arthur entered and closed the door. "Sit down, Mr. Harris," said the Admiral. Arthur took the chair to his left, facing the desk. The Admiral perused Arthur's orders for a minute, and looked at Arthur and smiled, handing them back to him.

"Mr. Harris," he said, "welcome to Corpus Christi Naval Air Station. Lieutenant Commander Thayer has briefed me on your status with the ONI. I served a tour as an Intelligence Officer myself, but I never chose to make that my career. You are considering ONI as a career. You may always opt later to leave ONI and follow another Navy career path. Either way, if you have the Navy in your blood, you will find satisfaction in your career. Because you are currently on a new type of ONI career track, and you are the only such Midshipman here this summer, your summer training experience will be a little different from the rest of the midshipmen here. You will begin with them, until you have soloed in the T-34. That will be about one week, if you work hard. After the T-34, you will be introduced to the F-4 Phantom II. You will depart for duty elsewhere, but I don't need to know where. Officially, you will not be there, but here, and all the records will show that you are here, not there. You will depart here with your flight instructor. Any questions?" Arthur thought for a minute, his thoughts racing.

"Sir, not at this time," said Arthur. "I am wearing contact lenses, which will enable me to see as if I met the vision requirements and to wear the oxygen equipment, but I understand that I cannot qualify as a pilot. If I have questions later, may I come see you again?"

"Of course, Mr. Harris. Just call my clerk and he'll give you an appointment, but your flight instructor will be much more able to answer your questions than I will. Now, because you have already walked through the heat to get here, I'll have my jeep take you to your barracks, where you will report to Sergeant Benoit, who will be your drill instructor for the first week or two."

"Thank you, Admiral," said Arthur. He stood, coming to attention facing the Admiral.

"Dismissed," said the Admiral. Arthur nodded to the Admiral, executed an about face and marched from the room. Back in the foyer, he reclaimed his duffel bag.

"Mr. Harris," said the clerk, "the Admiral's jeep is waiting out front."

"Thank you," said Arthur.

Ten minutes later, Arthur climbed down from the Jeep with his duffel bag and thanked the driver. He walked up the steps to the side of the World War II-era wooden barracks. The exterior was standard horizontal wood siding, painted a light tan, and the building sat up off the ground on concrete blocks. Entering, he looked both ways, and spotted the Sergeant's office at the end of the building. He walked down the aisle between the beds and knocked on the office door.

"Come in," growled a deep basso voice from within. Arthur opened the door, stepped in facing the desk, and snapped to attention. Although technically he outranked the Sergeant, he was under the Sergeant's charge for training and was required to treat him as his superior. Arthur took one step forward and handed his packet of orders to the Sergeant.

"Sir!" said Arthur. "Midshipman Second Class Arthur Harris reporting as ordered, Sir."

"At ease, Mr. Harris," said the Sergeant. "I am Sgt. James Benoit. While you are under my care, I will either make you or break you."

"Aye, aye, Sir," said Arthur.

"I'll break you only if you don't apply yourself," Sgt. Benoit said. "You don't strike me as the kind of kid who will be broken. I will expect you to excel."

"I'll do my best, Sergeant."

"That's all I ask, Son," said Sgt. Benoit. He looked toward a plan drawing of the barracks that was on the wall to the left of his desk. "You have bunk number 36. Find it, unpack and store your duffel, and relax. You're the only Second Class Midshipman in this year's flight orientation class. The others are all Third Class Midshipmen. Accordingly, I'll appoint you as Squadron Leader. Mess call is at 1800 hrs. You have two more hours to goof off. Starting tomorrow, you'll be working harder than you've ever worked before."

"Aye, aye, Sir," said Arthur. He brought himself back to attention.

"Dismissed," said Sgt. Benoit. Arthur executed a sharp about face and marched out of the office, closing the door behind him. He located his bunk and began unpacking his things and storing them neatly in the footlocker at the foot of his bed. He heard footsteps behind him and stood, turning to look. A naval officer wearing Lieutenant Commander's stripes, gold oak leaves on his collar, and aviator's wings on his chest, was walking up the aisle toward him, carrying a briefcase. Under the aviator's wings on his chest were three rows of ribbons. Arthur snapped to attention.

"As you were, Midshipman," said the officer. Arthur adopted the "at rest" position, feet apart, hands clasped behind the small of his back. "Just relax. Parade Rest is not necessary." Arthur relaxed. "I'm looking for Midshipman Second Class Arthur Cornwallis Harris III. Do you know him?"

"Sir, I am he, Sir," said Arthur. The officer extended his hand.

"Mr. Harris," said the officer, "I am Lieutenant Commander James Mason." Arthur took his hand, and they shook hands warmly. "I will be your flight instructor. I teach the class you will be taking and will be your in-cockpit instructor. I have been asked by ONI to accelerate your flight readiness." He looked around. They were alone in the barracks. "Like you, I am part of NOSI, reporting to Lieutenant Commander Thayer. After you are flight-ready, you and I will be deployed together."

"Mr. Mason, thank you," said Arthur. "I will do my best to be a good student and to learn all I can, as fast as I can." Mason sat on the bed and opened his brief case. From it he took two ring binders and handed them to Arthur.

"These are the texts from which I will be teaching. I am giving you copies so that you may study them. The other Midshipmen will be taking notes from my lectures and will study their notes. I want to make sure that you have the best material available so you can learn faster. Read the first two chapters this evening, as we will be covering them in class tomorrow morning. Tomorrow afternoon we will start flying."

"Sir, thank you again," said Arthur.

"You may curse me later for rushing you through," said Mason. "You are going to be in the air in combat before you are really ready for it." Arthur felt his heart skipping a beat and was very aware of the sweat running down his forehead. *Combat!* he thought. He felt both fear and excitement. He knew when he joined the Navy that he would face combat, but he didn't know it would be this soon. He hoped he would face it appropriately. This would surely help his career.

Other Midshipmen were arriving, straggling into the barracks. Arthur started leafing through the manuals he had been given. Mason stood and watched as the Midshipmen made their way to their own bunks. They seemed oblivious to the presence of the officer. Arthur closed the manual, placed it on his bunk, and jumped to attention.

"Attention!" he bellowed. "Officer on deck." All the Midshipmen snapped to attention, moving to stand at the foot of their bunks.

"At ease," commanded Mason. "I am Lieutenant Commander James Mason. I will be giving you your classroom training and am one of the flight instructors. Your days will be divided into four segments. The first segment you will spend with Sergeant Benoit. It will start one hour before breakfast mess, at 0500. You will spend another hour after breakfast with Sergeant Benoit, and you will report to me for classroom training at 0800. When we break for the lunch mess, you will be back under Sergeant Benoit's supervision until an hour after lunch. He will march you to the airfield and return you to me for actual flight familiarization. That is all, gentlemen. I will see you tomorrow morning." As Mason spoke, Sgt. Benoit left his office and proceeded up the aisle to stand behind Mason. As Mason finished speaking, he turned to face Benoit, at which point Benoit snapped to attention. "Sgt. Benoit, they are all yours." Mason executed an about-face and marched out of the building.

"Mr. Harris," bellowed Benoit, "I appoint you squadron leader. Take the men outside and form them up in a double column."

"Aye, aye, Sir," said Arthur. "Squadron, form up in four rows outside." The Midshipmen filed outside, forming up in four rows with their backs to the building. Arthur marched around to the front. All stood at attention. Benoit made his way around the formation, looking at each of the men, and took his place in front, about three feet in front of Arthur, but facing Arthur and the formation.

"You are all lousy excuses for officer candidates," bellowed Benoit. "I will change that while you are under my supervision. I will either make you or break you. Each of you will decide which it will be for you. Squadron, right face." Each of them, except for Arthur, executed a right face. "Mr. Harris, assume the lead position."

"Sir! Aye, aye, Sir," said Arthur loudly. He saluted Benoit, who returned the salute. Arthur executed a right face, marched to the head of the column, executed a second right face, took two steps to the center of the column and executed a left face. He was centered on the formation, at its head.

"Forward, Harch," bellowed the Sergeant. "Left, right, left, right, left...left...left..." The column marched smartly down the road toward the Mess Hall. When they reached it, Sergeant Benoit called, "Column, halt!" and "Left face." The Midshipmen were in formation facing him. "You will enter the building single file and enter the serving line. At ease. Dismissed."

Arthur soon knew that he would not starve to death during training. The chow was simple, but plentiful – "all you can eat." The servers piled his plate high with meat loaf, mashed potatoes, collard greens and green beans, with cornbread on the side, cherry pie for dessert, and iced tea. Coffee was available from a serving spigot in the middle of the floor. The Midshipmen ate at trestle tables very much like picnic tables. They could go back for seconds, but their time in the Mess Hall was limited to thirty minutes.

After Mess they wandered back singly or in small groups to their barracks, where Arthur studied feverishly for the next morning's classes. *This is my opportunity to begin a career of excellence,* he thought, *to make a name for myself and to realize my dream career. I must not blow it, and I must not allow distractions, fear, or idle thoughts to interfere. I must not allow myself time to think or to second guess. The decision has been made.* He pored over the material in the first few chapters, concentrating and absorbing as much of the information as possible.

"Lights Out" was scheduled for 2200 hrs., so before that time he put his books away. The Midshipmen removed their outer clothes to sleep in their underwear. A few had brought pajamas, but pajamas were not on the list of things that they had been given to bring. Their underwear was "regulation" underwear, white briefs and white tee shirts. Sgt. Benoit walked through as the men were preparing for bed and told those with pajamas not to wear them.

"Sailors wear their underwear for sleeping so they can jump more quickly into their uniforms if 'Battle Stations' is sounded," he said. "Wearing pajamas would delay you."

The next morning, they were brusquely awakened at 0500 by Sgt. Benoit blowing a police whistle while a bugle sounded Reveille somewhere outside. Sgt. Benoit told them they had fifteen minutes to get into working uniform and assemble in front of the building. They did so, sleepy-eyed. Sgt. Benoit started them off marching as he had the night before, and after a few paces ordered, "Double time, HARCH!" After a few more paces, he bellowed an explanation to the trotting Midshipmen.

"We are going to run for five miles," he said. "After that, we'll shower and go to the Mess Hall for breakfast." He kept up a steady chant to keep them all in rhythm. Before the first mile was up, the formation had spread a bit, with many gasping for breath, including Arthur. Distance running had never been his thing. Arthur gritted his teeth and tried to keep his breathing steady as he trotted onward. When the formation reached the point that it was hard to recognize it as a formation, Sgt. Benoit called a halt and got them all back in formation. All except Benoit were gasping for breath.

"You weaklings are sorry excuses for Navy men," he bellowed. "Now we're going to start running again, and we aren't going to stop until we've completed the five-mile circuit. By the end of the week, you'll all be singing all the way. Now, forward HARCH!" The men began marching forward. "Double time, HARCH!" he commanded. They all started trotting in step again. Sgt. Benoit started chanting in time with the cadence of the feet:
"When Master Chief was 101
He did PT just for fun.
When Master Chief was 102
He did PT better 'n you.
When Master Chief was 103
He did PT better 'n me.
When Master Chief was 104
He did PT more and more.
When Master Chief was 105
He did PT to stay alive.
When Master Chief was 106
He did PT just for kicks.
When Master Chief was 107
He up and died and went to heaven.
When Master Chief was 108
St. Peter let him in the pearly gate.
Left – left – your left, right, left,

Left – left – your left, right, left,
"Can't tell your left from your right, you lout?
Just follow Master Chief about."
"Mr. Harris, sound cadence."

Arthur began to chant.
"Left – left – your left, right, left,
"Left – left – your left, right, left,
"Can't tell your left from your right, you lout?
"Just follow Master Chief about.
"If you stagger, don't fall out,
"'Cause this is what your life's about.
"Left – left – your left right left,
"Left – left – your left right left,
"Sergeant now will take a turn."

Sgt. Benoit started another cadence chant, and at its completion, handed it off again to Arthur, who picked it up, improvised a couple of verses again, and handed it back to the Sergeant. This continued, with the Sergeant handing off first to one Midshipman, then another. The miles passed by with less effort, because they were all thinking of the cadence chants rather than their fatigue. By the time they got back to the barracks, real fatigue had set in, but they were still in formation – and they hadn't even had breakfast yet.

Sgt. Benoit told them that they would receive and pack their parachutes that afternoon, and the next morning, they would do their run wearing their parachute packs. After a few days of that, they would transition to the standard 50-pound combat pack.

"By the time you leave Corpus Christi Naval Air Station you will no longer be weaklings. You will no longer be boys. You will be men. You'll lose what fat you have, and each of you will gain at least ten pounds of muscle. Now fall out, shower, and dress for mess. Dismissed!"

Three of the Midshipmen fell to the ground at that point, too tired to move otherwise. Sgt. Benoit stalked up to them, nudged them with his feet, and barked, "Get up, you stupid idiots. Do that again and I'll send you packing and out of the Navy. You'll get drafted, and the Army will teach you to march, and you'll spend the rest of your military enlistment marching instead of sailing." The three scrambled to their feet and staggered off in the direction of the showers at the end of the building, where they had to wait at the end of the line.

In class that morning, Arthur answered the instructor's questions easily, having studied his textbook well. That afternoon, they received their parachutes and learned how to pack them, and then they took their first flights in the T-34 trainer aircraft, each with an instructor in the back seat, and a Midshipman in the front set.

Mason showed Arthur how to walk around the plane and inspect it, testing the flaps, looking at the disk brakes, and making sure the plane was ready. He showed Arthur how to put on his flight helmet and adjust the throat microphone. Dressed in flight suits (more like jump suits, as they were not pressure suits), they climbed into the cockpit and strapped in, plugged in their headsets and microphones, and Mason instructed Arthur in the steps required to start the engine and test the flaps using the controls. He worked through the pre-flight checklist with Arthur, and they closed the canopy.

Mason had Arthur taxi the plane to the end of the runway, and Mason took back the controls and talked through everything he was doing as he ran the plane down the runway and took off. He explained the takeoff flight pattern, and had Arthur take the controls and fly the plane away from the airfield, maintaining a steady climb rate. He talked Arthur around into the landing flight pattern with a steady descent rate, before taking the controls himself and talking through everything he was doing as he landed the plane. After braking at the end of the runway, he had Arthur taxi the plane back to the head of the runway.

"This time you'll take her off, Mr. Harris," said Mason. "Do you think you can?"

"I think so, Sir," said Arthur. "If I do something wrong, will you be able to take over?"

"Yes," said Mason, "but if you stall her too close to the ground I won't be able to recover and we'll crash. Make sure your revs and airspeed are appropriate and your angle of ascent is correct, and you'll be fine. Do you remember the necessary takeoff speed?"

"Yes, Sir," said Arthur, "You took her to a ground-speed of 85 knots and lifted her off gently."

"Exactly, Mr. Harris. You have the stick. Call the tower and get clearance."

Arthur did so, and taxied the plane onto the runway, ran the engine revolutions up to speed with the brakes engaged, and released the brakes. The plane began accelerating down the runway. About half way down, they had reached the speed of 85 knots and the aircraft had lifted its tail so that it was running horizontally on its two main wheels only. Arthur pulled back gently on the stick. The nose lifted slightly and the sound of wheels on tarmac ceased. They were airborne. Arthur carefully navigated the take-off flight pattern, and then left the airfield's air space and continued climbing for a minute.

"Mr. Mason," he said into the microphone in his flight helmet, "Do you want me to keep going, or turn back and land?"

"Go back and land, using the landing pattern I showed you. Then, we'll do it again."

"Aye, aye, Sir." Arthur banked, turned, and called the tower for landing instructions. He entered the landing pattern when the tower instructed him and began a steady descent. Everything went perfectly until he was but a couple of feet over the runway, where the plane stopped descending. Arthur felt a moment of panic.

"Push her down, Mr. Harris," said Mason. "You've got an air cushion under the wings and it is trying to keep you from touching down. You have to *push* her down the last few feet. Idle the engine and push her down." Arthur reduced the throttle to idle speed and pushed the stick forward until the wheels screeched on the tarmac and he applied the brakes. The plane cruised down the runway, reducing speed, until he reached the taxiway and turned onto it.

"Again, Sir?" he asked.

"Again, Mr. Harris," said Mason. Arthur taxied back to the head of the runway.

After two more repeats without incident, Mason had him take off and keep going. When they reached an elevation of 8,000 feet, he had Arthur level the plane out, and practice turning and returning to course. Arthur was flying lazy, elongated figure eights.

"Do you remember the textbook description of the loop?" asked Mason.

"Yes, Sir," said Arthur.

"I'll take the stick," said Mason. "I'll talk through it once and then have you do it." Mason increased the throttle, building up speed until they had reached 270 knots. "This aircraft's 'do-not-exceed speed' is 280 knots, so we'll stay a little under that. We will need pretty good speed for this maneuver." He pushed the throttle to maximum and built up airspeed to 280 knots. He pulled back sharply on the stick. The plane's nose came up and continued going up until they were flying straight up, their airspeed slowing rapidly. Mason held the stick in position, and the nose continued its trajectory until they were upside down, with the nose of the aircraft pointing in the direction from which they had come. They were regaining speed and descending again, building speed rapidly until they had reached the spot at which the maneuver had begun, flying right-side-up in their original direction at 270 knots again. They had flown a vertical circle.

"Now you do it," said Mason. "You have the stick." Arthur did exactly what Mason had done, executing the loop perfectly. "Very good," said Mason. "Imagine that you are flying along, minding your own business, and you discover a Soviet MiG on your tail, closing to shooting distance. This maneuver is a good one to attempt to break his lock on you and put you behind him, unless he also does a loop, in which case you are screwed. Now we'll do a barrel roll."

The barrel roll rotates the plane without changing direction, as if it were flying a spiral around the surface of a barrel. Mason executed it, and Arthur did one. Next, Mason had Arthur do a half loop, followed by a half-barrel roll so that the plane came out of the maneuver flying in the opposite direction at the original elevation. It was a vertical half-circle with a descending half-spiral at the end.

"That was something called the Immelmann Turn," said Mason. "It's a little bit tricky. You did a half loop, and went into a half barrel roll, but keeping the stick forward. The result is that you slid out of the loop in a spiral that put you right back where you were at the start of the maneuver but flying in the opposite direction. Your friendly MiG would have trouble following you. If he did, and you had altitude, you could go into a reverse loop, going down in a half circle and roll out of it again to put you back on your original heading but at a lower altitude. Most dogfighting maneuvers are a combination of portions of loops, barrel rolls, and turns. You can put half-maneuvers together in unexpected sequences that will be difficult for your attacker to follow and keep you in his gunsights.

"The Immelmann Maneuver is named after Max Immelmann, a World War I dogfight pilot, who invented another maneuver entirely, but slightly similar to this, that's now called a wing-over."

It took Arthur three tries to get the Immelmann Maneuver down pat. Mason proceeded to teach him other aerobatic maneuvers designed for the dogfights of plane-to-plane combat, before having Arthur fly the plane back to the airfield and land it. Arthur taxied the plane back to the hangar, parked it, and walked with Mason back to the barracks.

"Mr. Harris," said Mason. "You have a talent for flying and aerobatics. How far have you gone in the textbook I gave you?"

"About half way," said Arthur.

"Can you finish it tonight?"

"I can if Sgt. Benoit lets me," said Arthur.

"I'll have a word with him," said Mason. "Finish the textbook tonight and I'll have you take the written exam on it tomorrow. If you pass it, I can take you on to solo and start you on a jet." Arthur's eyes widened. "I'm going to give you a short course on the Phantom II jet in reconnaissance configuration, and then you and I are going to a carrier off the coast of Viet Nam, except that officially, you will never be there. You will have been here, at Corpus Christi NAS. Welcome to NOSI."

"Isn't a lot more training required before jets?" asked Arthur.

"Normally, yes," said Mason. "You're getting a very abbreviated version of flight training. You're not going to be a pilot. You just need to know your way around the aircraft so you can take the stick if the pilot gets shot."

He went on to brief Arthur on the current situation in Viet Nam. The US had combat troops in Viet Nam acting as advisors to the Army of the Republic of Viet Nam in their battle against the Communist insurgents, the Viet

Cong. In 1963, troops of the People's Republic of Viet Nam, North Vietnam, had invaded Laos and upgraded the trail that led through the mountains from North Viet Nam to South Viet Nam through Laos and Cambodia, near their borders with Viet Nam. Approximately 40,000 North Vietnamese troops had used the trail to infiltrate South Viet Nam and were embedded in Viet Cong guerilla units. In 1964, North Vietnam sent regular North Vietnamese Army units totaling about 100,000 men along the upgraded trail to South Viet Nam, where they massed in remote areas, and began striking out from there to destroy the "strategic hamlets" that had been built by the US and the South Vietnamese government.

In August of 1964, two US warships were fired on by North Vietnamese PT boats in the Gulf of Tonkin in international waters off the coast of North Viet Nam. President Johnson had used this as an excuse to push the Gulf of Tonkin Resolution through Congress, gaining authorization to commit ground forces to direct warfare in South Vietnam without the need to declare war. A US troop buildup was underway, and significant fighting was taking place. The Communists in Viet Nam were backed by the Soviet Union, but the Communist insurgents in Laos and Cambodia were backed by Red China. The US was in the war against the Viet Cong guerrillas and the North Vietnamese Army, Russian proxies. The US was being careful not to take action against the Communist-Chinese-backed rebels in the neighboring countries. In addition, no authorization had been given to place troops in North Viet Nam. US military action was authorized by Congress only in South Viet Nam and at sea along the coast.

The CIA was doing overflights with U-2 planes at high altitude, out of range of anti-aircraft missiles in the hands of the northern forces, but the cameras at the U-2's altitude had difficulty penetrating the canopy of the jungle. NOSI was starting to fly low-level surveillance

flights along the Ho Chi Minh trail to pinpoint movements of troops and supply convoys so US bombers could
try to take them out, but that meant flying over Thai and
Cambodian air space. Arthur was being accelerated so
that he could play a part in the low-level surveillance over
non-combatant territory, as a "deep cover" operation that
would not be acknowledged officially. The plan was for
NOSI to take over all such surveillance, leaving regular
ONI pilots to perform surveillance over North and South
Vietnam. Arthur, a few other Midshipmen, and a few selected ONI pilots were being transferred to NOSI to beef
up the new, super-secret unit.

The bombing operation was called Operation Com-
mando. Other US bombing operations targeted North Viet
Nam itself, aiming to destroy its industrial capacity to
support their war effort. Arthur was familiar with the
cameras used for low-level surveillance, because he had
worked with their output in Guantanamo. Mason would
fly an F-4 Phantom II jet, similar to the Crusader jets that
flew low-level unarmed surveillance from Guantanamo
when Arthur was there. The F-4, however, was a faster,
more powerful and more maneuverable plane.

The next morning, Arthur passed his written exam
with a perfect score. That afternoon, he prepared to solo
in the T-34. Mason watched him do the pre-flight inspection of the aircraft.

"Mr. Harris," he said, "I'll be accompanying you in
another T-34 as you do your solo. Now get aboard and
let's get in the air."

"Aye, aye, Sir," said Arthur. He climbed into the
cockpit and went through his pre-flight checklist. Then,
he closed the canopy and radioed the tower. After he received takeoff clearance, he took off, and following instructions from the tower, banked right by 45 degrees and
began his climb to altitude. He glanced out to the right
and then to the left to make sure there were no other air-

craft in his immediate vicinity and saw another T-34 off his left wingtip, flying in formation with him. A voice sounded in his earphones.

"Tango One Three Fiver," said the voice, "Tango One Three Six on your starboard wingtip. This is Lieutenant Commander Mason. Just ignore me."

"Tango One Three Six, roger. Tango One Three Fiver out." Arthur continued on the pre-planned flight route. He flew out ten miles, executed a 135-degree right turn, and flew straight until he had passed the airfield well to his right, and executed a 90-degree right turn and called the airfield for landing instructions. He descended as ordered and made another 135-degree right turn to enter the landing sequence. He landed the plane and taxied to the parking position. Mason's plane pulled in to park next to him. Both exited their planes. Mason walked over to Arthur and extended his hand.

"Congratulations, Mr. Harris," he said. "You executed a textbook solo flight. Drinks are on me. Let's take off our flight gear and go to the Officers' Club."

"Aye, aye, sir," said Arthur.

The morning after that, he began training in earnest with Mason, who had turned the class over to another instructor and would concentrate on getting Arthur flight-ready. Mason and Arthur stood beside the F-4 Phantom II jet, while Mason told Arthur about the powerful aircraft.

"This is the McDonnell Douglas F-4 Phantom II. You saw Crusaders in Guantanamo that were being used as low-level surveillance craft. Both planes are excellent fighter planes. The Phantom II takes a crew of two but can be flown by a single pilot. Because of the two-seat configuration, she is easily used as a photo-surveillance plane, with the photographer in the back seat. The Crusader is normally a single-seater but is made also in a two-seat version for training and surveillance. This Phantom is equipped with special, high-resolution inboard-mounted cameras for photo surveillance. The Phantom is powered by powerful twin turbojets. Her official maximum speed is Mach 2.23, about 1,472 mph, or about 1,300 knots, at 40,000 feet. However, the absolute speed record was set with a Phantom at more than 1,600 mph. Her cruise speed is 585 mph, or 506 knots. She set the record for Atlantic to Pacific speed run at a cruising speed of almost 870 mph, making the continental crossing in two hours and 47 minutes, with tanker refueling *en route.* She has a combat radius of 367 nautical miles, but she can fly 1,403 nautical miles at her cruising speed with three external fuel tanks. Officially, her top altitude is 60,000 feet but a Phantom set the record for altitude in a zoom climb at 98,557 feet after accelerating to Mach 2.5, or 1,650 mph, from 47,000 feet. When the engines stopped for lack of oxygen at 90,000 feet, he coasted her to her altitude record and nosed down, restarting the engines at 70,000 feet. These are all unofficial numbers. All the official numbers I have given you are *official* numbers. As you know, official statistics for military aircraft understate their capabilities. Their actual capabilities are Classified. The records I have told you are Classified Top Secret. She can climb at the rate of 41,300 feet per minute. Her record climb rate, set in 1961, from takeoff to 90,000 feet, was 371 seconds. No other jet can match her acceleration, speed, and climb rate, although she sacrifices some maneuverability for these capabilities. That said, she can accelerate out of a fight she doesn't like, and no one can catch her. She can be armed with a whole arsenal of weapons, from her 20mm, six-barreled Gatling cannon, through a variety of missiles and bombs, including nuclear weapons. She's a lean, mean, powerful fighting machine. She can fly as slowly as 120 to 130 knots and accelerate quickly to Mach 2. She can accelerate to supersonic speed flying straight up. You'll have fun with her.

This model of the F-4 was specially built for surveillance work. The normal Phantoms are not equipped with internal guns, relying on missiles and bombs alone. Her one flaw is a tendency to stall and spin at low speed, so you never want to fly her at her minimum speed, because a turn at that speed can cause her to stall, spin and crash. If you are flying slow and must turn, you should accelerate into the turn to maintain lift. You don't want to spin, crash and burn *outside* the Officers' Club. That's the name of a very potent cocktail." Arthur laughed. Mason continued. "However, except for practice, *you* will be flying her only if something happens to her pilot – me. I'll do my best to stay alive, and you had better do the same. Now, let's go through the pre-flight check list. You studied the manual?"

"Yes, Sir," said Arthur, his heart racing both with fear and excitement.

"What are the first three checks in the pre-flight check list?"

"The ground crew will have checked the exterior of the aircraft, and the manual does not say so, but I would do the same walk-around we did with the T-34."

"Good, but not necessary," said Mason. "Go on."

"Once at the cockpit, the first thing is to check the ejection seat, following the ejection seat checklist and notifying the ground or deck crew if anything is wrong with it. The next thing is to make sure that the center mirror in the forward canopy is tilted back sufficiently to allow the canopy to close, and make sure the canopy is clean. If it is not, have the ground or deck crew clean it. The third thing is to make sure the cockpit is clean, and if not, have it cleaned."

"Good. What do you do next?"

"I strap myself in, making sure my pressure suit is connected. I check to see all straps are snug."

"Good. Next?"

"I make sure all loose items and equipment are strapped down or otherwise secured so they don't float around during negative-G maneuvers."

"Go on."

"The crew chief will remove the pins from the ejection seat, but I, myself, will stow my pin bag." Removing the pins from an ejection seat was like pulling the pin on a hand grenade. After the pins are pulled, the explosive charges and rockets that will propel the seat out of the plane are armed. They will ignite when one pulls the ejection handle.

"And then?"

"I will follow the printed checklist. There are too many items to check to depend on memory."

"Good. Let's get started."

The rest of the day was spent in touch-and-go landing practice, with Arthur in the front seat and Mason in the back. In a touch-and-go landing, the plane touches down, and the pilot guns her and takes off again without braking. Mason explained that if he landed on the carrier and missed the arresting cable, he would have to gun her and take off, coming around for another attempt.

At the end of the day, Mason told him to skip mess with the other midshipmen and join him at the Officer's Mess, wearing his dress white officer's uniform. Mason wore the more formal Dinner Dress uniform that resembles a white-tie and tails outfit but without the tails. Over dinner, Mason told him that the next day they would practice carrier landings on a simulated carrier deck with arresting cable. Once Arthur mastered that, he would start flying the bird and learning combat maneuvers.

Every day, when not in flight training, Arthur spent time in the flight simulator, honing his flight skills. By the end of his third day, Arthur soloed in the Phantom II, taking off from and landing on the simulated carrier deck.

Mason flew with him for one more flight before the end of the day. After he had taken off and left the takeoff flight pattern, Mason told him to head out over the Gulf, turn northeast and ascend to 40,000 feet on a course to Houston, and accelerate to supersonic speed. At that altitude, the landscape sped by below.

Soon they were near Galveston Bay, and Mason had him turn toward Houston, decelerate to subsonic speed and call the tower at Ellington Air Force Base to get clearance for flying in Houston airspace under visual flight rules, telling Arthur he could do some sight-seeing. He was given permission, slowed to subsonic speed, and executed a dive to an altitude of 2,000 feet over the southwestern suburbs. Arthur descended slowly to 1,000 feet, searching the skies for any aircraft in the area and finding his way using ground landmarks, starting with the readily-recognizable campus of Rice University, and thence out Main Street to the Austins' subdivision.

He found the Austin house, dropped to a few hundred feet altitude, slowed to 200 knots, and flew over the house. He could see Hilda in the back yard, sunbathing. She sat up, shading her eyes to watch the noisy jet fighter approaching, which circled around and approached again. He banked right, left, right, waggling his wings in greeting, and she waved back. In a moment, however, he was past her. After a sweep of his eyes to establish that the skies were clear, he rammed the throttle to full and entered a vertical climb. Hilda watched him rise like a rocket into the sky, certain that it must be her Arthur showing off. When he reached a speed just below Mach 1, he eased the throttle. He was not permitted to exceed the speed of sound over land.

"I guess that was your girlfriend?" asked Mason.

"Yes," said Arthur.

"It's time to head back to base."

"Aye, aye, Sir," said Arthur. He climbed to 35,000 feet and flew south.

After they landed, Mason walked with him to the pilot's room, where they took off parachute packs and pressure suits and hung them on hooks in the flight gear storage room. From there, they went to their quarters, dressed, and met at the Officers' Club, where Mason said he would buy Arthur a celebratory drink. They settled onto bar stools and Mason waved the bartender over.

"My student, Mr. Harris, here, soloed today in the Phantom II," said Mason. Bring him a 'Spin, Crash and Burn' – and bring one for me, too." The bartender left to mix the drink, and Mason told Arthur, "That's a wicked drink, but tastes very good. You should only have one. It is seven different liquors and liqueurs blended with tropical fruit juices and topped with 151-proof rum." The bartender returned with two large glasses filled with strangely colored liquid. Mason raised his glass and so did Arthur.

"Here's to violating the law of gravity and living to tell about it," said Mason. They clinked glasses and Arthur took a cautious sip. It tasted good, but the heady fumes of the alcohol warned Arthur not to drink it too fast. They drank slowly, talking over the details of flying the Phantom II. They chased the drink with rare T-bone steaks, charred on the surface, with baked potatoes and vegetables, enhanced by a good red wine, and followed it all with ice cream, augmented with a warmed brandy on the side. Arthur slept well that night.

The next day Mason had Arthur practice carrier landings using the flight simulator, and then, after lunch, Arthur, with Mason in the back seat, flew the Phantom II to an auxiliary airfield where a mockup of a carrier deck had been constructed, complete with arresting cables and catapult, where he practiced landing and taking off.

The following morning, Arthur flew a course out over the Gulf on a bearing given him by Mason to intercept the carrier USS Lexington, a World War II era carrier. She had seen extensive service in the Pacific before being re-assigned to the Gulf of Mexico for use in pilot training, with Pensacola Naval Air Station as her home port.

Arthur contacted the air controller on the carrier, who informed him that he was visible on radar. The controller gave him a modification to his course and speed and or-dered him to descend to 5,000 feet altitude. A short while later, the controller ordered him to come down to 1,000 feet in preparation for final approach.

Arthur computed his final approach airspeed, taking into account the remaining fuel weight, the external load that consisted of a full load of dummy missiles, and the landing configuration for the carrier deck. He slowed to about 230 knots, lowered the gear and adjusted the flaps, descending to the altitude prescribed, in order to intersect the glide path at a comfortable distance behind the carrier. He slowed to the final approach airspeed a mile or two before intercepting the final glide path, cross-checking his angle of attack (AOA) and airspeed.

Arthur used his rudder and ailerons to roll out smooth-ly onto the final approach glide path, reducing power slightly and increasing the AOA to maintain the ON SPEED indication with the desired flight path angle. He lined up with the flight deck, approaching from the rear of the carrier. He worked to maintain optimum glide path using power and pitch, flying a 2-1/2- to 3-degree glide slope, which resulted in a descent rate of about 700 feet per minute. He kept power at about 83% and used small changes in engine RPM to control his glide.

As he drew closer, he panicked momentarily, because the slow pitching of the ship raised and lowered the deck perceptibly. He would have to time his touchdown pre-cisely so as not to reach the ship with the flight deck above the level of his wheels, or with the deck so low that he would have to push the Phantom II down to a hard landing. He adjusted his speed slightly so that he would arrive at landing point with the flight deck approaching its lowest point, so that he would touch down when the deck was neither rising nor falling, and the deck would then rise, preventing the plane from bouncing on landing.

He lowered the landing gear and applied full flaps, increasing the Angle of Attack (AOA) to maintain lift, simultaneously reducing power and increasing back stick pressure to achieve the ideal AOA and to maintain the computed airspeed. He adjusted his speed again due to the rolling of the ship, so that the flight deck would be level when he touched down. Even so, the time between entering his final glide path and touchdown seemed very short, and he was adjusting his AOA, speed, and angle of descent even as he came over the fantail. As his wheels touched the deck, he cut power to idle with one hand and deployed the drag chute with the other, setting the flaps to full and applying brakes as the arresting cable caught the tail hook. The plane slowed abruptly and stopped, slamming his body forward as if he had hit a brick wall. They were down.

Arthur jettisoned the drag chute and the deck crew hauled it in. It would be inspected and re-packed for reuse. Arthur opened the canopy.

"Reposition the plane for takeoff," commanded Mason.

"Aye, aye, Sir," replied Arthur. With the help of the ground crew, the plane was moved from the landing deck to the takeoff runway. The deck crew repacked the drag chute, reinstalled it and hooked the plane to the catapult. Arthur repeated the pre-flight checklist, announcing each checked item to Mason. Then, when all was ready, he closed the canopy and gave the "thumbs up" sign to the deck crew. He contacted the flight controller.

At the appropriate moment, he revved his engines with brakes on full, and on the signal from the deck crew, released his brakes at the moment that the catapult engaged, and pushed the throttle all the way to full. The back of his seat slammed into him with almost enough force to knock the wind out of him, and the plane shot forward and off the end of the runway, dropping momentarily toward the water before the afterburners kicked in and the powerful engines and the lift of the wings lifted him upward. He gained altitude rapidly, exiting the flight pattern assigned for takeoff, rolling out to the heading given him by the flight controller. Arthur switched his mike to "suit-to-suit" mode.

"Mr. Mason, Sir, should I go around again?" he asked.

"Yes, Mr. Harris. We'll do one more landing and takeoff. If the second goes as well as the first did, I'll certify you for carrier work and we'll switch places. I want to be sure you can land this thing from the back seat, if I am disabled. Then we can get on our way."

The second landing and takeoff went exactly as the first. They exchanged places and went around again. Again, Arthur, flying the plane from the back seat, executed a perfect landing.

"Mr. Harris," said Mason, "Congratulations. You are my first pupil to make his first carrier landings and takeoffs perfectly. Usually that takes months of training. I knew you were capable of doing it, and I'm glad you did it. Fly her home and let's go open a bottle of champagne."

"Aye, aye, Sir," said Arthur.

"Just don't get cocky. You are *not* a pilot and are *not* *qualified* to be one. You are only qualified to ride in the back seat and take over controls if I am disabled."

From the Officers' Club, Arthur called Hilda and told her about his flying experiences.

"It sounds like you have been having fun," she said.

"Yes, I have. Next, I'll be putting what I have learned to work. I will be doing intense work with the Phantom until I have really mastered her. I have to be able to fly her to ride in the back seat as a navigator."

"Be careful," said Hilda. "I don't want to have to attend a military funeral."

"I will be careful," said Arthur. "I don't want to be the subject of a military funeral, either. There are always risks in being in the Navy, but I'll be as careful as circumstances allow. I'll see you in August, on my way home."

CHAPTER 14

SURVEILLANCE

June and July 1965
Pacific Fleet and "Not in Cambodia"

On the long flight to Hawaii, Arthur sat in the mesh
sling seat of the cavernous C-130 transport plane and tried
to sleep, but couldn't because the seat was not designed
for sleeping. Military transport flights don't have First
Class sections. They don't even have coach class sections.
They're bare-bones aircraft fitted with webbed seats slung
so that the passengers face the rear – it's a "no class"
section. Members of the military fondly refer to the class
of service as "Cargo Class."

The C-130 in which they were flying was filled with
troops on their way to Viet Nam, along with an
assortment of cargo items strapped to the deck – mortars,
artillery pieces, jeeps and field generators, along with
large packages covered with tarpaulins, all strapped (or
chained) down.

Mason sat next to him, reading a pulp novel. Arthur
spent the time reviewing everything he knew about flying
the Phantom II jet. He relived in his mind his instructional
flights, his practice landings on the simulated carrier deck,
the aerial maneuvers, the dogfighting practice, and,
finally, the three carrier landings. Eventually, the drone of
the engines subdued his awareness and he dozed off.

He awoke with a start when the plane touched down on the runway at Pearl Harbor. After it had finished taxiing, he unbuckled, awakened Mason, and retrieved his duffel bag from where it was tied down against the bulkhead beneath his seat. The rear ramp of the plane descended, and they and all the troops walked down it to the tarmac. A waiting jeep ferried Arthur and Mason to a Navy version of the Boeing 707 passenger jet, called the E-6, equipped and used for anti-submarine warfare (ASW). Soon, they were again airborne, headed for Viet Nam.

The interior of the 707 was of the same "design" as the C-130 – bare, with mesh seats. Arthur and Mason were the only passengers. There was not much room for passengers. The plane's hold was filled with ASW electronic gear and recording devices and the sailors who manned that gear. The other troops who had flown with them to Pearl would have a couple of hours to stretch their legs and would re-board the C-130 for the long flight to Da Nang.

Eventually, their E-6, a faster plane than the C-130, landed at Da Nang Air Base and Arthur and Mason transferred to a waiting Phantom II jet. Mason had Arthur take the front seat, pilot her through takeoff and then gave him a flight path to the position of the carrier USS Midway in the Tonkin Gulf at Point Yankee, commonly called Yankee Station, where the carrier cruised in circles with Task Force 77, the Viet Nam Carrier Battle Force. She was part of the 7th Fleet, which operated in the southwestern Pacific, and was typically stationed at Point Yankee. The 7th Fleet was commonly called the Tonkin Gulf Yacht Club. It was from Point Yankee that US carriers launched air surveillance flights and air strikes, mostly on North Viet Nam. Air support for operations in South Viet Nam was usually provided by Air Force jets flying from nine different US Air Force bases in South Viet Nam.

As they approached the Midway, Mason told Arthur to make the carrier landing. Arthur contacted the Midway and proceeded to execute the landing. He executed it as perfectly as he had the training landings in the Gulf of Mexico. After they climbed down from the cockpit, Mason shook Arthur's hand.

"Mr. Harris," he said. "You're not officially a pilot, but I'm happy to have you as my backup pilot. You're as good as any pilot I have trained."

"Thank you, Mr. Mason," said Arthur. "It is my privilege to serve with you."

A helmeted sailor waved them toward the superstructure and opened a hatchway for them to enter. Another climbed into their plane and maneuvered it onto the elevator that lowered the plane to the deck below for fueling and mechanical service. As they entered the hatchway, an officer with Captain's insignia, four broad gold bars on his epaulets, eagles on his shirt collar points and the gold braid called "scrambled eggs" on the brim of his officer's ball cap, greeted them. Mason and Arthur saluted the flag aft and the Captain, who returned the salute.

"Permission to come aboard, Sir," said Mason.

"Permission granted, gentlemen," replied the Captain. "I am Captain O'Brien, Commanding Officer of the Midway. Welcome aboard." They shook hands.

"Captain," said Mason, "I am Lt. Cdr. James Mason. This," he gestured toward Arthur, "is Midshipman First Class Arthur Harris. We're both ONI."

"It is a pleasure to meet you, gentlemen," said the Captain, looking curiously at Arthur. "I guess I must assume that you are both not here," he said. He told Arthur and Mason that they would be flying surveillance flights over the Ho Chi Minh trail over North Viet Nam,

Laos and Cambodia, and that he would give them their envelope of orders when they were in his cabin.

"You will never officially be in Laotian or Cambodian airspace, or even here aboard my ship," said the Captain. "If you are shot down, and we cannot retrieve you without risk of official exposure, you will be on your own and will either escape, making your way back to Viet Nam, or you will become North Vietnamese prisoners of war. You want to avoid that at all costs. They do not treat their prisoners well. Once you return, you will not have been there. Do you understand? Do you both fully accept the mission as described?"

"Yes, Captain," said Mason, "I do."

"Yes, Captain," said Arthur. "This is my chosen career path in the Navy, and I understand the risks." The Captain looked steadily at Arthur.

"You are both here to launch the first deployment of a new special group within ONI," he continued. "I don't know what it is called, and I don't know why it is being formed, but I do not need to know, and so I don't know. What I know is that Regular Navy aviators are not allowed to fly over Cambodia or Laos. Good luck, Gentlemen. Go with God. Seaman Culligan, here," he motioned at the sailor standing beside and slightly behind him "will show you to your stateroom." Soon, Arthur and Mason were in their cozy little stateroom, which actually was large enough for both of them to stand up, or for one to stand up and the other to sit down at the desk, at the same time.

The next morning, before dawn, Mason took the front seat and Arthur took the back seat of their Phantom II, equipped with large-frame cameras for photo surveillance. They had already studied the maps and navigation charts they would use to fly across North Viet Nam to pick up the Ho Chi Minh trail and fly south along it. Arthur, in the role of navigator, had plotted the course and flight plan. Their Phantom II was lightly armed, because they were not flying out intending to do combat, and to conserve weight to increase cruising range. Theirs was supposed to be purely a reconnaissance mission, ahead of the bombers. Their task was to locate and photograph movements of troops and supply convoys and radio their coordinates to the B-52 bombers that would be flying high overhead, just minutes behind them. Escorting the B-52s would be a squadron of Phantom II or Crusader combat jets, prepared to intercept any airborne attack on the bombers and to mop up with missiles anything that remained of the bombing targets after the bombers had passed over.

Mason and Arthur's reconnaissance Phantom II was equipped with the four internally-mounted Gatling cannons, plus two sidewinder missiles. The configuration was slightly different from the purpose-built surveillance jet on which Arthur had trained at Corpus. If they were attacked, they could fire their missiles at the attacking craft and run for safe airspace. Under no circumstances were they to engage the enemy more extensively when they could avoid engagement.

Mason piloted the plane from the carrier over the mainland, flying at high altitude. Just before intercepting the Ho Chi Minh trail, he banked hard left to the South and began a steep dive, pulling out about 1,000 feet above the jungle canopy. He descended to just about 200 feet above the treetops and proceeded south along the muddy trail. Arthur took photographs at five-mile intervals. After about 25 miles, they crossed the North Vietnam border into Thai airspace. After another 25 miles they overtook a convoy of supply trucks churning their way along the muddy path. Arthur photographed the convoy while Mason radioed the coordinates to the bombers. Two minutes later, they were past the convoy and about ten minutes later their plane felt the vibrations of the shock waves from the carpet bombing unleashed by the B-52s behind them. About every fifty miles, the exercise was repeated – another convoy, more photographing and the bombing behind them as they continued. In between each target, Arthur and Mason both scanned the skies and their radar displays for hostile craft but saw none.

After a little over 400 miles, they crossed into Cambodian airspace, and 200 miles later the trail took a slight left and crossed into South Viet Nam, now in the mountainous country along the border with Cambodia. Mason climbed steeply, regaining the 60,000 ft. cruising altitude, and turned back along the computed flight path to Yankee. They landed on the Midway, changed into their dress khaki uniforms and retired to the Officers' Wardroom where they met with the Chief Intelligence Officer, Commander Walter Franks, and debriefed him on their mission. All told, it had been a routine mission.

After lunch mess, they changed back to their work khakis and pressure suits and returned to their Phantom II, which the ground crew had prepared for a second flight. This time, they would start farther north, nearer to Hanoi, because there were industrial sites along the northern part of the trail that produced the armaments that travelled south along the trail to supply the enemy forces, and the Air Force planned to bomb them. They verified the industrial targets, and the B-52's made the ground tremble. They continued south along the trail. This flight also was routine, until they crossed into Cambodian air space.

"Bogey high at three o-clock!" reported Arthur to Mason. He had spotted the bogey on radar, had searched for it visually and found it. It was distant and looked like a MiG 17, diving toward them from a high altitude. Mason turned the plane onto a trajectory designed to intercept the MiG's path, climbing rapidly toward the MiG with afterburners blazing.

"It's locked on to attack," said Mason. "Too late to run." At a range of about three miles from the MiG Mason launched one Sidewinder missile, and the MiG turned sharply to its right. Mason turned left and fired the second missile on a path designed to intercept the MiG's new path and put the plane into a sharp dive, rolling sharply right and pulling out of the dive just above the canopy.

Looking up, they saw two small explosions from their missiles, but the MiG was still flying, undamaged. It had turned north, fleeing the scene. Mason called the carrier and reported the contact. He returned to the point where they had departed the trail and resumed the surveillance flight.

After another fifteen minutes or so, Arthur again spotted a bogey, approaching this time from the 10 o'clock position at high elevation, and reported it to Mason. Mason responded similarly to the way he had responded to the first bogey, turning and climbing to intercept it. As the planes closed to the appropriate distance for launching missiles, Mason rolled out to the right, and dived at a shallow angle with full throttle and afterburners before pulling back on the stick, increasing throttle, accelerating to over Mach 2 and passing to the MiG's rear as he began ascending into a loop. They had already expended their two missiles on the first MiG. He executed the Immelmann Maneuver, coming out about one mile behind the MiG and bearing down on the MiG's afterburners, which were now engaged. He kept full throttle, gaining rapidly on the MiG, which had a top speed that was subsonic. He climbed slightly to approach the MiG from above, and the MiG dived sharply. Arthur knew that the MiG 17 was much slower than the Phantom II, but much more maneuverable in a dogfight. Mason had anticipated the MiG's dive, and followed it right down, maintaining a position just above the MiG's flight path.

As he approached within 100 feet, he fired the Gatling cannon, stitching a line of holes up the fuselage of the MiG. He pulled out of the dive, executing a loop to bring him back behind the MiG, which was still diving at a steep angle toward the deck. Mason had cut the Phantom II's airspeed so that as he came out of the loop the two planes were traveling at the same speed. Mason again fired the cannon, throwing a burst of lead up the MiG's tailpipe, pulling up and to the right in level flight. Mason and Arthur watched as the MiG plowed into the jungle canopy and erupted in a crimson and yellow fireball blossom.

Mason reported the kill to the Carrier, and requested permission to abort the mission and return to the carrier for fuel. The permission was granted, and Mason turned the plane to a northeasterly heading to take them back across South Viet Nam toward Point Yankee. He asked Arthur to take the stick for the flight home to the Carrier.

"I'm a little shaky," said Mason. "You take over for a while and fly us home. I need to do a little deep breathing."

"How often have you been in aerial combat?" asked Arthur.

"This was my first time," said Mason. "I have flown about thirty-five surveillance missions, but until now I had successfully avoided combat. The Phantom II is much faster than the MiG 17, but the MiG is much more maneuverable. When I was approached by MiGs before, they weren't diving on me like this one was, and I was able to fire up afterburners and outrun them. The fastest plane the North has in this war is the MiG 21, which will do about the same top speed as the Phantom II, but they only have a few of them. Mostly we see MiG 15s, 17s and 19s. The Phantom II can easily outrun all of those, but their maneuverability gives them an advantage in a dogfight. Our surveillance missions are not supposed to be combat missions, so always before, I just ran away. This time I couldn't, because the MiG came at me from in front and high. I couldn't just climb and run. I had to intercept."

"Roger, Sir. Breathe easy and I'll fly her," said Arthur. *I'm a little shaky, too,* he thought, *but I can still fly the plane. Mason was in control of the situation, but I was just along for the ride.*

Back on the carrier deck, a group of pilots met them to clap Mason on the back and congratulate him. Both he and Arthur hit the sack early after dinner, so they would be rested and ready for an early start in the morning. The next day, they did their surveillance flight without incident. For days, Mason referred to their first flight together over the combat zone as their "unintentional combat flight."

Over the next couple of weeks, Mason and Arthur flew about twenty surveillance missions. Only twice more did they encounter MiGs, and both times they were able to run away without incident.

On Monday of the third week, a MiG 21 dived at them from ahead, mimicking the maneuver of the first MiG they had encountered. Mason responded as he had before. This MiG, however, was much faster than the one before, able to match the Phantom II maneuver for maneuver. Mason maneuvered through a host of dogfight maneuvers, successfully staying in the attack position behind the MiG. Finally, he got the MiG in his crosshairs and released his missiles. The MiG rolled into a vertical dive at the last minute, and the missiles streamed past it harmlessly. Mason had rolled left into the beginning of a loop after releasing the missiles, and when he came out of his Immelmann turn neither he nor Arthur could see the MiG, nor could they see any evidence that it had crashed.

"Where did that fucker go?" yelled Mason. Arthur looked at the radar displays.

"She's above us, coming out of an Immelmann turn on our tail," replied Arthur.

"Shit!" said Mason. He banked hard right, dived sharply, and pulled up sharply, but the MiG matched his motions. The MiG was only about 1,000 yards behind him, and still slightly above. The MiG fired its cannon, and Arthur felt the impacts as the bullets hit the Phantom II's body. The engine indicators showed him the engines were untouched, and there was no fire or smoke. Arthur discovered that he was holding his breath, so he released it.

"The MiG hit us but we seem to be OK," said Arthur. Mason did not respond. Arthur could see his head bowed in the cockpit ahead. "Mr. Mason, are you all right?"

"I've been hit in the thigh," said Mason, his voice weak. "I'm losing a lot of blood."

"Can you apply a tourniquet? Your first aid kit is strapped to your right side."

"I think so," said Mason. Arthur looked at the radar and located the MiG, off to the right about two miles, and heading back at them. He watched Mason's head bobbing as he attempted to apply the tourniquet to his thigh. "Got it. Bleeding's almost stopped, but I'm very weak. I don't think I can fly this bird now. Take the stick and get us out of here."

"Aye, aye, Sir," said Arthur, "but the MiG's coming back for round two. I'm going to have to fight first."

Arthur banked sharply to the right, engaging the afterburner again and angled the nose up. He could no longer see the MiG visually, because the nose of the Phantom II was in the way, but he could see the MiG on radar, and saw that it also angled upward, apparently hoping to come under the Phantom II and shoot at her underbelly. Arthur slammed the stick all the way to the right and applied right aileron, executing a 180-degree turn, and pushed the stick all the way forward, putting the plane into a steep dive, which, with the stick and the aileron back in center position, put the plane into a spin. He watched the jungle swirl below him, and at an elevation of about 1,000 feet he returned the stick to center, applied a little left aileron, and pulled the stick back with a steady motion. The responsive plane came out of its spin into level flight just above the tree tops.

"What are you trying to do," asked Mason, "commit suicide?"

"I was hoping the MiG would follow us down but wouldn't be able to pull out…" He turned his head to look at the mirrors that gave him a rearward view and saw the fireball and mushroom cloud caused when the MiG crashed into the jungle. "…and that's just what he did." Arthur slowed the plane and turned to fly back by the crash site.

"Congratulations, Mr. Harris," said Mason. "You've earned your first kill and have saved my life. Report to Mother and let's go home." Arthur reported to the carrier and computed the fastest course back that would get them there without running out of fuel on the way. When they arrived, they were met on the flight deck by medical corpsmen, two of them carrying a stretcher and the third a doctor's bag. Arthur and the stretcher bearer lifted Mason out of the cockpit and lowered him gently to the waiting hands of men on the deck, who laid him in the stretcher and carried him to the superstructure, and inside to the sick bay, where a Navy doctor met them. He motioned Arthur out of the room.

"Wait out there," said the doctor, a Lieutenant. "I'll examine him and let you know his condition." He closed the door before Arthur could respond. A few minutes later, the door opened and the doctor stuck his head out.

"Mr. Mason will be fine," he said. "It's just a flesh wound. He lost a lot of blood, but we've sterilized and closed the wound and we're giving him blood now. In a couple of hours, he'll walk out of here with crutches. Come back in a couple of hours and help him to his stateroom." Relieved, Arthur thanked the surgeon and turned and walked to their stateroom. He returned after two hours.

Soon, Mason exited the surgery, leaning on crutches, his flight suit trouser leg cut off above the wound, which was bandaged with pristine, white gauze wrapped around the thigh. Arthur walked with him back to the stateroom, helping him on the ladders. Mason handed Arthur the crutches and limped to the desk chair and sat down.

"I guess I won't be flying tomorrow, he said. "You'll have a day off."

"Good," said Arthur. "I'm ready for a day off, especially after today."

Within a few minutes, a Filipino steward arrived with a white, card-sized envelope, handed it to Mason, and turned and left. Mason opened it.

"Well, Mr. Harris," he said. "We are invited to dine with the Admiral in the Officers' Wardroom. Admiral Benjamin is in command of our task force, and this carrier is the Admiral's flagship. We are being honored." A carrier usually had two wardrooms for officers – the formal "Officers' Wardroom" and the less formal "Dirty Shirt Wardroom." The Officers' Wardroom required full dress uniforms, while Officers still wearing flight suits could gather in the Dirty Shirt Wardroom. The ship also had an Admiral's Wardroom, for the Admiral and the senior officers, who were invited on a rotation basis. The Captain almost always dined in the Officers' Wardroom, but when he didn't, the Executive Officer presided. Thus far, Arthur and Mason had taken most of their meals in the Dirty Shirt Wardroom.

They showered, shaved, and dressed quickly in their khaki dress uniforms and proceeded to the Admiral's Wardroom, Mason using just one of his crutches. They stood behind their seats with the other officers until the Captain and the Admiral entered. The Captain took a seat at the side of the table across from Mason, both of whom were adjacent to the head of the table. The Admiral took the head.

"Admiral," said the Captain, "joining us tonight are Lieutenant Commander James Mason and Midshipman First Class Arthur Harris. They are ONI Intelligence Officers in a special new unit of the ONI that is being formed and are assigned to this task force. Today they were flying reconnaissance over the Ho Chi Minh trail in Cambodia, when they were attacked by a North Vietnamese MiG 21 in Cambodian airspace. Mr. Mason, who was piloting, engaged the MiG in a dogfight in which he was wounded in the thigh by a bullet from the MiG's machine gun. Mr. Harris took the controls and continued the dogfight, downing the MiG. As Navigator and surveillance camera operator, Mr. Harris has had some flight training, but is not officially qualified as a pilot, yet he flew the plane expertly, achieved his first kill, and safely flew the damaged plane back to the carrier and landed it without incident. I have written a request for commendations, which you will find on your desk in the morning." The Admiral extended his hand to Mason, who took it.

"Mr. Mason. Sorry for your wound. I'll write you up for a Purple Heart for this." He turned to Arthur and extended his hand to Arthur, who took it. "Congratulations, Mr. Harris. I think this may be the first time that a Midshipman who was not a pilot has flown in combat, engaged the enemy, and achieved a kill. I will sign the Captain's request for commendation, but you must both understand that today's incident never happened because you were officially not in Cambodian airspace, nor even on this ship. Your mission was classified. You may say that you flew over Viet Nam and were hit, and downed the MiG that attacked you, but you must never mention Thailand or Cambodia. You were never there."

"I understand, Admiral," said Arthur. "I understand the meaning of clandestine operations."

"Chaplain," said the Captain, nodding to an officer with a cross on his lapel, "Please say the blessing." The chaplain bowed his head and clasped his hands in front of his chest.

"Father, we thank thee for these, thy gifts. Bless them for our use, and ourselves to thy service, in Jesus' name. Amen."

"Gentlemen, please be seated," said the Captain. All took their seats, and The Admiral asked Mason to give a blow-by-blow description of their dogfight. Mason did so up to the time he was wounded.

"After the bullet went through my leg I was busy trying to stop my bleeding, and I got pretty weak. Mr. Harris continued the battle and should tell the rest of the story." Arthur picked up the story, giving a description of the remainder of the dogfight.

"Gentlemen, our Navy is blessed to have men like you," said the Admiral. "I am privileged that you are serving under my command."

"Thank you, Admiral," said Arthur, "but we did only what we had to do to stay alive and return to the carrier."

"You will go far in this Navy," said the Admiral. "Now, will you please pass the butter, Mr. Niemann?"

I already have gone far, thought Arthur. *I'm halfway around the world from home. I have killed a human being, and yet I don't feel guilt. I guess downing a plane is different emotionally from looking a man in the eyes and killing him.*

Conversations began around the table. The officer to Arthur's right asked him how he became involved with the ONI as a mere Midshipman. Arthur gave an outline of his deployment to Guantanamo, without revealing any classified details. The ebb and flow of conversations continued through the meal.

Before dessert was served, Mason addressed the Admiral.

"Admiral, may I be excused? I feel rather weak from my ordeal today and the loss of blood, and I need to lie down. Our mission was not supposed to be a combat mission, and our plane was not armed for combat. Inadvertent combat has gotten me down." The Admiral excused him, and Arthur rose and retrieved Mason's crutch, helping him up from his chair and handing him the crutch.

"You stay here, Mr. Harris," said Mason. "I can find my way to our stateroom without a problem. You're in the limelight tonight. Enjoy it." Mason left, and Arthur resumed his seat. Dessert consisted of apple pie with ice cream on top. Arthur enjoyed every bite, although his Grandmother made better apple pie.

The next morning, Arthur and Mason received a summons to the Admiral's stateroom before breakfast. When they arrived, Mason knocked on the door.

"Admiral, permission to enter – Lieutenant Commander Mason and Midshipman 2nd Class Harris reporting as ordered, Sir."

"Enter," said the Admiral's voice from the other side of the door. Mason opened the door and he and Arthur entered and snapped to attention. The Admiral was standing at his desk facing them.

"At ease, gentlemen," he said. "Please be seated." He motioned them to chairs facing him. Arthur and Mason stepped forward and sat.

"Mr. Mason, I believe you were Mr. Harris' flight instructor at Corpus Christi Naval Air Station."

"Sir, yes, Sir," said Mason, "that is correct, Admiral."

"You apparently did a very good job," said the Admiral. "Would you consider Mr. Harris qualified to be a pilot?"

"Yes Sir, except that his eyes require vision correction, and that disqualifies him under present regulations. He has not had the full course of training but seems able to do everything needed without it."

"If his eyes were not an impediment, what would be required now for him to receive his wings?"

"Well, he had a much, much shorter course than Navy pilots normally receive, but he had at least one lesson in each 'subject' they have to learn. He has soloed in the T-34 and in the Phantom, he has been submerged upside down in an ejection seat and extricated himself, he has been through high-altitude familiarization in a vacuum chamber ... I think he has done everything necessary, just not as many times as most pilots."

"Do you consider him less skilled because of the lack of repetition?"

"No sir."

"Assuming, then, that he had completed all the training, what steps would remain for him to receive his wings?"

"He has soloed in a jet fighter already, but he has not done his qualifying solo because it was not contemplated that he would become a pilot."

"Very well. Mr. Harris, after we have breakfast, I want you to put on your flight suit and pressure suit and solo in a Phantom II. It won't be *your* Phantom II, because its bullet holes are still being patched. We'll loan you a spare one."

"Thank you, Admiral," said Arthur. "Mr. Mason, do you think I'm really ready?"

"I think you can do it," said Mason. "You can take a Phantom off a carrier, fly several hundred miles at high and low altitude, engage in a dogfight, down your opponent and return safely to the carrier. The solo flight is a lot less demanding than that."

There was a knock on the door, and when it opened the Filipino stewards served the three men a breakfast of mountains of scrambled eggs, bacon, biscuits, butter, white gravy, and grits with butter, all chased with coffee and orange juice.

The condemned man ate a hearty meal, thought Arthur.

The flight deck was rolling slightly, influenced by the beginning of some monsoon winds, as Arthur watched the Phantom II jet rise on the elevator to the flight deck. A helmeted deck hand climbed in and taxied it to position for the start of takeoff. Arthur walked around it for the external pre-flight visual inspection, climbed into the cockpit and completed the checklist. He signaled thumbs up to the deck crew, who connected the plane to the catapult. A minute later, he was airborne, soaring into the heavens with afterburner blazing. He killed the afterburner and executed the maneuvers that Mason had laid out for him, eventually entering the landing glide path and executing a perfect landing.

As he climbed down from the cockpit, he saw that Admiral Benjamin was standing with Captain Franks and Mr. Mason, watching. Arthur walked over to them and saluted. The Admiral returned his salute.

"Well done, Mr. Harris," said the Admiral. "Please change to dress uniform and meet us in my Wardroom for lunch."

"Aye, aye, Sir," said Arthur.

Arthur stood behind his seat, as all the officers in the wardroom were standing behind their seats, when Captain Franks, followed by Admiral Benjamin, entered the wardroom.

"Attention!" barked Captain Franks. "Mr. Harris, front and center." Arthur executed a left face, walked two steps, which put him past the head of the table, executed a right face, and took two more steps, which placed him directly behind the Admiral's chair at the head of the table. He executed a final left face, standing at attention in front of the Admiral.

"Gentlemen, we have an historic event today," said the Admiral. "Today, for the first time in US Navy history, a Midshipman will receive pilot's wings. Mr. Harris, you have proven your capabilities, and I am waiving the vision requirement and the requirement that you be a commissioned officer before receiving your wings. You can see well enough with your contact lenses, and I see no reason to deny you your wings. Congratulations, Mr. Harris." He took one step forward and pinned the pilots' golden wings to Arthur's left breast above his Midshipman's service ribbons.

"You may wear your wings while under my command. When you leave my command, you will put them in storage until the Pentagon recognizes your status officially. Tomorrow I will ask you to fly the surveillance mission you have been doing for the last couple of weeks, but alone. Mr. Mason can't fly yet, and we have a shortage of pilots who are permitted to fly over Laos and Cambodia. You and Mr. Mason are the only ones. You can set the cameras to record automatically every five minutes in all directions, so you won't need a cameraman in the back seat. When you switch on the trigger, the gunsight camera will go into motion picture mode."

"Aye, aye, Sir," said Arthur.

"Very well, Gentlemen. Let's eat."

CHAPTER 15

HARD LANDING

Late July and Early August 1965
Location: Pacific Fleet and "Not in Cambodia"

In the morning, just before dawn, Arthur prepared to take off from the Midway, flying the Phantom II that had been Mason's until Mason was wounded. All the bullet holes had been patched, and none of the bullets that struck the plane had hit anything vital. The plane sported metal patches where each of the bullet holes had been. The patches were painted black.

"Scars of Honor," said the grinning Seaman climbing down from the cockpit, noticing Arthur touching one of the patches. Arthur grinned back.

"She earned them all," said Arthur, "and survived them."

The sky was clear but hazy as the catapult launched the Phantom into the air, with most of the fainter stars invisible. A few puffy clouds cruised by lazily at about 8,000 feet, where there was a mild thermal layer, but he climbed quickly above them, leveling off at 60,000 feet for his flight across North Viet Nam to the point where the Ho Chi Minh trail crossed from North Viet Nam into Thailand. Above 8,000 feet the sky had darkened progressively and at 60,000 feet it was a deep black, the stars were blazing points of light and the Milky Way a bright, hazy streak of white cloud stretching from horizon to horizon. At that altitude, most of the North Vietnamese surface-to-air missiles, SAMs, would miss him. There were no clouds and no atmospheric haze at 60,000 feet. His heart was racing, and he felt a curious mixture of excitement, pride, and fear as he began his first solo mission in the war zone.

Before long, sunrise cast long, hazy, blue shadows across the hilly jungle terrain below him, turned blue by the amount of atmosphere between the plane and the ground. As the sky changed to indigo and the stars started winking out, he descended in a steep dive to just above tree-top level and turned south for his surveillance run along the Ho Chi Minh trail. He reduced the throttle to a comfortable low-altitude cruising speed for surveillance, about 250 knots.

The sky had turned to a beautiful, tropical, cerulean blue and the surface haze was dissipating, evaporated by the hot rays of the sun. He flew carefully and precisely, watching his radar and the skies vigilantly for bogeys. He had one blind spot, in the direction of the sun, which was low in the sky to his left, but climbing. The cameras, which he had set to automatic when he came down to the trail, were recording on their timed sequence views through the gunsight and lateral views into the jungle on both sides. The gunsight camera would see the trail ahead, and a camera aimed down through the deck would see the trail below.

For the first half of the trail surveillance, there were no events. It was just as he crossed the border from Thailand into Cambodian air space that he spotted the bogeys. At the same time, his earphones crackled with static, and a voice spoke through the static.

"Mother Goose to Oscar Romeo Three Fiver, bogeys approaching at high speed from your niner o'clock at altitude fifteen thousand feet. Recommend you abort mission, Sir, and return to ship."

"Oscar Romeo Three Fiver to Mother Goose, I see them. It's too late – they have locked on. Engaging."

He turned sharply left into a hard bank, engaged the afterburners and pulled the stick back to climb sharply to engage the MiGs before they could begin their attack. He found himself looking upward at five MiG 21s, flying in a V-formation.

The MiGs would be armed with missiles, and the only armament Arthur had was the four 20-mm Gatling cannons that were basic equipment for his surveillance craft. He was carrying no missiles so that their weight would not decrease his cruising range. He increased the throttle to maximum thrust with afterburners blazing and pulled the stick back to its limit.

He flashed past in front of the MiGs flying vertically and executed a vertical three-quarter-loop downward combined with a roll that placed him into a position just behind the MiGs. He rolled out into the open end of the V-formation at the rear and cut the afterburners. He used the stick to put the lead MiG in his crosshairs. He had cannons that could fire either in single-shot or in automatic-fire mode. He clicked the selector to single-fire mode, but set it to fire all four cannons simultaneously, so that four shells would head for the target each time he pulled the trigger. He fired, and the MiG in the crosshairs exploded. The remaining MiGs rolled out to the left and dived to escape his attack.

Arthur also rolled out to the left, staying in formation with the MiGs, diving with them. They soon levelled out and began to climb in the beginning of a loop. He climbed with them and rolled out of the half-loop with them, still in formation. The MiGs tried to evade him by diving again for the deck, so he pulled up into a full power loop, but elongated on the downward leg, coming out of it once again in formation with the MiGs at low altitude.

They began to climb, and he climbed with them, firing at the lead MiG to the left. He felt, more than heard, a dull, "thump, thump," and realized that the trailing MiG on the right had moved behind him and had just hit his plane with two shots. A glance at the control dials showed all in order, so he started into a full-power loop and executed the Immelmann Maneuver. He followed that immediately with a reverse Immelmann, placing himself behind the MiG that had shot him. He fired all four cannons in single fire mode, and watched the MiG burst into flame and drop from the sky.

He flew in a circle, looking for the first MiG, but didn't find it. The remaining three MiGs were heading north, afterburners engaged. His F-4 screamed after them and, gaining rapidly, he called the Carrier.

"Oscar Romeo Three Fiver to Mother Goose. Killed at least one of the five bogeys. What does your radar show?"

"Mother Goose to Oscar Romeo Three Fiver, are you still in flying condition?" asked the crackling voice in his earphones.

"Affirmative, which is more than I can say for one bogey."

"Mother Goose to Oscar Romeo Three Fiver. We thought you had gone down. Congratulations. Two MiGs went down. Suggest you come home."

"Negative. In hot pursuit." Adrenaline raging, he fired once at the lead MiG and turned his nose slightly to the left firing at the left MiG. The lead MiG burst into flame and dropped toward the green jungle below. The trailing MiG peeled off to the left and scrammed, afterburners blazing. He circled, watching them until the lead MiG hit and exploded.

"Oscar Romeo Three Fiver to Mother Goose. Killed two. Other turned tail."

"We saw it on radar. Four kills confirmed. Please come home, Sir."

"Roger. Oscar Romeo Three Fiver out."

Back on the carrier, Mason was waiting for him.

"Tell me, Mr. Harris – how did a good Catholic boy from Alabama wind up here?"

Prodded by Mason's questions, Arthur laid out how he first became interested in intelligence as a career in his boyhood, and proceeded to tell Mason his life history, prodded occasionally by questions from Mason.

"So now you know my life history," said Arthur.

"I know a lot *about* you now," said Mason, "but I really don't know *you*. You're not an easy man to get to really know."

"Maybe that's why I chose Intelligence for a career," said Arthur. "I have to keep a lot of secrets as an Intelligence Officer." They stopped, facing each other, just a few feet from their Phantom. Mason looked steadily into Arthur's eyes, neither smiling nor frowning. Arthur tried to match the blankness of the stare.

"I think you'll make a good one," said Mason, turning back toward the plane and stepping forward.

Mason and Arthur walked around the Phantom II for their first pre-flight inspection together since Mason had been wounded. Mason marveled at all the black patches the crew had made to close the bullet holes. He laughed when he found the new name for the aircraft stenciled neatly on both sides of its nose: "The Flying Colander."

They climbed into the cockpit. As usual, Mason took the front seat. They completed their checklists and strapped in. Arthur prepared the cameras, and they took off for the usual surveillance run. Again, it went without incident until they crossed the Cambodian border.

Before this, all traffic they saw on the Ho Chi Minh trail had been travelling from north to south. They would come up behind a body of troops or a convoy, photograph it, and be past it before anyone could spot them. On this mission, however, they came upon a body of troops marching north along the trail. The troops spotted them coming and hit the jungle on both sides, falling prone and bringing their rifles to bear. They began firing at the low-flying jet at a range of about a half mile, and Mason returned strafing fire, killing many. However, a series of bullets stitched holes in the underside of the aircraft as they flew over the troops. Arthur saw Mason slump in his seat and blood sprayed on the canopy over his head. Arthur immediately took the controls himself.

"Mr. Mason, I have the stick," Arthur said. There was no response.

He looked left and saw Mount Bon Sar Pa, and so he banked right while increasing throttle to climb away from the trail with the mountains behind him. Had he turned left, he would have hit the mountain. He increased throttle further and pulled back the stick to raise the nose, hoping to climb, but nothing happened. He could bank but could not climb. His wing flaps worked, but the aileron flaps didn't.

Both engines began sputtering and stopped firing. He was on a glide path toward the ground over rice fields, with jungle ahead. He did his best to hold the plane steady and level. Arthur watched his altimeter. By now, he had shot down more MiGs than any other pilot so far in the Viet Nam War. He should be recognized as an ace, but he knew that he could not be, because he was officially never there. Now, he was over Cambodia again, and he realized that if he didn't eject he would soon be dead. He couldn't do anything for Mason, whose brains were splattered on the canopy overhead.

He prayed the Act of Contrition in Latin. "*Deus meus, ex toto corde paenitet me omnium meorum peccatorum, eaque detestor, quia peccando, non solum poenas a te juste statutas promeritus sum, sed praesertim quia offendi te, summum bonum, ac dignum qui super omnia diligaris.*

Ideo firmiter propono, adjuvante gratia tua, de cetero me non peccatorum peccandique occasiones proximas fugiturum. Amen."

He triggered the ejection and felt a hard kick in the rear. He shot upward into the air, just before the plane splashed hard into the rice paddy and skidded to a stop just short of the jungle.

Snapshots from his life flashed before him, as he hovered at the top of the ejection trajectory before plunging toward the earth. Oddly, his mind picked out the events about which he had not been fully truthful with Mason. He felt weightless, and the parachute deployed just before the ejection seat hit the ground. Pain hit his lower back, and after a few moments began to subside.

That was my first hard landing, thought Arthur, *and, I hope, my last. Thank you, Lord, for keeping me alive.* His heart was pounding rapidly and he was panting. He could feel that his face was flushed, and he had an erection that pressed uncomfortably against his flight suit. It had begun with the adrenaline rush following the bullets that ripped through the plane. *I guess danger is sexy*, he thought. He unstrapped, stepping quickly out of the ejection seat, and collapsed immediately into the mud, the pain in his lower back excruciating. He lay there, unable to move.

After a few minutes, the spasms subsided somewhat. He rolled over carefully and rose to his hands and knees, and then used the ejection seat to steady himself as he rose slowly to his feet. His back hurt, but he could stand and walk. He walked to the airplane, about 100 yards ahead of him, its nose in the mud, and climbed the rungs to the cockpit to check on Mason.

Mason was unresponsive, sitting in a pool of blood, with blood flowing from just below his breast bone and running out from the bottom of his helmet. The metallic, rusty smell of blood was overwhelming. Blood and tissue were splattered around the compartment, but especially on the canopy over Mason's head. Arthur pulled Mason's flight helmet carefully from his head and pressed two fingers into his neck, searching for a pulse. He found none, but found the entry wound for the slug that had killed Mason. The top of Mason's skull was a bloody mass of tissue. Bile rose into Arthur's mouth and he turned his head to vomit into the mud below.

Arthur reached into the cockpit and retrieved the M-1 carbine that was standard survival equipment for flyers, and the survival pack that contained first aid kit and survival supplies. He was already wearing, at his waist, his service-issued M1911 .45 caliber pistol, with his father's .357 magnum service revolver in an ankle holster mounted outside his pressure suit. He had spare clips for the revolver and two extra magazines for the M1911, in pockets designed for the purpose. His carbine had bailed out with him, fastened to his ejection seat, and he recovered it when he got out of the seat.

He climbed to the ground and turned around to find a man in North Vietnamese uniform running fast and almost on him, machete raised. Before Arthur could react, the machete sliced down his right shoulder as he twisted away from the blow, dropping what he was carrying to defend himself. It was a glancing blow, but it sliced through the flight suit and a moment later blood welled out, just before Arthur felt the pain. With his left hand, Arthur grabbed the man's right wrist in a crushing grip as it went down and, with his right hand, seized the machete by the top of the blade, jerking it from the man's hand. He took a quick, hard swing of the blade that struck his opponent in the neck. He watched with surprise as the head fell off, hit the ground and rolled. It lay there, looking up at Arthur, blinking, with its mouth working as if it were trying to speak. Only then did the body of the soldier crumple to the ground, blood spurting up from the neck stump. Arthur felt as if he were watching a movie on a distant movie screen, in slow motion; everything seemed unreal. He felt no emotions.

Now I've really lost my virtue, thought Arthur. *I have arrived in Cambodia and killed a man, but I'm officially not here.* A tune called "Nowhere Man" was running through his head.

The jungle was just ahead of the plane. Arthur picked up what he had dropped and ran for the jungle, both carbines in his left hand and the machete in his right, the pack carrying the first aid and survival kits over his left shoulder. He stopped, thrust the machete into a side pocket and through the fabric so it hung as if in a scabbard, and shifted one carbine to his right hand, and then continued toward the jungle. Once into the jungle, he ducked into the undergrowth and turned to look back at the plane. Its nose was crumpled upward and it looked very woebegone, like a puppy being housebroken whose nose was being rubbed in the urine on the floor. Arthur thought of the camera equipment and high-density film on the plane and debated with himself whether he should go back to the plane to retrieve them to prevent their falling into the hands of the enemy. Also, he wanted to retrieve Mason's dog tags.

No one else was visible, so after a few minutes of controlled deep breathing, he laid the pack and one carbine in the brush, chambered a round in the other carbine and stepped out of his hiding place, crouching to maintain a low profile and small target. No shots greeted him and he saw no one, so, sprinting, he splashed his way through the ankle-deep muddy water of the rice paddy to the plane. He opened the front of Mason's flight suit and took his dog tags, then dismounted the cameras and film canisters from the back compartment. He ran back into the jungle and deposited them in his hiding place, then looked back to the plane. No one was in evidence, so he decided to try to retrieve Mason's body. He returned to the plane, and with a great deal of difficulty ratcheted Mason's body little by little out of the front of the cockpit, using the carbine as a lever under Mason's armpit for assistance. He dropped Mason into the mud. He paused, waves of nausea passing through his torso and attacking his throat, but he swallowed rapidly, stilling them. He felt faint from the loss of blood and the exercise, as well as the waves of fear that almost overwhelmed him. Climbing down, he tried to lift the body into a fireman's carry across his back, but he couldn't. He no longer had the strength to do so. He was able to stagger all the way to the jungle, pulling Mason's body by the legs behind him, pausing every few steps to take deep breaths. He was feeling light-headed and dizzy.

Just as he reached cover, he heard shots and bullets zinged through the leaves beside him. He dropped Mason, turned around and dropped to the ground, bringing his carbine to bear. He saw three uniformed North Vietnamese soldiers beside the plane shooting at him with Kalashnikov rifles set on automatic fire. They weren't very accurate, but there was a lot of lead in his immediate neighborhood, so he stayed down, Mason's body providing a shield. Soon the NV troops stopped firing and dropped their magazines, loading new magazines. Arthur aimed carefully, firing six shots in rapid pairs, double-taps, two at each target. All three dropped into the mud and didn't move. He dragged Mason's body deeper into the jungle, found a depression and deposited the body in it, removing Mason's flight suit. He went back along the trail he had followed and chopped foliage from the bamboo and bushes along the way, using the machete that had wounded him. He filled the depression with what he had chopped. Kneeling beside the improvised grave, he prayed for Mason's soul – and his own.

Satisfied that the body was well-camouflaged, he scattered about half the foliage he had gathered back along the trail so it would cover the drag marks. He placed the cameras and film canisters into Mason's flight suit and tied the legs and arms together to create a handle or strap that he could carry hanging from his left shoulder. He returned to his entry point at the edge of the jungle. The drag marks in the mud from the plane to the jungle were already obliterated by new mud that flowed into them from the swampy rice paddy. He turned and continued in a straight line westward, cutting a trail as he went, and lugging the camera and film canister with him, bypassing the grave site by about 50 feet to its north. After about 100 yards, he turned left and continued his trail blazing south for about 20 yards. He used most of the brush he had cut in the last 20 feet to build a barrier across the trail. He hoped that if anyone followed him, they would find the barrier, think he was behind it, and spend some time approaching it carefully, even firing into it in the hopes of hitting him. His brain seemed unnaturally clear and thoughts passed through at blazing speed. His heart was pounding and he felt light-headed, but continued. *Adrenaline can be a wonderful thing*, he thought.

Back at the turn, he rigged a couple of trip wires, using a coil of fine copper wire from the survival kit, and set Mason's pistol up in the barricade, wedged firmly into the fork of two branches and tied in place with pieces of the copper wire, with the trip wire tied to its trigger. He placed one carbine similarly, set for fully automatic fire, and set a trip wire for it at an earlier spot in the trail, ten feet further away from the trip wire for the pistol. He racked both guns to lodge rounds in their chambers. He positioned both to aim at a point in the middle of the trail at about chest height. If the NV troops followed the trail, and tripped the first wire, the carbine would spray bullets until its magazine was empty. If they continued to advance and tripped the second trip wire, the pistol would shoot once in their direction, making them approach the barrier with more caution. With a bit of luck, one or more of them might even be hit.

Arthur returned down the trail to a point about halfway between the turn and the edge of the jungle, and then stepped carefully over the underbrush to the north of the trail and stole carefully northward through the jungle, not cutting a trail and taking pains not to leave signs of his passing, using his Boy Scout stalking skills. He carried a small branch with a cluster of leaves on the end to sweep away footprints, and he carefully worked his way through the underbrush to avoid snapping any small branches. He took care to zig-zag so that he did not leave any straight path behind him. After about 100 yards, he began a long turn to the west, checking his direction periodically with his survival compass. He did not dare go east because that way led to the Ho Chi Minh trail and its troop movements. His only hope was to head west and find the Mekong River, and somehow make his way down the river back into South Viet Nam.

After about thirty minutes of progress through the jungle, he stopped to rest, drank a small amount of water from his canteen, and took out his first aid kit. *I guess I'm going to get to use all the jungle survival skills I learned on Boy Scout survival trips,* he though. With his knife, he extended the cut in his flight suit at his shoulder so he could gain access to his wound. With a wad of cotton from the first aid kit moistened with water from his canteen, he carefully swabbed the congealed blood around the wound to clean and expose the gash. The bleeding resumed. He could see no way to close the wound, so he began packing it with cotton and gauze to stanch the bleeding.

By now, his wound was generating a great deal of pain with every movement of his right arm, and he was feeling quite faint. He had lost a quantity of blood, most of which was inside his flight suit. He had kept wearing his flight suit despite the heat so that he would not leave a trail of blood as he made his escape. Rummaging in the first aid kit for antiseptic, he found a package of antiseptic/antibiotic powder, which he thought was likely sulfa, given the yellow color of the powder. He had experienced an allergy to a sulfanilamide oral antibiotic as a child, developing hives. He decided to use it anyway. Hives he could live with. Dying from an infection he could not.

He pulled the packing out of the wound, sprinkled the powder into the open wound and immediately reinserted the packing. Realizing that his vision was fading, he heard a rattle of automatic weapons fire, followed about a minute later by the crack of a pistol shot from the direction he had come. This was followed by another burst of automatic weapons fire. Redness overtook his vision, followed by blackness.

After an unknown period, his eyes opened and he saw the canopy of trees above him. *I'm alive,* he thought. Two dark-skinned men were bending over him, looking down at him. They were dressed in black loin cloths and loose, black, long shirts. Both the shirts and the loincloths had colorfully beaded borders and decorations. Both men wore beaded headbands to hold their long black hair under control. Arthur thought of Apache tribesmen whom he had seen once in a village in New Mexico dressed in similar fashion and wondered if he were dreaming. He stood up and tried to run but discovered that his legs weren't moving because his feet were stuck in mud. He fell headlong, face-down in a puddle, losing his carbine in the process. He held his breath to avoid inhaling water, but felt his consciousness departing again. Moments later, four hands lifted him and he found himself being carried through the jungle.

After an unknown time his captors laid him on his back on the damp soil. They examined him quickly and one of them stood and ran deeper into the jungle, disappearing quickly.

"Not worry, Sir," said the remaining man. "Us ... Degar ... Montagnard. He go, get medicine man." The Degar tribes, the indigenous tribes of the mountains of Viet Nam, were known as "Montagnard" in French, meaning "mountain people." They were unwavering US allies who hated the Chinese, the Viet Cong and the North Vietnamese, but tolerated the South Vietnamese because they were enemies of the North Vietnamese and allies of the US. The man was pressing moss into the cut on Arthur's shoulder, stanching the bleeding that had started up again when he removed Arthur's packing. The man pulled a knife from the belt of his loincloth and cut the fabric of the flight suit further away from the wound, applying pressure with his other hand to the moss. Within minutes the man who had run away returned with another man who carried a doctor's bag. Two other men were with them.

"Medicine man," said one of them, pointing at the man with the doctor's bag. The "medicine man" squatted beside Arthur, taking a canteen of water from his kit. He took the moss off the wound and poured clean water over and into the wound. Arthur grimaced at the resulting pain, a grunt escaping through his lips. The medicine mand put a roll of gauze across Arthur's mouth, telling him to bite hard, and took another wad of gauze and pressed it hard on the wound. With his free hand, he reached back into the bag and brought out a bottle of Jack Daniels. He pulled the cork with his teeth and poured some whiskey into a tin cup held by another of the men and sprinkled some white powder into it. He stirred it with his finger, put the cup to Arthur's lips, and said, "You drink."

Arthur couldn't help but swallow several large gulps of whiskey that had an overriding burning taste that was both sweet and bitter. *Opium,* thought Arthur. The alternative was to drown from inhaling alcohol. Arthur felt the burn as the alcohol hit his stomach, and he felt pleasantly light-headed and the pain in his shoulder diminished. The medicine man poured some of the whiskey directly from the bottle into the cut. The pain came back with a vengeance and Arthur heard someone screaming and realized that it was he. One of the men put his hands over Arthur's mouth, smothering the scream.

"Please, sir," said the man, "not scream. Charley hear and come kill." Arthur's shoulder now felt numb, and he stopped trying to scream. The medicine man kept feeding him gulps of whiskey from the cup, and soon Arthur could not see without double vision. He felt pleasantly light-headed, not drunk. The medicine man sprinkled a yellow powder into the wound and took needle and thread from his kit and began stitching expertly, closing the wound. Arthur watched as if viewing someone else's shoulder. Part of his mind felt the stitching, but it seemed remote, apart from himself.

Another of the men took the bottle of whiskey and poured some more into the cup, sprinkling more white powder into it. He pulled a reed stalk loose from its roots. He used a knife to cut a section of reed about six inches long and used it to stir the mixture in the cup, holding it over the flame of a cigarette lighter held by another man.

The medicine man had finished his stitching. He took the bottle of whiskey and poured a little over the sutures. He took a handful of dried herbs from his pouch and plastered them on the sutured wound. After that, he bound the shoulder with clean gauze, fixing a sling for the arm and binding Arthur's right arm across his chest. He unbuckled Arthur's gun belt, re-buckling it with the holster reversed. He moved Arthur's ankle holster with the revolver from his right ankle to his left ankle.

"Your right hand not work. If shoot, use left hand," he said. He lifted Arthur to a sitting position and rested him against a tree trunk. One of the men ran back into the jungle and came back with Arthur's carbine, pack, and camera package. The man proceeded to strip and clean the carbine, which was more than a little bit muddy. The man with the cup handed the cup to the medicine man, who held it below Arthur's chin and put the reed into Arthur's mouth.

"You drink," he said. "Feel better. Is whiskey and opium powder. You feel better, you sleep soon."

"Who are you?" asked Arthur, his voice slurred from the whiskey.

"I Dr. Tran Thiu Trin," said the medicine man, bowing slightly "I do medical school in Saigon." Arthur remembered that Vietnamese put the given name last when giving their names, and that for a long time, Southeast Asia was a French colony known as French Indochina. Most of the educated Vietnamese spoke French, but they were now starting to learn English. The doctor's education likely was in French, and he had likely picked up English since America became involved in the war.

"Thank, you, Dr. Tran," said Arthur. "I am Harris, Arthur. I do not speak French, but I speak English, Spanish, and German. I am US Navy pilot." He turned his head to look up at the doctor. He had the impression that his vision turned later than his head, as if there were a delay in his perception. Everything seemed a little more distant than normal, as if he were looking through the wrong end of a pair of opera glasses.

"This Cambodia," said the doctor. "We not here. You not here. We Montagnard working with CIA. We take you our camp now." One man unrolled the long bundle he carried. It was two wooden poles about eight feet long with a six-foot strip of two-foot-wide canvas between them – a stretcher. He laid it on the ground, and three pairs of hands lifted Arthur gently and placed him on the stretcher. They placed the freshly-cleaned carbine beside

him, and stood, lifting the stretcher and trotting off with it
into the jungle. In minutes, their rocking gait had Arthur
sleeping soundly under the influence of the whiskey and
opium.

He awoke on a cot in a tent under drenching rain.
Winters in the southern hemisphere jungles are like this,
he reflected. *That's why they call them rain forests.*

"Ah, you awake," said the voice of Dr. Tran. He came
around from behind Arthur, a steaming cup in his hand.
"Fish broth, very healthy. You drink now, but slowly, not
burn self." He spooned a few mouthfuls of broth carefully
into Arthur's mouth, and then he helped Arthur to sit up
with his legs over the side of the cot. Arthur took the cup
and began sipping gratefully. The broth was very fishy in
taste but very good. He felt his hunger acutely as the broth
began trickling into his stomach. "If you keep down
broth, I give you fish, you eat fish." Dr. Tran disappeared
behind him and came back with an aluminum bowl. In the
bowl was a bed of rice with pieces of fish and some green
leaves on top. When Arthur had finished the broth, Dr.
Tran took back the cup, placed the bowl in Arthur's lap
and handed him a pair of chopsticks. Arthur carefully ma-
nipulated the chop sticks to place the food in his mouth,
one bite at a time. He had never used chopsticks left
handed before, and it was not easy. The doctor watched
him.

"Good," said Dr. Tran. "You live now. Tomorrow you
walk. We go through jungle to Mekong River, about 160
klicks. Five-six day fast walk. Boat take you to Viet Nam.
Then you go home."

The next morning, the Montagnard struck camp, packing the tents on wheelbarrow-like devices with long handles that they pulled behind them. They paused to eat a
lunch of cold fish and began their march westward. They

followed well-worn trails through the jungle, moving almost at a trot – a quite fast walk.

The third day, after they stopped for lunch, they heard sounds behind them, coming up the same path. The tribesmen hauling the "wheelbarrows" disappeared instantly into the jungle with the other tribesmen, and the doctor guided Arthur wordlessly into the jungle. They lay in the darkness behind trees and watched the trail. Within minutes, a group of twelve uniformed Chinese troops walked into view. From the corner of his eye, Arthur saw the Montagnards slowly rise to kneeling positions and sight their rifles. He knelt as well but drew his pistol because he was still one-handed and couldn't handle his carbine effectively. The doctor had his hand raised, looking from side to side. He dropped his hand and the tribesmen opened fire. Arthur followed suit. The Chinese troops dropped and crumpled where they were. The Montagnard squeezed off a second round of fire at their bodies, and trotted into the clearing, checking the bodies. One of the tribesmen trotted back along the path in the direction from which they had come. In minutes he was back. He said something in their language.

"He said all clear," said Dr. Tran. "No more Chinese coming." One of the men in the clearing trotted back into the jungle to where Dr. Tran and Arthur waited.

"All dead," he said. The tribesmen dragged the bodies into the jungle, concealing them from view with fallen branches and leaves. They covered the splotches of blood in the clearing with leaves. Finally, they pulled their "wheelbarrows" back into the clearing, broke out lunch and jugs of water, and they all ate a quick lunch of cold rice and fish before resuming their journey.

On the sixth day, they came to the edge of the jungle. Ahead and below them down a shallow bank was a broad, muddy river, so wide that the opposite shore was just a

thin green smudge between the grey river and the grey
sky.

"Mekong," said Dr. Tran to Arthur, gesturing toward
the river. "Now we find boats." They all started walking
along the river downstream to the left, remaining in the
jungle. After a while, they stopped. In a clearing ahead
was a small village consisting of one longhouse and three
round huts, all covered in thatch. Drawn up on the river
bank were twelve dugout canoes. Dr. Tran motioned to
one of the men, who disappeared into the jungle. Soon,
they heard chopping noises and angry shouts coming from
the jungle behind the village. A handful of men poured
out of the longhouse, guns in hand, and ran into the jungle
to investigate. Dr. Tran led the Montagnard and Arthur to
the boats, and they silently slipped three of them into the
water and climbed aboard, paddling silently downstream.
Just past the village, one of the canoes pulled in to the
shore, and the Montagnard who had created the diversion
ran from the jungle and boarded it. All resumed their
downstream journey paddling hard now. The canoes
slipped rapidly through the water.

Arthur was riding in the middle of one of the canoes,
Dr. Tran in the back and another Montagnard in the front,
both paddling. Arthur's backpack and package of camera
equipment were in front of him on the bottom of the canoe. The cameras were in a canvas package with a rope
handle, Arthur's pressure suit having been removed and
washed and packed in Arthur's pack. Arthur's khaki work
uniform was less visible than the bright orange pressure
suit. He carried Mason's insignia and dog tags in his
backpack.

The river wound its way lazily through the jungle, but
the tribesmen were anything but lazy. They paddled in
long, strong strokes, and the canoes slipped rapidly
through the water, their speed magnified by the deceptive-
ly lazy current. Arthur watched the shore sliding by them

to the left. The shore to the right was distant, a featureless strip of misty dark green. It began to rain again, and they stopped paddling periodically to use rice bowls to bail water from the canoes.

They passed two more villages like the first. At the second, there were men near the canoes, working on fishing nets. They watched curiously as the Montagnard flotilla streamed past but returned to their work as the last canoe sped past.

"We stop now and wait for dark," said Dr. Tran. "Phnom Penh ahead. King Norodom Sihanouk friendly to U.S.A. but us not really here, understand? Government also friendly with Commie Chinese. Commie Chinese also help Khmer Rouge revolution. We float through city in dark night." The canoes pulled over to the bank, and the men pulled them all the way into the jungle. Hiding in the jungle, they ate a supper of cold fish and rice while waiting for the darkness. The sky was overcast and it was still raining, so the night would, indeed, be dark. Dr. Tran rubbed dark mud on Arthur's face and on his tan uniform.

The night was very dark. As they floated quietly into the outskirts of Phnom Penh, it grew lighter from the lights in the houses. As they went through the center of the city, they crouched low in the canoes and drifted with the flow of the river, paddling slowly and very quietly. The steady patter of rain into the river water covered any paddling sounds they made. They were through the city and back in the jungle as dawn came. The rain stopped, the clouds parted, and sunlight streamed through the misty air.

Two more days of paddling brought them to the border, and another day took them through the gap in the mountains to the broad, flat alluvial plain of southern South Viet Nam created by the Mekong delta. Dr. Tran unpacked a field radio and used it to contact someone using Morse code. The canoes pulled to the bank at a village and all went ashore. Soon, Arthur heard the unmistakable chop-chop-chop sound of Huey helicopters – two of them.

The choppers came into view, flying up the river. One of them landed on the narrow beach and the other, bristling with Gatling guns, circled overhead. Using his left hand, Arthur shook hands with the Montagnard tribesmen, thanking them for his rescue, and Dr. Tran walked him to the chopper. Arthur shook his hand and turned, climbing into the cabin. The Montagnard handed up Arthur's backpack, package of cameras and his carbine. The Huey immediately took off, and the two helicopters flew rapidly down the river to Hanoi. The one carrying Arthur landed on the roof of the American Embassy, where Arthur disembarked.

The Huey took off again, and the two Hueys headed north toward the air base. An embassy staffer guided Arthur to the stairs and down to the office of the CIA Intelligence Officer assigned to the Embassy. The door was open. Arthur found himself facing a skinny civilian in an open-collared, short-sleeved blue shirt, sitting at a desk, and a uniformed Navy Commander sitting to the man's right in a chair facing the desk. A Vietnamese man dressed in a South Vietnamese military uniform bedecked with gold braid and medals was seated to the left of the civilian at the desk.

"Midshipman First Class Arthur Harris reporting," said Arthur. "Permission to enter."

"Come in, come in," said the man. "This office doesn't use military formalities. Come in and take a chair. I'm Charles Wallace." Arthur walked in and sat in the chair offered. "I'm the CIA Section Chief for Viet Nam. Sitting beside you is Commander Vincent Hardy, the Naval Attaché and Naval Intelligence Officer assigned to this embassy. Sitting to my left is Prime Minister Nguyen Cao Ky of the Republic of Viet Nam. He is here to discuss intelligence sharing between his government and ours.

"Mr. Harris, you are authorized to report to me in the presence of Mr. Wallace and the Prime Minister," said Commander Hardy. "Everything said in this room will be recorded and transcribed for the record but will be classified Top Secret. Officially, you were never there – or here."

"Aye, aye, Sir," said Arthur, and proceeded carefully to recount the events from the carrier takeoff until he climbed down from the helicopter on the roof of the Embassy.

"You're wounded, so you've bought a ticket home," said Commander Hardy. "You've earned a Purple Heart, but because your mission officially did not happen and you officially were not shot down in Cambodia, you won't receive one, at least not at this time. Lieutenant Commander Mason will be listed as MIA – Missing in Action -- over North Viet Nam. The plane officially belongs to the CIA and not the Navy, so the Navy will not show it missing. His family will be notified. Your name will appear nowhere in the record. So far as your official record will show, you are still at Corpus Christi Naval Air Station. However, once you are commissioned, you will officially receive your wings. Given your performance, the Navy has waived the vision requirements. You shoot better without your glasses than most pilots with perfect vision."

Commander Hardy and Prime Minister Nguyen Cao Ky stood, so Arthur stood as well and came to attention. "Mr. Harris," continued Commander Hardy, "You will receive the Viet Nam War Service Medal at an appropriate time in the future, and I will recommend you for an additional medal for valor under fire for your return to the plane to save the equipment and Mason's body, which we are in the process of recovering. If my recommendation is acted upon, you will receive the medal at a private ceremony at some time in the future, but don't hold your breath, because none of this really happened. You were never there."

"Thank you, Sir," said Arthur.

"Mr. Harris," said the Prime Minister, "you have also earned the Viet Nam Military Merit Medal, awarded by my government. I shall issue a letter to your government confirming this, and you will be allowed to receive the medal at an appropriate time."

"Thank you, Your Excellency," said Arthur.

"Now go back up to the roof," said Mr. Wallace. "Your Huey will be there to take you to Tan Son Nhut Air Base, where you will be cleaned up, your wound examined, and then the Military Transport Service will take you home. You want them to take you to Fort Rucker, or to Houston?"

"Sir, where will my shoulder be fixed?" asked Arthur.

"It can be fixed at Rucker or in Houston. At Rucker you'll have Army doctors; or in Houston you can go to Herman Hospital and a Navy surgeon who is now in civilian practice will patch you up."

"Sir, please have them take me to Houston. Going to Herman Hospital would provide cover, because it is a civilian hospital and I am not officially in the active Navy yet. Besides, it is a lot closer to Corpus Christi NAS, which is where I am right now, if my memory is correct."

"Mr. Harris, you are already thinking like an Intelligence Officer. That's good. Have a nice flight home, and maybe I'll see you back here after you're commissioned. I'd rather see you back here as a CIA agent, however. I don't like the idea of the Navy meddling in spy work."

"Thank you, Sir. May I be dismissed?"

"Yes, you're dismissed. Now go home."

"Aye, aye, Sir," said Arthur. He executed an about-face and left the room.

The Man Who Was Never There

CHAPTER 16

CONVALESCENCE

August-September 1965
Houston, Texas

Arthur sat on the side of his bed in a private room in Hermann Hospital in Houston. A Navy car had taken him to the hospital after the transport landed at Ellington Air Force Base outside of Houston. A Navy surgeon, Dr. Han Chong, a Lieutenant in the U.S. Navy Reserve and an orthopedic surgeon, had met him as he entered and took him straight to the room, where the bandage strapping his arm across his chest was removed and he shed his dirty tan uniform. Two attractive nurses helped him shower thoroughly using a hand-held shower wand, which was an interesting experience for Arthur, after which he donned a hospital gown. Lieutenant (Dr.) Chong stood facing him.

"Mr. Harris, your record will show that you dislocated your shoulder in training at Corpus Christi NAS, tearing the ligaments. I will perform a shoulder reconstruction, reconnecting the ligaments that were cut by the machete. I will go in through the machete cut, and sew it back up when I'm done. You will then have a surgical scar, not a war wound."

"Yes, Doctor," said Arthur. "I understand."

"You will be placed on a gurney and sedated, and wheeled to the surgery, where I will meet you. The anesthesiologist will put you under, and the surgery will take about two hours. I'll see you again tomorrow morning." He turned and left the room. Arthur reached for the phone and called first his parents and then Hilda. He gave the cover story Dr. Chong had given him, and Hilda promised to come see him tomorrow, if not today. When he ended the call to Hilda, he saw the gurney being wheeled into his room.

Two nurses escorted him to the bathroom, removed his hospital gown, made him use the toilet, gave him a second thorough but gentle shower using the hand-held wand, and gave his shoulder and the area around it a good (but gentle) scrubbing with dark brown liquid antiseptic soap that stained his skin. He supposed it was iodine-based. They clothed him in a clean hospital gown and helped him onto the gurney. They exposed his right shoulder, wiped it carefully again with a brown liquid antiseptic and covered him with a sheet. They attached a metal tray to the left side of the gurney and placed his left arm in it, strapping it down. They inserted an intravenous needle into the vein on the inside of his left elbow, taping it into place and connecting it to a bag of clear fluid that hung on a vertical rod at the foot of the gurney. Below the bag of fluid was another port into the tube. One of the nurses injected something through that port.

"I have given you a sedative," she said. "You will feel sleepy and relaxed, but it won't knock you out."

Arthur felt drowsy almost immediately. He felt much the way he did after the "medicine man" gave him the mixture of opium powder and Jack Daniels. He watched the lights in the corridor pass by overhead while wearing a foolish grin as the nurses wheeled him to the elevator and out of the elevator to the surgery. He remembered watching the doctor say something to him but he could not figure out what the man was saying. The doctor injected something from a syringe into the port on the tube, and another doctor put a mask over his face and he was breathing an interesting smelling gas. The doctor asked him to count backwards from 100, and he started counting – and the mist closed in and he went blank somewhere around eighty.

Awareness came slowly. He realized he was awake and thought it must be night until he realized his eyes were still closed and opened them. He saw white, and as his eyes focused he realized he was looking at a white ceiling. A glance to either side showed white curtains hanging from a metal rod suspended from the ceiling. He wondered if he could move anything, and his left arm lifted of its own accord and flopped back down on the bed.

"Good, you're awake," said a feminine voice. Arthur thought it sounded familiar. A face swam into view above him, looking down on him, and gradually came into focus. It was Hilda.

"Am 'wake," said Arthur, realizing his voice was very slurred. "I am awake," he replied, carefully articulating each sound. He felt like a drunk trying not to sound drunk. "How long have you been here?" He was speaking very slowly because of his effort at precision of enunciation.

"I came while you were still in surgery. They let me come in and sit with you while you are in recovery."

"Gooda shee you," said Arthur. "I mean, good to *sssee* you." Hilda grinned.

"You sound drunk," she said. "Take it easy. You'll come out of it soon."

"Iyam...I*yam*drunk," he replied. "Y'look cute... an'seksheee."

"Do you want anything to drink?"

"Then I'd get drunker."

"Like water."

"Oh." Arthur ran his tongue around his mouth and realized how dry it was. "Yeah." Hilda disappeared for a moment and was back with a paper cup with a flexible paper straw in it. She put her left arm under his neck and raised his head slightly, holding the cup low so the straw was against his lips. His eyes were looking down her blouse at her beautiful breasts. She wasn't wearing a bra. Although his mind was unfocused and wandering, certain things impressed themselves on his attention and memory. He opened his lips and closed them on the straw. In his mind, he saw his lips closing on her left nipple. He became aware of his arousal and diverted his eyes only to watch the sheet rise over his groin.

"Are you going to drink, or just hold the straw in your mouth. You have to suck."

He sucked, and cool liquid almost choked him. He coughed, sputtering.

"You also have to swallow," she said, pulling the cup away and wiping up the splattered water with a paper towel. He noticed that she was looking at the little tent over his groin. She laughed. "Well, *one* part of you is awake," she said.

"Yesh," he said, looking at the tent as well, "and hungry."

"There will come a time for food. In the meantime, try to drink some water." She held the cup down for him again, and this time he sucked water and drank. Thirstily, he emptied the cup, and noticed the pressure in his bladder.

"Shit," he said, "I gotta pish."

"Just a moment, sailor. I'll get the urinal." She was back in a moment with the cold metal urinal, which she inserted under the sheet and held in place for him, bending him down into it.

"Can't pish – too hard," he said. She laughed. Soon, however, the coldness of the urinal overcame his arousal and almost immediately, the urine began to flow and almost filled the urinal before he stopped. He tried to put

his right arm around her, but discovered it was strapped
across his chest and he couldn't move it at all. A sharp
pain pulsed in his shoulder from his attempt.

"Wow, that felt good," he said. "The pish, I mean."

"Your time at Corpus seems to have coarsened your
speech. You no longer sound like the gentleman you were
before the summer."

"Thatsh 'cause I'm drunk," he said. She laughed.

"Maybe you should close your eyes and sleep a little,"
she said. He heard her, but his eyes were already closed
and he was drifting into sleep.

When he awoke, she was standing there looking down
at him as if she had been there all along. She saw his eyes
open and smiled.

"How do you feel," she asked.

"I feel better now," he said. "How long was I asleep?"

"About five minutes," she said.

"It felt like a lot longer. I think I need the urinal
again." She disappeared and was back with it in a moment. "Shit! That's cold."

"Sorry," she said. He pressed his lips together and
clenched his teeth, frowning. He was trying to piss, but
Hilda's sexiness and her hand on his penis were somewhat distracting. Finally, the urine broke through and
again he nearly filled the urinal. She returned after emptying it and noticed the newly-erected tent.

"I'm afraid I'm horny," he said.

"That was a rapid recovery," she said.

"No, I don't think I can get up yet," he said. "I feel
very weak." She laughed.

"I was referring to the, uh, you know," she said.

"Oh," he said, "that. It does what it wants to do, even
when I don't want it to."

"I guess that can be inconvenient."

"Yes, especially in the middle of battle."

"How would you know about that? You're still in training." He was silent for a moment. Her lips were stern, but her eyes were smiling. He smiled.

"Your lips are smiling," she said, "but your eyes are not."

"There are things I can't tell you," he confessed, "but that is all I can say." She regarded him silently.

"Maybe someday you can tell me," she said. "I don't like secrets."

"I don't like keeping secrets from you," he said, "but while I'm in the Navy I am required to."

"I understand, but I still don't like it." She bent over him and adjusted his covers. She gave him a quick kiss on the lips. "I forgive you, because I understand that you have no choice in the matter. Now *I've* got to pee. I'll be right back." She disappeared from his view. A moment later, he saw another feminine face looking down at him.

"Ready to go to your room?" asked the nurse. His eyes glanced around, searching.

"Hilda..." he said.

"No," said the nurse, "I'm Martha..." Another feminine face appeared beside Martha's. "...and this is Mary. We're going to take you to your room, and you should take another nap, after which we'll feed you a liquid meal."

"Where's Hilda?" he asked.

"I don't know a Hilda," said Martha. He realized that the gurney was rolling down a corridor and rectangular fluorescent light panels were passing over him from his head toward his feet.

"You're taking me head first," he commented. Martha looked at him quizzically.

"Yes," she said.

"When I came to surgery you brought me feet first."

"It just has to do with the direction the gurney is facing when we start out." Martha was pushing from the foot. Mary was pulling and guiding from the head. Martha's breasts pressed against her white nurse's smock and her hips swayed seductively. His tent began to rise again. Martha noticed, a small smile on her face. Arthur was blushing. Martha looked at his face.

"No need to blush," she said. "I've seen it before. Let's get you to your room and we'll make you more comfortable."

"Hilda's my girlfriend," he said. "She was with me in the recovery room, in my cubicle. She went to the bathroom just before you came."

"When she comes out, someone will give her your room number," said Martha. Arthur continued watching Martha's body as she pushed the gurney. Arthur felt completely immersed in the moment, his attention completely occupied by what was happening, not thinking of the past or the future – almost not thinking at all, just observing and absorbing. Every detail of what was happening was apparent to him, in something of a light-headed hyper-clarity.

The gurney turned at right angles and stopped. Arthur heard elevator doors whishing open behind him. Martha pushed and the gurney entered the elevator. He saw the elevator doors close behind Martha. He felt some motion. A chime dinged and he heard elevator doors opening behind him. Martha pushed and Mary pulled to Arthur's left after the gurney had left the elevator. Down another hallway they went, the walls on both sides punctuated by brown wood doors. The wall on the left disappeared and he saw a counter with nurses behind it. The wall appeared again, and after the second door passed on the left, the gurney angled to the left and went through a doorway.

Mary and Martha maneuvered the gurney until it was immediately adjacent to a hospital bed on his right. Martha turned a crank, adjusting the height of the gurney so that it matched exactly the height of the bed. Martha and

Mary untucked the sheet under him, draping its edge over the bed. Martha went around to the other side of the bed, and Mary moved to his left side. She flipped the edge of the sheet up over him, went around and joined Martha. Their four hands gripped the gurney sheet above the bed, and they both pulled firmly. The sheet moved onto the bed, carrying him with it. They gently rolled him to his right. The pressure on his shoulder hurt a little. Martha held him in that position while Mary went to the other side. She pushed the gurney away and rolled the sheet up under him. Martha released him and she and Mary rolled him to his left. Mary held him there while Martha removed the gurney sheet, and Mary rolled him back onto his back.

"Do you need to use the urinal?" asked Martha. Arthur realized he did. Martha inserted a cold urinal under the sheet. Her hand guided him into it. He tried to urinate but couldn't. Mary walked to the hand-wash sink in the room and turned on the faucet. With the help of the sound of running water and the coldness of the urinal, he softened and began to pee. "There, now. I knew you could do it," said Martha, smiling. Arthur became aware of another face beside Martha's.

It was Hilda's, and it descended to kiss him thoroughly on the mouth, her right breast against his right hand, which was strapped into position over his left breast. Martha departed with the urinal. After the kiss, Hilda raised herself but remained bending over. Her breasts dangled enticingly. Arthur felt himself rising again to attention.

"I suggest you sit over here, Hilda," said Martha. "Arthur needs to sleep now." Hilda backed away and took her seat. Martha injected something into the port dangling near the top of the IV line. "I've given you a dose of morphine to kill the pain that will be about to start up. You'll sleep for about three hours, and I'll be back with some broth for you." Arthur felt the drug hit his system, and he drifted quickly into a dreamless sleep.

When he awoke, the room was in semi-darkness. He needed to pee. He raised his head and looked around. He was alone. He found the nurse call button on a cord pinned to his pillow. He pressed the button. Within a minute, Martha opened the door to his room.

"Good! You're awake," she said. She switched on the lights.

"I need to piss but didn't know whether I am allowed to get up to go to the bathroom."

"If a nurse is here, you can," she said. "Or, if Hilda is here, you can. Until we are sure you are steady on your feet, you must be escorted." She walked over to his bed. "Let me see you get up, but go easy; you're still under the influence of the morphine." She cranked his bed down to its lowest level and raised the portion under his torso. He raised himself on his left elbow, paused a minute, and sat up, swinging his legs carefully over the side of the bed. His head swam for a moment, but steadied. He remained sitting for a minute, his feet on the floor. Pushing down on the bed with his left hand, he raised himself to a standing position, and remained standing for a few moments, holding onto the rod that held his IV. He took one step and another, pushing the IV ahead of him with his left hand. Martha took hold of his arm at the elbow. "Now, walk toward the bathroom. I'll go with you." He walked to the bathroom, opened the door and entered. She closed the door behind them and took hold of his arm again.

"I'll be here in case you weaken. Go ahead and urinate." He pulled up his gown, realizing he needed two hands.

"I only have one hand," he said. Martha laughed and held his penis for him, aiming it in the appropriate direction. He proceeded to urinate into the toilet, and she flushed the toilet. She walked him back to his bed. Mary was waiting beside the rolling bed tray with a tray with a covered dish on it.

"I called Hilda," said Mary. "She is on her way and should be here shortly. She wanted us to call her as soon as you awoke."

"Was she at home?"

"No," said Mary, "She was at Fannin Bank, where she works. It's only a ten-minute walk from here. Why don't you try sitting in the chair?" He did, and she lowered the table and rolled it over to where he sat.

"I'll leave you two to get acquainted," said Martha, and left the room. Mary lifted the cover to reveal a steaming bowl of chicken noodle soup.

"Ah," said Arthur. "Jewish penicillin." Mary laughed. He picked up the spoon and began eating the soup. It was gone in a minute.

"You were hungry," said Mary. "Good job!"

"Yes, I was quite hungry. Still am," he said.

"OK," said Mary, if you can keep that down and still want more, I can get you more soup after thirty minutes. We want to be sure you can keep it down first. If you get through the evening without throwing up, you can have whatever you want for breakfast." The door opened and Hilda walked into the room.

"Hi, Arthur," she said. "Look at you! Sitting up and eating. You'll make a quick recovery."

"I hope so," said Arthur. "I want to spend the weekend with you before school starts. What is today?"

"Today is Wednesday, September first," said Hilda. Mary picked up the tray with the empty bowl.

"I'll get rid of this and order you more soup," she said.

"Can't I have a cheeseburger instead?" he asked.

"No way," said Mary. "Soup's the limit tonight. I'll put in for bacon, eggs, and toast with butter and jam for you for the morning."

"May I have grits, too?"

"OK, I'll add grits to the order," said Mary, laughing, as she left the room.

"With plenty of butter!" he called after her.

Hilda bent over, kissed him, and sat in the chair facing him. She was wearing a short mini-skirt, and his eyes wandered up her legs. Watching him and smiling, she said "Down, boy. Not yet. Mary will be back soon."

"She's pretty sexy, too," said Arthur, "but your skirt is shorter than hers." He realized he was saying what was immediately on his mind without modifying or editing it, so he was still drugged.

Mary returned with the soup and left again. Arthur ate the soup hungrily. Hilda escorted him to the bathroom and insisted on holding him to help him aim properly.

"If you do that, I can't aim at the toilet. You'll have to pick a higher target for me," said Arthur.

"Just lean over a little," she said, laughing.

"Won't help," said Arthur. "The floodgate is shut now." She took her hand away, and very soon he went soft, and the floodgate opened, but his aim was not accurate. Using a wad of toilet paper, she mopped up the over-spray.

Hilda visited him the next day after work and brought her own food so she could have dinner with him.

The following day, Friday, he was discharged from the hospital in the early afternoon. He asked Martha where his duffel bag was, and she told him that he arrived without one. A flight suit, however, and his khaki dress uniform were hanging in the closet. His backpack was on the floor. In it were his pistol, his revolver, Mason's insignia and dog tags, and some of the survival supplies. He noticed that the flight suit was clean and the cut at the shoulder had been mended. He dressed in his uniform, folded and rolled his flight suit and put it in the back pack.

Downstairs, the receptionist called a taxi for him, which took him the four blocks south to the intersection of Holcombe Boulevard and Fannin Street, where Fannin Bank was located. He asked the taxi to wait and walked in the front door. He walked up to a teller window that had no customer in front of it.

"I'm here to see Hilda Austin," he said.

"Are you a customer?" asked the teller, looking up and down at the young Navy officer with his right arm strapped across his chest with elastic bandaging.

"Yes, as a matter of fact," said Arthur. He kept his small checking account there. "I'll be right back, sir," said the teller. To Arthur's right, a businessman was making a series of deposit and withdrawal transactions.

Hilda was sitting in an office up the side corridor. A teller knocked on her door.

"Come in," said Hilda.

"A good-looking Navy officer is asking for you," said the receptionist. Hilda jumped up from her desk and ran to greet Arthur. A fond embrace and a long kiss followed. The man standing at the teller's window watched, a smile on his face.

"If that's the way you treat all of your customers at Fannin Bank, you're going to be very successful," he said to the teller, grinning.

"Oh," said Hilda, laughing, "we only treat *very special* customers this way. Arthur, I'll be able to leave work in about two hours. Can you take a taxi to my parents' house? I'll meet you there."

"Yes, my taxi is waiting out front." He kissed her and walked back to the taxi.

He spent the weekend at her parents' house, and Hilda returned Arthur to his apartment on Labor Day night. He hadn't been up to making the beach house trip. His duffel bag was waiting there for him in the apartment. He wondered how it had gotten through the front door. He struggled through his classes Tuesday with one hand. The elastic bandaging that strapped his arm across his chest came off Wednesday and was replaced by a sling. He still couldn't use his arm much, but he could at least take notes in class with his right hand.

He decided he needed to go see Father Joubert and go to confession. The mix of guilt he felt with the pleasure he remembered bothered him. He confessed to the killings in Viet Nam, and to the pleasure and satisfaction he had felt at killing the enemy and surviving. Father Joubert told him he was doing his duty to his country, and advised him to try to avoid the occasion of sin with Hilda. He granted him absolution, and for penance, told him to say ten Our Fathers and ten Hail Marys and to read the treatment of 'Just War' in St. Thomas Aquinas' *Summa Theologoca.* As he read the book he became less than convinced that the Viet Nam War was a "Just War," but convinced that his own performance was "just" under the definitions in the book.

His senior year went quickly. He and Hilda continued dating for a few months, but in November she arranged a date with Arthur for dinner, and broke the news to him. She had started seeing a bank officer at another bank whom she had met at a training workshop.

"Arthur," she said, while they were eating their appetizers, "I know you can't tell me what went on during the summer. I have strong feelings for you, but I can't become tied to a man who has as secret life on the side, and so I can't let myself fall in love with you. I have started seeing someone else, and I think we need to end our intimate relationship. I want us to remain good friends, however. After all, we'll always be kissing cousins." Arthur stared at her, shocked, saying nothing.

"Aren't you going to say something?" she asked.

"What should I say?" he said. "You sound as if your mind is made up."

"Are you angry?" she asked.

"I'm saddened," he said. "I'm not angry. I'm very much saddened. I had hoped that you would love me as much as I love you and that we could spend our lives together."

"Our lives really wouldn't be together if I couldn't trust what you tell me," she said. "Communication is very important to a relationship. Without full communication, the relationship is not real." Arthur lowered his eyes, looking at his plate.

"I'm not hungry any more," he said. "I'll pay for your dinner, but I need to go away and think for a while." He waved the waiter over and gave him enough money to pay for the dinner they had ordered, including a tip. He reached for Hilda's hand, lifted it to his lips, and kissed it. "Good bye, Hilda," he said. "We can remain friends, and I hope we do remain friends, but we'll have to stop seeing each other."

"I'm very sorry, Arthur," said Hilda.

"So am I," said Arthur. "So am I." He walked sadly back to his apartment, stopping at the liquor store at the Shamrock Club on the way. He bought a bottle of Jack Daniels, but instead of depositing it in the club for future use, he carried it back to his apartment. He spent the evening in the dark, drinking, but not enough to get really drunk. He turned on the desk lamp and wrote a long letter to JoAnne, pouring his heart into it, and telling her of his experience. He only told her that he had been on a secret assignment with the Navy that he couldn't tell Hilda about, and that this caused their relationship to end. He signed the letter, put it in an envelope, addressed it to her at Auburn University, affixed a stamp to the envelope, and walked to the mailbox in the Rice Village shopping center, where he mailed it. He walked back to his apartment – all eight blocks – staying on side streets, staying in the shadows, with his hand on his pistol under his jacket.

Am I paranoid? he thought. *Am I going crazy? Is my war experience driving me over the edge?* At the next corner, he turned and walked the block back to Rice Boulevard and tried to walk down the street as a civilian, not as a warrior skulking in the jungle.

He slept fitfully for about an hour and a half, tossing and turning, and gave up. He poured himself another drink and sat up reading a new James Bond novel. He finished it about nine in the morning. Unusually chilly pre-autumn air wafted in through the window. Just as he was putting the book away, there was a knock on the door. When he opened the door, his former roommate John Bartle, who was also an NROTC Midshipman, opened the door and walked in, staggering under a heavy load consisting of backpack and two large suitcases.

"You're starting early," said John, eyeing the open, half-empty bottle.

"I started last night," said Arthur. "Hilda broke up with me. I did something with the Navy this summer that's secret and that I can't talk about, and Hilda can't live with a man who keeps secrets. Why all the luggage?"

"Sorry to hear that," said John. "My cruise was uneventful, but I have flunked out of Rice. I have been ordered to active duty as a Seaman Third Class. I need a place to crash for a couple of weeks until I report. What happened on yours?"

"I can't tell you. I went to Corpus for the flight familiarization *cum* boot camp training. For part of the summer I was on duty that was classified and that I can't tell Hilda about – or you, for that matter."

"Oh," said John. He set his burdens down and sat on the side of his bed facing Arthur. "Want to talk about it?"

"What's your clearance?" asked Arthur.

"Secret, same as yours."

"You don't have the need to know." Arthur closed his book, and John looked at the cover.

"James Bond never married, you know," said John. "Relationships in which one partner keeps secrets don't work very well."

"I have learned that," said Arthur. "If I have another relationship, I'll have to make sure she doesn't know that I'm keeping secrets."

"Good luck with that," said John, laughing.

"I'll just have to have a good cover story for everything."

Arthur had a few dates with other girls on campus, after that, but nothing "stuck." JoAnne didn't reply to his letter. His mind kept returning to Hilda. He met Hilda for lunch a couple of times but did not attempt a date and she did not suggest one. By March, she had broken up with the bank officer. She called Arthur to tell him, but she declined an invitation from him for a date. Arthur decided that his career choice might well force him to a life of celibacy, if not chastity. It occurred to him that he should have become a priest, instead. At least then, celibacy would make sense.

Arthur had joined Players at the start of his junior year and enjoyed the experience. He continued in the Players in his senior year. He played bit roles, worked backstage, and designed stage sets, as he had done the year before. He designed a reusable set for Shakespeare productions that mimicked an Elizabethan stage and received recognition in the programs for each production for which he designed a set. As much as he enjoyed it, however, his experience with the Rice Players was a hobby – a diversion.

However, after his breakup with Hilda, he decided he needed to learn how to be a really good actor. If he were to be an intelligence officer, he had to be able to act convincingly. He approached Sandy Havens and asked for a private conference. When they were alone in Sandy's office in the basement of Hamman Hall, the performance hall used by the Rice Players and other campus organizations, he told him that he wanted very seriously to become a very good actor. "I need your advice on how to go about that at a college without a Drama Department," he said.

"I have an idea," said Sandy. "We're going to do Julius Caesar this year. I'm going to give you the role of Julius Caesar, as well as some other roles that do not play onstage at the same time as Caesar. You'll have to change personalities and appearance from scene to scene. Caesar will be your first major role. So far you have only played minor roles. Do you think you can do it?"

"Yes," said Arthur. "If I can't, I need to consider a career option that does not require acting. I assume that you will, as usual, appoint an understudy for the Julius Caesar role. If you don't think I can really handle it half way through the preparation, please tell me and give it to the understudy."

"You have a deal," said Sandy.

Arthur read and studied the play every evening until rehearsal work started. He had the role memorized and had practiced it in front of the mirror several times. When the cast did the first read-through of the play, Arthur did not use the script, relying on his memory. Sandy was impressed, as were the rest of the cast members.

His Caesar was well-played. He did his own makeup, and disguised himself as Murellus in the opening scene, and, after Caesar's death, he became Octavius. The personalities of all three characters were played quite differently. He changed the pitch of his voice for each role. Sandy told him afterward that his acting was superb, that he had "become" three different characters most believably. Arthur decided that his work with the Rice Players was providing good training for his future intelligence work. *I can become who I am not,* he thought.

CHAPTER 17

HUNTING AND HUNTED

June 1966
Long Beach Naval Base, California

By June, he had completed the degree requirements for the Bachelor of Arts in Architecture degree, but elected not to receive it at that time, to preserve his option with the Navy to return after his final training cruise to complete his Thesis Year. He wanted first to discuss with his family his decision to elect commissioning after his final summer training cruise to follow a Navy career. When school recessed for the Summer break, he caught a flight home.

"Dad, may I talk to you?" asked Arthur. It was Saturday morning, and he had arrived in Dothan the evening before. "Can we go for a drive? Don't you need to get something at the hardware store?" His father looked at him solemnly, folded the Saturday morning edition of *The Dothan Eagle* and rose from his easy chair.

"Let's go," he said. They walked through the dining room into the kitchen, where Arthur's Mom was washing the breakfast dishes.

"Honey," said Arthur, Sr., "We're going to the hardware store. I need to get something to stop the drip in the faucet in the back bathroom."

"Drive carefully," said Arthur's Mother. She always said that when anyone was going out and she wasn't going along. She was a committed – and experienced – back-seat driver.

Arthur Senior got into the driver's seat and Arthur took the front passenger seat in his father's four-door 1962 Chevrolet Bel-Air. His Dad backed the car out of the driveway and started up St. Andrew's Street towards downtown Dothan. "OK, Son," he said. "What do you want to talk about?"

"Dad," said Arthur, "I'm considering taking my commission and my Bachelor of Arts degree and doing a career in the Navy, instead of coming back to complete the fifth year of school for the Bachelor of Architecture degree, which wouldn't be much good to me as a naval officer."

"You could always change your mind after your enlistment and go back to school," said his Dad.

"Yes," said Arthur. "If you don't object strongly, I'm going to go ahead and opt for the Navy career, but I won't make a final decision about it until the end of this training cruise. I won't be eligible for commissioning until then, anyway."

"I'd rather you follow an architecture career," said his Dad, "but it's your life, and I do not object to your doing a career in the Navy. You can always retire from the Navy after twenty or so years, take your pension, and start another career. You'd still be a young man."

"Dad, I feel like I belong in the Navy."

"Then that's what you should do."

"Thanks, Dad," said Arthur. "I thought this was going to be a difficult discussion. How do you think Mom will take it?"

"She will be proud of you no matter what you do. But she will worry, with you in the Navy and a war on."

When they returned from the hardware store, Arthur told his Mom what he was considering, and she agreed with him that the Navy career was what he should pursue because that's what he really wanted to do. That evening, from the bedroom, he heard his mother and father talking quietly in the living room. He couldn't understand what they were saying, but then he heard his mother crying softly. He got out of bed and walked into the living room. His father and mother were sitting on the couch, his mother's face buried on his father's shoulder.

"Mom, what's the matter?" asked Arthur. He saw his mother take a deep breath and turn to face him. He saw the tears on her face.

"Your mother is worried about losing you," said his Father. "She's proud of you but knows there is a war on and that you might be killed."

"That's right," said his Mom. "I agree with your career choice, but I'm afraid – afraid for you, and afraid that we might lose you." Arthur sat beside her and put his arms around her.

"Mom," he said, "I'll try very hard not to get killed. The Navy is much safer than the Army, you know, and I'll be safe unless major war breaks out. The North Vietnamese lack the ability to mount a credible attack on our fleet."

"I know that," she said. "I'm worried about the Russians."

"The government is taking care not to draw the Russians into the conflict," said Arthur. His Mom hugged him fiercely.

"I know. I hope they succeed." She sat in his embrace for a while. Over her shoulder he saw his father smiling at him, but a frown creased his forehead.

"At Mass tomorrow," said Arthur, "let's light candles to the Holy Mother for our warriors' safety, including mine." They did so the next morning, and Arthur's father asked Father Jones for a personal blessing for Arthur. Arthur asked Father Jones for a personal blessing for his mother, although she was still a Methodist. Farther Jones solemnly pronounced the blessings, with the sign of the cross over each. It bothered him that he could not tell his family about his work in NOSI. *I have to deceive even my own family*, he thought. *How is that moral?* Yet, he did.

Driving his family home afterward, Arthur thought wryly how his religious faith had become separated from his life. He vowed to change that. He had been to confession, receiving absolution for his dalliance with Hilda, and for his killing in war, and resolved not to repeat sin in the future. At the same time, he reminded himself that the future was unknown. *I am even unknown to myself*, he thought.

For his final training cruise, he was assigned to the USS Eversole, a destroyer. He found her tied up directly to the pier at Long Beach, rather than to a row of other ships. She carried a white flag with one star on it in addition to the American flag. Arthur knew the one-star flag meant that she was the flagship of a battle group, with a commodore commanding. Commodore was a temporary rank assumed by a Captain in command of a battle group.

Two destroyers were tied up outboard of her, with a World War II-era diesel-electric submarine tied up outboard from the destroyers. Arthur stood and gazed at the Eversole with admiration. She looked much newer – and somewhat larger – than the Ingersoll, his first ship. He had read up on her history before taking the trip, using the library at the Navy Building on campus, which included classified volumes listing the capabilities of every ship in the current Navy.

On this cruise he would be an ordinary Intelligence Officer, not operating under NOSI command. He had called Thayer and asked not to be given a NOSI summer assignment so he could work in the fleet and qualify as a Surface Warfare Officer. Thayer had obliged, assigning him for his training cruise as a "normal" Intelligence Officer to the Eversole.

Eversole had been a World War II destroyer but she had been through the "remodeling" called FRAM II, converting her into a state-of-the-art submarine hunter. The upper forward gun turret had been removed, and in its place was a deck from which rockets and torpedoes could be launched. While the Ingersoll had single-gun turrets, Eversole's turrets had two guns each. Both the Ingersoll and the Eversole had 5-inch guns. The Ingersoll had four, one-gun turrets, while the Eversole had two, two-gun turrets. A small helicopter hanger had been installed where the anti-aircraft midships turret had been and what had been the 50-caliber anti-aircraft machine gun deck behind it had become a landing pad. Both ships had the same number of guns, but the Eversole's were longer, shot heavier projectiles and accepted longer powder cartridges.

The ship's "remodeling" converted her from a gun-rich attack destroyer to a modern, ASW (Anti-Submarine Warfare) destroyer, carrying the Secret DASH helicopter. DASH (Drone Anti-Submarine Helicopter) was a major part of the United States Navy's Fleet Rehabilitation and Modernization (FRAM) program of the late 1950s to render the navy more capable in ASW. The navy started FRAM because the Soviet Union was building submarines faster than the U.S. could build ASW frigates. Instead of building new ASW frigates, the navy used the FRAM upgrade to catch up by converting older ships that were otherwise obsolete in terms of modern naval ASW combat.

The navy was able inexpensively to upgrade the sonar, radar, depth charge system, and torpedo system on World War II-era destroyers, which was done in the FRAM I upgrade. However, the Navy still needed a stand-off weapon to attack out to the edge of the sonar's range. ASW cruisers carried a manned helicopter for this purpose, but the old destroyers had no room to add a full flight deck. FRAM II added the DASH helicopter. The DASH was a light drone helicopter that carried a sonar microphone on a long tether, and could release depth charges, including nuclear depth charges, or torpedoes. The DASH aircraft were considered expendable. Because they were difficult to control at a distance, many of them were thus "expended."

A sophisticated array of microwave and radar antennae had been mounted on a mast above the Bridge, and she had been equipped with state-of-the art sonar. The little hangar aft contained the little DASH helicopters, which somewhat resembled giant mosquitos. The DASH could be deployed over the horizon to a range of up to 22 miles, where she could drop her sonar mike in the water and listen passively for submarines, considerably extending the sonar range available to the ship by itself. If a hostile sub were detected, DASH could launch a torpedo or drop a depth charge. DASH effectively increased the range of detection and attack by 22 miles. However, she was piloted "blind", which meant that once she was over the horizon, the pilot could see only by radar. Many DASH 'copters were lost on the longer-range missions for that reason.

Arthur started walking again, carrying his duffel bag strap over his left shoulder, and holding his envelope of orders in his left hand. He ascended the gangway, dropped his duffel bag, did a right face, saluting the flag at the stern, and then did a left face, saluting the officer of the deck.

"Permission to come aboard, Sir," he said. The Chief who was doing Officer of the Deck duty returned his salute.

"Permission granted, Sir," said the Chief.

"Midshipman First Class Arthur Harris reporting for duty," said Arthur, handing over his envelope of orders. The Chief pulled out the orders, glanced at them briefly, and handed them back.

"Sir, I am Chief Bosun's Mate Jack Harper," he said. "Welcome aboard. Can you find Officers Country?" The area of the ship containing the officers' staterooms and the wardroom was called "Officers' Country."

"Yes, Chief, I have served a training cruise on a destroyer before."

"Good. Third stateroom on the right as you move forward. Lieutenant Commander Timothy Luke. He'll be your roommate and is in charge of Midshipman training on this cruise. He's the also the XO for the Eversole. You'll like him, I think."

"Thank you, Chief. I know Mr. Luke. I served with him on the Ingersoll three summers ago." Chief Harper saluted Arthur, who returned the salute.

Arthur entered the transverse passageway that was the station for the Officer of the Deck in port and where the bulletin board was posted with the Orders of the Day and the Duty Roster. After a long glance at the Duty Roster, he opened the hatch to his left and descended the ladder to the passageway forward through Officers' Country. He found Lieutenant Commander Luke where the Chief had said and rapped with his knuckles on the jamb of the hatchway.

"Permission to enter, Sir," he said. Luke was sitting at the little desk in the stateroom, going through some paperwork, and looked up, a smile of recognition lighting up his face.

"Mr. Harris! Welcome aboard," said Luke. "I am still waiting for the list of Midshipmen for this cruise, which hasn't made it this far yet." Arthur handed him his orders. Luke looked at them, separated his carbon copy from Arthur's, put his in a file drawer and handed Arthur's copy back. "Toss your duffel on the bottom rack. The note from the Chief says you are to be my roommate, so I guess he knows more about the incoming Middies than I do. The bottom rack is mine, but you may use it to unpack and stow your gear. You get the right-hand locker." Arthur quickly emptied his duffel bag, stored his gear and washed his hands in the sink. He removed his tunic and hung it in the locker.

"What's the uniform of the day?" he asked.

"If you're going out on deck, it is dress khakis. If not, it is work khakis." Arthur had arrived in dress khakis. Luke's shoulder boards bore the two broad stripes and one narrow stripe of a Lieutenant Commander. Arthur's bore the four narrow stripes of a Midshipman First Class.

"Short sleeved or long sleeved?" asked Arthur.

"Take your pick," said Luke. "Since it's ninety-five degrees outside, I suggest short sleeves."

"It's now 1600 hours. What time do we go to the wardroom?"

"Dinner mess is served at 1800 hours."

"What is dress for the wardroom?"

"Dress khakis."

"OK," said Arthur. He changed quickly to work khakis, the short-sleeved variety. "With your permission, Sir, I'm going to go walk through the ship."

"You've got my blessing, Mr. Harris," said Luke. Arthur left, giving himself a walking tour of the ship from stem to stern, observing the features he had studied before deploying for his cruise. He met several of the other officers, the chiefs and some of the crew. By the time he returned to the stateroom to change for dinner, he knew his way around the ship.

Officers' country was well-ventilated, but it was not air conditioned, and so its ambient temperature was equal to that of the outside air at best, or hotter, at worst. It was hot. However, the ever-moving air from the ventilation duct provided a little bit of a cooling effect so that the stateroom was bearable. When Arthur arrived back at the stateroom, Luke was still doing paperwork.

"Mr. Luke, may I sit on your rack?" he asked.

"Be my guest, Mr. Harris, just don't drip sweat on it." Arthur sat. A vent from the duct was blowing straight at him. He checked his watch; it was 1730 hours. He changed, dressing in his dress khakis, which were only slightly wrinkled.

"Sir, do I pass inspection?" he asked. Luke looked him up and down.

"You'll do," he said. "How far did you travel today?"

"I came from Dothan, Alabama," said Arthur, "with stops and changes of aircraft in New Orleans and Dallas." Luke grinned and shook his head.

"I don't know how it is that your uniform isn't as wrinkled as a prune," said Luke. "Yours is less wrinkled than mine."

"I stopped on the way from the airport and got it dry cleaned and pressed," said Luke.

"Smart. But, I already knew you were smart. Cost you an arm and a leg?"

"No, Sir," said Arthur. "They charged me $1.75."

"Not bad," said Luke. "I guess someone forgot to tell you that you can have your uniform cleaned and pressed here on board. There's not much demand for that while we're in port, but the steward who runs the dry-cleaning machine is on board and gets lazy if we don't keep him busy."

"So I wasted $1.75. Now I know," said Arthur, grinning. Luke stood up, laughing.

"You take the chair now while I get dressed," he said. Arthur sat down. When Luke was dressed, he and Arthur walked up the passageway to the Officers' Wardroom. They were greeted by Commander John Renn, who introduced himself as the Captain of the Eversole. With him was an officer with Commodore's stripes, four broad stripes and one narrow stripe, on his shoulder boards. Captain Renn introduced him as Commodore Wren, commander of the Antisubmarine Warfare Task Force of which the Eversole was the flagship. Arthur thought that the similarity of names would have been confusing but for the consistent use of titles for the Captain and the Commodore.

"Mr. Harris will be my Assistant Intelligence Officer on this cruise," said Luke. "I will rotate him through all the officer billets on this ship to make it easier for him to qualify as an unrestricted line officer."

"It is a pleasure to have you on board, Mr. Harris," said Captain Renn.

"Welcome to my task force," said Commodore Wren. Other officers were arriving and took their positions at the table, standing at attention behind their seats. The Captain took the head of the table, with the Commodore to his left, the "honored guest" position. Mr. Luke took the position to the Captain's right – as Executive Officer, he was the Captain's right-hand man – and he placed Arthur to his right. The other officers took their places – the Engineering Officer, the Deck Officer, the Supply Officer, the Ship's Doctor, the Assistant Engineering Officer, etc. Finally, the Chaplain, Lieutenant Rabbi Stein, took position at the foot of the table. The other Midshipmen on board for summer training were Midshipmen 4th class, and slept, worked and ate with the crew, as Arthur had on his first cruise. On command from the Captain, Lieutenant Stein asked God's blessing. He used the standard blessing from the Book of Common Prayer, but he omitted the reference to Jesus at the end.

"Gentlemen, at ease," said the Captain. "Please be seated." All took their seats. "Joining us this evening is Midshipman 1st Class Arthur Harris. He is the only First Class Midshipman with us this summer. He will be rotating through officer billets but will be Mr. Luke's Assistant Intelligence Officer. Please make him welcome." The Captain turned to the Commodore and began conversing, so conversations broke out all around the table.

"How did you like your flight familiarization summer training?" asked Luke.

"I enjoyed it," said Arthur. "I am hoping that by the time I am commissioned, they will have relaxed the vision requirements to allow officers using contact lenses to become pilots. That way I could do surveillance flights."

"Do you want to fly the U-2?" asked Luke.

"No," said Arthur, "the Navy doesn't fly U-2s. They are all flown by CIA pilots masquerading as Air Force officers. The Navy flies Crusader and Phantom II jets for low-level surveillance."

"Did you get to try out a jet during your familiarization?"

"Yes, I did," said Arthur, forcing himself not to smile. "I enjoyed it." Mr. Luke was smiling.

"Did you know that Commander Thayer, with whom you worked at Guantanamo in '62, is now deputy assistant Director, ONI?"

"No," said Arthur, "I didn't."

"He and I are old friends. I called him last night to touch base, since we'll be at sea mostly for the next six weeks."

"Next time you speak with him," said Arthur, "please give him my greetings."

"He told me to give you his greetings," said Mr. Luke. "I understand your last summer training was somewhat adventurous."

"Yes," said Arthur. "Flying is a great adventure for me."

"How much flying did you do?" asked Luke.

"Oh, I guess the usual. I soloed in the T-28."

"You did more than that, according to Commander Thayer."

"I really don't have any comment on that."

"And I really don't need to know the details," said Luke, "but I can tell you that you answered me correctly. Until you know that I have need to know, you can't tell me, even if you suspect I already know. How much do you know about the Eversole's anti-submarine systems?"

"I studied all I could find in the NROTC library before coming out here," said Arthur, thankful for the change in subject. "I know she's been through FRAM II, and I know what systems were installed during FRAM II. I read up on the sonar systems and the DASH."

"Then you're ready to start work," said Mr. Luke. "Good job."

"Well, I was an Eagle Scout," said Arthur. "The Boy Scout Motto is, 'Be prepared.'" Mr. Luke laughed. He talked with Arthur about the capabilities of the ASW systems on the Eversole and filled in the gaps in Arthur's knowledge. That conversation took up the rest of the dinner time.

"Gentlemen," said the Captain, as the dessert dishes were being cleared away, "I suggest an early bedtime for those of us not on watch. We will be firing up the boilers on the midwatch and making way at 0600 hrs. Good night, all. I'm hitting the rack." The midwatch was the watch period from Midnight to 0400 hours. The officers all began leaving the wardroom and walking to their staterooms.

The next morning, the three ships of the task force steamed out to sea in line formation (single file), led by their target submarine, USS Rasher, followed by the other two destroyers and Eversole. They would rendezvous with a fourth destroyer to complete the task force, which was part of DESDIV (Destroyer Division) 252, assigned to ASWGRU (Anti-Submarine Warfare Group) FIVE.

When they had cleared the harbor, the three destroyers formed up in a triangle formation with USS Eversole, the flagship, on point; USS Larsen to starboard, and USS Renshaw to port. Fletcher, which had waited for the rest to arrive on station, joined formation at the rear to make a diamond shaped formation. At that point Rasher took up position behind Fletcher.

The submarine left formation and headed west. All of those who had been on deck for departure were now below, changing into working uniforms. Arthur and the officers not on watch straggled into the wardroom for breakfast. Arthur and Luke sat together. The Captain was on the Bridge, but the Commodore was in the Wardroom.

"Mr. Harris," said Mr. Luke, "I am assigning you first to the Sonar Room. Your first job will be to find the Rasher. Once you do, you will feed me her bearing, range, course and speed. I'll be on the Bridge, but we'll be connected by headphones and microphones. Chief Morrison is running the Sonar Room and will show you the ropes."

"Why isn't the Sonar Room called the Sonar Compartment?" asked Arthur. "All the other 'rooms' on the ship are called 'compartments.'"

"Can't tell you," said Mr. Luke. "Tradition, I suppose, but I have no idea why. It is sometimes called the 'Sound Hut' but that's the old name used by people of Korean War or older vintage."

"As you know, I did some sonar work on the Ingersoll," said Arthur.

"I remember," said Mr. Luke. "The Ingersoll had Korean War vintage sonar equipment. The Eversole's equipment is much updated. You'll be impressed."

"After a day in the Sound Hut," said the Commodore, "your ears will ring for hours."

"I'll get used to it, Commodore," said Arthur. "I did on my first cruise."

"With the Eversole's equipment you don't have to listen to the pinging all the time," said Mr. Luke. "The displays are sophisticated enough that you can use them instead of your ears except when you are in passive sonar mode. Even then, the scopes will show an image of the sounds you are receiving."

"What odds do you give us to find a Russian sub?" Arthur asked Mr. Luke.

"Pretty good odds," he replied. "If there is a Russian near enough to hear our active sonar, she'll come closer to try to observe and learn more about us. If you spot that, you'll go to passive mode and record her sounds and print the sound chart. I'll tell you why later." Arthur smiled, remembering that he had done that of his own accord on his first cruise.

After their breakfast Arthur and Timothy Luke excused themselves and went to their stateroom. Luke closed the hatch.

"Now I'll tell you what I couldn't tell you in the wardroom," he said. "ONI is building an analytical database of Russian submarine sounds. Each ship has her own distinct sound signature. We are hoping to be able to build a signature catalog that will allow the identification of an individual submarine by her sound signature alone."

"That would be pretty impressive," said Arthur.

"It already is. We have a catalog on board of the Soviet subs that have been signatured, but most of them are from their Atlantic fleet. This cruise will be the first to start tracking the Russians in the Pacific. On the Ingersoll, we tracked and recorded Soviet submarines when we encountered them, but we were not actively looking for them, and the program of collecting recordings had not yet been devised. On the Eversole, that is our primary mission. We'll start out by doing ASW exercises with the Rasher as the target – but when we find a Russian, the Rasher will join the hunting as part of our team."

"Wouldn't a nuke be better than the Rasher? A nuclear attack submarine?"

"Not really. You see, the advantage of a nuclear submarine is its speed. It can, if it is headed in the right direction, outrun a torpedo. But nuclear subs are noisy. They can shut down to quiet running mode, but their cooling-water circulating pumps must keep running until the reactor cools off. If the reactor cools off, the sub can't put on a burst of speed and get away. So, they keep their reactors hot, keep the pumps running, and otherwise make themselves as silent as they can. A diesel sub, running submerged on electric power in quiet mode, is much quieter than a nuke.

"Another advantage of the nukes is their ability to run deep. They can go much deeper than conventional submarines. They can find a thermal boundary, a thermocline, even a very deep one, and get under it, becoming invisible to sonar that is above the thermocline. A conventional sub can do that too, but only at relatively shallow depths. A conventional sub can cut power entirely and disappear from the passive sonar scopes. A nuke can't do that."

"Will we be using mostly passive sonar?" asked Arthur.

"We will be using passive sonar all the time," answered Luke. "But we will also use active sonar. We can't go quiet, like a sub can, so we will run active sonar until we find a target, and switch to passive sonar and listen to it. If it is a Russian sub, we'll record the sounds and print the sound signature chart, and when we get back, ONI's computer will run an analysis of them and develop a computerized database of the signatures. Someday the Navy will have onboard computers that can compare a newly-recorded sound signature to the signatures in the database to identify an individual ship, but computers are too big and need too much electricity to use them on board a ship now. That's why we still use the WW II mechanical computers for fire control. Come on, let's go to the Sonar Room."

Arthur took his study notebook from his locker and the two men walked up the ladder to the sonar room, located at the same level as the Bridge. Immediately behind the Bridge was the Communications Room (Com Room, also called the Radio Shack), with the Combat Information Center (CIC) above it right under the radar antenna, and the Bridge in front of it. Behind the Com Room was the Sonar Room. Timothy Luke passed the Sonar Room and entered the Com Room, and Arthur followed him.

"This," said Luke, "is the Com Room. Signalman First Class Short runs it. It is equipped with short wave, AM and FM broadcasting equipment. It can also send signals by Sonar. Not only does it communicate, but it listens for enemy communications using an automatic scanning method that lets Short listen to any signal the scanner finds on any frequency. He has a number of code reference manuals for the codes believed to be used by the Russians. He also has our code manuals. He can receive and record a transmission and decode it with the code books.

"That room beyond" – he indicated a small compartment through another hatchway – "is the Crypto Room. Our crypto machine is in it. We can take a message that needs to be sent out, encrypt it, and send it. We can receive an encrypted message, decrypt it, and send it to the Captain. Only someone with a Top-Secret clearance can go into the Crypto Room, but only in my presence or that of Signalman 1st Class Short, and only on a need-to-know basis. Most of our routine messages in or out use the telex machine. You will do some duty on this cruise in the Com Room. Now let's go to Sonar."

They turned and went to the room they had just passed. Luke un-dogged the hatch, they both went in, and he dogged it shut again. "This is a soundproof compartment. Well, almost soundproof. When we do gunnery, you can hear some of the noise of the guns, transmitted through the metal of the ship. Actually, you feel it more than hear it. Mr. Harris, this is Chief Morrison. Chief, Midshipman 1st Class Arthur Harris. Mr. Harris is also an Intelligence Officer and is already cleared for Top Secret, so there is nothing on this ship that is closed to him. I'll leave you to show him the ropes. Happy hunting!" Timothy Luke un-dogged the hatch, and let himself out, dogging the hatch back in place from outside.

"Mr. Harris," said Chief Morrison, "Welcome to Sonar. First, I'll show you the secure hatch dogs. In the event we are boarded by the enemy, we can lock ourselves in here using this second set of dogs, which is only on the inside of the door. Once we double-dog the hatch using the secure lugs, no one can get in without burning a hole in the hatch. At all other times we leave the secure dogs undogged. We double-dog the hatch only under simulated or actual boarding of the ship by enemy forces. That's the origin of the phrase, 'I double-dog dare you.' I know you have worked with sonar before, but this is state-of-the-art sonar. We still have the earphones so we can listen to incoming sounds, and we have speakers we often turn on to listen without having to wear earphones, but we have a set of displays here that is new. With the new displays, we can pin down the position, speed and direction of travel of any object that is picked up by the sonar. We can watch a sound signature of a designated target, in a range of frequencies and magnitudes, like an earthquake recorder. It works both in passive and active mode. In passive mode, it displays the signature of the sounds emitted by the target. In active mode, it breaks down the returning echoes, allowing an analysis of the shape of the object producing the echo. With it we can easily tell the difference between a whale return and a submarine return. All the data from this scope can be charted on paper and saved. It can also be recorded on this tape recorder. We do both, and when in port, we send a package to ONI in Washington where they do additional analysis with their computer. This book is our sound catalog. Russian ships and submarines whose sound signatures have been captured are in this book. We can visually match a sound chart from this with the sound chart on the signature scope."

"I assume that you can adjust the displays to show more or less distance, and therefore less and more detail?"

"Yes. These new displays allow us a great deal of flexibility. I'll explain all the controls as I use them."

"Thank you, Chief."

"Coffee?"

"Thanks, I'd like some."

"We make our own coffee here, as do the CIC and the Bridge." He lifted the percolator and poured steaming coffee into a ceramic mug, handing it to Arthur.

"Thanks," said Arthur. He sipped his coffee, savoring the bitter taste of the strong, hot, unsweetened brew. As he did so, the loudspeaker in the room crackled and the Captain's voice boomed into the room.

"Captain to Sonar. Start hunting." The Chief thumbed the switch on the microphone that was mounted to the upper left corner of the desk in front of the Sonar Display Panel.

"Sonar to Captain. Aye, aye, Sir." He turned to Arthur. "Sir, please stand right behind me and watch me carefully. I'll explain everything I am doing. On the next run, you'll sit and I'll stand."

"Very well, Chief," said Arthur.

"I'm going to hunt in active mode for a short while, switch to passive, back to active, alternating. We can't go quiet, so any submarine out there is going to hear us anyway, but when we're in active mode we'll have trouble hearing them except as an echo, so every so often I'll switch to passive mode and just listen. Here goes active mode." He flicked a toggle switch and a sharp "Ping!" noise came over the loudspeakers. The scopes recorded returning echoes as bright spots. One large bright spot appeared and a subdued "Ping!" noise came over the speakers simultaneously, somewhat muffled, somewhat distorted, but definitively a ping.

"Sonar to Bridge," said the Chief. "We have a target bearing 330 at 43,000 meters, inbound."

"Very well, Sonar," said the Captain's voice. "We see the target on radar. It is a surface ship. Looks like a freighter. Let me know if anything else turns up."

"Aye, aye, Sir." The Chief turned to Arthur. "Sir, notice the bright spots near the center of the scope. Those are the other ships of our task force. You didn't really hear their echoes because their proximity blended the echoes in with the outgoing sound. Sound travels in sea water much faster than in the air. The sonar measures the time between the outgoing signal and the echo and divides by twice the speed of sound in seawater to display the distance on the scope. The returning echo was slightly higher in pitch than the outgoing echo, so I know from the Doppler effect that the target is headed towards us rather than away from us. This scope," he pointed at the upper left scope, "displays the relative speed in text right under the echo. The distance between us is decreasing at the rate of ten knots. Had she been going away from us, the pitch of the echo would be lower than the pitch of the outgoing pitch. Oh, here's another!" Now Arthur could hear a second echo return, at a higher pitch.

"Sonar to Bridge," said the chief. "We have another target, distance 12,000 meters, incoming, closing at 15 knots, bearing 90 degrees."

"Very well, Sonar," said the Captain's voice. "She's not on radar. Must be our sub."

Arthur could hear the vibration of the ship's engines increasing in pitch, and the ship started rolling with rolls of greater amplitude. The echoes on the scope near them remained in the same relative positions, but the two targets rotated until the second target was directly at the top of the scope, showing that the ship had turned to head toward the submarine.

"I'm going to passive mode," said the Chief, flipping the switch back down. The sharpness of the bright spots on the scope decreased dramatically and they became fuzzy little blobs on the screen, just a few shades lighter than the deep green of the background. The Chief turned up the volume and handed a second set of earphones to Arthur, who put them on.

"If you listen closely, you can hear a grinding noise at about the C below middle C. That's our freighter's engine. Mixed in with that you can hear a sort of whiny noise at B-flat just below middle C, 60 cycles per second. That's the engine of the sub. That tells us she's running on her electric engine without Diesel recharging. The Diesel engine runs at lower pitch and is louder than the electric. Almost all electric motors in the world run at B-flat just below middle C. We'll be in striking range in a minute. At 15 knots closing speed, we'll be on top of her in less than fifteen minutes." They continued watching the scopes and listening for about ten minutes.

Arthur heard a new sound – a squealing noise, diminishing rapidly in volume.

"That's a torpedo. Watch the scope." A small white blip sped upward from the center toward the approaching echo of the sub. It reached the sub, and then appeared on the other side of the sub's blip, still moving. "Sonar to Bridge. You were dead on but you missed her. She's running deep."

"Very well, Sonar. We'll try depth charges." A new squealing sound could be heard, increasing in pitch, and a small white blip began dropping down the scope from the sub.

"Sonar to Bridge. Incoming torpedo." The ship leaned suddenly to port and felt like it was bouncing.

"Captain is starting evasive action," said the Chief. He turned sharply to starboard." Arthur watched as the torpedo blip seemed to turn left and streamed on past the center. "Sonar to Bridge. She missed us." Now the ship leaned sharply to the right as she came around to engage the sub again. The blip moved to the center of the scope over a few minutes. As it passed through the center of the scope, the Chief reached and turned the headphone volume way down. Arthur heard two loud thumps in the earphones. Along with the second thump came a "clang" sound.

"Sonar to Bridge. Second depth charge contacted the sub." Depth charges are drums of explosive material set to go off at the water pressure encountered at specific depths.

"Very well, Sonar. Secure from ASW exercise. Come out on the Bridge and watch."

Arthur and the Chief went out to the flying Bridge and watched as the Rasher surfaced, bow first. She executed a wide turn, joining formation with the Eversole, about 100 feet out. A few officers appeared in the conning tower and waved at the Eversole. Arthur and the others on deck waved back. Abruptly, the men visible on the submarine ducked out of sight and the submarine nosed down, disappearing quickly below the waves.

"Back to work," said the Chief. He and Arthur rushed back to the Sonar Room. "Going active," said the Chief. They both watched the scopes for echoes, listening to the pings. They quickly found the sub, as it pulled away to the starboard. They followed its track as it made a great circle to the rear, eventually disappearing in the echoes of the Eversole's wake.

"Sonar to Bridge," said the Chief. "Target is hiding in our wake."

"Very well, Sonar," said the Captain's voice. "Let's see if we can flush her out." The Captain's voice sounded over the ship-wide loudspeakers. "Deploy subsurface practice mines," he ordered.

"The Captain is deploying dummy subsurface mines behind the Eversole," said the Chief, "hoping that the sub will change course to avoid them. That might or might not work. The sub could go deeper than the mines and miss them. It's a risky move for the sub, but she is using active sonar. You can hear her pings. She should be able to spot the mines and may be able to avoid them. At the same time, her active pinging will pin down her position for us and we can launch torpedoes at her."

"Chief," said Arthur, "She's gone silent. She stopped pinging and I can't hear her engine, either."

"Sonar to Bridge," said the Chief. Target has gone silent. Recommend changing course to take her out of our wake."

"Very well, Sonar," said the Captain. Come right 90 degrees." Again, the pitch and roll of the ship changed as the ship came about to the new course.

"Now we'll go active and see if we can find her," said the Chief. He flipped the switch that started the Eversole's sonar pinging. Nothing showed on the scopes, however. There was a hazy scattering of returns along where the wake had been.

"I think she's found a thermocline," said the Chief. "Now, she'll be hard to find, especially if she stays silent."

With the Chief constantly advising the Captain, the Eversole changed course to pass directly over the last known location of the submarine, on the theory that a sonar ping straight down might penetrate the thermal layer, known as a thermocline, while a ping at an angle might be deflected. However, the sounds of the Eversole herself would get in the way and spotting the sub would be a long shot. As they passed over the location where they believed the submarine lay, waiting, they caught no identifiable echoes.

"Sonar to Bridge," said the Chief, "we see nothing."

"Chief, there's an echo to port," said Arthur.

"I take that back, Captain," said the Chief. "We have an echo bearing 200 degrees at a distance of about 6 kilometers."

"How did she get over there?" asked the Captain. "She can't go that fast submerged. Are you sure that's our target?"

"No, Captain," said the Chief. "That's probably our Soviet shadow." The Chief was busy turning on switches and loading tape onto the tape recorder.

"Bridge to Sonar," said the Captain, "we will engage the target."

"Aye, aye Captain," said the Chief. All gear is operational and ready to record. Going passive."

"Very well, Sonar. Torpedo, depth charge and mining stations, stand by."

The Chief turned off the active pinging. The spot on the scope that identified the target reduced in brightness but remained. He and Arthur listened closely to the sounds and watched the three oscilloscope-like displays, one recording variations in pitch, one recording variations in frequency, and one showing the overall sound signature of the combination of sounds coming from the submarine.

"She's nuke, and she's Russian," said the Chief. "Hear the intermittent gurgle in the pump sounds? Hear the vibrations? That's a November Class nuke. November was the first generation of Russian nuclear attack submarines. Despite their noisiness, they are hard to track when they rig for silent running because their hulls are rubber-coated, making them difficult targets to ping." Arthur listened carefully, identifying the sounds pointed out by the Chief. He looked at the sound graph and opened his study notebook.

"Chief, that submarine is K-42," he said, after a few moments of leafing through his notebook.

"How do you know?" asked the Chief.

"From her sound signature." He showed the Chief the chart in his notebook. I recorded her in the Summer of '63."

"Sonar to Bridge," said the Chief. "We have a November Class Russian nuclear attack submarine, believed to be K-42."

"Very well, Sonar," said the Captain. "Changing course for slow intercept. Let me know when we are within torpedo range."

"Aye, aye, Captain," said the Chief. He and Arthur watched the scopes as the two grew gradually closer together.

"Sonar to Bridge," said the Chief. We are within torpedo range, bearing 270 degrees.

"Chief," said Arthur, "it looks like we have already launched," said Arthur, pointing at the two torpedo tracks on the scope heading on an intercept course for the Russian.

"Sonar to Bridge," said the Chief. "Torpedoes are on good intercept track."

"I did not give a launch order," said the Captain. "Who launched?" No one replied.

"Sonar to Captain," said the Chief. "Echo for submarine emerging from directly underneath us on bearing to intercept November."

"I'll be damned!" said the Captain. "Rasher must have been hiding beneath us and launched torpedoes." Arthur and the Chief watched the torpedo tracks on the sonar scope. It appeared the Russian was trying evasive maneuvers, turning away and increasing speed. However, it was too late. Arthur and the Chief heard the loud thumps of the practice explosive charges as the torpedoes struck the Russian submarine. Practice torpedoes are equipped with charges similar to loud firecrackers. They would do no damage to the sub but would make a noise that would carry some distance underwater.

"Bridge to Sonar," said the Captain. We have her on Radar. She has surfaced." The Eversole turned on a direct intercept course and, within minutes, the conning tower of the Russian submarine could be seen. Eversole pulled alongside and reduced speed. The Russian crew was on deck, standing at attention and saluting.

"This is the Captain," said the speaker system. "Man the rails and return salute." Arthur and the Chief joined the others on the Bridge to return the salute being offered by the Russians. Arthur carried a camera with a telephoto lens and snapped pictures of the submarine and her identification number to be matched with her sound signature. She was, indeed, K-42. Just then, Rasher surfaced between the Eversole and the Russian. Her officers emerged on the conning tower and returned the Russians' salute.

The Russian captain waved at the American ships and all the Russians scrambled below as the Russian submarine slipped below the waves and disappeared.

For the next two weeks, Eversole's task force played cat and mouse with the Russian submarine. Rasher scored two practice "kills" on the Eversole, but Eversole's task force scored ten kills on the Russian, and five of the kills were from Rasher, proving that a WW-II era diesel-electric submarine could overcome a Russian nuclear attack submarine. The Russian played observer, never launching an attack, but surfacing when an attack upon it hit the target. Arthur and the Chief carefully recorded every encounter. Eventually, the Russian surfaced, its captain waving to the Eversole, and K-42 slipped below the waves and headed away at a speed the task force could not match. November was headed home, and no doubt would have to file a detailed report on how vulnerable she had been.

Arthur and the Chief went to the Bridge to speak with the Captain. Arthur took his notebook with him. The Chief outlined the project underway to record sound signatures of Soviet submarines and showed him Arthur's chart from the Summer of 1963.

"Captain, Mr. Harris anticipated ONI's project by three years. In this notebook is his work from the summer of '63. The sound signature he developed for K-42 enabled him to identify her as soon as we got a good graph on her."

"Mr. Harris," said the Captain, "I'll include that in my report on this exercise. Good work, Mr. Harris."

Eversole and her task force made a course for Pearl Harbor.

The next morning, however, Arthur was in the Sonar Room when he spotted a sonar return from a relatively large submarine. He called the Chief over to look at it. Both put on their headphones and started the recorder. After about fifteen seconds of listening, the Chief took off his headphones.

"She's one of ours," he said. "She's big, so she's a missile submarine." He keyed the microphone. "Sonar to Bridge.

"Go ahead, Sonar," said a voice from the Bridge.

"We have an echo for a Boomer – a large nuclear submarine of the class that carries ICBMs. She's one of ours."

"Very well, Sonar," said the Captain's voice. "Give me bearing and direction and we'll intercept."

"Bearing 175 degrees, distance 22 kilometers, travelling at a speed of thirty-five knots, on a course that will intercept ours in about 25 minutes."

"Very well," said the Captain. "Steady as she goes. We'll pretend we don't see her, let her get close, and torpedo her." Arthur and the Chief watched the blip on the scopes grow steadily closer.

The Chief was pouring himself a cup of coffee when Arthur spotted two torpedo tracks departing the submarine.

"Sonar to Bridge," said Arthur. "Target has launched torpedoes."

"Begin evasive maneuvers!" commanded the Captain.

The ship rocked, rolled and pitched unexpectedly as the Captain took her through evasive maneuvers, but with each maneuver, the torpedoes changed course and continued their approach. In a matter of minutes two sharp "bang" sounds rang through the Eversole as the torpedoes struck her and discharged their practice loads.

"All engines stop," commanded the Captain. "Deck crew, man the port rails and prepare to salute." Arthur and the Chief joined the Bridge crew on the port side. In a moment, a very large, torpedo-shaped cylinder emerged from the water nose-first and settled onto the surface. Arthur had never seen a missile sub up close before and was amazed at how large she was. The submarine's officers emerged in the conning tower and the Eversole's captain ordered his crew to salute. The submarine's crew returned the salute, and the submarine began accelerating.

"All engines ahead flank speed," said the Captain. The Eversole began surging forward, white water churning at her fantail. The other three destroyers were on station behind the Eversole, and Rasher started in the middle, directly behind the Eversole, but was soon left behind, having a top speed on the surface of 20 knots. Before long, the ASW task force was steaming at maximum speed, about 35 knots, but the boomer was rapidly pulling ahead of them. She turned and began "swimming" in lazy circles around the task force. After the second circle she sub-

merged and Arthur and the Chief returned to the Sonar
Room. They watched the scopes as the submarine drew
steadily ahead of the task force until she disappeared from
sonar.

"How fast can she go?" asked Arthur.

"Fast enough to swim circles around us on the surface,
and she's faster underwater. On the surface, officially, she
can go about 35 knots. Underwater, officially, she can do
about 40 knots. However, since we were doing 35 knots
she was moving considerably faster than that." ASW exercises continued until the task force approached Pearl
Harbor.

Eversole's little task force steamed into Pearl Harbor,
the crew lining the rails in dress white uniforms. The Captain gave the crew three days of shore leave. As on his
first cruise, Arthur and the non-duty officers explored Diamond Head, the beaches, and most of all, the night life.
Timothy Luke and Arthur shared a hotel room at the
Sheraton Princess Kaiulani Hotel, not one of the newest
hotels, but one they could afford. Of course, they did the
mandatory visit to Don Ho's famous night club and restaurant and enjoyed the show. This was their last night of
"liberty" and so they made the most of it, bar-hopping
from strip joint to strip joint. They ended the evening at
the bar in their hotel, confident that they could find their
way to their rooms from there, even if they were drunk.

They found a table in the corner farthest from the bar,
in the room deserted except for them and the bartender.
They wouldn't be overheard. Loud jazz music played
over the speakers in the bar. Speaking in low voices, they
discussed the ASW exercises they had just been through,
especially the surprise attack by the Rasher from underneath the Eversole. Luke and Arthur planned on writing
an article on the tactic to send to the Naval War College.
They would not write about the identification of submarines using their sound signatures, however, as that was a

developing, Top-Secret Compartmented project. "Compartmented" meant only those involved in the project or directly above them in a reporting chain of command could know anything about it, regardless of their security clearances. They would, however, write a report for ONI on it.

"Our return cruise to Long Beach," said Luke, "will be a continuation of the ASW exercises. How would you like to do it on board the Rasher? You'd get the submariner's view of ASW warfare."

"I'd like that," said Arthur.

"I'll ask the Commodore if he would be so kind as to cut you orders for that in the morning."

"Thanks, Mr. Luke. I think it would be beneficial for me to have experienced this from both above and below the waves."

"Speaking of which, the waves in our glasses have disappeared and seem to be subject to a drought. Want one more before we call it a night?"

"OK, but just one more," said Arthur. "I don't want to go to sea with a hangover."

"We won't be going to sea tomorrow," replied Luke. "We'll get the ships ready, load new ammo, supplies, and the like, and we'll go to sea the next day." He waved at the bartender and made a swirling motion indicating another round. Luke had been drinking Jack Daniels, but Arthur had been drinking Cutty Sark. He was no expert on scotch, but Cutty was a brand he could afford, and so he stuck with what he knew, even though Luke was buying. He preferred the bite of the scotch to what he felt was the cloying sweetness of Jack Daniels. He had not liked Jack Daniels since Cambodia. They chatted while sipping their drinks.

"How is the database of sound signatures coming?" asked Arthur.

"Well," said Luke, "it's a lot better for the Russians' Atlantic Fleet than it is for their Pacific Fleet. They have a lot more subs in the Atlantic, so there are more targets to record. Besides, we have more ASW task forces in the Atlantic. Our Pacific fleet is more oriented toward aerial warfare, and we mostly protect our carriers rather than chasing submarines. The task force you are with right now is the first task force in the Pacific dedicated exclusively to ASW exercises with the intent of finding and identifying Russian submarines."

"You mean we are making history?" asked Arthur.

"Only if we succeed in building a usable database," answered Luke. "What we are getting, so far, leads us to believe that we will have a set of sound signature graphs that are unique for each Soviet submarine. What you did with K-14 proved that it is useful. The Soviets have about 35 nuclear-powered submarines, of which 23 are ICBM-firing – boomers. They have about 200 diesel-electric attack submarines. It would take some time to go through sound charts comparing them before being able to reach a reasonable conclusion as to the identity of a signature that has just been captured. This technology will not really be useful until we have computers capable of making the comparisons at computer speeds, rather than at human speeds. In addition, those computers would have to be small enough to fit in a sonar room on board a destroyer or submarine. Electronics technology is improving rapidly, but it isn't there yet. Nevertheless, by the time we build the set of signatures, I hope we will have something useful, with small computers capable of handling the data. I have good hope for that. The ONI now has a computer built using transistors instead of vacuum tubes. Still, circuits are going to have to get much smaller for the computer to be small enough to be fit into a Sonar Room."

"Well," said Arthur, "If we come across another Soviet sub, we can try comparing its signature with those we have on file on board, just as an exercise."

"Good," said Luke. "That's your assignment when we next find a Soviet sub. If you succeed, the next time we hit port, the drinks are on me."

"Deal," said Arthur. "Just give me a copy of the sound charts we have that I can take to the sub. Otherwise, I don't have a chance of succeeding."

"Tell the Chief to have them made tomorrow," said Luke.

They paid their bar bill and left a generous tip – the bartender had been generous with his pours – and headed for their room. They were due back on board at noon tomorrow, to prepare for departure the following morning.

The next day, amid the hustle and bustle of loading supplies on board the ship, the Captain's voice came over the loudspeakers: "This is the Captain. Mr. Harris, please report to my quarters." Arthur left his place and walked briskly to the Captain's stateroom. The hatch was open, so he knocked on the jamb.

"Sir! Midshipman 1st Class Harris reporting as ordered, Sir. Permission to enter."

"Enter," said the Captain. He was sitting at his desk. "Please take a seat, Mr. Harris." Arthur sat in the indicated chair. The Captain handed him a Manila envelope. "This envelope contains new orders, authorized by the Commodore. You will report today to Rasher for the return cruise to Long Beach. Oh, and take this with you. I signed for it when it arrived. It is a package from your father." He handed Arthur a slender, rectangular box about 3-1/2 feet long and about six inches square in cross section. In the middle of the box was a shipping label from his father to Arthur at his FPO address. Toward the end of the box was the logo and address of Wilkinson

Sword, the famous English sword maker. Arthur looked up to meet the Captain's smile. "I think your father has given you your officer's dress sword," said the Captain. "I think he approves of your career choice." Arthur grinned.

"Thank you, Captain. I think he does approve. I might as well tell you now, sir, I want to opt to accept commission, assuming I am qualified, at the end of the cruise, rather than to return to Rice for my fifth year."

"I have anticipated as much. Mr. Harris, it has been a pleasure having you as part of my crew. I give you now my invitation to join me for dinner at the Officers' Club the evening after we return to Long Beach, at 1800 hours. I will notify the Admiral and will ask for your commissioning ceremony to take place after dinner. He will join us for dinner. Now, go pack your gear and report to the Rasher. At the end of the cruise, upon your commissioning, you will receive your Surface Warfare badge and Aviation Officer badge and be qualified as an unrestricted line officer. You will be given the option of continuing as a Surface Warfare Officer, going to Submariner's School, or going to Intelligence School. I think you will choose the last of these, but I wanted to make sure that you understood that you will have all three options."

"Thank you, Captain. I accept your dinner invitation with pleasure."

"Dismissed," said the Captain, smiling.

Arthur stood, snapped to attention, nodded to the Captain, executed an about face, and walked to his stateroom, carrying his package, where he opened it. It was, indeed, an officer's dress sword, beautiful with its gold guard and pommel and snakeskin handle wrapped in gold wire. Its bright blade bore elaborate engraving. The gold bullion tassel was already attached to the pommel, so Arthur wouldn't have to look up the instructions on how to attach it. There was a leather carrying case, as well, to keep it protected and dry in between the times he would wear it.

He inserted the sword into the carrying case and hung it in his vertical locker next to his dress white uniform, which he knew he would wear for his commissioning.

Unfolding his duffel bag, he carefully packed all his belongings, transferring the folded clothes from his "sea chest" locker and carefully rolling and packing his hanging uniforms, except for his khaki dress uniform, which he left hanging. Finally, he removed his khaki work uniform, rolled it up, and packed it, and, towel wrapped around his midsection, walked to the officers' shower, where he showered quickly, and returned to the stateroom, where he shaved and combed his hair. He dressed in his khaki dress uniform, making sure his Midshipman's service ribbons and insignia were in place. Carrying his duffel bag over his left shoulder, he placed his cover on his head and walked to the midsection of the ship. The Chief Sonarman was Officer of the Deck. Arthur approached him and returned the Chief's salute.

"Chief," said Arthur, "I am transferring to Rasher. It has been a privilege to serve with you."

"And I with you, Sir," said the Chief. Arthur executed a right face to the stern, saluted the flag, executed a left face, marched across the deck to the next destroyer, stepped on board, executed a right face, and saluted the flag. He executed a left face and saluted the Officer of the Deck on that ship, who returned his salute. "Permission to come aboard," he said, handing the ensign his orders. The Ensign glanced at them and handed them back.

"Mr. Harris, you may proceed." Arthur saluted, received the return salute, and marched to the third and then the fourth destroyer. He repeated the process each time, finally marching across and onto the deck of the Rasher. A Chief Bosun's Mate was Officer of the Deck. He turned to the stern, saluted the flag, turned back to the chief, saluted, and received the return salute.

"Permission to come aboard," he said. "Midshipman 1st Class Arthur Harris reporting for duty." The Chief glanced at Arthur's orders and waved him towards the prow, where he found the Rasher's Captain supervising the loading of torpedoes from a barge tied alongside. A pyramid-shaped metal frame supported a winch over the hatchway, which was being used to hoist the torpedoes into the hold below. Arthur snapped a salute, which the Captain, who was a Commander by rank, returned.

"Sir! Midshipman 1st Class Arthur Harris reporting for duty," said Arthur, handing the Captain his orders. The Captain grinned at him.

"Mr. Harris, welcome aboard. I have been expecting you. Take your duffel bag below to the officers' state-rooms. You will be in the first one back on the port side. Your roommate is the Executive Officer, Lieutenant Commander James Murray. He is ashore, supervising the delivery of the torpedoes. I think you'll like him. He used to be called 'Jim,' but I'm Jim Hastings, so to keep us straight we call him 'James.' Do you go by 'Art,' or 'Arthur?'"

"Well, Sir, to my mother I was always Arthur, and I've kept the tradition."

"OK, Arthur, call me Jim. One thing I must warn you about: protocol on a submarine is very lax compared with what you are used to. We use first names on board, not last names, and officers mix freely with the crew. We're pretty informal. We don't salute all the time, either. After all, most of the time we are below decks, as it were, and under water. So, go find your rack and move yourself in, and come back up here."

"Aye, aye, Sir," said Arthur. The Captain grinned at him.

"By the time you leave, you'll be used to saying 'OK, Jim,' instead of 'Aye, aye, Sir.' Go make yourself at home." He held out his hand, and Arthur took it, receiving a warm handshake.

"OK, Jim, I'll see you in a few minutes," said Arthur.

The task force spent the next week, as it steamed from Pearl Harbor to Long Beach, trading roles of hunter and hunted. As they approached Long Beach, Arthur wrote a classified report on the effectiveness of identifying ships by sound signatures and forwarded it by encrypted radio to ASWGRU Five and to Washington to ONI headquarters.

They steamed into port at Long Beach and spent the first night on board. The next day, the officers supervised as the crew made the boat shipshape, and Arthur showered, shaved, persuaded the ship's clerk and barber to cut his hair, and donned his dress whites and carried his sword. Tonight, he was having dinner at the Officers' Club as guest of the Commodore and the Captain of the Eversole.

Arthur arrived at the entrance to the Officers' Club promptly at 1800 hrs. The Marine guard at the door was dressed in dinner dress uniform. He checked Arthur's name off his list and a steward led Arthur to a table at the head of the dining room. At the center of the table was Commodore Wren, with Captain Renn to his right, and Lieutenant Commander Luke to the right of Captain Wren. The other officers of the Eversole filled out the table continuing to the right. To the Commodore's left was Commander Jim Hastings, and to his left, Lieutenant Commander James Murray. The other officers of the Rasher filled out the complement of the table. Three of the other tables in the room had the officers of each of the other three ships in the task force. There was a fourth table at which Arthur was surprised to see Captain O'Brien from the Midway and some of the Midway officers whom he recognized, as well as Thayer, who now wore the stripes and silver oak leaves of a Commander. There was one empty seat at the table, with a Flying Cross Medal in place of a dinner plate, but otherwise set as for dinner. Arthur snapped to attention and nodded at the Commodore, who nodded back.

"Commodore, where should I sit?" asked Arthur.

"When we dine, you will sit at Commander Thayer's table. First, however, we have a little ceremony to perform." He walked around the table and stood facing Arthur. All the officers were standing, and Arthur noticed that the Commodore and all the other officers in the room were wearing swords. Senior officers were dressed in dinner dress, with junior officers (Lieutenant and below), including Arthur, wearing dress whites. Arthur remained at attention. Commander Hastings, Captain of the Rasher, and Commander Renn, Captain of the Eversole, came around the table and took positions on each side of Arthur, facing him. Acting in unison, they unsnapped and removed Arthur's Midshipman 1st Class shoulder boards and unpinned from his chest his Midshipman service ribbons. Both captains stepped back but remained two steps away, facing Arthur.

"Mr. Harris," said the Commodore, "I have two documents for you to sign. First, this is your appointment as an Ensign in the United States Navy." He showed Arthur the document and laid it on the table. Holding the second document, he said, "This is your Officer Appointment Acceptance Form. Please sign it where indicated." He laid it on the table and handed Arthur a fountain pen. Arthur bent over and signed both documents and returned to attention. "This, Mr. Harris, is your oath of office. I will administer it, and then you will sign it. Raise your right hand and repeat after me:

"I, your name, do solemnly swear..."

"I, Arthur Cornwallis Harris III, do solemnly swear..."

"To support and defend the Constitution of the United States..."

"To support and defend the Constitution of the United States..."

"Against all enemies, foreign and domestic..."

"Against all enemies, foreign and domestic..."

"And will bear true faith and allegiance to the same;"

"And will bear true faith and allegiance to the same;"

"That I will obey the orders of the President of the United States..."

"That I will obey the orders of the President of the United States..."

"And the orders of other officers appointed over me..."

"And the orders of other officers appointed over me..."

"According to the regulation and the Uniform Code of Military Justice..."

"According to the regulation and the Uniform Code of Military Justice..."

"So help me God."

"So help me God."

"Congratulations, Mr. Harris. You were appointed an officer and a gentleman by Act of Congress when you received your appointment as Midshipman. Now, in addition, by Act of Congress, you are a commissioned Ensign in the Navy of the United States of America. Please sign your oath. I remind you that your oath has no expiration, and it binds you for the remainder of your life."

Arthur bent over, signed the oath document and returned to attention. The two captains stepped toward him. In unison, they attached the black shoulder boards with one broad gold stripe each that signified his rank as Ensign and stabbed onto his left chest the gold emblem of the Surface Warfare officer and the gold wings of an Aviation Officer, handing him the retainer clips. One of them took Arthur's sword from its case and handed it to the other, who attached the sword to the harness Arthur already wore under his tunic. They returned to their seats but remained standing.

Captain O'Brien of the Midway and Commander Thayer then marched to position on either side of Arthur.

"Take two steps backward," whispered Commander Thayer. Arthur and the two officers stepped backward, and Commodore Wren returned to his seat, remaining standing. Captain O'Brien stepped forward, executed a left face, then another left face, and stood facing Arthur.

"Ensign Arthur Cornwallis Harris III," he said, reading from a document he held in his hand, "while serving as a Midshipman Second Class on the USS Midway, CV 41, flew reconnaissance missions over land in the Vietnam War theater of operations. He was the photographer in a two-seat Phantom II piloted by Lieutenant Commander James Mason. On one of their first flights together, they were attacked by North Vietnamese MiG jets and scored a kill. They took fire, and Lieutenant Commander Mason was wounded. Midshipman Harris then flew the missions alone while Mr. Mason recuperated. On a subsequent flight, flying alone, Mr. Harris was attacked by five MiG 21 Jets. He returned fire, scoring four kills, which remains a record for the Viet Nam conflict. After Mr. Mason's recovery, they flew together again. On a mission performing low-level surveillance, they were struck by North Vietnamese small arms fire from the ground. Mr. Mason was killed and the plane partially disabled. Mr. Harris took the controls and guided the aircraft to a crash landing. He ejected before the jet hit the ground and was attacked by a North Vietnamese soldier wielding a machete. Mr. Harris was wounded in the struggle but was able to seize the machete and dispatch the North Vietnamese soldier. He went to cover in the jungle and killed several North Vietnamese soldiers who

had come to the wreck. He returned to the aircraft and retrieved the classified surveillance equipment and Mr. Mason's body, taking it into the jungle and burying it. He
retreated into the jungle, where he was rescued by
Montagnard tribesmen allied with American forces. Accompanied by the Montagnard tribesmen, he was able to
return to friendly territory, from which he was extracted.
Accordingly, the President of the United States hereby
awards him two medals: the Purple Heart, for being
wounded in battle; and the Navy and Marine Corps Medal, for exceptional valor under fire from the enemy. In addition, he was awarded by Prime Minister Nguyen Cao
Ky the Republic of Viet Nam Service Medal. For service
at Guantanamo Bay Navy Station during the Cuban Missile Crisis, he is awarded the Navy Expeditionary Medal."
He pinned the four medals on Arthur's chest, under the
Surface Warfare emblem. "Mr. Harris, thank you for your
service to our country, and for your bravery and valor.
There are also additional service medals which you will
receive upon your arrival at your next posting. Congratulations, Mr. Harris."

The room erupted into applause. Captain O'Brien returned to his seat. The Commodore walked back around
the table to take position facing Arthur. Commander
Thayer took up a position beside the Commodore, facing
Arthur.

"Gentlemen," said the Commodore, addressing the
room, "we have one additional ceremony to perform. At
this time, Mr. Harris is leaving the fleet for reassignment
to the Office of Naval Intelligence. There is no official
ceremony for that sort of thing, but we will improvise
one, based loosely on the Change of Command ceremony.
Mr. Harris, I am placing orders here with your other documents releasing you from my command and assigning
you to Commander Thayer's command at the Office of
Naval Intelligence."

"Draw your sword, Arthur, and salute the Commodore," whispered Commander Thayer. Arthur drew his sword and used it to salute the Commodore, who drew his own sword and returned the salute.

"Mr. Harris," said Commander Thayer, "I receive you into my command." He drew his sword. Arthur saluted him, and Commander Thayer used his sword to return the salute. All three men returned their swords to their scabbards. The Commodore took Arthur's hand and shook it warmly and firmly.

"Good luck, Mr. Harris," he said. Commander Thayer also shook Arthur's hand.

"Padre," said the Admiral, "it's your turn now."

Father James Michaels, Chaplain of the Midway, came forward.

"Let us all take a moment of silent prayer to remember, by the name and rank we knew him, Lieutenant Commander James Mason, whose place is vacant tonight, and who has posthumously been awarded the Navy Flying Cross." He paused, for about thirty seconds.

"Dear Father, ruler of the Universe, receive our friend James Mason into your loving embrace. May his soul, and the souls of all the faithful departed, through the mercy of God, rest in peace. Look down upon us gathered here today. Bless the food which we are about to consume from thy bounty and bless us to Thy service. In the Name of the Father, and of the Son, and of the Holy Spirit. Amen."

"Gentlemen," said the Commodore, "please be seated." The chaplain gathered Arthur's documents.

"Mr. Harris, I'll hold these for you and give them to you when you depart this evening," said the chaplain. He returned to his seat, and Arthur took his seat at Thayer's table. The Admiral immediately called everyone back to stand at attention. At each place was a wineglass.

"Gentlemen, charge your glasses," commanded the Commodore. Bottles of port passed around each table, each man filling the glass of the person to his right and passing the bottle to his left. The Commodore raised his glass. All in the room raised theirs. "The President of the United States," said the Commodore.

"The President," said all.

"The Navy – may she always have a following wind."

"The Navy," said all.

"The Chief of Naval Operations," said the Commodore.

"The CNO," said all. The Commodore lowered his glass. Arthur raised his glass.

"To all present, for otherwise we would be absent."

"All present."

"To our wives and sweethearts – may they never meet."

"Our wives and sweethearts!"

"Gentlemen," said the Admiral, please be seated. Stewards please serve the meal."

The meal was a multi-course meal, with a different wine for each course. After the dessert, strong coffee was served, and the entire party adjourned to the bar, where each ordered the drink of his choice and cigars were passed around. The evening ended in the fog of alcohol and the smoke of cigars. Arthur retired to his room at the Bachelor Officers' Quarters on the base, proud and happy to have achieved his goal – he was now a Navy Surface Warfare Officer, Aviation Officer and an Intelligence Officer, looking forward to a career of 20 or so years in service to his country. He was embarking on a new chapter of his life, in the secret world of intelligence operations.

He felt profoundly happy, but then he remembered that when a Roman general rode god-like through Rome in a chariot for his Triumph Parade, a slave stood next to him holding over his head a golden crown of laurel leaves, whispering in his ears, *"Memento mori,"* "Re-

member death," meaning "Remember, you are mortal."
You are not a god.

He slept soundly, interrupted by a disturbing dream in which he was running through the jungle away from his crashed plane, carrying a bleeding, naked woman in his arms, pursued by North Vietnamese soldiers who were shooting at him. The woman kept whispering, *"Memento mori."* He awoke sweating, but after a few minutes he returned to a dreamless sleep.

CHAPTER 18

SPY SCHOOL

September 1966 – February 1967
The Farm

The morning after his commissioning in Long Beach, Arthur had caught the train to the east coast, because there was some sort of strike involving the airlines, and he could not get anything resembling a direct flight. He had a little time, so the train was both cheaper and more scenic. He opted for a reserved coach seat rather than a sleeper. He reasoned that if he could sleep standing up during battle stations in the engine room, wedged between two insulated pipes, he would be able to sleep sitting on the train with his seat reclined. Besides, the ONI would reimburse him for the reserved coach seat. If he wanted to upgrade to a sleeper, he would have to pay for the upgrade out of his own pocket. He had better use for his money, as little as he had. He found the seats comfortable and spacious. As a member of the military traveling under orders, he wore his dress khaki uniform and was given a fifty percent discount on the fare, for which the Navy would reimburse him.

The train took him from Los Angeles to Las Vegas, down into Arizona and across New Mexico. It stopped outside Santa Fe, and the passenger portion of the train was left on a siding while the freight portion, with the engine, continued. After about a half-hour, the temperature inside was stifling, and passengers had opened all the windows and doors. There was little to no moving air, so opening the windows didn't accomplish much. Waves of dry, dusty heat washed into the cars. Soon, another train came by, and stopped to attach the passenger cars behind its freight cars, and the air conditioning started back up. This train took him through Texas to Houston. He changed trains there, and the new train took him through New Orleans and Mobile, and up by way of Dothan to Atlanta. It blew by Dothan at full speed without a stop.

"Doesn't this train stop in Dothan?" Arthur asked the Conductor when he came through the car on one of his routine walks.

"Sir, it stops in Dothan if we have passengers to un-load there, or passengers to pick up, or express packages or mail to drop off or pick up. We don't have any of those this trip."

"Ah. Thank you."

"You got friends in Dothan, Sir?"

"My family lives there and I went to Junior High and High School there."

"Nice town. I got an uncle and aunt there. You enjoy your trip now, Sir." He touched his cap brim with his fin-gers in a sort of salute and resumed his walk through the cars.

Arthur changed trains again in Atlanta to a train that ran from Miami all the way up to Portland, Maine. Arthur regretted that the most scenic part of his trip, Nevada, Ar-izona and half of New Mexico, had been at night, and he had slept through it.

He got off in Williamsburg, and caught a shuttle bus to Camp Peary, along with about a dozen other people about his own age. He arrived four days before classes started and checked in at the BOQ on base. The rest who were headed for "the Farm" and who had been on the train with him stayed in Williamsburg to see the sights, but Arthur was nearly out of cash and couldn't afford to do that. He went to the academic building and obtained the textbooks that would be used for the classroom part of his training and spent the Labor Day weekend in his BOQ room studying. Now, he was in a chilly auditorium/lecture hall for the orientation talk.

August and September are the hottest months of the year in the South. Camp Peary in Virginia was a hot place on the day after Labor Day when Arthur reported to the school run by the CIA at Camp Peary. Despite the heat of summer, Arthur was chilled as he sat in the auditorium waiting for the instructor to begin. In the south, air conditioning tends to be very effective. Wearing civilian slacks and a short-sleeved shirt, he was dressed as he would have been for class at Rice. On arrival he was assigned a cover name, Joseph "Joe" Green, and told to use only his cover name while there. No one must know his real name.

Seated around him in the auditorium were about sixty young people of approximately Arthur's age, both female and male. The women, in particular, seemed cold, crossing their arms and legs, using their hands to rub their upper arms. *The air conditioning certainly works,* thought Arthur.

The official name for Camp Peary was "Armed Forces Experimental Training Activity (AFETA). Originally a training camp for Seabees during World War II, it now functioned mainly as the CIA training school, although Navy Seals also trained here, as well as FBI agents undergoing counterespionage training. NOSI did not maintain its own training program – it put its clandestine Intelligence Officers through the CIA school.

Camp Peary consisted of 9,275 acres of wooded, swampy land fronting on the York River very close to historic Williamsburg. 8,000 acres of the Camp are unimproved. Called "The Farm" by members of the CIA, which its insiders called "The Company," Camp Peary was originally a farm. After the Navy started using it as a training base for Seabees, the portions away from the river and along the highway remained in use as a farm. Those who have trained at it refer to it "affectionately" as "Camp Swampy." Most of its facilities are not visible from the surrounding roads. Those that are, are innocuous. Its acreage includes the original Magruder's and Bigler's Mills, the original structures still standing but converted to other uses. It contains an airfield with a 5,000-foot runway near Bigler's Mill.

"Ladies and Gentlemen," said an over-amplified male voice, "welcome to The Farm. I might as well warn you up front that this is not a dude ranch. You will work hard here, and some of you will not find this to your liking and will depart without completing the course. The majority will continue to a career with The Company. There are a few of you here from other services, and we welcome you. When you complete, if you are good enough, you may be invited to hang up your uniforms and join The Company.

"You may call me Joe – Joe Magnum. That is not my real name. None of you will know my real name. I am a clandestine employee of The Company. Only the officer who handles personnel matters knows my real name, and no one who encounters me through my work will ever know my real name. Other than he, no one who knows my real name will ever know my code name; and other than he, no one who knows my code name will ever know my real name. Even my immediate family will never know that I work for The Company. The same will be true for all of you, if you survive this course and continue in the clandestine service.

"I cannot emphasize this enough. No one must ever know you are an intelligence operative except your co-operatives, and they will not know who you really are. You must never let anyone other than a co-operative know that you are an intelligence operative. You MUST maintain your cover at all times. Your mother, your father, brothers, sisters, those closest to you, including your spouses and your children, must never know.

"I ask each of you to look at the course synopsis folder you were handed on your way into this room. In the upper-right-hand corner is a name. That is the name you will use until and unless you are given another name to use, or leave the program. You are not to disclose to each other, or to your instructors, or to anyone with whom you speak while you are here, your real name. Each of you will now become two people – the real you and the clandestine you." Joe Magnum walked away from the podium to an overhead projector that stood in the central aisle of the auditorium. Arthur looked down at his folder to read again his name: Joseph "Joe" Green. *Giuseppe Verdi,* he thought to himself, *Joe Green. I am Joseph Green, or in Italian, Giuseppe Verdi.*

"Now," continued Joe Magnum, "for the next couple of hours I will give you an outline of what your training will cover. It will last six months. You will have a break for Christmas, and may go home, but all that you may tell your parents is that you are receiving additional training. Those of you who are military will call it additional military training. Those who are training for The Company will say you are taking advanced courses at William and Mary College to prepare you for possible diplomatic service. If pushed, you should say you are studying negotiating techniques and learning to program computers. Unless those asking you are computer programmers, you can say almost anything about computer programming and they won't have a clue whether you are making it up. One of your first classes here will teach you the rudiments of computer programming, so you will be able to talk as if you know something about it.

"OK. This is Spy School. Here you will learn the fundamental elements of tradecraft that will enable you to function as an undercover or clandestine operative. We will begin with a three-week interrogation course." He turned on the overhead projector and a slide projected to the screen over the stage that simply contained the words, "Interrogation Training."

"There will be classroom work to learn about the different modes of interrogation you might use or might be subjected to. This will take about a week. You will have a one-day break, and then you will practice what you have learned. You will be interrogated by masters at interrogation. We will not do anything that will injure or maim you, but you will be subjected to every mode of coercive interrogation known to man short of that. All of you, ultimately, will break under this interrogation. What you will learn is precisely where the breaking point is for you, and we will teach you techniques to delay the breaking point. You will learn ways to trick your interrogators into thinking they have broken you and you have spilled the beans. However, *our* interrogators are so good that they will know when you are trying to trick them.

"The interrogation will proceed without a break until the end of the second week, or until you break, whichever comes first. I am sure that all of you will break first. We will give you a break for one day, and you will resume training." He switched to the next slide and continued switching slides as he covered the remaining topics.

"Covert Surveillance. You will learn to observe without being observed. You will learn to follow without being followed. You will learn to see without being seen, hear without being heard, and record what you are seeing and hearing without being recorded in turn. You will learn to be there without being perceived as 'being there.'

"Sleight of Hand. You will learn to appear to do one thing while doing another. You will become more than an amateur magician. You will learn to pass objects hidden in your hand to another agent without anyone around you being the wiser. You will learn to plant bugs while all around you are suspicious of you. You will learn to make things disappear without anyone noticing you are doing it. You will learn to pickpocket. You will also learn to put things into people's pockets without their being aware of it.

"Collection. You will learn to receive information, documents and objects from another agent without being detected. You will learn to pick locks, to break and enter, and to steal information without being detected.

"Manipulation. You will learn to be a con artist. You will learn how to identify personality types and their weaknesses and use their weaknesses against them. You will undergo psychoanalysis, so you will learn your own weaknesses, how to mask them, how to compensate for them, and how not to allow others to use those weaknesses to intimidate you. You will learn to lie convincingly, to cheat, to trick, and to camouflage what you are doing.

"Camouflage. The art of hiding in plain sight. You will learn to do one thing while appearing to do another. You will also learn physical camouflage, like that used by the military. As a covert operative you must not stand out; you must blend in with your surroundings. You must appear such that no one gives you a second glance. You will also learn emotional and behavioral camouflage to enhance your blending in. To be a con artist, you will learn how different personality types behave and their weaknesses, and you will learn the manipulative tools of lying, cheating, trickery, camouflage, and evasion.

"Analytical Combat. You will learn to use combat exercises – or any adversarial exercise – to draw out the enemy and learn his strengths and weaknesses, rather than fighting immediately to defeat him. You will learn to play with the enemy like a cat playing with a mouse before killing it. If any of you are fencers, you know that this sort of tactic is essential to winning fencing matches. The fighter who enters the field of battle ignorant of the strengths and weaknesses of his enemy, no matter his prowess in battle, will likely lose. Once you have engaged in analytical combat, you can attack and defeat the enemy. I am using here the language of physical war, but it is just as applicable to any contest of wills – chess, for example.

"Defense. No matter how skilled you are, someone, somewhere, is more skilled than you, and you many find yourself backed into a corner and needing to defend yourself. You will learn techniques of evasion and escape, and if those don't work, you will learn to use a variety of types of weapons. You will learn as well to improvise weaponry. An umbrella, a chair, a stick, a rock, a pencil – any type of object – can be used as a weapon. You will learn to improvise your defense based on the situation in which you find yourself. You will also learn how to use effectively all the standard types of weapons – rifle, pistol, machine gun, grenade, knife, machete, sword, bayonet, club, axe, bow and arrow, crossbow, spear – anything that has been used historically as a weapon. You will learn all these things not just in the classroom, but also in the field.

"In short, you will learn espionage tradecraft, fighting and survival.

"When you have completed our course here, you will have learned the rudiments of espionage. Your learning does not stop here. Every assignment will teach you new lessons. If at any point in your career you stop learning, you will leave the work of spycraft by being killed, by being fired, or, if you are lucky, by resigning.

"OK, let's take a fifteen-minute break. Go piss, shit, get another cup of coffee, or whatever it is that you do on breaks. We reconvene in fifteen minutes and begin our study of interrogation."

Arthur tried to hold his breath, but could do that only so long, and soon his lungs were trying to inhale. The water poured into his mouth and he found he couldn't breathe without feeling like he was breathing water. He was coughing, sputtering, trying to draw in air, and failing. He was lying on his back on a board, tilted about thirty degrees, with his head down and feet up. He was tied to the board hand and foot. His face was covered with a cloth, and water was being poured on it. He felt like he was drowning. He coughed again, expelling all the air from his lungs, which tried to inhale again. His throat clamped shut and he lost consciousness.

He awoke. *How many times can I endure this?* The cloth was no longer covering his face. He was still tied to the tilted board, and he was wet and cold. A man with his face covered by a black fabric mask showing only his eyes was leaning over him.

"He's awake," said the man, and stepped away. He had a vaguely eastern European or Slavic accent. Another man stepped into Arthur's field of vision, also wearing a black, fabric mask.

"You will tell us your real name," he said, in a similar accent. "You have told us your name is Joe Green. We know that is not true. You will tell me your real name...No... I guess you are still thirsty."

He covered Arthur's face again with the cloth. Arthur immediately felt that he was choking and started coughing. It was difficult to draw in air through the wet fabric. Water was again splashing on his face, the panic rising in his chest. He coughed, gasped, coughed again, gasped again. The water stopped pouring. He knew he could not hold out much longer – the panic was too great. He could feel his heart beating so rapidly he could not count the beats. The cloth came away from his face. He blinked and opened his eyes, gasping. The cold, steel-grey eyes of his inquisitor looked at him piercingly.

"You tell us…No… You are still thirsty." The cloth fell back in place and water was again choking him. He coughed, sputtered, gasped, coughed, and made gurgling sounds when he tried to inhale. Finally, the cloth came away, and Arthur knew he was defeated. He gasped desperately for air.

"Now you tell us, no? Tell me your real name." Arthur was still gasping for breath. He tried to speak, but only a gurgle came out. He coughed until he couldn't cough because he had no more air. He gasped a few breaths, turned his face to the side, and vomited on his inquisitor's legs. The man slapped Arthur's face, hard. "You should not have done that." The cloth went back into place. Water filled his mouth. His bladder decided to discharge, and urine soaked his already saturated shorts and ran downward toward his head across his belly and chest. He expelled the water with a cough.

"My name!" gasped Arthur. The cloth came away again.

"What is your real name?" asked the inquisitor.

"I am Giuseppe Verdi," said Arthur. The other man glanced at a panel of dials connected by wires to various parts of Arthur's body.

"He tells the truth," said the man.

"Now you may breathe for a while," he said, and disappeared out of Arthur's range of vision. The plank rotated to a level position. Arthur breathed heavily, rapidly and noisily, sounding like an asthmatic struggling for breath. The man cut Arthur's bonds and helped him into a sitting position, which he was allowed to keep for about a minute. He vomited again, yellow bile.

"You talk to Chief now. You tell him what he want to know," said the man. Arthur nodded dumbly. The door opened, and Joe Magnum walked in, grinning.

"Giuseppe," said Joe, "You're the first one in your class successfully to resist waterboarding, to trick your interrogators into thinking you have broken, and to be released. You'll make a good spy. Dimitri," he turned to the inquisitor, "he fooled you. His real name is not Giuseppe Verdi. Giuseppe Verdi is Joseph Green translated into Italian. It's the name of an Italian opera composer. Joe Green, you have survived the interrogation class with flying colors. You broke, as expected, but even then you defeated the process because you deceived your inquisitor. Joe Green is your code name here, and by translating it into Italian and giving the Italian version of your code name, you even tricked the lie detector gauges. How did that work? How did you convince yourself that Giuseppe Verdi was your real name?"

"I just told myself that here, I was Giuseppe Verdi, masquerading as Joe Green."

"Well, it worked. Enjoy your break tomorrow. You've earned it. See you Monday morning at 0700 hrs."

"Thank you, Sir," said Arthur. He staggered back to the locker room, where he showered, changed into clean clothes, placed his interrogation clothes in his laundry bag, and staggered to his room at the BOQ. A staff member followed him in, placed a plate with food and a full glass on the desk with knife, fork and spoon wrapped in a cloth napkin, smiled at Arthur, and departed. Arthur wolfed down the food, drank the glass empty, and collapsed onto the bed. After a minute, he pushed himself up, removed his outer clothes and fell back into the bed wearing briefs and tee shirt.

As he drifted into sleep, it occurred to him that he had no idea what he just ate or drank, nor even whether the staff member who served him was male or female. He slept until mid-morning the next day, Sunday. He had missed breakfast, but lunch was not too far in the future. If he hurried, he could still make Mass at the chapel at 1200 hours. He arose, drank a glass of water, took a dump, showered, shaved, brushed his teeth, and dressed. He picked up the laundry bag holding his dirty clothes, catching his breath at the pungent smell of stale urine.

He picked up the *CIA Deception Manual*. He walked to the end of the corridor and down the stairs to the small laundromat in the basement. He put his clothes in the washing machine, added soap and bleach, and turned on the machine. While it washed his clothes, he started reading the introduction to the manual, studied the table of contents, and began speed-reading Chapter 1. The *Deception Manual* was the introduction to tradecraft used by spies. It would be the topic of class starting tomorrow morning, followed by weapons training in the afternoon. When his clothes were washed, he put them in the drier, and continued studying. When the clothes were dry, he folded them, smoothing out the wrinkles, and returned them to his room. He ran to the chapel, just a few hundred yards away, and heard Mass. It occurred to him that it was ironic that Mass was said daily here, in the "heart of wickedness," as some referred to the CIA. He noted that he was experiencing a conflict between life and faith, but that was not new.

He ate a hearty lunch, at a trestle table in the mess hall, surrounded by his fellow students. The other students were talking somberly about their failure points in the interrogation sequence, and one of them, Helen Thomas, turned to Arthur.

"Joe, I heard that you broke, but didn't really break, because you gave another false name, and the interrogator believed you. How did you think fast enough to do that when you couldn't even breathe?"

"Well," said Arthur, "my name here is Joseph Green. When I was first given my name, I realized that it is English for the Italian opera composer Giuseppe Verdi, so I associated the two in my mind on the first day, in case I needed to give another name at any point. Not knowing what was coming, I planned ahead anyway."

"Giuseppe," said Helen, "you done good. Meet me at the Officer's Club this evening at 1700 hours for happy hour. I'll buy."

"Thanks, Helen," said Arthur. "I look forward to a good, stiff drink and amicable companionship."

Arthur arrived at the Club at 1630 hours and picked out a table in the corner. He sat with his back facing the corner and watched the entrance. When the steward came over, Arthur ordered a ginger ale and handed the man fifty dollars.

"I'm meeting a woman here at 0600," he told the steward. "She offered to buy me a drink. Let her pay for the first one, but for the subsequent drinks, tell her someone else paid for them." The steward grinned.

"Yes, sir," he said. Arthur detected a trace of German accent.

"*Sprechen Sie Deutsch?*" asked Arthur.

"*Ja, mein herr. Ich spreche Deutsch und Tschechisch,*" said the Steward. "My mother was Czech, but my father was German."

Arthur sipped his ginger ale and wandered out to the porch, leaving his jacket on the back of the chair to claim the table. He sat in one of several rocking chairs and zoned out, watching the landscape do nothing. His reverie was interrupted by a pleasing female voice.

"Woolgathering?" asked Helen. Arthur grinned.

"Indeed I am. Haven't had much of a chance to do nothing in a while."

"They won't serve us drinks out here," she said.

"Then let's go inside," said Arthur. He rose, and they walked together to the door, which Arthur opened for her. He glanced at her common-sense tan slacks and blue knit blouse, covering but not concealing her well-shaped breasts. Her erect nipples were very evident. *Here we go again*, thought Arthur. Her blond hair was bobbed and straight. He motioned her toward the table he had "reserved." They had barely taken their seats when the steward was standing before them, waiting for their order.

"I'd like a Manhattan," said Helen. "I'm buying."

"Gin and tonic," said Arthur.

"Any particular brand of gin?" asked the steward.

"Doesn't matter. Once you add the tonic, I won't be able to tell the difference. Now, if I were ordering a Martini, it would be different."

"An unpretentious man," said Helen. "I like that." He looked into her startling green eyes, mesmerized by them.

"How do you know I'm not just pretending to be unpretentious?" asked Arthur. "After all, the whole point of our course is deception." Helen laughed.

"Well," she said, "you're not pretending to have blue eyes and dark blond hair," she said.

The steward returned with their drinks.

"*Ich danke Ihnen*," said Arthur. "*Das Wetter ist warm heute, nicht wahr?*"

"*Ja, mein herr. Es ist so warm, es ist heiß*. That will be $2.50, please," said the Steward.

"I'm buying the drinks," said Helen, handing him three dollars.

"Thank you, Ma'am." The steward took the money and walked away.

"Do you speak German?" asked Arthur.

"I recognize it when I hear it," said Helen. "When you speak it, you sound German rather than American."

"My German professor in college told me I had a good ear for languages," said Arthur.

"What did you two say to each other?"

"I told him, 'Thank you. The weather is warm today, isn't it?' and he responded, 'Yes, sir. It is so warm it is hot.'"

"I'll take your word for it, but I wonder why you think it necessary to show off in front of me. You have already impressed me, or we would not be here together."

"Sorry. Just blame it on my feelings of inferiority." She laughed.

"Inferiority or inadequacy?" she asked.

"Inferiority, definitely," he responded. "I am exceptionally adequate." She laughed, and he laughed with her.

"Also, a bit oxymoronic," she said. "Have you been reading ahead in the manual for this week's lessons?"

"I've started, but I didn't get very far," said Arthur. "You?"

"Yes," said Helen, "I read the first chapter. I'm going to try to stay a chapter ahead. The last thing I want to do is to be surprised in class and wash out." They chatted about the first chapter and its discussion of the various means of deception – trickery, lying, cheating, play-acting, etc.

"Your drink is empty," said Arthur, "and so is mine." He waved at the steward, making the circular motion indicating another round of drinks. Within moments, the steward was back. He took their empty glasses and placed the full ones in front of them. Arthur took a sip, savoring it. "This is good gin," he said to the waiter, "I think you have given me Tanqueray."

"Indeed, sir," said the steward.

"*Das nächste Mal*," said Arthur, "*bringe mir Tonic mit keinen gin in der gleichen Art von Glas*." (Next time bring me tonic with no gin in the same kind of glass.)

"*Javohl,*" said the steward. Helen tried to hand him some money, but he shook his head. "Ma'am, it's all paid for by someone else," he said and walked back toward the

The Man Who Was Never There

bar. By this time, the room was filling up. Arthur spotted Joe Mangan at the bar, and waved, nodding his head as if in thanks. Helen looked.

"That was generous of him," she said. "I guess that's your reward for outwitting the interrogators." Art shrugged.

"I guess so," he said. "I need to buy him a drink when I can."

Arthur and Helen continued chatting about the deception manual subjects. After a while, Arthur suggested they order dinner, and had the steward bring them a menu. She ordered the garden salad and grilled chicken. He ordered the fried calamari appetizer and fried chicken. They switched to wine for the meal. Arthur suggested a good Sauvignon Blanc, and Helen agreed with the selection.

At the end of the dinner, Helen asked for the bill, and the Steward told her it was all paid for. She fished a fifty dollar bill out of her purse and handed it to him.

"Bitte bringen Sie das Geld wieder zu meinem Freund und für die Getränke bezahlen und essen mit dieser," she said. (Please bring the money back to my friend and pay for the drinks and meal with this.)

"I see you can be deceptive, too," said Arthur, grinning. She grinned back at him.

"I think we're just doing our homework together," she said.

"At the next opportunity," said Arthur, "I think we should do our homework together 'off campus.'"

"I agree," she said. "Just remember that we aren't allowed off campus until we graduate, except for the brief break for Christmas."

"'...and no mingling of the sexes in private is permitted on campus,' I might as well have opted for Catholic seminary instead of Spy School." The waiter brought their dinner and refilled their wine glasses.

- 321 -

"*Le plaisir est plus doux dans l'anticipation que dans le souvenir,*" She said.

"Ah, yes. Pleasure is sweeter in the anticipation than in the remembering," he replied. "So you're a philosopher, too."

"There is much about me you do not yet know," said Helen.

"Two can play that game," said Arthur, laughing. They ate their meal, chatting about the art of deception.

They walked slowly back to the women's BOQ, where Helen favored him with a quick kiss before disappearing inside. Arthur walked back to the men's BOQ, whistling a vague tune. With a start, he realized it was "Nowhere Man."

The rest of the course went quickly. There was a lot to learn, in addition to the field exercises in a town mockup, through which each had to go, spotting "enemy" popup targets and shooting them before they had a chance to shoot and recognizing "friendly" popups and holding fire. There was a survival camp in the swamp, with no backpack, no implements and no tools, for two days and two nights. All were expected to make fire, catch game, cook and eat it, make a sheltered place to sleep using the underbrush, all the while evading detection by roving bands of "enemy." Every day they had firearms training on the range, at which Arthur excelled, having shot with his collegiate rifle and pistol team. Helen also excelled, and it turned out that they both had opted for the same set of collegiate sports – wrestling, shooting, and fencing. They learned self-defense techniques – how to disarm and kill an armed assailant while unarmed; how to fight hand-to-hand with a variety of real and improvised weapons; and how to detect a trap and avoid attack.

They parachuted from airplanes at low altitude, and they parachuted from airplanes at high altitude, parasailing to precise targets at a distance. They learned scuba skills and how to sneak ashore at night from a boat two miles out without making any noise or causing any ripples, both with snorkels and with scuba gear.

They lost weight where they had fat and gained weight where they needed muscle. There was precious little time for socializing, but Helen and Arthur managed to see each other with fair regularity at the Officers' Club. Christmas break was short – it started the day before Christmas Eve and ended the day after Boxing Day. Arthur went home to see his parents and told them all about his experience at the Houston Music Theater, where he was working while being in the reserves and waiting for an active duty assignment – his cover story. He regretted the separation between his family and himself – a separation of which only he was aware.

At 0800 hours on "graduation day," all the remaining students were gathered in the auditorium once again. Magnum took the stage.

"You are all the ones lucky enough – or unlucky enough, depending on your point of view – to complete the course here and graduate. All of you have already been sworn in either as officers and gentlemen or gentlewomen – or as intelligence officers. Sorry, guys, but mere intelligence officers aren't created gentlemen by Act of Congress, only the military guys. A couple of you have been offered transfers from your military service branch to The Company, and one accepted but one declined. Unfortunately for The Company, the one who declined was the top of this class." He was looking directly at Arthur. "Are you sure you won't change your mind, Joe?"

"Sir," said Arthur, "as I told you yesterday, I would be happy to work with the Company when seconded to it by the Navy, but I really want to maintain my career as a gentleman."

"There has to be a smart-ass in every crowd," said Magnum, a grin on his face but a frown on his brow. "My report on you will recommend that The Company request your service from the Navy whenever the Navy is willing to lend you to us.

"Now, on to graduation. As I said, you have already been sworn in, so we'll now do the graduation pledge. All stand and raise your right hands...now, repeat after me:

"I pledge to trust no one and suspect everyone..."

"I pledge to trust no one and suspect everyone..."

"To keep my head down and dodge every bullet..."

"To keep my head down and dodge every bullet..."

"No matter what happens, to act as if everything is perfectly normal..."

"No matter what happens, to act as if everything is perfectly normal..."

"Because in God we trust..."

"Because in God we trust..."

"But all others we verify."

"But all others we verify." Chuckles spread through the room.

"You guys will all take the *official* oath when you report for duty at The Company. All right, guys, you're dismissed. See you some day, somewhere, under the covers." Everyone laughed.

"Joe" and "Helen" walked out together.

"Meet you at the gate in fifteen," said Helen.

"See you thereish, thenish," replied Arthur.

Fifteen minutes later, when Arthur arrived at the gate with his duffel bag slung over his shoulder and wearing his dress khakis, Helen was lounging against the gatepost chatting up the guard, a Marine corporal. Arthur joined them, swung his duffel bag down to the ground and leaned it against the guard shack. The guard and Arthur exchanged salutes. Helen looked him up and down, smiling approvingly.

"Joe, you might as well pick your burden up again," she said. "We need to hurry. I have a train to catch." Arthur hoisted his duffel bag to his shoulder again.

"Where's your luggage?" he asked.

"I had a friend take it on ahead for me. I'll catch up with it before the train leaves." She took two steps and kissed him on the mouth. "Let's get going, Giuseppe."

They walked out together. There was a line of taxicabs waiting. They took the cab at the head of the line and climbed in. When Arthur asked the cabbie to take them to the train station, station, she laughed.

"Where are you going, sailor?" she asked.

"You said you had a train to catch."

"Yes I did, but I didn't say when. We're going to the Aldrich House, where we will have a lazy lunch with wine. I have a room reserved there. My train is tomorrow afternoon." Laughing, Arthur gave the Cabbie the corrected instructions. The Aldrich House was in historic Colonial Williamsburg, not far from the gate. They could have walked it, but the weather was a bit warm for that. But so was the taxi; its air conditioning did not work. The air conditioning in Aldrich House did work, and they needed it, for they both worked up a sweat before lying beside each other, enjoying the wash of cold air across their naked bodies. Arthur felt a pang of guilt, but kicked it away, sure that God would forgive this natural and enjoyable act.

The next morning, sitting in the B&B's dining room waiting for Helen to come down for breakfast, Arthur opened the manila envelope containing his new orders and reviewed them. There was a set of orders sending him to Pensacola Naval Air Station in a week, where he was scheduled for a flight refresher session followed by testing.

Helen arrived looking fresh and beautiful, her hair arranged in a businesslike bun at the back of her head, dressed in a trim, tan, business suit with the skirt just above the knees and a light blue blouse buttoned up to the neck, the jacket open.

"You look ready for the Board Room," said Arthur, rising and holding her chair for her as she sat down.

"I'm still a little young for that," she said, eyeing his uniform and service ribbons. "You look ready for the fleet."

"Indeed. That seems to be where they are sending me," said Arthur. Where are you bound?"

"Classified. Need to know only," she said. "You can write me in care of CIA headquarters and they'll post it on."

"I'll do that," said Arthur. He handed her a piece of note paper on which he had written his FPO address. "Here's where you can write me. They'll find me somewhere and deliver it to me. But I'm not under cover, so you'll have to use my real name. They would never have heard of Joe Green, or Giuseppe Verdi, for that matter. When I go operational, they'll give me a new cover name and identity." Helen looked carefully at the note paper and put it into her purse.

"Ensign Arthur Cornwallis Harris III," she said, "it is a pleasure to make your acquaintance." Her cheeks dimpled as she smiled at him. "Are you sure you shouldn't be in Her Majesty's Service, with that name?" Arthur laughed.

"I was born here, although my grandfather, Arthur Cornwallis Harris I, and my father, Arthur Cornwallis Harris II, were both British subjects. There were never more than two of us with that name alive at the same time, and so we just used 'Senior' and 'Junior' to distinguish ourselves."

"So, did your friends call you 'Junior?'"

"I wish. They knew I was the Third, so they called me 'Turd.' When they didn't call me that, they called me

'Corny.' As a result, I have eschewed nicknames, even 'Art,' and insisted on using my whole first name, Arthur."

"Ah. Art Corny the Turd. I can understand your penchant for formal names." She laughed. "So, when do you leave? "

"I'm catching the train this afternoon," he replied. "I called, and they told me the train to Atlanta leaves at 1400 hours. I'll change there for a train that stops at Pensacola on its way to New Orleans and Houston. You?"

"I'm starting out on the same train. I am reporting to an office located generally west from here. At that time, I will learn where I will be assigned and what I will be doing. Classified, need to know, you know, and I don't need to know until I get there, so they won't even give me a hint."

"I can't tell you where I am being sent, either, because I don't know. I'm going to Pensacola for a flight refresher and receiving deployment orders there. Where are you being sent?"

"You don't need to know."

"I think they are very wise. Otherwise, I know a few interrogation techniques that might make you spill the beans."

"Beans, my dear sir? I think not. I am having bacon and eggs with grits for breakfast, and I'd just as soon not spill them. I don't have to check out until noon, so we can go back upstairs for a little practice of our undercover techniques before we go our separate ways."

The games were fun, but too soon, Arthur was sitting on the train headed south to Atlanta, where he would change trains for one going through Dothan to Mobile. He had hoped to see Helen on the platform, and perhaps to sit with her, but he lost track of her when he stopped to buy his tickets. She already had hers and went ahead to the platform. He did not find her. From Mobile he took a bus to Pensacola, followed by a taxi to Pensacola NAS. When he arrived at Pensacola NAS, he checked in at the BOQ. Soon, there was a knock on the door to his room. He opened it to find Commander Thayer facing him.

"Mr. Harris, it is a pleasure to see you again," he said. "I'm here also for a flight refresher and re-certification course."

"It's good to see you, too, Sir," replied Arthur. "Please come in." He held the door wide, and Commander Thayer entered.

"I'm in the room next to yours. I just stopped in to say, 'Hi,' because I know you have a batch of studying to do tonight before the written exam tomorrow. I am depending on you to pass it and go on to the refresher and in-flight test."

"I'll do my best," said Arthur. "I feel pretty confident."

"Good," said Thayer. "I'll leave you to your studies. Please join me at breakfast before you go to your exam." Arthur opened the door for him.

"I'll do that. Good night, Sir."

At breakfast, Thayer filled Arthur in on the current organization of ONI. The Director, ONI, was Rear Admiral Eugene B. Fluckey, who had been appointed to head the office last year. Thayer was Commanding Officer, NOSI. They both chuckled when Arthur called him the NOSI CO, pronouncing "NOSI" and spelling "CO." Thayer expressed his pleasure that Arthur had the highest score that year from The Farm, promising to use him as an operative whenever possible, and asking if he would object to working "alongside" the CIA when he didn't have assignments in NOSI suitable for him. Arthur assured him that he would look forward to such missions.

After breakfast, Arthur aced the written exam, and began flying that afternoon. By the end of the week he had demonstrated every standard maneuver with the Phantom, as well as some non-standard twists and turns, including one that he had invented himself and demonstrated to his instructor. He called it the "stall and plunge." Operating at altitude, he raised the nose sharply to put the plane in vertical position and reduced the engines to "idle," with the elevator turned hard right. The plane started upward from inertia, turning quickly to the right and stalling, with the nose continuing its trajectory until the plane was in a nose-down vertical position. He increased the throttle to maximum and engaged the afterburners to go screaming straight for the deck, breaking the speed of sound before leveling out. He explained that he hoped the maneuver would allow him to escape air-to-air missiles, as they could not change direction as quickly and were likely to lose their lock on the plane.

"Mr. Harris," said the instructor wryly, riding in the rear seat, "if you use that trick in battle and survive, please come back and tell me all about it."

"I did, Sir."

"You did survive, or you did tell me about it?"

"Both, Sir – I did survive, and I just did tell you about it. I have already used it in battle." They both laughed.

Having completed his recertification course for combat in the F-4 Phantom, Ensign Harris was promoted to Lieutenant, Junior Grade. The unit with which he had flown over the Ho Chi Minh Trail was also awarded the National Defense Service Medal, which was received by each of the unit members, and so Arthur received that medal as well. But it was Arthur Harris' work that composed the bulk of the basis for the unit award. The other unit members would receive it where they were; Arthur received it at Pensacola NAS. At the end of the ceremonies, Arthur was handed the envelope with his new orders. He was to report to Thayer in Washington.

Thayer received him warmly but said he had some bad news for him. He gave Arthur orders that had him stand down from the active navy and proceed to Houston to register with the Houston Navy Reserve Unit. The paperwork simply said he was "Released from Active Duty." Thayer told him that NOSI was being partially de-staffed, and because it had been so secret, the Navy was hesitant to send its NOSI members out to the fleet. Because of the Draft, the Navy had no problem recruiting top-quality officers, and so it could afford to lose a few like Arthur. Thayer said he was exploring options with the CIA to place his people who were being de-staffed, but he did not know how long it would take.

"We have been getting a lot of pushback from the CIA, which claims we are encroaching on their territory," said Thayer. "Do you remember Charles Wallace?"

"The CIA Section Chief who debriefed me after my crash?"

"He's the one. You might consider him now the enemy of NOSI – and as a result, your enemy. After your debriefing in Nam, he raised a big stink about what you had been doing. He doesn't particularly object to ordinary ONI activities. He doesn't know that NOSI exists, but he knows we have been doing things below the radar, like your missions over the Ho Chi Minh Trail, and he doesn't like that. He doesn't want the Navy engaged in clandestine missions, feeling that only the CIA should engage in clandestine activities. Accordingly, we are stepping back for the time being from the arena, so to speak."

"As you may suspect, Sir, I am disappointed and disheartened," said Arthur. "What do I do now?"

"Go home, hug your Mom and Dad, throw a football around with your brother, and go back to Houston and get a job. Register with the Reserve Unit. I, or the CIA, will be in touch with you."

"Aye, aye, Sir," said Arthur. Thayer could see that he was very disappointed.

"Don't worry, Arthur," he said. "I won't forget you. You do have a future, although neither of us knows yet its shape."

On the train to Dothan, Arthur fantasized about confronting Wallace and strangling him on the spot.

FUGUE

May 1967
Houston

Arthur visited his family, and while there invested $500.00 to buy a used 1958 Chevrolet, which he drove to Houston. His mother had sold the Olds to their yard man, who was driving around Dothan with lawn mowers hanging out the back, the trunk open. Arthur was bitterly disappointed that his Navy career had been suspended and that he had been transferred to the Reserves. He was also disappointed that he could not "inherit" the Olds and restore it. Being transferred to the Reserves could end his career dreams.

He returned to his inexpensive apartment near Rice University at 1700 Sunset Boulevard. In a letter to Thayer, Arthur provided his address and telephone number. He registered with the US Navy Reserve Unit, where he was told he would report every Wednesday evening for Reserve Meetings, and one Saturday per month for drill. He would have to do a two-week training "cruise" every summer.

He called Clovis Heimsath to inquire about a job but was told there were no openings for anyone who lacked the 5-year professional BS in Architecture. He drove to the Houston Music Theater, which had unknowingly been his cover story while he was at The Farm. His time at Rice with the Rice Players sort of gave him "credentials." They hired him. It was an evening job, which gave him time in the daytime to explore his options. His title was "House Manager." He had to show up an hour and a half before show time, unlock the theatre, turn on the electricity and get the air conditioning running, and let the staff, actors and musicians in. He would manage the "house," and his staff for that consisted of the ushers (unpaid volunteers) and a janitor (paid). The job didn't pay a lot, but it paid enough for his rent and basic living expenses. He would also receive reserve pay.

A month passed without further word from Thayer, so he assumed that Thayer's effort to find him a slot and second him to the CIA wasn't working out. His calls to Thayer were unanswered. He decided to try to contact the CIA on his own. He would not be able to rely on his own CIA contacts, because he knew only the cover names they used during his stint at the Farm, and he had no idea where they had gone from there.

So, he turned to the telephone book, and found a number listed in Houston for the Central Intelligence Agency. He decided to call it.

(END)

Meet our author

William Arthur Wheatley

Born in 1944 in Tennessee, William A. Wheatley spent
the next ten years in Mexico, where his engineer father
was building power plants. His grandmother and his
mother, both teachers, gave him a good education. The
family moved to Dothan, Alabama in 1955, where his father worked as an engineer with the Corps of Engineers at
Fort Rucker.

As a boy, he read all the books in his family's extensive library, which included all the classics. He read Forster's *Lieutenant Hornblower* serialized in the *Saturday Evening Post* in 1951, dreaming of becoming a naval officer on a sailing frigate. He also read Ian Fleming's first two James Bond books – *Casino Royale* and *Live and Let Die*, enjoying them immensely. He noted that Bond was both a spy and a Navy commander and determined to follow a similar path.

While in high school, he took a geology course at the local community college, learning to read and analyze the aerial photography used in geological mapping. He enrolled at Rice University as an architecture student and joined the Navy ROTC unit.

The Cuban Missile Crisis broke out in his freshman year, and the Navy sent him to Guantanamo for two weeks to analyze aerial photos, which started his career with the Office of Naval Intelligence (ONI). In summer training before his senior year, he flew in the back seat of a Navy jet doing low-level surveillance over Cambodia, but officially he was never there. After college, he was commissioned and sent to Camp Peary, the CIA spy school, and then he was seconded to the CIA. In civilian life he was an architect/construction manager, often on troubled projects in interesting parts of the world, cover for intelligence operations.

He lives in Philadelphia with his wife, Giovanna, and continues working and writing. His sons and grandchildren live in Houston. He travels whenever possible, enjoying especially visits to his wife's family in Italy.

Made in the USA
Middletown, DE
12 December 2019